"INTRIGUE AND SUSPENSE REIGN SUPREME" (Booklist) IN FIONA BUCKLEY'S ELIZABETHAN MYSTERIES FEATURING URSULA BLANCHARD

"Buckley writes a learned historical mystery. Ursula, too, is a smart lass, one whose degrees must include a B.A. (for bedchamber assignations) and an M.S.W. (for mighty spirited wench)."
—*USA Today*

"Queen Elizabeth maintains a surprisingly vital presence . . . although it is Ursula who best appreciates the beauties—and understands the dangers—of their splendid age."
—*The New York Times Book Review*

"Ursula is a force to be reckoned with—audacious, intensely loyal, and beguiling."
—*Publishers Weekly*

"Through the eyes of Ursula, a woman both compassionate and ruthless, Buckley effectively dramatizes the tangled personal and political obligations of the Elizabethan court."
—*Kirkus Reviews*

"Fantastic historical fiction . . . filled with royal intrigue. . . . Fiona Buckley . . . makes the Elizabethan era fun to read about."
—*Midwest Book Review*

By Fiona Buckley

To Shield the Queen
The Doublet Affair
Queen's Ransom
To Ruin a Queen
Queen of Ambition
A Pawn for a Queen
The Fugitive Queen
The Siren Queen

TO SHIELD THE QUEEN

FIONA BUCKLEY

Pocket Books
New York   London   Toronto   Sydney

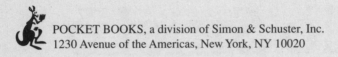 POCKET BOOKS, a division of Simon & Schuster, Inc.
1230 Avenue of the Americas, New York, NY 10020

Originally published in Great Britain by Orion
First published in hardcover in the United States in 1997 by Scribner

ISBN-13: 978-0-7434-8907-2
ISBN-10:   0-7434-8907-1

This Pocket Books trade paperback edition April 2006

10 9 8 7 6 5 4 3 2 1

POCKET and colophon are registered trademarks of
Simon & Schuster, Inc.

Manufactured in the United States of America

For information regarding special discounts for bulk purchases, please contact
Simon & Schuster Special Sales at 1-800-456-6798 or business@simonand-
schuster.com

For my agent, David Grossman

To Shield the Queen

§1§

Richmond Palace

John Wilton was a small man, knotted and wiry, with short, dusty brown hair which stuck up in spikes. He had a snub nose and discoloured teeth. I can't remember what colour his eyes were and I never knew his age. Men like John seem to be born in middle life, and there they stay. He had started out as a groom employed by my husband's family and become, eventually, my husband Gerald's manservant. Now, when Gerald was gone, he would gladly have become mine, except that I couldn't afford him.

He believed in hard work and honesty and sometimes carried the latter too far. John would speak his mind when he felt it necessary, regardless of risk, regardless of the other person's social standing. He was as plain and trustworthy as a loaf of good brown bread. In that April of 1560, when Queen Elizabeth had been on the throne for less than eighteen months, the sect we now call the Puritans had barely begun to emerge and I doubt if John had ever heard of them, but in a later age, he might well have joined them.

1

And I have done few things in my life harder than dismounting from his pillion and bidding him farewell that afternoon, at the landward gate of Richmond Palace.

Some people would have thought me ungrateful! I was there, after all, to enter the service of her majesty Queen Elizabeth, and Richmond Palace was one of the newest and most beautiful royal residences, a place of ample light and airy grace, with turrets and fountains and generous windows and singing weathervanes which made a melodious sound when the wind blew. It was a privilege to be allowed into it and it was rather more than a privilege to be doing so as one of the young queen's Ladies of the Presence Chamber. God knows, I had parted from others who meant more to me than John. I had watched my husband die of the smallpox and been forced, too, to say goodbye to our daughter Meg, and leave her behind in the care of her nurse Bridget. What was a mere manservant compared to husband and child?

However, John was my last link with them; with my too-short married life and the small, loving child who was Gerald's gift to me. Now I must lose even him and no amount of palaces or pinnacles or even the most charismatic of princes could make up for that. But there it was. However great the honour of becoming a Lady of the Presence Chamber, a stipend of thirty pounds a year would barely keep Meg and her nurse. I couldn't find the wherewithal to pay John too.

I talked to him, while we waited for someone to come and guide me into the palace. I gave him messages for Meg and Bridget and then repeated them, dreading the moment of parting and at the same time wishing it could be over. The delay was prolonged. The guard had a messenger at hand and sent him to announce my arrival, but it was a quarter of an hour before he came back, bringing a page to act as my guide, and a serving man to carry my panniers full of personal belongings.

At the last moment, when the porter had shouldered my luggage and was already disappearing through the arch of the west gatehouse, and the page was waiting with rather obvious patience for me to follow him, tears came into my eyes and I had to blink hard to control them.

John noticed. He swept off his cap, which made his hair stand up like the spines of a hedgehog. "I hope to get work not far from Bridget and the little one," he said. "I'll remember your messages, mistress, never fear, and I'll keep an eye on them for you. And if you ever need me, Mistress Blanchard, just you send word and I'll be there as fast as I can, on any nag I can get hold of."

"Thank you," I said shakily. "If I do need you, be sure that I shall call. Goodbye, John, and a safe ride home."

As he mounted his horse again, panic almost overtook me. At the age of twenty-six, I was virtually alone in the world, left to fend for myself in this place which was so beautiful and luxurious, and was also utterly unfamiliar and full of unknown demands, not to mention perils. The perils were not precisely unknown (I had learned about those from my mother) but they were no less alarming on that account.

However, I must not begin my service to the queen by giving way and making a fool of myself. Somehow I kept my countenance. As John clattered away from the gate with the two hired horses which had brought us and my personal belongings from Sussex, I didn't watch him go. Instead, I braced myself; not to forget my sore heart, which wasn't possible, but to ignore it, and to be alert and attentive as a queen's lady-in-waiting must be if she is to please her mistress.

* * *

Once through the archway, I realised that the porter and my baggage had disappeared completely. I could only hope to be safely reunited with my belongings in due course. The palace was immense.

I was quite used to fine houses. I had been brought up in a manor house, and with Gerald I had been part of the entourage of Sir Thomas Gresham, financier, whose way of life, divided between London and Antwerp, verged on the princely. Richmond, though, belonged to another order of dwellings altogether. I had expected to emerge into a courtyard, but I found myself instead being led along a sanded path through a formal flower garden, bordered with lavender. Few of the flowers were in bloom yet, but under the shelter of a wall, I saw patches of forget-me-nots and violets; and a bed patterned with the rich yellow and velvety purple of heart's-ease.

I made a conscious effort to take an interest in my surroundings. The garden was bounded by long two-storey buildings, guards' quarters by the look of them, and beyond those to the right, there must be an orchard; blossom-laden boughs were just visible above their roofs. To the left, where the River Thames flowed, the sky was empty and luminous. I couldn't see the river but I could hear the shouts of boatmen. The slim turrets of the palace proper were still far away ahead. It was no wonder that I had had to wait so long for my escort to appear. It was several minutes before we passed through another arch and came at last into the courtyard, where some saddled horses were awaiting their riders. Faintly, from a window on an upper floor, I could hear music.

We turned left and mounted a broad flight of steps up to an iron-studded main door. Inside, the palace was splendid, but bewildering, a maze of corridors and galleries. The sun poured in through slender mullioned windows. Once I glimpsed the sparkling river outside; a moment later I caught sight of a tilt-yard from which came the sound of clashing weapons and drumming hoofs. We went out into an enclosed garden and across it, and then up more steps and in at another door.

There were people everywhere, strolling or standing in clusters to talk, or hurrying about on presumably urgent errands, or, in one case, in a rage. As we passed through a long gallery with a flat carved ceiling and some spectacular hangings depicting scenes from Roman history, we had to flatten ourselves against the assassination of Julius Caesar to make way for a young woman, dressed expensively in green and gold brocade with a great cone-shaped farthingale and wearing, in addition, an expression sour enough to turn wine to vinegar on the instant, as she swept past us in the opposite direction with another young woman just behind her, frantically apologising about something and scurrying to keep up.

The page glanced back at them and let out a small, derisive snort. It was demeaning to question a page but when I was myself, not weighed down by sorrow, I was inclined to be inquisitive, a trait which Gerald had virtually encouraged, since finding things out was part of his business. Besides, I was still concerned with taking an interest and I could not too soon begin to learn about the court. So I ignored protocol and asked the page who the angry young woman was.

"Lady Catherine Grey," said the page. "I don't know the name of the other."

He said no more. But even if the Gresham household in Antwerp hadn't quite prepared me for the royal court of Queen Elizabeth, it had been a place where famous names were spoken and the political scenery surveyed. I had heard of Lady Catherine Grey.

Until the queen married and had her own children,

her heirs were her cousins, descendants of her father's sisters. Catherine was one of them. In Antwerp, people called her the Protestant heir. So that was Lady Catherine Grey. She didn't look very regal, I thought, and wondered what the queen would look like.

The page, finding his way apparently by witchcraft, brought us at length to a room where a number of ladies were seated, stitching and gossiping. The room was tapestried but well lit through many large windows, and rosemary strewn on the floor filled the air with sweetness. Mingled with this was the characteristic smell of fabric, of silk and linen and fine wool. It came from the hangings and the numerous workboxes and also, I realised, from the brocaded and embroidered dresses of the ladies. I was instantly conscious of my plain dress, dark for mourning and without a farthingale because one can't ride a horse in one. I had better dresses with me, but none was really new and fashions were changing all the time.

The page led me up to one of the ladies. She glanced round enquiringly, needle suspended over an embroidery frame. He bowed, gracefully. "Lady Katherine, I bring you Mistress Ursula Blanchard."

Catherine was a common name, though people varied the spelling. We had thought of calling Meg by it but decided against it just because there were so many Catherines about. This one was older and more dignified than Lady Catherine Grey, refined of feature, her skin pale and clear. She was in a dress of dove grey, with blue embroidery which picked up the colour of her calm blue eyes. I curtsied to her and she smiled.

"Of course. You are expected. Thank you, Will."

I tipped the page and he took himself off. I stood nervously, aware that all the other ladies were looking at me with interest. Lady Katherine, however, patted an empty seat beside her, a velvet-upholstered stool, and I sat down gratefully.

"Thank you, madam."

"I'm sure you must be tired. We will go presently and look at your room. I am Katherine Knollys, cousin to her majesty on the maternal side. I am one of her principal ladies. Mistress Ashley is in overall charge of all the ladies but she is indisposed today, so I instructed that you should be brought to me instead. I intend visiting her this afternoon, however, and as I shall have to pass close to our quarters, I'll take you with me and show you myself where you will be sleeping. Later, I will present you to her majesty. She is closeted with some of her council members at the moment."

"And with Robin Dudley," remarked another lady, young, with a fragile build but very bright grey eyes.

"Very likely, Jane," said Lady Katherine repressively. "He is the Master of Horse, after all. I believe the queen wishes him to purchase some new riding horses. Jane, this is Mistress Ursula Blanchard, who has come to join us. Ursula, this is Lady Jane Seymour, niece to the queen of that name, the mother of poor King Edward who died so young."

I inclined my head to Lady Jane. For all her sparkling eyes, she didn't look much stronger than her cousin Edward, who hadn't lived to see his sixteenth birthday. I often gave thanks to God for my own good health.

Lady Katherine began to present me to the other ladies. I smiled and said the right things, and wondered how hard I would have to battle for my position in this private hierarchy. In Sir Thomas Gresham's house, I had had Gerald to give me status. Gerald was successful, an up-and-coming young man of breeding. He was respected and his wife automatically shared in that respect. Here, I thought forlornly, I would have to win recognition for myself. The queen's women were all so very elegant and confident. My looks would not help. Gerald had once said that he first wanted me because of my black hair and long hazel eyes and my pointed face which made him think of a kitten, but Gerald was never one to follow fashion. Most men preferred something more rounded and fairer. Brunettes went out of favour when Anne Boleyn's dark head was cut off, nearly a quarter of a century ago.

Also, these ladies were all daughters or wives of important men. Most of them had titles.

And in addition, I thought wryly, they were probably all legitimate.

I wondered how much Lady Katherine Knollys knew about me. She was introducing me simply as the widow of Gerald Blanchard, gentleman. In turn, I tried to absorb what I was told about the others, but there were too many of them and, although some bore names as famous as Seymour, I knew I wouldn't remember more than one or two of them, not yet. I was indeed very tired, not only from the two-day ride from Sussex, but also from the strain of my farewells and my sadness. I was glad when, at length, Lady Katherine rose and took me off to my quarters.

"You feel dazed, I expect," she said as she led me through another lengthy gallery. "I know a little of your story. Sir William Cecil told it to me and Mistress Ashley. You have certainly had a troubled life, but you will be too busy to brood, I promise. Do you dance gracefully?"

"Dance?" The change of subject took me by surprise. "Well—reasonably so, I think. But . . ."

"You are in mourning, but that won't be for ever," said Lady Katherine briskly. "The queen likes to dance and also to watch her ladies do so. Later, we must see what you can do."

"Does Lady Catherine Grey dance well?" I asked.

8

"Catherine Grey? Why do you ask?"

My inquisitiveness had surprised her. I might have to curb it if I wished to fit in at court. I said mildly that the page and I had met Lady Catherine Grey on the way through the palace. "I—noticed her," I said. "She was so splendidly dressed. I asked who she was."

Katherine Knollys laughed. "Oh, I see! Splendidly dressed! I daresay she was in a splendid temper as well, only you are too discreet to put it that way. Am I right?"

"Well, er . . ."

"A foolish maid of honour mistook her for someone else and went through a doorway ahead of her. The queen will only allow her to be a Lady of the Presence Chamber and not of the Privy Chamber. It causes misunderstandings. Though it might help if Catherine were not in a perpetual sulk over it. Oh, I may as well be candid; you will soon hear all about it anyway. She is still a person of importance, of course. Lady Jane Seymour has lately become her close friend and will I hope be a steadying influence. Lady Jane is a dear girl, though perhaps a trifle too spirited. Here's your room. Here at Richmond, you can have your own, though you will have to share at some of the other residences."

The room into which she took me was in a corner of the building and it was a very odd shape, almost triangular, although it did have one very short fourth wall. It was panelled, with a leaded window overlooking the courtyard and it contained a small tester bed, a clothes press, a window seat with a storage chest beneath it, and a washstand. To my relief, I saw my panniers on the floor beside the bed.

"There's a truckle bed underneath yours, for your maid," said Lady Katherine. "Have you brought a maid or were you intending to hire one here in London?"

9

"I meant to do without," I said. "My means are—well, modest."

"Do without a maid?" Lady Katherine, who had been stooping to make sure that the truckle bed was there, turned to me, her finely plucked eyebrows rising.

"Yes. I can easily manage. It's quite all right."

"My dear Mistress Blanchard, it is *not* quite all right. A lady-in-waiting must have her own maid. It is not a question of whether or not you can manage; it's a question of how the other ladies will regard you. Especially when your—well, your antecedents—become known, as they will. The court is like that. Whatever else you go without, a maid, my dear, is essential."

Lady Katherine decided that my sudden quietness was because I was so tired. She sent for wine and cakes and said her own woman would help me unpack and dress for my presentation to her majesty. Then she left me alone while she went to give orders to her maid and I sat on the window seat, sipping white wine and nibbling cinnamon pastries and inwardly cursing in terms profane enough to scandalise a fishwife.

If only, oh if only, Gerald could have lived. I thought of his square brown face and his friendly brown eyes and longed for him as desperately as I had on the day he died. If you had to take his life, I said silently and furiously to God, couldn't you at least have waited until he could leave me a little better provided for? He had been doing well in Gresham's service, but he hadn't had his good salary for long enough. He had saved so little.

The Blanchards, neighbours of my own family in Sussex, were well-to-do, but Gerald was a younger son which meant he must make his own way. His father would have given him a present of money or perhaps a small farm, if Gerald had taken a suitable bride, but I didn't qualify. Oh yes, the Faldenes were well off, too, high enough up the social scale to have a tradition of court service even though we were not titled. But Ursula Faldene was not a well-dowered daughter of the house. I was the unfortunate disaster which had befallen an earlier Faldene daughter when she went to the court of King Henry VIII to serve his second wife, Anne Boleyn, and misbehaved herself with a court gallant whom she would not identify. Or possibly, couldn't identify, my Aunt Tabitha had once, disagreeably, suggested. "How many of them were there, I wonder?" she had said to my mother.

"There was only the one!" my mother protested. "But he was married and no, I won't name him."

"Only one? Prove it!" retorted Aunt Tabitha.

When I married, Gerald's family consisted of his father Luke Blanchard, and his elder brother Ambrose, cold-faced men, both of them. I never saw Gerald's mother, but I know he took after her. His candid, merry countenance must have been her legacy. In my own family, my grandparents had died some years ago, leaving Uncle Herbert, his dreadfully virtuous wife Tabitha, and their children, my cousins. There had been a scheme between the Faldenes and the Blanchards to marry Gerald to my cousin Mary but I ruined that. The two families weren't on speaking terms now. I would have been cut off without a dowry, except that I'd never had one in the first place. I wasn't expected, or supposed, to marry.

In bygone days, the Faldenes used to cope with surplus or embarrassing females such as my mother by depositing them in nearby Withysham Abbey, but all that came to an end when King Henry, because the Pope wouldn't grant him a divorce from his first queen and thus set him free to marry Anne Boleyn, thumbed his nose at the Holy Father, broke with

Rome and divorced himself. While he was at it, King Henry also disbanded the monasteries and nunneries of England. Withysham was no longer an option. My grandparents therefore took my disgraced mother back. From then on she was little more than an unpaid servant in her own home, and I was reared to be the same.

I do remember, when I was small, receiving occasional signs of affection from my grandfather. I recall him giving me sweetmeats now and then and he let me learn to ride. I remember him walking beside me, the first time I was put into a saddle, and steadying me while the groom led the pony round the stable-yard.

However, he died when I was eight and my grandmother followed within the year, and from then on my mother and I were at the mercy of Uncle Herbert and Aunt Tabitha, except that mercy was a commodity in short supply in their household.

In time, I came to see that they were a couple whose public life and private life were completely different.

Outwardly, they were respectable and kindly folk who gave to charity, entertained or were entertained by their neighbours in our part of Sussex, on the northern edge of the downs, and never failed to ask politely after the health of guest or host and the families thereof.

In private, Uncle Herbert's principal passion was money. He never bought anything without haggling over it; it hurt him to see anyone making a good profit out of him. Faldene tenants had to pay their rent to the last farthing on the exact day stipulated. Most households gave the servants lengths of clothing material at Christmas, and usually such materials were hardwearing and not too costly, but Uncle Herbert used to give the servants his cast-offs, and believe me, my uncle didn't cast anything off until the nap was gone and it had at least three patches. His favourite occupation was sitting in his study and going through his ledgers in the hope of squeezing another groat or two into the credit column of the estate transactions. Uncle Herbert, in fact, hated giving to charity, and in private, said so.

As for the punctilious enquiries over other people's well-being: if only Aunt Tabitha had been half so anxious about the health of those under her control!

Faldene House was in the modern style, with towers and crenellations which were impressive, but were there for ornament, not for use as lookouts or battlements. It had been built early in the century, replacing a much older house.

It was poised charmingly on a hillside overlooking Faldene Vale, a downland valley which was half-filled with woodland as a bowl may be filled with wine, while our cornfields and meadows lay spread over the sides of the valley. When the wind was fresh, cloud shadows would race across those hillsides, and ripening crops would ripple like water.

A splendid place, Faldene, but as a home, it was not happy. My uncle and aunt, so apparently concerned for the welfare of others, were petty tyrants.

Aunt Tabitha, thin and active and straight of back, was given to final pronouncements on all matters moral. She liked sitting in judgement on slacking maidservants and disobedient children, or on me when I had been caught reading poetry or playing with a ball when I should have been scraping carrots or mending sheets. Uncle Herbert was a contrast to his wife in appearance, for he was heavily built and grew more so as the years went on. However, he was good at delivering victims to Aunt Tabitha's judgements, because indoors he wore soft slippers. For all his bulk, no one was better than Uncle Herbert at creeping up and catching people out. Once caught out, you could be casually struck or formally beaten, and the causes were often trivial.

Aunt Tabitha also resented anyone who fell ill. The fact was, that she never ailed a day herself and was apt to regard any child or servant who went sick as a malingerer. She was quite capable of pulling someone out of bed if she thought their headache or fever was imaginary. I know. After the age of thirteen I was subject at times to violent headaches, with nausea, and I suffered much from Aunt Tabitha's crude refusal to believe in this malady. My mother suffered, too, during the first stages of the lung-rot which killed her (though I believed then and believe now that the years of cold unkindness from her family had much to do with it). When it was clear that the illness was real, my aunt did let her rest in bed, but grudgingly, with much talk of her "charity" towards her fallen sister-in-law.

My mother died when I was sixteen. Until then, she did her best to protect me from my family. She was in their power and therefore always had to be humble and polite towards them, but she was essentially a clever woman and she did her best by me. Aunt Tabitha meant me to grow up into another dogsbody; fetching, carrying, stitching, skivvying. But my mother managed to teach me to play the lute and the virginals and persuaded my aunt to let me share my cousins' tutor by saying that I was over-lively and that this would keep me out of mischief. I had the sense to apply myself. Indeed, I was actually encouraged to study once Uncle Herbert had grasped that he could turn my education to advantage by using me as a clerk and secretary.

As I grew up I spent many hours in his study, learning how to maintain ledgers and write letters in an elegant hand. Whatever I learned, though, was for my relatives to use. When my mother was gone, it was made clear to me that I was expected to spend the rest of my life gratefully serving those who had so generously taken me in. Marriage? No, that was for respectably born young women.

When they discovered that I had supplied the deficiency for myself and stolen Cousin Mary's prospective bridegroom while I was about it, Aunt Tabitha hit me so hard that I fell down, Cousin Mary threw herself on the floor and pounded it with her fists, howling, and I thought Uncle Herbert would burst a blood vessel.

In other circumstances I might have pitied Mary, but I knew they would find her someone else fast enough, and she hardly knew Gerald. She didn't love him. Gerald and I already knew we would have to marry without the consent of either of our families and our plans were already made. I escaped from Faldene that night and we ran away together. We took refuge with a friend of Gerald's in the town of Guildford, on the way to London. We were married two days later in a nearby church, with the friend and his wife and parents as witnesses, and then went on to London, where Gerald was due to take up a post in the household of Sir Thomas Gresham.

I was soon absorbed into the life of the large, friendly Gresham establishment, attending dinners there and being asked to hawking parties. My childhood riding lessons came in useful. I hadn't ridden much since my grandfather died, but I had the basics, and soon developed some skill. It was much better fun than being dependent on a pillion. Gerald encouraged me. Gerald always encouraged me, in everything I did, just as I encouraged him.

Four years later, when Queen Elizabeth came to the throne and sent Gresham out to Antwerp, we went too. With us went our little daughter Meg, her nurse Bridget Lemmon, and John Wilton. When he first decided to leave Sussex, Gerald had asked John to come as his personal man. John was willing, and signed on in our little ship of matrimony.

And then the ship foundered on a black, evil rock of disease and stranded me, widowed, in Antwerp, with a small daughter, two servants, some rather expensive lodgings and just enough money for a couple of months.

Sir Thomas had come to know that ours was a runaway match, and when he first heard of it, he questioned Gerald about it, but he had liked me from the start and apparently accepted Gerald's account of my unhappy life at Faldene. Now he was kind but seemed uncertain what to do with me. I had my pride. "I will write to my home," I said bravely.

In fact, I wrote both to the Blanchards and the Faldenes, explaining my position and asking their help, for Meg's sake, if not for my own. She was four years old and pretty. My father-in-law might be willing to do something for his own granddaughter, I thought.

I was wrong. Master Blanchard did not care if Meg and I died of starvation and nor, apparently, did Gerald's brother Ambrose. They wanted nothing to do with us and would prefer never to hear of us again. The letter in which Master Blanchard Senior expressed these unattractive sentiments contained the outrageous remark that he was being generous in even bothering to answer what he called my whining appeal.

The Faldene response was different. They were prepared to forgive my ingratitude and wilfulness and take me in, along with the fruit of my sin (that meant Meg, and since she was legitimate, the sin in question was presumably the theft of Gerald from Cousin Mary). And to Faldene I would have had to go, with Meg, to face a life of unpaid servitude, except that Gerald's work had brought him to the notice of the Secretary of State, Sir William Cecil. Sir Thomas had commended Gerald by name on occasion, it seemed, and thought of writing to Cecil to explain my plight. The ship which brought Faldene's answer to Antwerp also brought an offer for me to follow in my mother's tradition and come to court to wait on the queen.

There were drawbacks: that thirty pounds a year stipend for instance. The queen's ladies usually had families behind them to support them. Nor could I have my daughter with me. It was better than going home to Faldene, though, and I agreed.

I did go briefly to Sussex first, because I wanted to visit my mother's grave, and while I was there, I wished to find a cottage to rent for Bridget and Meg. It would be easier to find one, I thought, in a place I knew.

I stayed with John Wilton's sister, whose husband had a small farm there. I did not need or want to call at Faldene House, although when I went to look at the grave, I was close to the house and it seemed odd to see it and not go there. After all, I had been reared there, however grudgingly. I did not altogether escape seeing my family, though. I was placing a bunch of bluebells on my mother's sadly overgrown resting place, when Aunt Tabitha chose to walk through the churchyard. She saw me, stopped short, and then came briskly up to me.

"Well, well. Ursula! What are you doing here? Are you intending to call on us?"

"I thought you might prefer it if I didn't," I said quietly. "I am paying my respects to my mother's memory, as you see."

She stared at me as if wondering whether she could still bully me and I stared back, determined that she should not. "This, I take it," she said, "is the child."

I was holding Meg by the hand. I told her to make her curtsy and presented her to my aunt, who looked at her disparagingly and said, "Are you taking her to court with you?"

"No. I am making arrangements for her elsewhere."

"Better leave her with us. We can see she is reared in the true faith and taught to be useful."

"In the true faith?" I said, and then realised that a faint tang of incense was clinging to my aunt's clothes. I knew the smell, for when I had lived at Faldene, Queen Mary was still on the throne and mass was not only legal but obligatory. "You still hear mass?" I asked sharply.

Aunt Tabitha looked offended. "We attend church regularly as the law enjoins," she said. "If, in private, we follow our own beliefs, it is no one's business but ours."

The conflict between the old Catholic religion and the new Protestant one was something that no one, noble or humble, could ignore. In the days of Elizabeth's predecessor Queen Mary, it had been, literally and hideously, a burning question.

Even after Elizabeth came to the throne and brought with her some semblance of calm, it was still the stream that drove the mill wheel of international politics and the cause of half the family feuds in the land. Elizabeth had made the land Protestant but some of her councillors were sympathetic to the old religion; most of them men who had served as Queen Mary's councillors. The queen could not afford to do without their experience and didn't try, and no one was being sent to the stake for Catholic sympathies.

18

However, you could be fined or even imprisoned for hearing mass, or celebrating it. If mass was being said at Faldene now, it was illegal.

"You will of course do what you think right," I said, "but I most certainly will not burden you with Meg."

"You never did know the meaning of the word gratitude, Ursula. I can only hope you don't go the way of your mother. There'll be plenty of lusty, well-off gallants at that red-headed heretic's court, I don't doubt!"

I took my leave of her coldly and led Meg away.

Now, sitting on the window seat in my room at Richmond, I thought grimly that I would survive somehow. I would keep myself decent; I would make my way at court, and I would keep Meg out of Faldene's clutches, too.

But to prosper at court apparently meant hiring a lady's maid. Dear God, how was I to afford that? It would take half my stipend! Feverishly, I tried to think of ways and means. There was a small garden with the cottage I had found for Bridget and Meg. Bridget could read, though only just. I would write her a clear, simple letter, telling her to grow vegetables and keep hens, and try to sell things—eggs, pullets, onions, lettuces. It wouldn't be enough, but I must just do my best.

The door opened and back came Lady Katherine Knollys with her woman. "Would you believe it? I've already heard of someone who might suit you!" she announced. "One of the maids of honour is being sent home for being caught in compromising circumstances with a young man, and leaves court tomorrow. She comes from the North, but her tiring woman is a Londoner and doesn't want to go with her. She intends to seek another position. I suggest that you interview her in the morning."

"Thank you," I said tonelessly. "You are very kind."

I was presented to her majesty later the same day. I had changed into a black velvet gown, decorated only with a few seed pearls. The gown had a small farthingale and a little white linen ruff and with it I wore a silver net for my hair, and a silver pendant. It was a becoming ensemble, which was fortunate because it gave me confidence. Being presented to Queen Elizabeth of England was quite an ordeal.

To begin with, Lady Katherine gave me a terrifying list of dos and don'ts. I must curtsy thus, and speak only if invited to do so but then must speak clearly and without stammering. And although I was here, as much as anything, because my mother had served the queen's mother, I must not allude to Anne Boleyn in any way, or even to Kate Howard, Anne's cousin, who had also been married to King Henry, and had been beheaded, like Anne, for adultery.

"Her majesty never speaks of them. She may well think of them privately, especially her mother," said Lady Katherine. "She has shown great kindness to the Boleyns and their kin, of whom I am one—my mother was Queen Anne's sister—but the past is never mentioned. You must also . . ."

I felt positively frightened before I even entered the room where the queen was to receive me. With Lady Katherine, I had first to cross a crowded antechamber, and then pass through an inner door with guards who placed their pikes across it until Lady Katherine gave our names, when they let us pass with a clash of pike-handles on the floor as they set their weapons upright again.

Inside, was a big room with an ornately painted and gilded ceiling and tapestried walls. This too was crowded, with courtiers male and female, and my sovereign was seated on a dais at the far side of an immense expanse of floor, across which I must walk, at Lady Katherine's side, under the eyes of what seemed to me like an audience of several hundred.

Quaking inwardly, I tried to keep my head up and my gaze fixed on the glittering figure of the queen. Viewed from afar, that was all she was: just a sparkling effigy on a chair with a high, pointed back. The odd thing was that as we approached, she did not become more human. Yet she was only a young woman, not yet twenty-seven, only months older than I was myself. It was extraordinary.

At the foot of the dais, Lady Katherine and I sank into our curtsies. A cool, even voice told us to rise, and as we did so, Lady Katherine began on a formal introduction, while I took my first good look at my sovereign.

I saw . . .

An astounding dress of ash-coloured satin, iridescent with gold embroidery, the waist so tiny, so pointed, that it was hard to believe that a human body could be held within it. I saw many ropes of pearls; a close ruff of lace, with more pearls at the edges; matching wrist-ruffs; a pearl headdress; pale red hair crimped into a cap of curls.

Her clothes were like the outer defences of a castle. I had to gaze hard to see past them, to the shield-shaped face, the golden-brown eyes under faint, arched eyebrows; the well-defined mouth. These too were defences of a kind for they told one nothing: her face was truly a shield. The eyes were watchful, determined to reveal nothing of their owner's thoughts; the eyebrows were immobile; the shapely mouth devoid of passion. She looked more like a faery being than a human one.

A hand, long and slender, the nails softly burnished, the length of the fingers deftly shown off by

21

jewelled rings, was extended to me to kiss. "So you are Mistress Ursula Blanchard, formerly Faldene, and your mother, Anna Faldene, once served—at court."

I heard the faintest pause before the words "at court." Carefully, I said, "That is so, your majesty."

"You may address me as ma'am. We see that you are in mourning, Mistress Blanchard. That is for your husband?"

"Yes, ma'am."

"We will do what we can to fill your days and heal your grief. Here at court it would be perfectly proper for you to relieve your black clothes with a little more white or silver. A white or silver under-kirtle, perhaps, with matching sleeves. You have our permission."

"Thank you, ma'am," I said, recognising that this was an order in disguise.

"Black and white become you, however," said Elizabeth. "They are my colours: did you know?"

"N-no, your maj— ma'am. No, I didn't know that," I said, stammering a little in spite of all Lady Katherine's strictures. I looked the queen in the face, hoping she hadn't noticed or at least was not irritated.

She hadn't and she wasn't. Suddenly she smiled, and fleetingly, I saw the girl beneath the satin and gold and pearls, the living, breathing princess inside the castle.

"Welcome to our court, Mistress Blanchard," said Queen Elizabeth.

The memory of that sudden, *human* smile stayed with me all the rest of that day, but when that night I retired alone to the tester bed in the corner room, sorrow and anxiety overtook me again. I lay there, longing uselessly for Gerald and Meg, and on top of all that, desperately worried about money.

The magic of Elizabeth's smile was forgotten. I

remembered instead that she had practically ordered me to buy white or silver sleeves and under-kirtles, which I couldn't afford, and that I must also, somehow, pay a maid I didn't want and still support my daughter.

And so it began, my slide towards unlikely adventures, down a slippery incline called economic necessity.

§ 2 §

Slippery Footing

I woke next morning heavy of heart and jaded from my restless night. However, my window showed me that the weather was still bright, and sunshine is encouraging. I made an effort, rose in good time and faced the business of the day. One of my first tasks was to interview the lady's maid Katherine Knollys had found for me.

To my relief, the woman was so anxious for a post that she didn't haggle about her pay. Fran Dale was past her youth, with no savings and no family and was already regretting her refusal to go back to Yorkshire with her former mistress. In fact, she was on the point of retracting her resignation when I appeared, like a gift from heaven. I hired her, I confess, at a bargain rate, and tried hard to think of her as a bargain and not as a maddening expense. I did have some money left from Gerald's small savings and his last salary payment. What I would do when that ran out, I preferred not to think.

The next thing was that Lady Katherine Knollys introduced me to the queen's principal lady, Kat

Ashley, who came as a surprise, for she was not the impressive figure I expected.

She was well spoken and clearly well educated, and she was certainly well dressed, but her plump face and her slightly protuberant blue eyes had an expression which made me think at once of tavern-keepers and village beldames. She had been in Elizabeth's service since the queen was a child, and Elizabeth was employing her for love rather than suitability, I thought. Yes, the girl I had seen yesterday, looking out of the queen's golden-brown eyes, was human enough, and capable of affection.

However, when, that morning, I was taken to attend on Queen Elizabeth for the first time, the affectionate girl had been eclipsed by a very angry monarch. When Lady Katherine Knollys and Mistress Ashley brought me into the gallery where the queen was, we found it lined with courtiers, all keeping quiet and standing still, while her majesty marched up and down the black and white chequered floor, satin skirts swishing, costly shoes clumping and slender hands clenching and unclenching with an angry flash of gems. Just as we entered, she halted in front of a quailing individual in the dress of a messenger.

"Oh, stop cringing, man. It is not *your* fault! We shall not cut your head off for bringing bad news. But if I had that impertinent chit here I might be tempted to cut *her* head off!"

Swinging round, she caught sight of me and my companions. All three of us curtsied. Elizabeth fixed her gaze on me. "Ah, our new recruit, looking puzzled and alarmed. You must become informed of our concerns, Mistress Blanchard. We have just received word that Mary Stuart, Queen of Scotland in her own right and Queen of France by right of her marriage to its king, is not content with all these great honours but is styling herself Queen of England as well, and although we have sent a protest by way of our ambassador, she continues to have the heralds cry all three titles before her as she goes to chapel! What do you think of that, ha?"

She barked the question as a man might. I said, "I am truly shocked to hear of this, ma'am."

She nodded and appeared mollified, but not for long. A paunchy middle-aged man in an elaborate mulberry velvet doublet at this point asked permission to speak. Elizabeth veered to face him. "Yes, my lord of Arundel? We are listening."

"It is only, ma'am, that Queen Mary is but seventeen and very pious. Perhaps all we are hearing is an expression of her youthful ardour for her faith, and her desire to see it bloom once more in lands from which it has been banished."

Across the gallery, a fair-haired young man clad in an azure doublet, extravagantly puffed breeches to match and skintight tawny hose which revealed how long and muscular his legs were, caught my eye and rolled his own eyes upwards, as if to say, "Lord preserve us from such nonsense." A soberly dressed older man beside him nudged him reprovingly.

A swarthy, hard-faced gentleman standing close to me glowered in the direction of Arundel and muttered, "Pompous ass!" I glanced at him curiously and he gave me a little bow. "Sir Robin Dudley, Master of the Queen's Horse, at your service."

"This is Mistress Ursula Blanchard," whispered Lady Katherine. "Newly come to court."

Dudley nodded but said no more because, like everyone else, he was too interested in Elizabeth, who was surveying Arundel in a way which made it clear that she agreed with Dudley and the young gallant in azure. For a moment I thought she was actually going to utter the words "You silly little man!" She did not, although I felt sure she had considered it.

After a pause long enough to make Arundel blush, she said, "Piety? There is little difference between my faith and hers. We worship the same God; the rest is a dispute about trifles. No, my friend, what this concerns is power. A pious wish to expand what they call the true faith is as good an excuse as any for a country, or a ruler, with an urge towards conquest. Let us take up arms for God, they cry! And let us also, while we are about it, swallow up the rich pastures, the fine wool and creamy cheeses, the tin and iron of England! Faith? Bah!"

"Ma'am, I meant only . . ."

"I know you did, Arundel. I know. You wished to reassure us. We are not unmindful." Having embarrassed him, she had evidently decided to soothe him. As he bowed and murmured his thanks, she turned back to the messenger. "A reply to our ambassador will be made ready for you to take back to France. We will thank him for the pains he takes to keep us informed. You may withdraw."

The messenger retired with obvious relief and the queen beckoned to Dudley, and began to talk to him. The anxious crowd of onlookers, seeing that the queen had recovered her temper, relaxed.

Lady Katherine Knollys whispered to me, "You know about Mary Stuart, of course?" and I nodded.

Lady Catherine Grey was known as the Protestant heir for the very good reason that until Elizabeth married and had children, there was an alternative successor in the Catholic Mary Stuart.

Mary Stuart was another descendant from one of King Henry's sisters. Ever since Elizabeth came to the throne, she had been claiming—to the indignation of Elizabeth and most of the council—that she ought to be our ruler instead, because King Henry's marriage to Anne Boleyn hadn't been legal and therefore Elizabeth was not legitimate.

27

Fortunately, so far her claim was mere words, with little prospect of ever being anything else. Even the crown she did possess, the Scottish one, wasn't secure. The Protestant Scots were in arms against her regency and although Elizabeth considered that for a people to rise against their sovereign—even an impertinent chit of a sovereign with designs on Elizabeth's own crown—was a terrible thing, she had sent help to the rebels. England was beleaguered by Catholic powers, such as France and Spain. We could do without a Catholic Scotland. It was already well known that Sir William Cecil had threatened to resign as Secretary of State if Elizabeth wouldn't help the Scots, and in the end she had agreed.

Mary Stuart evidently hadn't taken the hint. This was scandalous and worrying; but to me it was not only that. Like a warhorse which hears a trumpet, I found myself excited, pleased to be back in the heart of political affairs, just as I had been in Antwerp. I grieved for Gerald and ached for Meg, but nevertheless, in coming to court I had done the right thing, for I had somehow or other come home.

I settled down. I laid out a little money on a messenger to take my instructions to Bridget about buying hens and planting onions, and quietly sold a few pieces of jewellery. Lady Katherine Knollys was right: if I were known to be hard up, it would damage my standing among the other ladies. Lady Catherine Grey, in fact, sniffed my problem out almost at once and made several edged remarks, but fortunately I got on quite well with the rest and even gained a little admiration when I enlivened some of our sedentary hours of embroidery by telling them stories of life in Sir Thomas Gresham's service in Antwerp. Lady Jane, who didn't share Catherine Grey's haughty attitude towards me, and often tried to jolly her out of it, was particularly enthusiastic. "Oh, do listen to Ursula!" she would cry, when I started an anecdote.

I was careful what I said about Gresham, though. Most of my tales concerned amusing domestic panics behind the polished and expensive Gresham hospitality; or salty items of gossip about notables whose reputations did not matter in England. It was Lady Catherine Grey, whose vocabulary did not include the word "discretion," who one day said, "Why don't you tell us some of the real stories about Sir Thomas, Ursula? Or were you and your husband not highly placed enough to know them?"

"Real stories, Lady Catherine?" I spoke lightly but I frowned at her. We were waiting for the queen to finish a conference with her treasurer, William Paulet, and we were gathered with our books and needlework in a large room through which other people could wander at will. The Spanish ambassador was wandering through it at that moment, though he was still, fortunately, out of earshot, talking to Kat Ashley by the window.

"Yes. About Sir Thomas's real work in Antwerp. Oh come on, Ursula. Tell us."

"Sir Thomas," I said, "is a financier who is in the Netherlands to raise loans for the queen from the banks of Antwerp and Brussels."

"*I've* heard that he's also raising funds by any means that he can think of—including bribing or blackmailing people and forging requisition documents, all so that he can spirit gold and silver bullion out of the Antwerp treasury and into the holds of ships bound for the Tower of London."

"You know more than I do," I said in cool tones.

"If it's true, it's a strange way to behave in a country where he's trying to make friends with important people," Lady Catherine said.

"No, it isn't," said Lady Jane Seymour, kindly

29

extending a hand for the needle which Catherine had allowed to come unthreaded, and putting the silk back through the eye for her. "You know how religion gets into everything. It's like an oil flask leaking into a saddlebag." There was a ripple of laughter from the other ladies. More careful than Catherine, Jane glanced round and made sure that de Quadra was still at a safe distance before adding, "The Netherlands are a Spanish province and Spain is Catholic. That makes the Netherlands treasuries fair game."

"And this is not the right time or place to discuss such things," I said abruptly. "You gossip too much, Lady Catherine, and I fear you invent half the things you say."

"Gently, Ursula, gently," said Lady Katherine Knollys reprovingly.

"I am sorry," I said. Here at court, neither curiosity nor an acid tongue were well regarded. On these occasions, I longed most terribly for Antwerp and for Gerald. Gerald had loved both my acerbity and my enquiring mind.

However, it was important to silence Catherine Grey, because she was, of course, quite right. I was sorry that gossip about Gresham was evidently abroad in the court. He had indeed robbed the Netherlands treasuries, and while he was about it, he had also learned more about King Philip of Spain's intentions and resources than King Philip would have wished either Gresham or Queen Elizabeth to know. Information about Sir Thomas's activities would greatly interest Philip's representatives in the Netherlands.

I knew about those activities because Gerald had been caught up in them. Not highly placed enough to be informed of such things? If that remark hadn't been so obviously intended to sting, it would have been funny. My open-faced, friendly husband had a remarkable talent for finding out who was vulnerable: who was in debt, who was hiding a record of embezzlement from a current employer, who was concealing a mistress from a wife he didn't want to hurt or a wealthy father-in-law he dared not offend. Gerald, in fact, had been making his way as one of Sir Thomas's recruiting officers for collaborators and spies.

Lady Katherine Knollys had probably heard the whispers about Gresham, too, and despite her rebuke I think she knew why I had been so sharp with Lady Catherine Grey. She now soothed me with a smile. "But I can't fault your discretion, Ursula," she said. "For that, I commend you."

De Quadra and Kat Ashley were approaching. Katherine Knollys began a harmless topic of conversation. Catherine Grey bent over her work, looking sullen.

I returned to my own work, admitting to myself that in a way, I enjoyed the need for caution and being aware of people like de Quadra, with their amiable expressions and their ever-open ears.

If only, I thought, I could find a way of earning just a little more, I would in time, when I had grown used to being without husband or child (and learned not to be inquisitive or sharp), be very happy in the queen's service.

I found the court more exciting every day. The excitement hummed in the air and throbbed in the ground. It was in the glitter of the river as it wound past the palace of Richmond, in the singing of the musical weathervanes, in the splash of oars as brightly decorated barges brought dignitaries to audience with the queen; in the clash of pikes on the ground as noble guests were saluted, in the trumpets which announced that the queen was leaving her apartments, setting out to her council or to church or to hunt.

Above all, it was in Elizabeth. As the days went on,

I learned my way about the palace, and I came to know the queen at least as well as any of her attendants knew her, although always one felt that there was more to know, aspects which she would never reveal, which would remain forever hidden behind those ramparts of satin and embroidery and jewellery. What was not hidden, however, was the power of her personality, which radiated from her like the glow from a fire. To be in her company was to be where colours were brighter and air was keener and words had double their usual meaning. Which meant being fiercely exhilarated and also very careful, both at once.

Working for her could be tiring. Sometimes she was out very early, having taken a fancy to walk in the gardens or park or, in wet weather, in the palace galleries. Her ladies had to accompany her to prayers and then be there for the morning practice of dancing or music. As yet, because of my newly widowed status, I did not dance, but I had to watch.

We always had to be near at hand even when the queen was busy with council or audience, and we had to go with her when she rode out in her coach to be seen by her people, or went hawking, or watched a tilt or a tennis match. However, if urgent business came up at any time, she would abandon whatever else she was doing and deal with it. This occurred several times within my first weeks, for the war in Scotland was reaching a critical stage, and messengers arrived constantly. When this happened, the council members would be called together and Sir William Cecil would be seen striding rapidly in the direction of the conference chamber.

I very soon learned to recognise all the people of importance. The young man in azure and his soberly dressed companion, whom I had seen on my first morning, were, I learned, connections of Dudley's, but people were vague about their names. They were not apparently notable. Dudley himself was very notable. Because he was so dark, people called him the Gipsy behind his back. The queen would sparkle whenever he came into the room and he was often in her company. He was the centre of the wildest rumours. His wife was never seen at court and one of the livelier rumours said that he was gradually poisoning her so as to be free to marry the queen.

He was not a council member, though. I soon discovered who was and who wasn't. The hierarchy of the palace allowed the queen's ladies to be on conversational terms with most people. In fact, I did better even than that, for within my first few days I met Cecil and his wife Lady Mildred personally. They asked me to their rooms.

"We wanted to see you," Cecil told me. "After all, we brought you here."

"Your husband served Sir Thomas well," Lady Mildred said gravely, "and through him, the queen. Your mother, too, was well liked in her day. The Faldene family is still remembered at court although it is years since any of you were here. Your mother left it long before our time, of course, but some of the older people can recall her."

They had led me to a comfortable, cushioned settle and Sir William was pouring wine for us all. He had a neatly combed fair beard and intelligent blue eyes, with a permanent crease between them, of anxiety and concentration. Being Elizabeth's Secretary of State was not a restful occupation. Before keeping this appointment, I had felt shy of meeting him, but it was his wife, oddly enough, who struck me as the more formidable of the two. Her face was full of strength and intellect. She made me nervous even when she was being friendly, as she was now.

"It's said of your mother," she told me, "that she

33

was kind to Queen Anne. She was still at court when Elizabeth was born and I believe tried to comfort the queen when she began to slip out of the king's favour, because the child was a daughter and not a son."

"I think that's true," I said. "My mother spoke of her court life now and then. She was fond of the queen. She didn't believe the charges that were brought against her. I remember saying that to Sir Thomas Gresham, once."

"He remembered, and passed it on to me." Cecil nodded. "And I have told her majesty. You are aware that she never speaks of her mother?"

"Yes, Lady Katherine Knollys warned me about that."

"She greatly admired her father," said Cecil, "and she can't remember her mother, as far as I know, but she is consistently good to those who are linked to her mother, by blood or by kindness. That is why she agreed to give you a place here. We hope, most heartily, that you will do well."

"Most heartily," Mildred confirmed.

Cecil handed me my wine. "We shall not pay you special attention after this," he said, "but not because we've forgotten you. It would be wiser, that's all. At court, one is always on a slippery footing and it's as well not to arouse envy."

Considering the state of my finances, I was more likely to inspire pity or scorn, although I didn't say so.

"And you can come to us if ever you are in any difficulty," said Lady Mildred, and Cecil nodded in agreement.

"In effect, you have no family," he said. "Sir Thomas has told us all about you. There was, alas, no place in his household vacant which you could fill, and when we said we would sponsor you at court, he was relieved. If necessary, we will be your family. We would like you to promise that you will turn to us if you are in any trouble."

I was so touched that my eyes stung. It was a long time since anyone had offered me that kind of support. I gave the promise, although I wasn't sure how far I meant it. I could see plenty of difficulties ahead, and all of the same sort, but one couldn't ask people like the Cecils for alms, for the paradoxical reason that they might actually offer some. I would not trade on their goodwill. I was no whining beggar, whatever my father-in-law might say.

Gossip about possible or impossible marriages for the queen went on all the time. Everyone expected her to choose a husband soon, and tongues wagged constantly on the subject. She had refused Philip of Spain; she couldn't under present circumstances marry Robin Dudley, but there were other foreign princes and other homegrown noblemen too.

The Earl of Arundel, Henry FitzAlan, was said to have hopes but I had seen for myself what Elizabeth thought of him. He was not only a quarter of a century older than she was, with a bulging middle, but also had something like a genius for irritating his sovereign lady. In addition, he was one of the Catholic councillors inherited from Queen Mary. "In days gone by, he alternated between regarding Elizabeth as a menace to the peace of the realm, and a poor young girl in need of protection," Lady Katherine Knollys once told me. "I think she finds both memories uncomfortable."

Arundel, in fact, was chasing a dream. When the bright young folk of the court got together and laid odds on the chances of the various contenders, they estimated his at five hundred to one against.

For the moment, the queen showed no inclination

to choose anyone. "We have our war in Scotland to deal with first," I heard her say once, when another councillor, the Earl of Derby, tried to raise the matter with her informally. Derby was another of Queen Mary's former councillors, and he had favoured the union with Philip of Spain. I wondered what he thought of the Scottish war, because I supposed that from his point of view, England was on the wrong side. He never, of course, said as much, but he certainly had a long face when news came that the foe wished to negotiate.

Cecil was sent to Edinburgh to represent England at the peace talks. He came back in July, with a peace treaty signed, but by then, the atmosphere at Elizabeth's court had changed. Gone were the days when the queen would abandon any diversion, no matter how absorbing, if a matter of business came up.

Cecil had returned with a difficult mission successfully accomplished, the Catholic influence in Scotland reduced almost to nothing and England that much safer because of it, only to find that Elizabeth, who should have been loading him with rewards and giving banquets in his honour, had scarcely any attention to give either to him or to the responsibilities of reigning.

That was the time when the sizzling nature of the attraction between the queen and Robin Dudley, her Master of Horse, really became apparent.

§3§

Dudley's Dilemma

"Apparent" was a mild word for it. It was the kind of attraction which sends the ambient temperature up whenever the two people concerned are together, and they were together a great deal. When the queen danced, either for her private amusement or on official occasions, Dudley would be there to partner her. When she walked, in gallery or garden, Dudley was in attendance. When she rode, he rode beside her; when she went out in her coach, he rode beside that and talked to her through the window. She normally dined in private, or with a few chosen companions. Dudley was chosen nine times out of ten. Wherever they were, they followed each other with their eyes.

The only place in which they were not together was the queen's bedchamber. Kat Ashley took care that two of the queen's ladies always slept in the anteroom at night. I now knew that Kat Ashley had not always been a model of discretion in the past and in my opinion she still wasn't—I thought she allowed the queen's women to gossip far too much—but she was

careful about that final point. The queen might call
Dudley her sweet Robin but they were not lovers.

Or not yet.

Everyone thought they soon would be, and even
before Cecil came back from Scotland, the situation
had most of the council fairly biting their tongues
with rage. Dudley wasn't popular. His father had been
beheaded for treachery, and he himself was no more
than a knight. He was no one's ideal candidate for the
kingship.

Most of the council were quite outspoken on the
matter, at least when the queen and Dudley couldn't
hear them, and as for Sir Thomas Smith . . .

Smith wasn't a council member, but one of Cecil's
legal advisers. For a courtier and a lawyer, he was
amazingly rough tongued. "A sound political marriage, that's what England needs," he declared, one
hot morning when we were sitting on our horses in the
main courtyard at Richmond, ready to go hawking,
and waiting for the queen to appear. The day promised to be scorching, but nothing could have been
much more scorching than Smith's powerful voice as
it went on to announce that what the country didn't
need was a swollen-headed horse-master swanking
about in ermine.

"Dudley's married already, mercifully," the Earl of
Derby pointed out. Edward Stanley of Derby was
much the same age as Sir Thomas, but he was polite
where Sir Thomas was outspoken, spare and dapper
where Sir Thomas was large and untidy, Catholic
where Sir Thomas was Protestant.

Of the two of them, I preferred Sir Thomas. There
was something cruel about Derby's thin mouth. It was
said that in Queen Mary's day, he had encouraged her
enthusiastically in persecuting heretics, and that because of this, he rarely came to court. He was believed
to be here now simply because he wanted to keep an

eye on sweet Robin. Robin Dudley was the one subject on which Derby and Smith agreed. They might differ on everything else, but Dudley they unanimously loathed. It almost drew them together.

"Only, of course, because he's married, there's a risk of scandal," Derby added ominously.

"There's a worse risk than that. If his wife dies . . ."

"Ah, yes. She's said to be ill, is she not?" said Derby. "But Cecil visited her on his way back from Scotland and he says there's nothing wrong with her."

"Mighty disappointing for Dudley, if so," said Smith.

Arundel, who was also nearby, said, "Shhh," in a reproving tone, but there was no stopping Thomas Smith, who continued to give tongue in those all too resonant accents.

"The sooner the queen's suitably married, the better. For all her crown and sceptre, she's a woman and she needs a man and some children like any other woman, and the country needs an heir. Someone ought to tell her."

"We have," said Derby. "The council, I mean. Though in more respectful terms. But while Dudley's on hand, it's useless." He removed his russet velvet cap and wiped his sweating hairline with a handkerchief. "It's too hot for hawking today. In another hour the park will be no better than a frying pan."

"And I had a late night last night," drawled a tall, arrogant-faced individual called Sir Richard Verney. He was one of Dudley's men and I wondered whether he minded hearing his employer spoken of so scathingly, and whether he reported what he heard to Dudley afterwards. No one seemed to be worried about it. "Personally," Verney complained, "I'm likely to fall asleep in the saddle."

"You shouldn't sit up till dawn at card parties," said somebody. Everyone laughed.

Fiona Buckley

"Well, it won't be any hotter than that damned Irish gelding Dudley's bought for the queen," Smith said. He scowled at the animal in question. Caparisoned suitably for its royal rider, it was being held by a groom. It kept on trying to circle round him and we had all moved our mounts away from its heels. "Anyone would think that she *wanted* to break her neck," said Sir Thomas.

"I've warned him about that horse," said Verney, "but he never listens to advice."

"I know. I was there. I heard. He told you not to be such an old woman, and three grooms and a coachman heard him too," said Smith with a chuckle. Verney's high cheekbones flushed with annoyance. It occurred to me that people didn't worry about criticising Dudley in Verney's presence because he probably agreed with them.

"One day," he said grimly, "he may wish he'd heeded me. Ah. Here comes the queen."

"And Dudley," muttered Sir Thomas Smith.

The court had moved about during the summer but we were back in Richmond by July. It was one of Elizabeth's favourite palaces and she was particularly fond of riding and hawking in the park. She wouldn't call off a hawking expedition just because of a heatwave. I was among those present because of my ability to ride on my own and not just as a pillion passenger. Few ladies possessed this accomplishment, and the queen valued those of her women who did. When she found that I was one of them, she gave me leave to borrow certain animals from the royal stables.

However, I had to take whichever was available and this time I found myself on a little blue roan mare called Speedwell. Speedwell was young and only recently broken in, and was still liable to shy at everything, from a blackbird flying across the path to a deer breaking cover to somebody sneezing. Riding her meant being constantly alert, and in this sultry weather, it was a strain.

The queen and Dudley might be too engrossed in each other to notice the weather, but the rest of us were wilting before we were well out into Richmond Park. Sir Thomas Smith, astride a massive weight-carrier, was crimson in the face before we even left the courtyard.

It was very, very hot. The gentle hills of the park quivered with heat haze and the open stretches were like griddles, on which the grass and bracken were turning yellow. In the woods, the leaves hung as though weary and when we came in sight of a pool, the glitter of the water was enough to make one's eyes ache. The beaten earth paths were baked hard, and here and there we saw the shimmer of transparent wings, where ants' nests were swarming. Flies buzzed round horses and riders.

Dudley and the queen rode, as usual, side by side, Elizabeth on the excitable Irish horse, a bay with a broad white blaze, and Dudley on a powerful black. He was so much a part of it that even those who disliked him most still watched him with unwilling admiration. He carried a goshawk which could take a rabbit. The queen had a hobby hawk which could not but which was still capable of taking bigger prey than the merlin usually carried by ladies. Most of the gentlemen had goshawks like Dudley but one or two were sharing. Among these was a stranger, a lean dark man, who, I now gathered, was Arundel's guest and had arrived at court the day before. He had kept quietly back and out of the conversation in the courtyard but was now riding beside his host and taking a turn now and then at flying Arundel's bird. I wondered if he wouldn't rather have stayed indoors with a cool tankard of ale. I knew that I would.

The women in the party, apart from the queen and myself, included Lady Katherine Knollys, who rode her showy but well-mannered chestnut mare with an air, and Lady Catherine Grey who was balanced uneasily on top of a phlegmatic brown gelding. She was no horsewoman and only came hawking because it was the proper thing to do, and as the heir to the throne—well, in Protestant eyes, anyway—she must be seen regularly close to the existing incumbent. Or as close as she dared to come. She seemed afraid of getting too near to Elizabeth's restive bay.

Behind us, as usual on these outings, were the attendants and falconers, some mounted and some stumping along on foot. People flew their hawks and handed over the haul of larks, blackbirds and thrushes to the mounted attendants, who took them back to be stowed in the bags on the shoulders of the foot people. The bags didn't fill very fast, for the haul was poor. Even the songbirds preferred to rest in the shade in this temperature.

The flies were infuriating. I swatted at them with a frond of bracken I had plucked by leaning perilously out of my saddle, and prickled with sweat in my heavy riding dress, and was thankful when at last we turned for home.

The queen and Dudley still led the way, with Lady Catherine Grey on Elizabeth's other side, although she still kept a wary space between them. The palace turrets were drawing blessedly closer and I was thinking in terms of cool drinks and a rest, perhaps, on my bed, when Arundel caught sight of a wood-pigeon on the wing, seized his goshawk from the wrist of his guest, who chanced just then to be carrying it, and flung it into the air.

What happened next, happened quickly. The hawk, taken by surprise, dithered on the wing for a moment and its shadow alerted the quarry, which fled for the safety of a wood where the branches would keep the hawk from swooping. Its alarmed, flapping flight brought it directly over our heads. By then, the hawk had seen it and given chase. She dived, steeply and fast, plunged below the pigeon, rose and struck her quarry in mid-air. Hawk and pigeon together descended into our midst with a vehement beating of wings and a flurry of dove-grey feathers. They landed between the queen and Lady Catherine Grey and right in front of Speedwell, and all three horses, even Lady Catherine's placid gelding, simultaneously plunged, snorting.

Lady Catherine clutched wildly at her saddle pommel while her horse pranced sideways. Speedwell stood up on end, pawing the air, and the queen's horse laid back its ears and bolted, straight off the track and across a rough downward slope full of tussocks, rabbit holes, sharp dips into narrow tracks, and all manner of perils for a horse too frightened to look where it was going.

Dudley swore and spurred instantly in pursuit, but although the bay pecked once, it did not fall and Dudley caught up within a hundred yards. Stretching out a powerful hand to the bay's bridle, he hauled it round in a curve, slowing it down. In a few moments, they were on their way back to us at a controlled trot, with the queen laughing and telling Dudley she could have pulled up unaided if he had left her to it, and teasing him because his face had gone bloodless.

Meanwhile, Lady Catherine's mount had backed into the horse which Arundel's guest was riding and he, in response to Lady Catherine's squeals of fright, had gallantly seized her gelding's bridle to steady it.

I had to steady Speedwell myself and stay in the saddle as best I could. Arundel, the only other person near enough to reach me, was too busy gaping in horror at the drama round the queen to notice my plight. Lady Catherine's rescuer glanced concernedly towards me, apologising with his eyes for the fact that his hands were too full to be of any use to me. I gripped the pommel between my knees, kept my seat even though Speedwell was nearly perpendicular, dragged on the curb, and pulled her jaw towards her chest. She settled back on to all four feet and I spoke to her soothingly, while edging her away from where the hawk was now mantling fiercely over her prey.

Arundel, face pale and jowls wobbling, dismounted to gather up hawk and quarry. As the queen and Dudley rejoined us, he stammered out an apology, but the queen continued to laugh, as though danger had merely stimulated her. "It was scarcely your fault, Henry. How were you to know the pigeon would decide to fly back over us?"

"Nevertheless, madam, I cannot say how much I regret . . ."

"No harm done," said Dudley, but added, with an edge on his voice, "The day's sport is over. No more flying at game, if you please, ladies and gentlemen. Lady Katherine, will you ride beside her majesty, please? Your horse is steady and will have a calming influence on hers."

No one demurred, although as we set off again, Sir Thomas Smith lumbered up to Arundel on his semi-carthorse and growled under his breath that Dudley gave himself airs and threw out orders too freely.

"The queen chooses to permit it," said Arundel, "so what have we to say?"

"Plenty!" Smith snorted. "The queen is a young girl and lacks wisdom. Someone should tell her to take care of herself. A nice mess the country will be in if she kills herself before there's an heir of her body, though I hope not of Dudley's body too. If Cecil's wrong and Lady Dudley really is dying—does anyone know the truth about that?"

"No," said Lady Catherine Grey. In her usual heedless way, she ignored the fact that Dudley was probably within earshot, and added, "But it is to be hoped that if Amy does die, the queen will not so forget herself as to marry her horse-master."

Dudley certainly heard, for I saw him give her an unfriendly glance. They were relatives by marriage but I had noticed that they didn't like each other. Lady Catherine always shrank a little when Dudley came near her, as though his intense masculinity somehow offended or even alarmed her, and I had seen him eye her in a way which reminded me irresistibly of a cat looking at a sparrow which, just now, it is too lazy to stalk.

Then, unexpectedly, he reined back to bring himself alongside us, and grinned at us boldly. "The trouble is, everyone has a favourite candidate and they're all different. Take Arundel here! We know who he favours."

Henry FitzAlan of Arundel, already pink as a result of being too warm, went pinker still and glared at Dudley.

Dudley grinned again. "Then there's Derby," he said, sliding smoothly past the embarrassing subject of Arundel's own rejected suit and turning his attention to the equally annoyed Edward Stanley. "You've been sighing with regret ever since Philip of Spain wedded his French princess and fell off the end of the queen's list of possibles."

"We've had him already," snapped Smith. "When he was married to Queen Mary. Most people didn't want him back."

"The realm could have gained greatly from friendship with Spain," said Derby.

"There I agreed," said Arundel. "It might well have

been better to have him back as our queen's husband than arriving as an invader to take England by force, which is what many people fear."

"Oh, he won't do that," said Dudley easily, and to my surprise, caught my eye. "He can't afford to mount an invasion. He's up to his Hispanic beard in debt. Ask Mistress Blanchard there. She knows."

To my embarrassment, they all stared at me and began pushing their horses closer to Speedwell. Arundel's guest said in astonishment, "I don't understand."

"This is a friend of mine, Matthew de la Roche," said Arundel. "Matthew, this is Mistress Ursula Blanchard, who has recently joined the court. Her husband died last winter."

"They were in Antwerp at the time, with Sir Thomas Gresham," said Dudley. "Her husband was well placed and I have sometimes heard Mistress Blanchard speak of Antwerp myself. You always preserve admirable discretion," he added, addressing me directly, "but there is no need for that in present company. Council members and their advisers can be trusted. Why not speak for yourself?"

Coming from Dudley, it amounted to an order. "Gerald—my husband—did work for Gresham," I agreed. "And yes, he did mention to me that King Philip was known to be in debt." Gerald, in fact, had been the one who discovered the details. "King Philip of Spain has been borrowing heavily from the Brussels bankers," I said. "It is true that he isn't at present in any position to mount an invasion."

"Ah. Sir Thomas Gresham. A famous name, these days. That explains it," said de la Roche. "Gerald Blanchard?" He smiled at me. "A French surname and an Irish Christian name. Unusual."

"My husband's mother came from Ireland. I believe she named him," I said. "The name Blanchard comes from his grandfather. He was French by birth. He married the daughter and heiress of the house and lived there with her."

"And you, Mistress Blanchard? Are you all English, or do you have varied origins, as your husband did?"

"I'm entirely English—my maiden name was Faldene. Your own name sounds French, too." He also had a trace of accent, I thought.

"My father was French," he said, "but my mother was English. I'm also a cousin, in a remote way, to FitzAlan here. But from what part of England do you come?"

"Sussex," I said.

"Ah. I thought I knew the name Faldene although I haven't met the family. I have settled in Sussex myself. I have been most of my life in France, but when my father died last year, my mother grew homesick for England, and I came over with her to buy a property here. Sadly, she too died not long ago. But I shall make the best of the place we bought—although it needs much setting in order. It has kept me so busy that I have had no time for social contacts."

His voice, accent and all, was pleasant. He was not a conventionally handsome man, not with that long chin and those wide, bony shoulders, but there was an attractive quality of vigour about him, and I liked his eyes. They were dark and diamond shaped, set under dramatic black eyebrows, and they had in them a glimmer of amusement. His way of studying the person to whom he was talking, as though truly anxious to know what they were thinking and how they felt, reminded me of Gerald.

I bit my lip. Something rustled in the undergrowth, and Speedwell once more snorted and pranced. I quietened her. Around us, the tension had settled down. Dudley had stopped provoking people and lost interest in me and was talking hawks with somebody else. De la Roche said, "You ride well, Mistress Blanchard. Is that your own horse?"

Lady Catherine Grey answered for me. "No, Ursula has no horse of her own. She borrows from the royal stables."

"No horse of your own?" De la Roche sounded quite shocked. "But why ever not? Someone as skilled in the saddle as you are should have her own mount. You must buy a horse without delay. Arundel, can you not recommend a dealer for Mistress Blanchard?"

A moment ago, I had liked him. Now, without warning, I was convulsed with fury. I was so sick of my straitened circumstances and the embarrassment of trying to hide them, in this court where to be hard up was to be second rate.

You must have a maid. A white or silver under-kirtle, perhaps, with matching sleeves. Buy a horse without delay. Spend money I hadn't got!

"I can't buy a horse," I said. I forgot about not being sharp. "I can't afford one!"

"Can't afford one? But, you are a Faldene and surely they are a family of some eminence. And your husband was a successful man. I don't understand . . . Mistress Blanchard! I beg your pardon. I see I have said something I should not."

I had turned away my head but he had still glimpsed the tears in my eyes. They were mostly tears of rage. I found myself looking at Lady Catherine Grey instead of de la Roche, and she was clearly amused by my discomfort. I straightened my back and addressed de la Roche once more.

"Yes, I'm a Faldene. So was my mother and she never changed her name. Do you know what I'm saying?" I saw the contempt in Lady Catherine Grey's face but I was too angry to care. "I was brought up at Faldene on sufferance," I said. "A child with no father. My husband was a younger son. He had no

48

property of his own and he married me against his family's wishes. He died before he could gather any substance to speak of. I have very little—except a small daughter whom I love, and must support. Now do you understand?"

I waited, simmering, to see if contempt would now appear on the face of de la Roche.

It did not. Instead, he said seriously, "In such circumstances, did neither of your families . . . No, forgive me, it is not my business. But . . ."

I had banished the tears, by sheer willpower. "My own family offered me shelter of a kind," I said. "I preferred to enter the queen's service and earn my stipend. It is modest but I am glad not to be living on grudged charity. I have no complaints. However, I cannot afford to buy, or keep, a horse."

"I am *very* sorry." Master de la Roche looked quite shaken. "I did not know. Please accept my apology. I had no wish to hurt your feelings. I have the utmost respect for anyone, like yourself, who bears up under such misfortune. If there is dancing this evening, and I ask you to partner me in a galliard, will you accept?"

I looked into those dark, diamond-shaped eyes and I saw contrition, and sympathy, and something else.

I saw admiration, not just for a young widow making her way in the world under difficult circumstances, but the admiration of a man for a woman he desires.

We were in the midst of languorous summer, and Gerald had been gone now for more than six months. Deep within me, momentarily, something stirred in answer.

I stamped on it at once. No, said a shocked voice inside my head. No! He isn't Gerald. There can be no one for you but Gerald.

However, what was being offered, I could not utterly reject, either. I hadn't danced since Gerald's

49

death, but perhaps now it was time to ease the bonds of sorrow. "Of course, Master de la Roche. I shall be delighted to dance with you," I said. "And I am sorry," I added, "if I was discourteous just now."

Matthew de la Roche laughed. "Mistress Blanchard, I prefer conversation to have a little salt in it, like a good dinner."

I laughed, too. I was being pleasant, making amends. I hoped he would see no more in it than that. I hoped there *was* no more in it than that.

During the next few days, Matthew de la Roche was hardly ever out of my sight. It seemed that I had ridden out hawking as an unattached young widow and come back with a suitor. I didn't want a suitor, or so I told myself, but I let him dance with me that same day because I wanted to dance. After that I could not have got rid of him without being rude and I didn't want to do that either.

It was quickly obvious that he was behaving towards me as Dudley was behaving towards the queen. He was always there. We danced together; he rode out with me. He invited me to watch him play tennis or practise tilting. He did both very well and I knew that he was proud of his skill and enjoying showing it off to me.

When, with others of the court, I accompanied the queen out walking, I found him at my elbow. He was at my elbow the following Sunday when the public were admitted to the Presence Chamber to see the queen pass on her way to the chapel. He seemed to like me in the same way that Gerald had, because he thought my dark hair and pointed face attractive and because the edge on my tongue was to him exciting instead of objectionable.

In so many ways, our minds were in accord and I

was drawn to him physically. Before long I knew that it was like the attraction of a cliff edge, for I was not only fascinated but also afraid, and I wasn't alone in my doubts. The day came when I was called to Kat Ashley's room. Lady Katherine Knollys was there too. They looked at me anxiously.

"Ursula, my dear." Mistress Ashley patted the window seat beside her.

Sensing that some serious matter was about to be raised, and not knowing what it was, I remained standing. "Yes, Mistress Ashley?"

"This is so difficult. We are only concerned with your welfare. But even the queen has noticed that Arundel's guest, Matthew de la Roche, is very much in your company. We understand that he is a widower. Does he have serious intentions towards you?"

"I don't know, Mistress Ashley." Kat Ashley always made me uneasy. She took the same avid interest in matters of love and marriage, as any village woman whose favourite occupation was gossiping round the wellhead.

"There is nothing against him as far as anyone knows, but no one seems to know a great deal." Lady Katherine, who had also remained standing, spoke seriously. "However, I must tell you, Ursula, that the queen is very much opposed to any sign of scandal among her ladies."

Alarmed, I said, "Has the queen actually . . . ?"

"Expressed concern? Yes, she has, although she has not criticised your behaviour. You have done nothing yet to give rise to scandal, but you must be careful. I should also," said Lady Katherine, "be careful in another sense. It may not be against the law to have Catholic sympathies—if it were, half the council would be in the Tower; Henry FitzAlan of Arundel and Edward Earl of Derby for example!—but all the

51

same, de la Roche was brought up in France and presumably in that faith. It is a point you should consider before . . . taking any final decision."

I nodded. Matthew had told me about himself. I was aware that he was a widower, and I knew that the young wife who had died in childbed had been French. I also knew that both he and she were Catholic. I had been very silent when I heard that. "I will be careful," I said.

"I was sure you would be sensible," said Lady Katherine. "The queen is impressed with you, you know, Ursula."

The summons from the queen came the next day.

Elizabeth had been shut away all morning. Kat Ashley was with her but all the rest of us were out of doors, taking advantage of the bright light to get on with various kinds of stitchwork. I was making a pair of white silk sleeves with silver leaves embroidered on them. It was cheaper than buying them ready made.

We had chosen to sit out in a walled garden, a favourite place of ours because it was so pretty, with its rose arbour in one corner and the fruit trees trained round its mellow brick walls. It had a scythed lawn with a yew tree in the middle, and neat, geometrical flowerbeds aglow with phlox and gillyflowers and here and there the tall spikes of lupins, and delphiniums like blue flames. The flowerbeds were edged not with lavender, as in the big entrance garden, but with box, which had its own, more subtle fragrance. It was a charming place.

We were sorted out according to rank. The exalted Ladies of the Privy Chamber occupied the rose arbour, while the humbler Ladies of the Presence Chamber had the square of grass round the yew tree. To my regret, I was seated next to Lady Catherine Grey, who had admired my work, but added that such meticulous stitching was tiring; would I like the name of her own gown-maker? The woman was expensive, of course, but *so* skilled . . .

Lady Catherine Grey had a real talent for the acid-in-honey kind of remark. It put my much simpler form of sharpness to shame. I was a frequent target because I was hard up and I had rebuked her for gossiping about Sir Thomas Gresham; and at the hawking party I had admitted in her hearing that I was illegitimate. But I was learning how to retaliate. Smiling at her, I said I enjoyed the satisfaction of doing good work and then added, "Of course, it requires concentration."

Lady Catherine was quite a skilled embroidress but she was incapable of concentrating for long at a time and sometimes abandoned projects halfway through. Lady Jane quite often finished them for her. I saw some of the others glance at us with covert amusement.

It was said that Lady Jane Seymour's brother, Lord Hertford, was sweet on Catherine and she on him, and it was true that they often danced together, and that she always watched him, and looked resentful when he danced with anyone else. She was pretty in a way and might have been nicer if she had met with more kindness, but her parents, dead now, had been noted more for their ferocious ambition than for their loving natures, and Elizabeth candidly disliked her. Most of the people close to Lady Catherine seemed either to value her or detest her because of her royal birth, and none of them, except for Lady Jane and her brother, were at all interested in her as herself. Perhaps Hertford, if her sulkiness didn't discourage him too much, would one day make her happy and soften her edges.

They certainly needed softening. Lady Jane did try but without noticeable success. When a page came into the garden, spoke to Lady Katherine Knollys, and then came across to me to say that the queen wished to see me in her private apartments, I was glad of the excuse to get away. I gave my needlework to one of the others to look after and followed the page indoors. The summons was a surprise and I was afraid I had inadvertently done something wrong, or else was about to face another inquisition about the state of affairs between myself and Matthew de la Roche. He was off somewhere with Arundel just then and I was relieved because his constant presence worried me. I was not yet finished with Gerald. I needed, still, to remember and to mourn and I did not want to be distracted.

Elizabeth was waiting for me in one of her private chambers, a long, narrow room, with a window at the far end, overlooking the river. The sunlit water threw ripples of light on the white-painted ceiling. The queen was in a chair by the window, with her back to the light. She was not alone. Dudley was there too, standing beside her chair, and Kat Ashley was seated on a stool near the door, engaged on a piece of sewing.

The page withdrew, closing the door. I curtsied and rose, and Elizabeth beckoned me to come forward. She was in informal dress, a long, open-fronted gown, peach-coloured and patterned with silver, over a loose white undergown, free of stays and hoops. Dudley was in shirtsleeves above his puffed breeches. Elizabeth half-turned her head and gave him a nod and it was he who began the talking, and not about Matthew.

He wasted no time on preamble. "Mistress Blanchard, I imagine you have heard that I have a wife, who is ill."

I said yes, I had heard this. Looking from one face to the other, I saw that Dudley's mien was unusually grave and that Elizabeth seemed, for once, to be tired, almost haggard. It struck me that she was too intelligent not to realise that she was giving rise to damaging talk. No matter how much she wanted Dudley, she must know that a queen could not dally with a married man, and that a queen should, in any case, choose a husband with exceptional care, to please her council and her people as well as herself. And that Dudley, even without a wife, wouldn't please them at all. If she were in love with him, as we all believed, then she must be at war with herself.

What Dudley felt was much harder to guess. Did he still have affection for his ailing wife or did he simply long for her to depart from the world and leave him free? I could tell nothing from that hard, dark face. Dudley had immense male magnetism but I could not imagine falling in love with him. I could not love where there was no kindness.

I valued kindness. Gerald had been kind, at least to me, if not to his hapless band of reluctant spies. That used to puzzle me, and once I asked him if he ever felt sorry for the officials he victimised into collaborating with him. He said yes, often; that many of them were pathetic rather than wicked but his duty was to Gresham, and beyond Gresham, the queen; and to me and Meg because we were the family he loved and must support. I supposed, doubtfully, that he was right. At least, in Gerald, the kindness was there. I thought Matthew had it, too, but in Dudley I could sense no kindness, no softness, whatsoever.

"It is also being said," he informed me now, "that my wife's illness is due to poison. In fact, that I am trying to get rid of her in order . . . to marry elsewhere." The hard eyes fastened on my face. "Have you heard that, too?"

The whole court had heard it. There was little point in looking horrified and declaring that no one had ever suggested such a thing. "Yes, sir," I said.

"And do you believe it?"

I wondered if he seriously expected me, if I did believe it, to say so to his face. I spoke carefully.

"It would be a very terrible thing to do and it could place you in danger, sir. I find it very hard to credit," I said.

Dudley's genial smile revealed the amazing depth of charm which he had at his command. He glanced at Elizabeth. "Mistress Blanchard has a remarkable grasp of the situation."

"Proceed," said Elizabeth.

"I will be frank," said Dudley. "You are short of money, are you not, Mistress Blanchard? I heard you say so to Matthew de la Roche, not so long ago, in a quite forceful manner."

"That is true, sir," I said. What in the world was all this leading up to?

"We cannot offer you a bigger stipend than that of the other ladies of your rank," put in Elizabeth, "but we are willing to lend you, as it were, to undertake an honourable task, suitable to your condition, for extra pay. You would continue to receive your stipend. Dudley is fully informed about you and has our permission to say what he is about to say."

Dudley bowed. Then he turned back to me.

"Lady Dudley—she is still often known by her girlhood name of Amy Robsart—is genuinely ill, Mistress Blanchard. Sir William Cecil, who called on her on his way back from Edinburgh, says he saw nothing wrong with her but she puts on a show for visitors. The truth is that she has a growth in one of her breasts and the doctors doubt if she will see next Christmas. She has also heard the rumours that I mean her harm. We have been estranged for some years. Ours was an impulsive marriage and it didn't prosper, but I do *not* wish her ill. She has a woman attendant always with her, of course, a Mistress Pinto, but my wife is in great distress of mind and body. Her fears are feeding rumour and I wish those rumours to be stopped. Mistress Pinto knows of this, but her task is a heavy burden for just one woman. I want you to join my wife's household, assist Mistress Pinto, and convince Lady Dudley, if you can, that she has nothing to fear from me. You are not linked to me or to my wife either by blood or previous service. If you are there when the end comes, and can confirm that my wife died naturally, by the will of God, you will be protecting my reputation."

"And mine," said Elizabeth. "In this matter, what touches Sir Robin's honour, also touches mine."

Scandal would not smooth the way to the altar, I thought, and was startled when she added firmly, "It is our wish that Lady Dudley's life should be preserved as long as possible. That means giving her peace of mind. Will you assist in that? It would help us, and would, I think, be a way of helping you."

Elizabeth did indeed have a personality full of mystery. I was sure, immediately, that she was not merely saying the right things, but meant them, although in that case . . .

I was not given time to pursue this puzzling idea. "I myself can do little for Amy," said Dudley. "I visited her not so long ago and she wept and trembled at the sight of me." He shrugged, more in exasperation than pity, I thought. "The kindest thing I can do for her is keep away from her. But if you will succour her, I can offer you . . ."

The sum he named made me gasp. It should solve all my financial problems for at least three years.

It had crossed my mind that if Matthew asked me to marry him, I would not have to worry about money any more. I had even wondered if I ought to encourage him for Meg's sake. But here was a way to earn, which did not involve marriage before I was ready for it, would demand no disloyalty to Gerald's memory.

57

"Where is Lady Dudley living?" I asked.

"In Berkshire, near the Oxfordshire border," Dudley said. "Close to Abingdon. The house is called Cumnor Place."

I had no idea what lay ahead of me. At the time, it seemed to me that I was to be highly paid for simply comforting a frightened, sick young woman and trying, kindly, to stop her from spreading rumours. It might be distressing; but it didn't sound difficult and I would have money to spend on Meg. She must by now be growing out of everything she had had when I parted from her. She would need new caps, gowns, shoes. I looked at Elizabeth.

"Ma'am, is it your wish that I should go to Lady Dudley?"

"Yes, Ursula, it is our wish. We have your interests in mind," Elizabeth said. "It may be as well for you to be away from the court for a while. There is a matter on which you may wish to meditate, undisturbed. Is there not?"

She meant Matthew. I saw from the amused glint in Dudley's eyes that he knew all about it, and I reddened.

"But it is not our command," said Elizabeth. "You are free to choose. Do you need time to consider?"

No, I didn't. I did want time away from Matthew, and I needed Dudley's money. I thought of the gowns and caps and shoes for my daughter and said yes, at once.

§4§

Cumnor Place

Elizabeth clearly felt I should be separated from Matthew and I agreed with her. I knew that I must tell him why I was leaving the court. He had been paying his addresses to me and I had not dismissed him; I owed him some courtesy. He and Arundel were expected back that evening and I would see him then, I thought.

However, before evening came, I received a note from him delivered by the page Will, who ran many of the errands connected with the queen's ladies. He handed it over with a knowing look, which annoyed me, but I gave him the expected gratuity, and went to break the seal in private.

It was an apologetic little letter, saying that an urgent matter had arisen connected with the refurbishment of his house. He must leave at once and would be gone by the time I received the note. He would return in perhaps two weeks, and hoped to have the pleasure of seeing me then. I would be constantly in his thoughts.

I would be in Oxfordshire long before the two

weeks were up. There was nothing to do but write a reply which he could be given when he came back.

My letter thanked him for his, explained that I had gone, at the queen's wish, to attend on Lady Dudley, who was ill, and civilly hoped that his business with the house had gone well. It was a pleasant, polite letter, but I was careful in what I wrote. This was not a love letter, just a few words to a friend. As yet, I could go no further.

Dudley presented me with generous funds, and said that he would provide an escort. When I was introduced to them, I found that they were the fair-haired, azure-clad young gallant and the quietly clad middle-aged man who had caught my eye on my first day.

I remembered being told that they were connected in some way to Dudley. It seemed that they were not often at court but occasionally visited him there and sometimes took messages to his wife. The middle-aged man was called Thomas Blount, and was a cousin of Dudley's by marriage. The fair-haired young fellow, who greeted me with an extravagant bow and a declaration that he was eternally at my service, and was now disporting himself in rose-pink instead of azure, turned out to be Lady Dudley's half-brother, Arthur Robsart.

For all his elegance, he, like Blount, had come without a servant. When this point arose, while we were all discussing how the party to Oxfordshire should be made up, he added that he normally lived in Norfolk, and smiled at me with raised brows, as if inviting a reply.

"Ah yes. I believe I have heard of the Norfolk by-laws that forbid the inhabitants to travel with attendants," I said solemnly.

Arthur suddenly grinned and the young fop turned

on the instant into an entirely masculine and somewhat mischievous young man. "Some parts of it are
fairly rustic and it's a good way from court. Plain
living is more admired away from cities. My wife
Margaret is Norfolk-born and her tastes are simple.
So are mine, in many ways. I prefer to travel unclut-
tered and I only wear rose satin at court because it's
the thing to do. When in Rome imitate the Romans."

"Or make fun of them," said Blount, who though
serious of face, was not humourless.

"Exactly," said Dudley. "Arthur makes fun of
fashion, Mistress Blanchard. He puts on satins in
pretty colours fit for a maid of honour, as a backhanded way of gibing at our peacocks and popinjays.
Can we keep to the matter at hand? I'm sending a
manservant of my own with you because I shall want
him to bring back word of your safe arrival. His name
is Martin Bristow and he knows the route. Now,
Mistress Blanchard, you are a gentlewoman going to
stay with another gentlewoman, so you had better
take your maid. Can she ride? If she can't, she'll have
to follow you. Pillion passengers slow everyone down
and I want to get you there quickly."

No one who is perching sideways on a cushion
behind the saddle, hanging on to the belt of the rider
in front and without stirrups, can keep in place for
long at anything faster than a dignified walk. I had
ridden behind John on the way from Sussex, so that
the spare horse could carry the luggage, and we had
taken two and a half days over it.

"I'll ask her," I said.

Fran Dale was turning out my modest wardrobe
and repairing things ready for the journey, and rather
than call her from her work, I went to her. It turned
out that although she disliked riding—"I can't abide
long journeys, and that's the truth, ma'am, and it's

why I didn't want to go traipsing up to the North with my last lady"—she *could* ride and was willing to put up with it if her employment depended on it.

"It does," I told her, and assured Dudley that my maid could accompany us, if he could supply us both with mounts.

"I think you should also have a manservant of your own," he said. "You should have proper status if you are to be a personal attendant on Lady Dudley. I'll pick someone out for you."

I instantly thought: John Wilton! I could afford his services now, and for the foreseeable future too. I explained. I didn't know precisely where John was, but his sister Alice, with whom I had stayed on my brief visit to Sussex, would probably know. So might Bridget, since John had said he would watch over her and Meg.

Dudley agreed. Despite his wish for haste, we had to leave a day or two for a courier to go ahead and announce our impending arrival and there was just time to send to Sussex. Bristow, a smart young fellow who regularly rode round the countryside on Dudley's errands, set off, carrying with him some money for Bridget and some lengths of bleached linen, woollen cloths of blue and grey, and some rose-coloured damask from which she could fashion new clothes for herself and Meg. He was back in two days with John and also with an endearing note from Bridget.

Gerald and I had chosen Meg's nurse because she was kind and wholesome and experienced with children. She was the eldest daughter of one of the Blanchard tenants and had ten younger brothers and sisters. Few people are perfect, though, and Bridget had two drawbacks. One was that none of her family washed very often. We overcame that by being stern in unison until we had convinced her that although we were good humoured and would feed her well and wouldn't hit her, we meant it when we said that she must wash all over at least once a fortnight, and wash Meg, too.

The other drawback was that although she could read and write a little, it was a very little. That hadn't mattered at first, but when I came to court, I had worried about it. I would need to send instructions to her, and I would want to receive reports.

However, she had managed. I read the letter several times over, blessing it as a physical link between myself and the Sussex cottage where my child lived.

I got your letter, Mam, and vicar here helped me read it. I'm makin shift to write this myself. I am plantin the gardin like you sed, Mam, an heve got hens. They are sittin and I hope to hev chiks. Meg is well and arstin for you offen. Yrs respeckfully, Bridget.

I sighed over that letter, longing unbearably to be with them both, aching for my daughter, who was asking after me, but I must turn my mind towards Oxfordshire.

I was very, very glad to see John; at the sight of his plain, trustworthy face and his spiky hair, a little of my bygone happiness seemed to live again.

"You leave tomorrow," Dudley told us.

On the afternoon before we left, I walked in the park with the queen, along with various other ladies and courtiers, for until my actual departure I was still on duty. We were joined by Bishop de Quadra, the Spanish ambassador. His short, black-clad figure found its way to my side, apparently by intent.

"Mistress Blanchard, may I speak with you?" De Quadra had talked to me before, casually, during the many hours which the whole court spent standing about in anterooms and galleries in attendance on Elizabeth. His English was clumsy but he spoke French and so did I. He spoke French to me now. "I hear," he said, "that you are bound for Cumnor Place tomorrow, to reassure Lady Dudley that although her life may be in danger from disease, it is not in danger from assassins."

"Yes, that is so," I said.

"For your sake," said de Quadra, "I hope that what you intend to tell her is the truth."

"What?"

My face showed my amazement. De Quadra considered me thoughtfully, his own olive-skinned features expressionless. "I believe," he said, "that your husband was no friend to my master King Philip. Possibly, therefore, you distrust me, but in fact, I wish you no harm. You are young, and a woman, and I understand that you have a child dependent on you. I speak to you not out of any personal interest, but as a human being. Take care. You may be stepping into danger."

"Danger?" I was startled.

"An art you should acquire," said de Quadra, with perfect seriousness, "is that of holding important conversations while making them look trivial. Look as though we were discussing the weather, as you English so much love to do. Or discussing the people around us. I wonder what Edward Stanley of Derby and Sir Thomas Smith are talking about so earnestly? Those two amuse me. Sir Thomas is so big and outspoken, and my lord of Derby so neat and courteous; Sir Thomas such a rabid Protestant and Derby with so much Catholic passion in his past, yet they are often together. I believe much of their conversation is a duet of hatred for Dudley. I wonder who the third man in the group is."

I glanced at the little group, who were strolling

64

together a few yards away. I wasn't interested in them but I didn't wish to offend the Spanish ambassador. "I suppose he's another friend," I said.

"If so, he is not on their social level."

I looked again, and saw that de Quadra was right though I couldn't make out why. The man was quite well dressed. "What is it about him that tells one that?" I said.

"Oh, come, Mistress Blanchard. He looks at their faces when they speak and bobs his head to show his willingness to agree, and he is matching his pace to theirs, not the other way about. If you are to be involved in political affairs, you should cultivate habits of observation."

"But I'm not going to be involved in political affairs! I'm only going to comfort an ailing woman and hope thereby to quieten some rumours."

"If and when Amy Dudley dies, her husband will become free to marry and may seek to marry the queen. That is most certainly a political affair." He used the French word *affaire,* dryly, with a double meaning. "You English," he said, "have a saying that where there is smoke, there is fire. In my experience, there is truth in that. The rumours that you hope to quieten are, I presume, the whispers that someone intends harm to Lady Dudley. They are persistent. There is much smoke. To me it suggests a flame somewhere."

I experienced a jolt in the stomach, not of surprise, but of alarm, as though a secret fear had been roused to life. "My lord bishop," I said urgently, "if you know anything definite, please tell me."

De Quadra shook his tonsured head. "I know nothing specific. However, the rumours are not only persistent but strong. You speak of quietening them. I would counsel you to beware of them. If you go to Cumnor, Mistress Blanchard, I advise you to be very alert to all that goes on in that house. For your own sake, take care."

We set out on the Friday, each of us with a few belongings in saddlebags. The bulk of the luggage would follow by packhorse. Like pillion riders, packhorses slowed travellers down. Dudley had mounted me on a dainty little mare called Bay Star, and Fran Dale had a stolid, broad-backed white gelding. I had asked Dudley to give her a safe, comfortable horse, in the hope of reducing her complaints to a minimum.

I kept Dale because she was a very competent lady's maid and completely honest, but her favourite phrase was "I can't abide . . ." The list of things that she couldn't abide, apart from horse-riding, included moths round candles, loud noises, nasty smells, the flies that buzzed round horses in summer, and any place which was neither London nor the court. She had round blue eyes, a skin which must once have been good but was now marred by lines and smallpox scars, and a permanently aggrieved expression. John found her annoying. That first day he told her roundly, twice, to stop grumbling.

Despite Dudley's wish for haste, we soon saw that the journey would take at least two full days. We had avoided pillion passengers or packhorses, but Dale was a very poor rider and her white gelding was a maddening slug. However, we made the best time we could and if we didn't overtake many other riders on the road, we at least went faster than the farm wagons and donkey carts. The roads we took were well used, with grass and bushes cut back on either side to discourage footpads from lurking.

We set out on a fine morning, and Arthur Robsart got us all singing as we went. He had a good tenor voice and when, after a respectful hesitation, Martin Bristow joined in, he turned out to be a good singer, too. We were quite a jolly party and despite our unremarkable pace, we got through Maidenhead on the first day. By the afternoon, Master Blount was saying that we ought to reach Wallingford by nightfall. We would be well on our way by then.

During the afternoon, a darkening sky and a distant rumble told us that a storm was coming. Dale promptly announced that if there was one thing she couldn't abide, it was thunder.

"That's a new addition to the list," I said sardonically. She gave me a hurt stare, which I ignored.

Blount said, "I am not so well acquainted with the inns along here. Bristow?"

We all turned to Bristow. He was one of the smart and knowing sort, a little cocky for my taste, but he had already shown himself to be an efficient guide. He knew which inns gave horses good fodder and which didn't.

"Can we take shelter anywhere near here?" Arthur enquired.

"There's an inn called the Cockspur a quarter of a mile ahead," Bristow said. "It's a good enough place, if plain. The landlord doesn't cheat you."

"I don't think we'd mind all that much if he did," said Arthur, with one eye on the darkening sky.

We raced the storm, by breaking into a canter. Dale's lethargic steed didn't want to but Bristow seized its bridle and John gave it a crack with his whip and it decided to oblige.

The rain began just as we reached the inn. It was a rather ramshackle place, with thatch in need of repair and a yard full of potholes, but it was quite big. There was a first floor with a gallery linking the rooms, and a row of dormer windows looking out of the thatch above. The landlord, who met us in the porch, his bulky cylinder of a body wrapped in a white apron, was polite and apparently recognised Bristow. He asked respectfully after the health of Sir Robin Dudley, shouted for a groom to help John and Bristow with the horses, and whisked the rest of us to what he said was a private parlour.

This was more like a large cupboard, and we were sorely crowded, but it was clean, with panelled walls and a hearth. The sky was now so black that we could scarcely see each others' faces, but the landlord lit candles and went to find food and drink for us. A few moments later, John appeared, carrying a couple of saddlebags.

"I thought I'd best bring our belongings inside, Mistress Blanchard," he said. Then he added, "I'd like a word with you, ma'am, if I may."

I went out with him, and we stood in the porch, watching the rain swish down and turn the potholes into pools. "What is it?" I asked.

"I've been wanting to speak to you quietly since yesterday evening but I couldn't get the chance, ma'am. I didn't know where to ask for you, in that great palace, and once we were on the road, someone's always been near enough to hear. Mistress Blanchard, you gave me to understand you were going into the country to be company to Lady Dudley, who is ailing."

"Yes, John, that's right." I noticed, for the first time, how I always called him John, as Gerald had done. One normally addressed servants by their surname, but not John Wilton. To us, he always had been, always would be, John.

"I go about," said John. "I hear the talk at markets and whatnot. And I talked to the other grooms at court. Seems there are rumours about, well, about the Dudley household."

"Yes, there are. But then, with people so much in the public eye as the Dudleys," I said, "there is always gossip."

Lightning lit up the sky, followed by a crash of thunder, and the rain suddenly increased, as though the flash had released it. Puddles danced with raindrops and there was a sweet smell in the air.

"I don't want to give offence, ma'am." John always took care to address his employers correctly, even when arguing with them. "But I must speak my mind. Something funny happened to me yesterday evening and I reckon you ought to know about it."

"Something funny?"

"I don't mean comic, Mistress Blanchard. I mean peculiar. I was approached."

"Approached?"

"Aye. By someone I didn't know who was lounging round the stables watching other folks work. I was cleaning Bay Star's tack ready for you today and this fellow come drifting up to me and said was I John Wilton. So I said yes. And then he said was I travelling Abingdon way with you today, so I said yes again, since it's no secret as far as I'm aware . . ."

"No, it's no secret," I said. "We shall certainly pass through Abingdon. It's the last town before Cumnor. Go on."

"Well, he asked if I'd like to earn a bit extra, so I said how—though I didn't say it in a very friendly fashion. I don't take to people as talk in near-whispers. Makes me wonder what it is they're afraid to say out in the open. But my tone didn't put him off. He said there was a private message to be carried. Then he waffled a bit. He said the great lord he worked for wanted a letter delivered secretly, and that it was a delicate affair of state. But it all sounded thoroughly havey-cavey to me, so I said no."

"Who was the letter for? And who was sending it?"

"That I can't tell you. Things didn't get that far."

"Didn't you ask?" I said, quite sharply.

"I didn't want to know," said John candidly. "And

besides, I doubt if he'd have told me until I'd more or less agreed to help. It could have nothing to do with the Dudleys, ma'am. The fellow mentioned Abingdon and maybe that was the point, and it was just that we were bound in the right direction. But I didn't like it. I wouldn't do anything to mix you up in anything that wasn't respectable, and I just hope that you're not mixed up in such a thing anyway."

"John, I've simply been employed to help Lady Dudley, who is very ill. I am to lend a hand to the companion she already has and try to convince Lady Dudley that her husband means her no harm. To help give the lie to the rumours you mention, in fact. I'm sure there's nothing wrong about that."

"Well, it sounds all right," John admitted. "Only, I didn't like that fellow and his talk of secret messages."

At heart, neither did I. All too well, I remembered de Quadra and his hints. "If anyone else ever comes to you with such a suggestion," I said, "try to find out more. Be a little more inquisitive, John, for goodness' sake. If there is anything going on around Lady Dudley that shouldn't be, then I don't know about it—but if it's there, I *ought* to know about it. Do you understand?"

The storm persisted and in the end we stayed the night at the Cockspur. We set out early the next day, dined en route in the little riverside town of Abingdon, and reached Cumnor Place in the late afternoon.

The weather was cloudy but the rain had done the crops good. All round us, the meadows were green, and we saw flourishing orchards and ripening corn. The land belonged to Cumnor Place, Bristow said, and John remarked that the estate seemed prosperous. However, Cumnor Place itself, when we got there, didn't look prosperous at all.

There was no one on duty at the gatehouse, and we rode straight through the open gate and along a further path to the courtyard. I saw at once that in the days before Anne Boleyn and the Reformation, this had been monastic property. There is no mistaking ecclesiastical architecture. Cumnor had two storeys, built round a secluded courtyard, and there were still cloisters along one side. Doorways, windows, all had the distinctive pointed arch, the shape that spoke of prayer and incense.

"It reminds me of Withysham, the old abbey near Faldene," I said to John Wilton. "Your sister told me she had heard that Withysham was going to be repaired and used as a house, just like this. It's odd to think of old monasteries being put in order to be used as country homes."

"This could do with being put in order, although it's a home already, mistress," said John, eyeing it without enthusiasm.

He was right. Of course, it wasn't a near-ruin as Withysham had been, the last time I saw it, with lengths of broken-down wall and weeds everywhere. Nevertheless, it was neglected. Grass had sprung up between the cobbles in the courtyard and several slates were missing from the roof. The walls were heavy with ivy, in urgent need of trimming.

A pair of lurcher dogs ran out barking to greet us, and geese cackled in the courtyard, but we were already dismounting before any of the human inhabitants appeared, and when they did, it was unhurriedly, as though no one were much interested.

A couple of grooms were the first to present themselves. They came through an archway and went to help John and Martin hold the horses. Then a short dark man in a dull, dark suit emerged from a doorway in the cloistered side of the house, to greet Thomas Blount and Arthur Robsart by name, and announce

71

himself to me as Anthony Forster, Treasurer of the Household.

"You will be Mrs. Blanchard, of course. We are expecting you. You are very welcome." He didn't sound over-delighted to see me.

Master Blount said irritably, "Where on earth is everyone? Are all your servants asleep, Forster?"

"They are over in the church, Master Blount. We gave them leave to attend a wedding. One of our maids is marrying a fellow from Abingdon. We couldn't be sure when you would arrive. Ah, Mrs. Blanchard, let me present my sister-in-law, Mrs. Odingsell . . ."

A dignified lady with chilly grey eyes had followed Master Forster out. Thomas Blount and Arthur Robsart bowed to her and I curtsied. From yet another doorway came a large lady with iron-grey hair crimped into waves in front of an exotic crimson velvet cap and the rest of her swathed in a voluminous loose dress of magenta satin. She wandered out yawning as though she had just been woken from an afternoon rest, and asked what the to-do was about.

When I had been explained to her, by Forster and Blount together, she remarked, "Oh yes, we had a letter." I had been wondering if this were Mrs. Forster, but she now informed me that she was Mrs. Owen, evidently thinking that this should impress me. It didn't, because I had never heard of Mrs. Owen (or Mrs. Odingsell, come to that). Dudley had not thought to give me the fine detail of how the house was organised and I hadn't thought to question either Thomas Blount or Arthur Robsart. However, the velvet cap and the magenta satin didn't suggest a housekeeper, so to be on the safe side, I curtsied to her as well. This seemed to meet with approval.

The two ladies withdrew into the house, through their different doors, and in a mild flurry of saddlebags being unstrapped and horses being led away, Dale and I were parted from our travelling companions. I glanced, puzzled, at the retreating forms of Blount and Arthur as they went off towards Forster's doorway. Forster smiled at me. His eyes had a twinkle, but they were too knowing to be attractive.

"They are to have rooms in my wing. Because of her poor health, Lady Dudley rarely accommodates guests in her own wing. They will wash and change and then come to see her. But you will be part of her household and I am taking you and your maid to her straight away."

As he led us towards a third entrance, he added, "The house is oddly arranged. Have you been told about it?"

"No. I know very little about Cumnor."

"Well, Mrs. Odingsell and I live in the wing behind us. To your left is the part of the house occupied by Mrs. Owen, and the rest, where we are now going, is the domain of Lady Dudley. In fact, there are three quite separate households, although all share a common kitchen. It would be too expensive to provide a kitchen for each wing. We manage very well on the whole."

I doubted it. My girlhood as a semi-servant at Faldene had taught me a lot about this side of life. I could imagine all too well the squabbles in the kitchen over the use of the spit and the best cauldron, and the way food would arrive on the dining tables lukewarm after being carried through the house or across the courtyard on a cold day.

The studded oak door by which we entered was presumably Lady Dudley's front door. It was set in an arched stone porch, with slender lancet windows, much obscured by the ivy, at each side. I saw Dale looking about her with distaste. Any moment now, she would announce that she couldn't abide old abbeys, or windows with ivy tapping on them. Indoors, we entered a wide vestibule with a staircase to the upper storey. It was a double flight, with a little landing halfway up, and on the landing stood a woman.

Not Lady Dudley, I thought. I knew that Amy Dudley was quite young, and this woman was at least as old as Dale, and dressed, in any case, in much too plain a style. She stared at us in silence, and it was Forster who spoke first.

"Mrs. Pinto! This is Mrs. Blanchard, who has come to assist you." As everyone here seemed to do, he used the shortened form of the word mistress, which was coming into fashion then. Gerald had disliked it, and so did I. "Mrs. Blanchard, this is Mrs. Pinto, Lady Dudley's companion."

Mrs. Pinto came slowly down the stairs to meet me. She did not take my offered hand, and I let it fall to my side. She had blunt, rounded features in which one could see the remains of a pudgy prettiness, but her eyes were coloured like flint and not much softer.

"My lady is upstairs," she said. "She spends much of her time in her room, poor soul. Sometimes she feels too tired to come down. She stays in her chamber and prays and sews. I suppose you wish me to take you to her."

There was no question about it. Lady Dudley's woman Mrs. Pinto was looking at me as though I were a mangled and disgusting rodent, dangling limply from the jaws of a cat. Forster observed it too.

"I will leave you ladies to become acquainted," he said cravenly, and with a hasty bow, removed himself. I heard Dale draw in a disapproving breath, although whether because of Mrs. Pinto or Mr. Forster or both, I couldn't tell.

It was embarrassing. I did my best. "I would indeed like to meet Lady Dudley," I said politely to Mrs.

Pinto, and then added in a clear voice, "I hope we will be friends, you and I. I wish only to be useful."

Mrs. Pinto did not deign to answer this. She turned on her heel and led the way up the stairs. I followed, with Dale trailing after me.

We were led to a bedchamber, big and shadowy. It was L-shaped, with windows looking out both to the courtyard and the grounds, but the windows were too narrow for the size of the room, and gave only a poor light. The bare stone walls were without any tapestries. Looking about me, I thought that the room couldn't have been much more austere when it was used by the monks. The bed was luxurious enough, but the only other furniture in the room was a chest-cum-seat under the windows, a small table on which stood a branched candlestick, lit to dispel the gloom, and beside the table, a chair in which a woman was sitting.

"Lady Dudley," said Mrs. Pinto, in a voice of doom, "as expected, Mrs. Blanchard has arrived. This is she."

Lady Dudley started to her feet. She was certainly young, but she had none of the glow of youth. The fingers gripping the back of the chair were not slim, but thin; the hair gathered into her little jewelled cap should have been gleaming ash-blonde but instead was as dull as straw. Her face was pale, and the hollows under the charming cheekbones were far too deep.

Most telling of all, her sloe-blue eyes were sunken and shadowed, and although they were luminous, it was not with the sparkle of health but with something nearer to the shine of phosphorescence.

And when they met mine, I saw that they were also terrified.

§5§

Light and Shadow

I curtsied at once. "Ursula Blanchard, at your service, Lady Dudley." Rising, I found her still regarding me with that look of fear. Her first words were both startling and pathetic.

"My husband sent you, did he not? Are you his creature? Have you come to kill me?"

There was a paralysed silence, except for another intake of breath from Dale. Mrs. Pinto stared at me with something close to triumph, as if to say, Aha, you see, you haven't deceived us.

I spoke gently. "No, Lady Dudley, I have not. Your husband did send me, but my purpose is only to help and comfort you, to assist Mrs. Pinto in any way I can—" better try to smooth the bristling Pinto down a little—"and to amuse you if I may. I can play the lute and the virginals and sing a little."

I smiled at Lady Dudley encouragingly. She seemed almost too frightened to understand me, but although she was trembling, she did not plead or weep. Beneath her terror was a desperate dignity which moved me, suddenly and intensely. I must reach her; quieten her dread somehow.

What I said next was probably not at all what Dudley had had in mind when he gave me my orders, but it seemed right.

"I will also," I said, "taste everything you eat or drink and—in Mrs. Pinto's presence—handle every garment you are to wear, before you put it on. I will do all in my power not only to convince you that you are not in danger, but to keep it at bay if, by chance, I am wrong. I said I was at your service. I mean it."

In time I would look back across the years, and see my younger self at Cumnor Place, standing at the window of Amy Dudley's best parlour, on the first floor, looking down into the courtyard. I have come to think of her as Amy rather than Lady Dudley, for the name suits her youth and helplessness better than a solemn title.

The parlour, like everywhere else in Amy's quarters, is inadequately furnished. Stretches of bare floor lie between the scattered tables and chairs and the one settle; acres of bare stone wall between the only two pieces of tapestry. They cover the two doors and are meant to keep out draughts. There are plenty of those. Cumnor Place whispers with them, and all of it, not just Amy's bedchamber, is shadowy. The house is at least two and a half centuries old. There is a pervading smell of old stone and sometimes I almost fancy that the building, like a living thing, can remember the monks who once dwelt here, or that their shades still inhabit it. At night, by candlelight, it is eerie.

In a corner of the parlour is a little prie-dieu; very simple, nothing Popish. There's an English Bible on it, and a couple of candles in plain candlesticks. Amy, in her loose morning wrapper and warm slippers, because although it is still summer, she always feels cold, is kneeling there, at prayer. Her voice is low but I can hear the words, all the same. She is asking God to have pity on her, to heal her ills, to deliver her from her desperation.

I know what she means by ills. I have now been here for a week. Under Pinto's cold eye, I help Amy to dress and undress. Cecil had claimed that when he saw Amy there was nothing wrong with her, but he had only seen her dressed. I have seen her naked. Her left nipple is scarlet and discharging and beside it is a bulging lump which seems to have consumed all the natural glossy plumpness of a young woman's breast. Her physician, Dr. Bayly from Oxford, has warned her that she is dying.

He sounds a tactless man but I wish he still called, for Amy trusts him. However, he fell out with Anthony Forster. Amy told the doctor that she feared her husband was trying to hurry her out of the world by poison and thought Forster might be arranging it. Bayly believed her, accused Forster to his face, and was ordered off the premises. It was after this, as far as I could tell, that the rumours that Amy feared she would be murdered, began to spread across the country.

I had been waiting for a natural opportunity to ask what had aroused Amy's suspicions in the first place. When she told me of the quarrel between her doctor and Forster, it seemed to be the moment. It was my second morning and Amy, who had woken feeling weak, was taking breakfast in bed. I was sitting beside her, having eaten a slice of her toasted bread and drunk one of the two wine caudles which I now insisted should be supplied. Pinto was looking on, coldly (mainly, I think, because she hadn't thought of this precaution herself).

"But, Lady Dudley," I said, "what gave you the idea in the first place that anyone, Forster or your husband or anyone else, meant you harm?"

"My lady was sick," said Pinto aggressively. "Three or four times, a while after dinner but not after any special dish. Oh, she was so sick! It was pitiful to see her! It was a blessing that she has so little appetite, in my opinion! Whatever was in her food, she didn't eat enough to do her harm."

I had noticed how little appetite Amy had. At that moment she was nibbling her toast as though even that were too much for her. "I am glad you're here to taste my food," she said to me. Her brow clouded. "When I was sick, as Pinto says, I had pains in my limbs, too. Forster said that such things can happen to people with maladies such as mine, but Dr. Bayly was puzzled. The trouble stopped after he had it out with Forster. It was a few months ago now."

I was conscious of a queasy feeling in my own stomach. I didn't like the sound of this.

"Mrs. Blanchard," Amy said earnestly, "I live here, out of the world, but the news of the world still reaches me. The queen is enamoured of my husband, and he—well, if he were free to marry her, he would be king of England. I know my husband. He is ambitious and proud, and he ceased to care for me long ago. He has placed me here, in Forster's power—and I don't like Forster. He controls this household. He doles out money for me, grudgingly, and people visit him who don't visit me, but they talk about me. Ask Pinto there."

"Pinto?" I said.

"Tell Mrs. Blanchard," said Amy.

Pinto shrugged. "It was some while ago. I was going to Forster's wing to look for one of the maids who was doing work over there when she was needed here . . ."

79

"Yes, Pinto. Our old grievance." When Amy was well, I thought, she must have been very sweet, with a sly sense of humour. "But go on."

"Well, I was hurrying along the cloister when I heard voices through a window. Forster was talking to visitors in there. I heard Lady Dudley mentioned. That's all. I didn't hear anything else. Only I didn't like the tone, somehow."

"And I don't like Forster's eyes," Amy said. "There is something in them. He says reassuring things to me but his eyes say something different."

"He made out to be as shocked as could be about the idea of poison," Pinto put in, "but my lady *was* sick, several times, earlier this year, and for no good reason."

"I ached and my stomach hurt," Amy added. "Forster may say, as much as he likes, that my illness was the reason and that I am prey to melancholy fancies, but I am still afraid."

The young Ursula whom I see in my memory, surveying the summer sky, is pretending to wonder whether the fine weather will hold. Young Ursula, actually, has stalked to this window to conceal her face because, today, when Amy began her pitiful prayers, she was overtaken by such anger that she feared she would burst.

Just as I was angry with God for letting the smallpox take Gerald, I was angry with him for letting this hideous disease attack poor Amy. I was also furious with Dudley, for peacocking about at court, playing the lover to Queen Elizabeth when he not only had a wife, but a wife in such extremity. And not only that. He had virtually deposited Amy in a human gloryhole. Whether or not it harboured schemes against Amy's safety, I had never seen such an incredible household in my life.

Forster had said it was really three households, and

this was more or less true. Arthur Robsart and Thomas Blount, although they had brought money and letters for Amy, were being treated as Forster's guests. If they dined with Amy, as they had done once or twice, when she was having a good day, it was in response to a formal invitation, as though they were being invited to a house five miles off.

In fact, Arthur, although he was Amy's brother, had actually declined one such invitation. Though he seemed fond of his sister, he spent little time with her. I thought he found her company depressing. I could understand that, for I too was oppressed by the atmosphere of fear and malaise in Amy's rooms. When he did come, I was glad to see him, for he brought jokes and songs with him, even if briefly. He would be going home soon, and I told him I would miss him.

But if the heads of the households kept their lives more or less separate, the way the servants were organised was a complete muddle. Each wing had its own staff, but that merely meant that each servant was on the payroll of either Lady Dudley, Mr. Forster or Mrs. Owen. Lady Dudley, however, as the bearer of a title and the wife of the queen's Master of Horse, had a stipulated right to give orders to anyone in the house. However, it didn't stop there, for Anthony Forster, who actually owned the property and paid all the farm workers, clearly considered that both he and the chilly-eyed widow, his sister-in-law Mrs. Odingsell, were free to do exactly the same thing, a belief shared also by the indolent Mrs. Owen.

Mrs. Owen, I now knew, was the wife of the original owner of the property. Mr. Owen was a physician who had once attended King Henry. He was still alive, but like Mrs. Forster (who existed but apparently spent most of her time elsewhere) he was not in evidence at Cumnor. Mrs. Owen seemed never to have grasped

81

that she was now a mere tenant and not the owner's wife. Amy hadn't the spirit to control any of them and perhaps had never had it, even when she was well.

The result was chaotic. People were regularly stopped when on their way to perform one errand, and sent in the opposite direction to perform another. As Amy had observed, across her breakfast tray, it was an old grievance.

Pinto—one of the few people who seemed clear about her duties and determined not to be enticed away from them—still regarded me with suspicion as a possible assassin sent by Dudley. However, she and I were positively shoulder to shoulder on the day when one of Amy's maids came and said that she'd been bringing the fresh sheets for Lady Dudley's bed as asked, but Mrs. Owen had met her as she crossed the courtyard from the wash-house, and told her to take them to her room instead. Pinto and I got them back with difficulty, and almost formed a partnership in the process, although it didn't last.

As for the kitchen, things there were even worse than I had imagined, since the cooks not only squabbled over who was to use which spit and which cauldron, but half the time weren't sure whose meals they were cooking in the first place. If Forster really had tried to poison Amy, he'd be taking a risk, I said to myself cynically. The doctored dish might well turn up accidentally on his table instead of hers, and as the cuisine was usually dreadful, he might not notice if it tasted cold.

In my one week at Cumnor, I had been prostrated twice by violent headaches which ended in attacks of nausea. I had suffered from them at Faldene, but when I was with Gerald, they had stopped. Now, the effort of getting things done at Cumnor, mingled with my fury at this impossible and unkind situation, had brought them back.

That and the uncertainty. Amy's fears, now that she had explained them to me, were horribly convincing. De Quadra's hints nagged at my mind and so did the mysterious message which John Wilton had refused to carry. My orders were to assure Amy that she was safe, but was it true? If not, was Dudley the threat? If he was, why had he sent me to protect his target?

The possible answer to that was detestable. It would mean that I was here as his shield, not as hers. My appointment would be something he could claim as proof that he cared for his wife's welfare. He would suppose, no doubt, that I could do nothing much in the way of protecting Amy effectively. This thought made me angrier than ever.

I was still standing at the window, brooding on these things while I gazed out, when a horseman came into the courtyard. I stood rigid, eyes widening. I put out a hand to open the window so that I could lean out, and then hesitated.

Behind me, Amy rose from her devotions and called to me. "Mrs. Blanchard! Would you help me, please? I would like to dress. Master Blount and my half-brother are to dine with us. It's the last time. They're leaving the day after tomorrow and tomorrow they're engaged to dine in Abingdon. And I would like some mulled wine."

I turned to her at once. It was better like this, anyway. Better not to appear too eager. I must not seem to promise what I might never perform.

The man who had just ridden in was Matthew.

I did not see who greeted him or brought him inside, but one of the maidservants approximately attached to Forster's staff appeared when Pinto and I were helping Amy into her farthingale and gave her a note from Forster. Amy read it and then looked at me.

"It seems you have a visitor, Mrs. Blanchard. A Mr.

Matthew de la Roche. He wishes to call on you, and Forster asks if he may be received here. Are you willing to see him?"

"I . . . yes, of course, Lady Dudley. How very kind of him to call."

"Who is he?" Amy enquired. "A connection?"

"No. He . . . he's someone I met at court." Pinto and Amy were both gazing at me with interest. I felt myself turning pink.

"A suitor?" said Amy in a wistful voice.

"Well, yes," I said. "But I am still in mourning and as yet he is no more than an acquaintance. I shall not desert my post with you, Lady Dudley. I promise you that."

I was so very sorry for her. She was no more than a couple of years older than I was, but her blossom-time was already gone. She had been courted by Dudley, had married him and lost him, and for her there would be no new beginning. I too had had a husband and lost him, but I was strong and well and now being offered fresh opportunities. If she were resentful, I could not blame her.

Pinto was resentful, all right. I saw it in her eyes, but Amy said, "If Dr. Bayly was right, then I shall not hold you back for very long, Mrs. Blanchard. If Robin is patient just for a while, nature will set him free, and save him, and possibly Forster, an unpleasant task."

Dutifully, I said what I was being paid to say. "Lady Dudley, I assure you, I promise you, that Sir Robin wishes you no ill and . . ."

Amy hushed me with a gentle wave of her hand. "Perhaps. Perhaps not. But I am sure now that *you* intend no harm to me, Mrs. Blanchard, and I wish you happiness. Even if it means that you must leave me." This was tantamount to saying she was fond of me, and Pinto positively glowered. "I will ask Mr. de la Roche to join us at dinner," said Amy, unheeding. "May I make a suggestion?"

"Yes, of course, Lady Dudley."

Amy gave me a smile. "Put off your mourning. Just a little."

I took Amy's advice. After all, to exchange a black dress for a cream one was nothing much. Many a young widow would have remarried by now, and in my straitened circumstances nine young women out of ten would have been energetically trying to lure Matthew to the altar, no matter how much Kat Ashley and Lady Katherine Knollys advised caution.

Gerald and I had broken the pattern and married for love. I knew what that was like. If I married again, then I wished it once more to be for the man's own sake, and not simply for the shelter he could offer me.

I was not sure if that man could be Matthew. I was older now than when I had run off with Gerald. Then, I hadn't understood what a gamble I was taking, but I realised it now. I was lucky: Gerald was all I believed he was. I might not be so fortunate a second time. Much as I liked Matthew, there were things about him which made me uneasy. Kat Ashley and Lady Katherine Knollys had hardly needed to point them out, for I already knew.

Still, there could be no harm in asking Dale to look out, for once, a dress that wasn't wholly or partly black. It had crossed my mind before I set out that perhaps I would soon want to relax my mourning, and in my luggage I had a cream satin gown with a pale gold latticework of embroidery on the sleeves. It wasn't too showy; indeed, like most of my clothes, it was somewhat out of date. It had no ruff, just a V-shaped neckline and a turned-back collar with a little embroidery to match the sleeves.

When I tried the dress on, I looked well, especially after I had brushed my dark hair glossy and put it into a gold-thread net with a few pearls here and there, and hung a gold chain and pearl pendant round my neck. These items were the only good jewellery I had left, having sold the rest. The ensemble was pleasing. It would do.

Amy's dining chamber adjoined her parlour. Because I must see that Amy herself was dressed before I could attend to myself, I arrived late and everyone else was already assembled. There was a sense of occasion, and for once, the atmosphere of shadow and fear which so persistently hung about in Amy's rooms was dispelled. Everybody had exploded into slashed satins and gold chains and freshly laundered linen and I knew that the reason was Matthew.

Matthew, very splendid in plum-crimson and tawny, dominated the room, and when all eyes turned to me as I entered, I knew that he had told them all he was here to court me. Amy, who had chosen a most exquisite gown—even though white was not the best choice for someone who already looked like a ghost—at once began half-deferring to me, as though I were somehow on show.

There was no doubt about it. I was in the presence of matchmakers.

I felt momentarily irritated, but the admiration in all the male faces was warming, and so was Matthew's evident gladness at being with me again. I was amused, too, when Arthur Robsart said, "My faith, Mistress Blanchard. I thought you were a quiet cygnet but now you are a swan. What an elegant dress!"

As usual, the food was not particularly good, but at least, with so many of us sharing the same dishes, I need not taste Amy's portions, and there was so much laughter and witty conversation that the uninspired cooking didn't matter. Matthew retailed the latest court news, with shrewd comments of his own, in his agreeable French accent. Arthur Robsart made puns, and Blount put in dry jests now and then. Even Amy laughed sometimes. Soon I was thoroughly enjoying myself.

Most of the time, life with Amy was very bleak. Arthur's visits had brought a little lightness, but they were always so short. There had been nothing like this and I was giddy, almost effervescent with the relief of it.

After the meal, Amy declared that we must have some music. Forster was skilled with several musical instruments, she said, but he had not joined us, so we must do without him. However, there was a lute in the parlour and Ursula must play. "She plays so well, Mr. de la Roche. Have you ever heard her?"

"I think not, Lady Dudley."

"Then come!" cried Amy and made us all repair to the parlour, where she put the lute into my hands, insisting that I should play some popular songs which they could all join in singing.

Amid the laughter and the wine, I had let myself forget about the matchmaking. I had responded unthinkingly to the admiration of the men, to the fact that one of them had pursued me from Richmond to Oxfordshire. Now I realised with renewed force and considerable embarrassment that I was being displayed to Matthew like a horse being trotted up and down to show its paces, and that everyone was assuming I wanted this. And then I saw the lines of pain round Amy's eyes, and realised too that her seeming merriment was all a pretence.

It wrenched at my heart. I took the lute, but the laughter had died out of me. I played adequately but not with sparkle, although the singing was enthusiastic enough to cover for me. I kept to familiar melodies, and was glad that Matthew knew them all and was able to take part.

I was beginning to wonder, by this time, what would happen next. Matthew had not come all this way to leave without talking to me privately. But when that moment came, what would he say?

I became nervous, played several wrong notes, and said apologetically that I was tired. The party began to rise to its feet and bow over Amy's hand.

Amy said, "Mr. de la Roche has ridden all the way from Richmond to see Mrs. Blanchard and no doubt there are things they wish to discuss. I have had my writing room opened for you, Mrs. Blanchard."

I had never been in the writing room before. It was rarely used and was usually locked. It looked as if it had once been the abbot's study. There was a scarred oak desk and matching chair which might well date back to the monastic days, a silver writing set, some shelves, and a modern settle which looked out of place. The place had been dusted but it smelt airless, and I opened one of the slender windows. Then I stood with my back to it and my hands folded at my waist, and said, "It was very kind of you to come so far to see me, Master de la Roche. I appreciate it."

"My name is Matthew, and I'm not here out of kindness, but because I wanted to see you. I came back from Sussex early, on purpose to see you, and found your letter. How could you go off like that—without even saying when you would come back? How *could* you?"

"I had no choice, Matthew. Someone was needed here, to help Lady Dudley, and I was chosen—by the queen and by Dudley. Besides, I'm being well paid. I need the money," I said candidly.

"Money! Ursula . . . oh, my dear," said Matthew. "I know that we met only very recently, but you must have realised that you have only to crook your little finger and I would be willing to place everything I am and have, including my name and my house and every ounce of gold I possess, at your disposal."

He was so very attractive, and so concerned for me. Yet here in this room, face to face with him, I felt hounded by him. I wanted Gerald. Matthew was a comparative stranger and Gerald had been the other half of myself. "Matthew!" I pleaded. "Don't!"

He looked astonished and no wonder. "I'm sorry," I said miserably. "Over dinner I suppose it seemed as though I were flirting with you, leading you on, but I was just enjoying myself. I think I took too much wine. It's so sad here, as a rule."

I did not add the word "frightening." I still did not know if Amy's fears were real or imaginary, but Matthew heard what I did not say.

"Yes, that I can believe. I know the court gossip. For all the merry talk at dinner, this place is full of shadows and you should not be here, Ursula. You're young and alive, and for you, this is entombment. I want to take you away from it. Tomorrow if you wish!"

I shook my head. "No. Please try to understand. It's too soon. I don't know enough about you and you don't know enough about me. I can't just marry you to . . . to take shelter from the rain!"

"Why not? You'd soon find out," said Matthew with assurance, "that I had more to offer you than that!"

"Matthew, I'm engaged to remain here as long as I'm needed. When I'm not . . . not needed any more . . ."

He stepped forward suddenly, and taking my shoulders, he studied me searchingly. "When do you expect that to be?" he asked.

"I don't know. I can't tell."

"You are recently widowed," he said slowly. He dropped his hands. "I have rushed you too much, perhaps. I am sometimes impulsive, especially when my feelings are strong, and from the moment I first saw you . . ."

"Matthew, please don't . . ."

"Listen, Ursula, my very dear Ursula. I must in any case go away again tomorrow. I have many things to attend to. My steward, Malton, is in a great fuss because I am having part of my house rebuilt, and the workmen are not doing what they were told to do and the wrong building materials have been delivered—and I have other matters on my mind, as well. I went back to Richmond only because I wanted to see you, because I found, as soon as I had left the place, that I needed to tell you what I felt for you. Now, I must return to Sussex. I didn't expect an answer from you immediately, to tell you the truth, but I needed you to know. My name, my house, and every ounce of gold I own. They are all yours if you choose. By the time we meet again, you will have had time to think. Will you undertake, at least, to think about Matthew de la Roche?"

It was hardly an onerous demand, yet I was silent. He waited, and when I did not answer, he said, "What is the difficulty? Your husband? Ursula, you are young. Healing will come. Then you'll want to make a new start."

"Yes, I know. But . . ."

I did know. That first stirring of desire, on the day of the hawking party, had told me. One day, Gerald would slip away from me, into the past. It was not so much that I would say goodbye to him; more that he would say it to me. But it wasn't only Gerald.

"Ursula, what *is* it? What's the matter? Is it your daughter? I'll rear her as my own, I swear it. Or does the queen disapprove? She sent you here although she must have known that I was courting you."

"She has doubts, yes, but I can marry without her consent. Only, you see, I . . ."

"You share her doubts? Is that it?"

"I've nothing to bring you," I said. "I've no dowry. And also—you are Catholic."

"The dowry is of no importance. As for the other . . . yes, I recall that you fell very quiet when I first spoke of it. This is the real hindrance, I take it. Does it matter so much? I would not interfere with your wishes in the matter of your own worship, or that of your daughter."

It was best to be frank. "You were in France, were you not, when the queen's elder sister, Queen Mary, was on the throne?"

"Yes. Why?"

"Then perhaps you don't know how it was here, but there were things done in her day, in the name of religion, which I can't forgive," I said. I began calmly, but then anger burst out of me. "There was a man from Faldene who was burned for heresy. The great campaign against heresy started the following year, but Queen Mary was about to marry Philip of Spain and this man had made a speech against the marriage as well as against the Church . . ." I swallowed. "I didn't see it. It was done in Chichester and I wouldn't go, but Uncle Herbert and Aunt Tabitha went. I was still living with them then; it was just before I ran away with Gerald. They wanted me to go with them. They said my mother had served Queen Anne, who had driven the land away from Rome. They said my mother had been tainted by heresy and that I should see what came of it. But I *wouldn't* go, I *wouldn't*. Can you imagine what it would be like to be . . . ?" I shuddered.

"When they came back," I said, "they called me and made me listen while they told me all about it. My uncle stood with his back to the door so that I couldn't run out of the room and when I tried to put my hands over my ears, Aunt Tabitha caught hold of my wrists and dragged them down. When they let me go, I ran to my own room—it was just an attic but at least it was private—and cried and cried. I can't repeat what they told me. I can't bear to remember their faces. They took such pleasure in it. And later on," I said, "when the campaign got under way, I heard that it was against the law even to show pity. People were dragged to . . . to *that* and couldn't even have the last blessing of seeing someone cry for them!"

"Ursula, we're not all like that. If the true faith were one day restored here in England . . ."

"Such things would happen again."

"Not necessarily. And could you prevent them by refusing me? If they did happen, you would be safer with me. Ursula, I am offering you love and care, and a home. I leave, of necessity, tomorrow, but I will come back to find you and ask for your answer. Will you promise to think?"

"I don't know. I . . ."

"For the love of God! I'm only asking you to *think!*"

"Very well." After all, he had paid me the compliment of riding all the way here to see me. "I promise."

He kissed me, a long but careful kiss, intended to begin arousal but not as yet to set it blazing. When he let me go, I did not know if I were glad or sorry.

Matthew left early the next day. Amy sent me out to say goodbye to him as he was mounting his horse in the courtyard, and he told me to remember my promise. He would have leaned down to kiss me, but the groom who was holding his horse remained studiously blank of face, to my embarrassment, and he wasn't the only witness. "Better not," I whispered. "Pinto's watching from the parlour window. She doesn't like me."

"She is jealous?"

"Not because of you! She thinks I'm a danger to Lady Dudley or possibly a rival for Lady Dudley's affections. She might well be glad if I went away with you," I said. "When I go back into the house, I don't want her hinting that I'm no better than I ought to be."

"As I said, she is jealous. She envies you your youth, the doors that are open for you and not for her. Be careful, Ursula. I mean it." He was serious. "If you don't remarry, you could turn into another Pinto. *Au revoir,*" said Matthew, "and beware!" He rode away, leaving that ominous warning to echo in my ears.

Feeling in need of steadying company, I snatched a few minutes to go through to the stableyard and say hallo to John Wilton. He spent most of his time with the horses, and since my arrival I had seen little of him. He told me that all was well with him and asked if I had any errands or commissions. "Not just now, John," I said, looking with affection at his spiky hair and remembering how he and I and Gerald had ridden through the night to Guildford, the night I ran away from Faldene. "But I'm glad to know you're here," I said earnestly.

I went indoors and back to Amy. Yesterday evening, she had asked if I had "settled anything" with Mr. de la Roche, and when I said no, that I was not yet ready for such a step, she had said, "Do think about it, Ursula," and then added, "but I'm glad you're staying for the time being."

Now I saw all too well how much she needed help and company. The effort of bearing up during the dinner party had exhausted her. She was tearful and in pain. We fetched soothing possets for her, helped her to her prie-dieu to pray and Pinto played draughts with her for a while until Amy said she wanted to go back to her room and have her dinner in bed, on a tray.

After Amy had had her meal, tasted as usual by me, she decided to sit in the parlour and do some embroidery, but she soon felt too tired to go on with it and asked me to read to her instead.

Although Pinto was of gentle origin and had had a little education and could play the lute and sing—to tell the truth, quite as well as I could—she hadn't come from a background which valued intellect in women. Her literacy level was no better than that of Meg's nurse Bridget. Pinto could sign her name and she could write a label for a bottle of ointment or rosewater or preserved plums, but she could only do it slowly, and reading, for her, was a matter of picking out one letter after another and doubtfully stringing the sounds together. She couldn't read aloud to entertain her mistress, and she didn't like hearing me do it.

When I read to Amy, Pinto would sit and listen with her mouth primmed up, and if she could find something in the choice of material to object to, object she would. I used to try and persuade Amy to choose, because then Pinto would keep quiet, but today Amy, as she often did, said, "Oh, I'm too tired to decide. Pick something for me, Ursula."

So I searched among her books and found some verses by a poet called William Dunbar, and read her a poem in praise of the City of London, and Pinto said when I finished that it was dull. So I tried another poet, by the name of Skelton, who wrote verses in praise of various ladies, and Pinto said he sounded like a philanderer and she was surprised that I thought his work suitable for her mistress. Not greatly to my surprise, Amy then said she was weary and

asked us to help her back to bed. After we had done
so, Pinto made a few edged remarks, suggesting that
my poor choice of literature had bored or irritated
Lady Dudley. I finished the day feeling literally as
though I had spent it banging my head against a stone
wall. A headache was looming.

I went to bed early and the headache subsided, but
I couldn't sleep. Matthew had unsettled me. Suddenly it seemed hateful to exist like this, fending off
Pinto's resentment and tasting Amy's meals for fear
of poison.

Dale had once remarked that it wasn't her place to
say so but she didn't like to see me acting as taster; it
wasn't nice. I now realised that I heartily agreed with
her. The simple normality of the dinner party had
shown up, by sheer contrast, the unpleasant nature of
everyday life at Cumnor. What a way to live, I
thought. What a *horrible* way to live.

And suppose, said a nasty little voice inside my
head, just suppose Amy is right? Just suppose there
was poison in that broth you tasted today?

I was quite sure there wasn't, as apart from my
fading headaches, I felt perfectly well, but it seemed
to me quite possible that an attempt had been made
on her life earlier, and that Dr. Bayly had frightened
the culprit off. If so, what if the attempt were later
resumed? I might hope that Amy's earlier attacks of
nausea, and her present fears, were only her sick
fancies, but what if they were not? How was I to tell?

As I lay there, I was conscious of the age of the walls
around me. Pictures drifted through my mind, of
processions of cowled monks, carrying candles, making their way through the house to their devotions in
the nearby church. In my imagination, the cowls had
something threatening about them, as though they hid
faces one would rather not behold.

The night was warm and I had looped back the

bedcurtains. By the moonlight slanting through the window, I could see Dale as she slept on the truckle bed against the wall. I could hear her breathing, too. She was a comforting human presence and I was glad of her.

I could also see the door of the room, the gleam of the iron hinges and the push-down handle. I was actually looking in that direction when the handle moved.

I sat up, heart pounding wildly. The door was opening. A figure, carrying a candle like one of the monks in my reverie, entered softly and closed the door after it. I made a strangled sound of terror and the figure turned quickly towards me, holding the candle up so as to cast light on my face.

"Hush. It's all right. Don't be afraid," said the voice of Arthur Robsart.

"Master Robsart?" My panic subsided, leaving bewilderment. "What on earth . . . ?"

"Shh." He came silently across to me and placed the candle on a small table beside the bed. He was wearing some kind of loose dressing robe, much embroidered and tied with a silken cord which gleamed in the candlelight.

He then sat down on the edge of the bed and, to my rage and disbelief, leaned forward to take off his slippers. "Don't let's wake Dale," he whispered. "I'll snuff the candle in a moment. We can draw the curtains, and I'll slip away before dawn. She'll never know I was here. I take it that I'm welcome?"

"You most certainly are not! When did I ever . . . ?"

"Yesterday, at dinner. You were iridescent, sweetheart; like cloth of gold in full sunlight. It was as plain as could be that you were longing for a lover, but Master de la Roche has gone away again and left you. I must go, too, in the morning, but for tonight, I'm still here and I've noticed during the past week that you rather liked me. I would never try to seduce a virgin," said Master Robsart virtuously. "That would be quite immoral. You have been married, though, darling, you know what it's all about. I felt sure that if I came to you tonight, you wouldn't order me away."

"You were sorely mistaken! I am but recently widowed and still mourning for my husband. I have no interest in any other man, and if I had, Master Robsart, I would hardly choose you! You have a wife! Please go away at once."

"Hush, hush. We don't want to start a scandal. Come now, sweetheart." The obtuse young fool was about to take off his robe. I didn't think he had much, if anything, on beneath it.

"Dale!" I shrieked.

"What? What? What is it, ma'am? Oooh!" She sat up on her truckle bed and stared at Arthur in amazement.

"Dear Dale," said Arthur. "I'm sure you're an excellent and trustworthy maid to Mistress Blanchard, and that means you're discreet, but virtue should be rewarded . . ."

"I'm glad you think so!" I said waspishly.

". . . and I will happily reward yours to the amount of a gold angel."

"I should stand out for several gold angels if I were you, Dale," I said, "but I'll pay them to you for *not* promising discretion. I shan't need it." Secure in possession of the funds Dudley had already provided for me, I added to Arthur, "If Dale thinks she deserves a pay rise, she has only to ask. Now will you please go?"

"But darling, why?" Arthur did have the decency to do up his girdle again although he still seemed disposed to coax. "Where's the harm? You needn't worry about my wife, I assure you. She won't know."

"Unless you leave at once, I shall make it my business to tell her. Good God! Do you behave like this often? How many love-children have you fathered?"

"None that I know of. I take care," said the lighthearted tomcat perched on the side of my bed. "But even if I did get you with child, you needn't worry . . ."

"I'm quite sure I needn't! I don't intend to give myself cause!"

"You know I'm Amy's half-brother?" enquired Arthur.

"Yes, but what . . . ?"

"Wrong side of the blanket," said Arthur cheerfully. "Same father, but he wasn't married to my mother. He acknowledged me and paid for my upbringing, though, and I bear his name. I'd do the same for any child of mine. There's nothing to fear."

"Master Robsart," I said. "Please listen. I don't *want* a love affair with you."

"A few days ago you said you would miss me when I went away. All week I've been growing more and more certain . . ."

"You were amusing company, nothing more. Now, will you please *get out?* If you don't, I shall scream at the top of my voice and rouse the whole house and I don't think Lady Dudley will be pleased. It could be bad for her, too," I added, ruthlessly using his sister's poor health as a lever.

"Oh, very well." Arthur put on his slippers again. "I thought it was worth trying," he said philosophically. "One can't win every time."

"Oh, *really!*"

"You don't understand yourself," he added, as he stood up. "Recently widowed or not, you want a lover. What went wrong between you and de la Roche?"

"What?"

"He came here courting you, didn't he? He made no secret of it. And you want him, I saw it at that dinner, but when he left I thought I'd been wrong. I wasn't wrong, though. You're giving off signals like a flagship. You want a man and if it isn't me, then it's de la Roche. Why did you let him go?" said Arthur, and then picked up his candle and sauntered out of the room, waggling his fingers at me in an impertinent farewell as he turned to close the door.

"Ma'am!" said Dale in a staggered voice.

"I know. Outrageous behaviour! Bolt the door, will you, Dale?" I said.

I didn't sleep at all that night. I lay there open eyed as the hours went by, and grieved because I knew that Arthur had been right. I saw the truth now. I did want Matthew. When he was near me, my bones shook.

There are no sane explanations for it, the way that a certain set of features, a certain build, the laughter lines at the corners of a particular pair of eyes, the timbre of a special voice, can overwhelm one's senses. He had a long chin and a strong nose; his eyes were dark and narrow, his bones long and loosely jointed, his voice deep. All these things are commonplace, but added together they made Matthew, Matthew, *Matthew*. Now my eager body and my hungry heart shouted at me to forget religion and Gerald and Amy Dudley, and marry Matthew at once.

But he had gone away and I didn't know where. He had said he would come back although he hadn't said when. For all his protestations, he might meet someone else or simply change his mind; might stroll out of my life as Arthur had just done.

I had had my chance. I might well have thrown it away, too.

§6§

The Scent of Danger

I have been five weeks at Cumnor Place, I thought. Five long weeks. Amy is as ill and as nervous as ever she was and I am no nearer learning the truth. Are her fears soundly based or not? I don't know. And oh, how I wish I could hear from Matthew.

It was a month since Matthew had left, and Thomas Blount and Arthur Robsart had left early the next day. For all I had heard of Matthew since, he might never have existed. I had had no message, no letter. There was nothing I could do. I could not go back to court to seek word of him. I had not left Cumnor Place once; not even for a walk round the home farm or a short ride. Amy needed me too much. Duty and compassion (not to mention the feeling that I must earn my pay) bound me within the walls of Cumnor as firmly as their vows bound the monks of bygone days.

I crossed the parlour to pause, as I often did, at the window. If only Matthew would ride in again. But the courtyard was empty.

In the parlour, just behind me, Amy and Pinto were sitting, Amy trying listlessly to do some embroidery, and Pinto mending some garment or other. I had got nowhere with Pinto. She still feared that I was Dudley's creature and her suspicious eyes watched me all the time. I had continued to taste Amy's food, and I often felt that Pinto wished someone *would* poison it, for my benefit. I was sure that she would love to see me fall down in convulsions. And as for that man Anthony Forster . . .

At that moment, the short, square figure of Forster emerged from his own door. He looked up, saw me, and beckoned.

I turned to Amy. "Lady Dudley, Mr. Forster seems to want me. He's in the courtyard. Shall I go down?"

"Yes, oh yes. See what it's about."

I had expected her to say that. She was intimidated by Forster and his sister-in-law and anxious not to displease them. I sometimes wondered whether Forster and Mrs. Odingsell had any closer relationship but I thought not. To begin with, Mrs. Odingsell was one of the rigid breed of Protestant and it was difficult to imagine her enjoying carnal relations even with a husband, let alone a lover. The vicar of the nearby church apparently saw nothing strange in their household, and regularly dined with them, and Forster played the organ in church every Sunday.

However respectable they might be in that sense, I still considered them odious. I didn't actually believe that the upright Mrs. Odingsell was plotting against Amy's life, although Forster might be, but they both bullied Amy in subtle ways. Forster starved her of money, and their habit of using her servants and encouraging Mrs. Owen to do so as well, was becoming slowly more marked, and more insufferable. I now understood that Forster (whose stingy streak put me strongly in mind of Uncle Herbert) followed a deliberate policy of keeping his own wing understaffed so that he could get work done for nothing by purloining the services of Amy's people, while she was too timid to stand on her rights and give orders to his.

Lately, he and Mrs. Odingsell had even taken to purloining me. I had a maid and manservant of my own and was still officially one of the queen's ladies, but I had several times been called into the Forster wing, even when Amy needed me, to help out with female tasks such as setting a table, or helping to turn a mattress. John Wilton had also found himself being used as an odd-job man. He was displeased and had once taken it upon himself to remonstrate with Forster, although it made no difference. To Forster, this sort of thing just meant economic sense. What, I wondered crossly, did he want now?

I wasn't needed to lay a table this time. "Ah, Mrs. Blanchard," he said, as I joined him. "Mr. Hyde is here. He has been with me all morning, and now he wishes to pay his respects to Lady Dudley. Can she receive him?"

Mr. Hyde. I stood there, using one hand to keep a capricious wind from blowing my skirts about and the other to keep it from whisking my cap off, and thought how very pleasant it would be to jump up and down on the cobbles with both feet at once, shake my fists in the air and scream.

Thomas Blount, Arthur Robsart, Matthew de la Roche, had all gone but we did not altogether lack company. Mr. Hyde was Forster's brother-in-law, another of the relatives by marriage who seemed, with Forster, to fill the place more usually occupied by blood relations. He lived in Abingdon and had visited Cumnor several times in the past month. He came to see Forster, but he always wanted to "pay his respects" to Lady Dudley. Mr. Hyde's idea of paying his respects made him into a menace.

Mr. Hyde, in fact, was a rotund and amiable nitwit who firmly believed that if someone were ill or anxious, nothing would do them more good than to be regaled with juicy pieces of gossip. Once, he brought us a lurid tale of an Abingdon woman who had died suddenly, and whose husband had been arrested on suspicion of having poisoned her. A neighbour had seen the husband kissing somebody else's wife and now everyone believed the worst. The second time, he brought a further instalment of the story, to the effect that the man had been released for lack of evidence, but no one round about had any doubt really that he was guilty.

Pinto used to make the most vituperative remarks about him and on these occasions I had every sympathy with her. Dale's comments on the subject of Mr. Hyde were also a pleasure to hear. Dale was welcome to say she couldn't abide *him*.

However, Amy's distress was heartrending. After both of these visits she went to her prie-dieu the moment Hyde was gone, prayed for a long time that her husband might not be faithless and that no one should try to harm her, and then burst into tears and had to be helped to bed. Another visit from Mr. Hyde was exactly what she did not need, and Mr. Forster, I thought savagely, ought to know it. He'd been present throughout all the previous visits.

"I didn't hear him arrive, no," I said. "I was looking at Lady Dudley's furnishings, earlier. She has quite a generous allowance from her husband. Surely she could have more tapestries in her rooms and some new furniture? Some of her chests and tables are very old and quite badly scratched. I've worked out what replacements would cost, and I'm sure they could be provided."

Forster's knowing eyes fairly sparkled with amusement at the idea of a young female like myself working out figures. "You can cipher well enough for that, can you?"

"Oh yes," I informed him, for once blessing Uncle Herbert, who had taught me to maintain his ledgers. I wished I could get a glimpse of Forster's. If the unused money hadn't found its way into his coffers, my name wasn't Ursula. I smiled at him limpidly. His expression turned faintly uneasy.

"It seems a little pointless," he said. "I am the household treasurer, after all. You can safely leave such matters to me, Mrs. Blanchard. About Mr. Hyde. Can he see Lady Dudley now? He and I then intend to ride back to Abingdon where I am to dine with him. I don't want to come up myself; I have one or two things to do."

Pinto and I, in one of our rare moments of agreement, had offered, after Hyde's last visit, to refuse him admittance, but Amy had said no. "It will offend Forster," she had said.

"I'll ask her," I said. "If she says yes, I'll come and fetch him to her. But, Mr. Forster, please ask him, this time, to be a little discreet in what he says. Lady Dudley is not well and she is easily upset."

"Of course," said Forster.

Amy, predictably, said that Mr. Hyde could come to the parlour and Forster probably did say something to him, because Hyde's first words were: "I'm sorry to hear you're not so well today." However, if Forster had warned him to watch what he said, he either hadn't been convincing, or Hyde had a short memory. Within five minutes, our maddening visitor had launched into his latest piece of gossip, which concerned a gipsy woman who had been taken up for saying that the queen was pregnant. He didn't mention Dudley, of course—even the maladroit Mr. Hyde wasn't as foolish as that—but he hardly needed to.

The moment he left, just as Pinto and I knew she would, Amy slid to her knees beside her little altar and began to pray aloud that her husband might come back to her, and that the tales of his obsession with the queen were lies.

"You can see why she's frightened," Pinto said to me in a low, fierce voice. "If that story's true, then what?"

"It can't be true," I said. "The queen lives her whole life virtually in public." On this subject I felt sure of myself. "It isn't possible."

". . . *let it not be so, oh Lord. Let his heart turn to me again* . . ."

"And how would you know? You weren't a Lady of the Privy Chamber. I'm not ignorant; I know how these things are arranged. You were just one of the women that go about with the queen when she's out in public," said Pinto, rather as though she were saying, "You were just a worm."

". . . *but if it is true,*" said Amy, hands gripped together before her, "*then, oh God who succours the helpless, let both of them be . . . be . . .*"

We turned, alarmed, as Amy not only burst into tears, but began to pound upon the altar with her linked hands. They looked as frail as though the bones were only dried twigs, and yet she hammered so hard with them, on the prie-dieu, that one of the candlesticks jolted to the floor.

"My lady!"

"Please, Lady Dudley . . . !"

We ran to her. Pinto put a hand on her mistress's shoulder but Amy ignored it. She shook her head from side to side and her voice rose.

". . . *If it's true then let them both be damned for it!*"

She put her head down on those skeletal hands and began to wail. Again in partnership, Pinto and I helped her up. She couldn't stand. We half-carried her, still wailing, across the intervening anteroom to her bedchamber. Two of her maidservants, alerted by

105

the noise, came running to us, and Dale hurried from our quarters, a clothes brush in her hand.

"It's all right. Lady Dudley is distressed, that's all." I waved them all back. "Someone bring a soothing draught. The usual one—tell the kitchen!"

We got Amy into bed and the draught was brought. I remembered to sip from it before giving it to Pinto to hand to Lady Dudley. Pinto put an arm round Amy and helped her to drink, very tenderly. I always felt more kindly towards Pinto when I saw how good she was to her mistress, but Pinto did not feel more kindly towards me. As soon as Amy was settled, she called for a maid to sit with her, took my arm and almost dragged me back to the parlour.

"Now then," she said, as she shut the door after us, "did you know about this story before you came here?"

"What story?"

"That the queen is with child, of course! We all know who the father is, if so. *Did you know what is being said?*"

"No, I did not. And I tell you, it is *not* true. Junior lady I may be, but I assure you once again that the queen's life is so arranged that such a thing would be impossible without the whole court knowing."

Pinto looked me up and down, unpleasantly. "Why should I believe a word you utter? *He* sent you here, didn't he? If he's got the queen with child, he's got no time to lose and nor has her virginal majesty."

"Pinto, if I were to report what you have just said, you would find yourself before the magistrates in a very short space of time."

"Then report me! And break my mistress's heart. Or is that what you want? It might help her on her way, and if this rumour's true, helped on her way she'll have to be, won't she? The two of them daren't wait for God to call her. So why shouldn't I believe you're here to jog God's elbow?"

"You've thought that from the start," I said wearily. "How do I convince you? The queen and Dudley are not lovers; there is no child; I am here only to give Lady Dudley comfort, and how do you think *you're* helping her, Pinto, by quarrelling with me? Do you think Lady Dudley needs an atmosphere of strife and suspicion all round her? You stupid woman!" I found I was losing my temper. Amy's outburst, the worst I had experienced yet, had shaken me badly. "The only threat to her is from her illness," I said loudly, "and if you loved her as you claim to do, you wouldn't want her to think otherwise!"

Her flinty eyes didn't change. I uttered an infuriated noise which even to my own ears sounded animal—somewhere between an exclamation and a growl—and flung myself away from her, out of the door and down the stairs, making for the open air. I marched out into the courtyard, into which John Wilton was escorting two horsemen who had evidently just arrived. Lately, one of the jobs Mr. Forster had found for John was to put him on duty in the gatehouse.

"Here's Mistress Blanchard," said John as I neared them. "Very likely she'll know. Ma'am, these gentlemen are enquiring after Mr. Forster. I know he's gone to Abingdon but I don't know when he'll be back. Maybe you can tell them."

"He's dining with Mr. Hyde," I said. "I suppose he'll be back for supper. May I know your names, gentlemen?"

However, the man on the goodlooking and probably very expensive chestnut gelding, the tall man with the good clothes and the haughty profile, I had already recognised. He was Dudley's retainer, Sir Richard

Verney. The other, who introduced himself as Peter
Holme, was the man de Quadra and I had seen in
Richmond Park, talking to the Earl of Derby and Sir
Thomas Smith.

"Would you like to see Lady Dudley?" I asked.
"She is—er—resting at the moment, but after dinner
she may be able to receive you. Can I take her any
message?"

"Lady Dudley is unwell, is she not?" said Verney.
"We really have no need to trouble her. Our business
is only with Master Forster. By all means transmit our
respects to her."

Forster's butler, Ellis, had come out of the house
now, and was advancing towards us. As I handed the
visitors over, I glanced upwards and saw Amy's face
at her bedchamber window. She made signs at me to
come to her. I made my excuses and hurried indoors.

Pinto was still in the parlour. As I reached the top
of the stairs, I glimpsed her through the door, stitching at something, her face sulky. I slipped across the
anteroom and into Lady Dudley's bedchamber. Amy
was sitting on her front window seat, clutching her
wrapper round her. Her cheeks were stained with her
recent tears and the eyes she turned towards me were
full, once more, of the fear I had seen on the day that I
first came to Cumnor.

"That was Verney, wasn't it? My husband's man."

"Yes, Lady Dudley. Look, I don't think you should
be out of bed. If I straighten the sheets for you . . ."

"Never mind about the sheets! Is Verney coming to
see me?"

"No, I understand his business is with Master
Forster. He sends his respects."

"The time Pinto overheard Forster and some visitors talking about me," said Amy, "the visitors were
Verney and that other man who was with him just
now."

"Peter Holme," I said.

"Is that his name? I don't know him, but he's come with Verney before, and they talked about me to Forster. Verney comes from my husband. What are they doing here this time, Ursula? Have you any idea?"

"No, no, I haven't. But, Lady Dudley, surely it's natural that people calling here and seeing Master Forster, might mention you. Why should there be anything sinister in it? I feel sure there isn't."

"Do you? I don't," said Amy. I offered her my arm and she let me guide her back to bed, but her frightened eyes did not leave my face.

"I want to know why they're here," she said. "Don't ask them outright, because if you do, you'll just be given some harmless excuse. I want to know their *real* purpose. You're clever, Ursula. Can't you find out?"

§7§

Private Conversations

Soothing her by promising to do my best, I settled Lady Dudley and retreated to my own room to think.

On the face of it, her instructions were absurd. Except by saying to Verney, "Lady Dudley wants to know what your business is," how could I possibly find out? And what was the point, anyway? There couldn't be anything wrong about it. Why should there be? I struggled to work it out. Dudley *couldn't* be the queen's lover, not without the whole court knowing, and therefore Elizabeth could not be carrying his child. Even if he did want to marry her, he must know perfectly well that Amy was dying, which in due course would release him. He had no need to injure her, although Amy firmly believed that somebody had tried and her story of attacks of nausea, which had stopped after Dr. Bayly became suspicious, was uncomfortably suggestive.

Verney was Dudley's man and Forster was Dudley's treasurer. This visit was probably something to do with Dudley's finances.

Peter Holme, evidently, was Verney's servant. I had

no idea why he should have been talking in Richmond Park to the Earl of Derby and Sir Thomas Smith, but what had that to do with Cumnor or Lady Dudley? All these gentry had interests in common: they gambled, hunted, bred horses and dogs, and sold each other young animals or stud services. They often communicated by sending a servant along with a message. There were half a hundred perfectly innocent reasons for that conversation in the park.

However, for over a month I had lived with Amy's fears, and I couldn't forget that someone had tried to send a covert message, of unknown content and destination, through John Wilton. Nor could I forget that my attention had been drawn to Peter Holme by de Quadra, almost in the same breath as his warnings that the rumours surrounding Lady Dudley could be the smoke which meant, somewhere, a genuine fire.

If I cared for Amy, I thought, then I ought not take anything or anyone for granted. Be alert to everything that goes on in that house, de Quadra had said. He was right. It was part of the business of protecting her, just as tasting her food was. She wanted to know what was going on between Verney, Holme and Forster, over in Forster's wing, and she might well have good reason. It was therefore my duty to find out. It was that simple.

Only it wasn't simple at all, because I couldn't for the life of me see how to do it.

Midday came. Amy ate in her room and after I had performed my usual service of tasting her food, Pinto stayed with her while I went downstairs to the dining room and ate with Dale. Though dining at the same table as myself, Dale knew her place and did not try to talk, which was as well, because I was still trying to think.

They were muddled thoughts. In truth, I knew that I wanted nothing to do with this, that I longed to be elsewhere, back at court, or in the Sussex cottage with Bridget and Meg. I ached for Meg, grieved for Gerald . . . and yet, when I tried to imagine Gerald's face, it kept on turning into Matthew's face instead. I wanted Matthew most of all. I should have followed my instinct, I said to myself. I should have agreed to marry him and left Cumnor with him. But all the time, another part of my mind was wondering how, just how, I could carry out Amy's orders.

The afternoon was quiet. I sat sewing in the parlour with Dale. I stitched at the white silk sleeves I had been making on the day when I was called to see the queen and Dudley. I was still embroidering them. When, at last, barking dogs, cackling geese and the sound of hoofs announced that Mr. Forster had ridden home, I went down to meet him.

If I could manage to be the one who told him that he had guests, he just might say something about them which would tell me why they were here. Mrs. Odingsell, however, was there first. When I came up, she was already in the courtyard and telling her brother-in-law about the new arrivals.

". . . they've spent the afternoon strolling round the home farm but they're in their room now. Do you want them called down to the parlour?"

"Can I be of service?" I enquired helpfully, coming to Mrs. Odingsell's side. "Shall I call them for you?"

"Oh, not yet." Forster seemed irritated. He swung down from his horse. The dour-faced groom, Roger Brockley, was waiting to lead it away. Brockley, in fact, though unsmiling, was really one of the better features of Cumnor for he was extremely competent. "I'm covered in dust from my ride," Forster said. "I want to wash and change. Tell Ellis I want supper for three at the usual time, in the little dining room. We shall wish to be private, if you will excuse us."

"Naturally." Mrs. Odingsell inclined her head with

112

dignity. "I will speak to Ellis. Thank you for offering your help, Ursula, but there's no need, this time."

They went indoors and I returned slowly to Amy's parlour. Dale was still sewing. Outside, clouds were gathering and she remarked that the sky was getting dark. "Going to rain cats and dogs in a minute and I just hope it don't thunder. I can't—"

"Abide thunder," I said absently. I stood gazing across the courtyard towards Forster's part of the building. I knew where the small dining room was, and from where I stood, I could see its windows, four of them, regularly spaced and identical. The room was on the first floor, above the sloping roof of the cloister, but I could hardly climb on to the cloisters and crouch there to eavesdrop. Nor could I very well press my ear to the door inside the house. How would Ellis or the maids get in and out with the dishes or fresh supplies of wine? The idea was so ridiculous that I had to stifle a giggle. Then a mental picture rose before me, of the inside of the small dining room. I had laid the table in there on occasion. Surely . . . ?

"Dale," I said, "I have something to do for Lady Dudley. Tell the kitchen to leave me a cold supper. I shall be back later. And don't ask questions."

"Yes, ma'am. No, ma'am," said Dale, startled.

Suppertime was not far off. I must hurry. I had the forethought to use the privy first: if it proved possible to carry out my plan, a call of nature could ruin it. I was already dressed in clothes which allowed me some freedom of movement. When one's work involves fetching and carrying, not to mention turning mattresses, elaborate dresses are a nuisance. I had never again put on the cream gown I wore when Matthew came. Today, I was in a dark gown with no farthingale and now I had only to remove a rustling silk underskirt and change noisy shoes for quiet slippers.

113

The doors of the three households, both inside and out, were usually unlocked by day; the internal doors were even left unlocked at night. People could come and go much as they chose. I went openly to Forster's small dining room. If anyone saw me there, I would say I was making sure that all was in order. The servants might think me somewhat officious, but nothing more. After all, I thought wryly, they were used to seeing me lay tables. A few minutes later, I was giving colour to my story by adjusting the position of the candlesticks. I was also berating myself for stupidity. I was obviously out of my wits. My idea wasn't going to work; how could I ever have thought it would?

What I had remembered, and seen in my mind's eye, were the tapestries round the walls of the room. There were gaps for the windows and the door and a stretch of panelling on either side of the door, but otherwise, the walls were hidden. If, I had thought, I could conceal myself behind those tapestries . . .

A foolish notion. For one thing, they didn't come right down to the floor. I couldn't hide behind them because my feet would show. In fact, even the rest of me would make a noticeable bulge, for the hangings were close against the wall. Ursula, my dear, you are a silly girl. You'll never make a spy and there's nothing to spy on, anyway. You're imagining all this. You've let Amy infect you.

However, I was at Cumnor to help Amy and to take her orders, and she had told me to find out what Verney was up to, so I paused for a moment to look round carefully. There were no other possible hiding places in the room. I couldn't squeeze into the cupboard under the sideboard, because I knew it was full of glassware, and although the deep window seats lifted up and had storage chests beneath, I knew that they were full of tablecloths and napkins. I looked at

114

them with annoyance. Three windows, three useless
window seats . . .

Three? But the small dining room, viewed from
across the courtyard, had four windows. I went to the
hangings and peered behind them. Oh yes, of course,
and how typical of Forster.

The tapestries in the small dining room represented
the virgin goddess Artemis turning her ardent pursuer
Acteon into a stag and setting his own hounds on him:
a dramatic and spirited tale to which the design did
not do justice. Artemis was portrayed as a female so
fat and blank of face that one couldn't imagine any
handsome youth bothering to chase her, and Acteon
wasn't handsome anyway. In the panel where he was
reaching up to clutch in alarm at the antlers sprouting
on his head, he looked like a bucolic amateur actor
whose headdress was slipping. The bodily propor-
tions of the hounds were odd to the point of defor-
mity.

It was a poor, cheap tapestry, and it had obviously
been bought ready-made instead of commissioned to
fit the room. In fact, it was several feet too long and
Forster had simply ordered the extra footage to be
hung over one of the windows, obscuring it.

Here was the fourth window, complete with a
recessed seat on which one might perch without
causing a bulge, one's feet well clear of the foot of the
hangings.

Voices were approaching. I had half a second to
decide whether or not I was to do this crazy and
dangerous thing.

I couldn't! Yet Amy was afraid and perhaps had
cause, and the experienced de Quadra had thought
her danger could be real. I hitched myself quickly on
to the window seat. I at once discovered that my toes
still stuck into the tapestry and pushed it outwards. In
a panic, I twisted half-sideways, so that my feet were

parallel to the fabric instead. It was awkward but it would have to do. There was no going back now. The door of the dining room was opening.

The people who came in, however, were the butler Ellis and a maidservant. I couldn't see them but I heard them speak to each other, heard wine being unstoppered and Ellis saying something about another serving spoon. I heard the maid scurry off to fetch it, and then come back. Presently, I heard them both leave.

The wall of fabric in front of my nose was frustrating. I felt stealthily at my girdle, where I had a huswife pouch containing a case of needles, a thimble, a couple of spools of thread and a little pair of scissors. I listened intently to make sure that the room really was empty, and then, using the point of the scissors, I made a small hole in the hangings. With my eye to this I could see the table.

When the door opened and Forster ushered his guests through it, I drew back at once, illogically sure that because I could see them, they could see me. I sat trembling, while they took their places. I heard Ellis's voice again, and wine being poured, and then Forster said, "All right, Ellis; that will do. We'll look after ourselves now. See that we're not disturbed, will you?"

The door closed. Fearfully, I ventured once more to apply my eye to the slit I had made. Forster and his guests were indeed alone, helping themselves to wedges of pie. Candles had been lit because of the dark weather. I had quite a good view, since none of them had his back to me. Verney's proud profile and Forster's blunt one were outlined against the light from a branched candelabra on the sideboard and Holme was facing me. I could see his upper half quite well although his face was shadowed.

Forster was observing, in the tone of one who is not

116

starting the discussion but bringing it to a close, that it seemed to him that all the details were now settled. "We can only hope that everything goes smoothly," he observed, and without waiting for an answer, engulfed a mouthful of pie.

Whatever their business was, they had already discussed it. Forster hadn't waited until supper to talk to his guests, after all. Silently, I cursed. Holme did say something in reply, but as he too now had his mouth full, I couldn't make out what it was. It was difficult to hear, anyway. The threatened rain had begun and the wind was throwing squalls of it against the window behind me. When I picked up the thread of the conversation again, they were talking about Amy's ex-physician, Dr. Bayly.

". . . shocking behaviour on the part of Lady Dudley's doctor," Verney was saying, in the drawling voice which went so naturally with that arrogant profile. "His wild accusations must have been an appalling embarrassment."

"He's an opinionated old fool," said Forster irritably. "I threatened to have him in court for defaming my character if I had any more of his nonsense. The vicar was scandalised by it. He said to me . . ."

Rain hit the window again, as though the sky were emptying its slops. When the squall had passed, the conversation had again changed course. For some reason, they were now discussing Abingdon Fair, which was due to begin in just over a week, on 7 September.

"I hope it won't rain," Forster said. "One year, it poured steadily throughout all four days of the fair."

"That certainly would be a disaster," Verney remarked, "and it would also be very bad luck."

Forster laughed. "My dear sister-in-law is very shocked to hear that the fair will be open on the Sunday. She thinks it most ungodly. Mrs. Odingsell believes that people should go to church on Sunday morning and read the Bible all the rest of the day. She runs the house well but a merry and enlivening presence she is not." They definitely weren't lovers, I thought. "More wine?" enquired Forster, and leaned forward to replenish the goblets which his guests at once held out.

There was a pause, broken only by the sound of mastication. Then Forster remarked, changing his tone, "What about my contract, by the way? I understood that you were bringing it with you. I'm not prepared to proceed without it, as I hope I've made clear. I ought to have thought of it much sooner."

I peered intently, trying to get a better look at Holme. I couldn't somehow place him. He had a wide, pugnacious jaw and squashed-together features, as though a giant had put a palm on the top of his head and rammed it downwards. His voice was lightly countrified in accent, but not in grammar. He was broad shouldered and neatly clad in a russet doublet which any man might wear, from a farmer on a Sunday to a lord at ease by his hearth. In the presence of Sir Thomas Smith and the Earl of Derby, he had been obsequious, and when I saw him in the Cumnor stableyard, I had supposed that he was Verney's manservant. However, at this table, he seemed to be on equal terms with Verney and Forster.

"I have it with me," Holme was saying. "Sir Richard here was so keen to get on with settling details, up in the bedchamber, that I didn't have a chance to mention it before your butler announced supper."

"Though our principals are not happy about it," Verney observed. "You would get your remuneration without this, Forster. I never like to put such confidential matters in writing. I was not pleased when you wrote to me to ask for the contract, and still less when you sent the letter by your man Bowes."

Bowes was one of Forster's staff, a versatile individual (Forster's servants had to be) who seemed equally willing to clean silver under Ellis's eye, tune Forster's musical instruments or ride to London with letters. I had thought him a decent type of man. Verney and Holme evidently didn't agree with me.

"I don't trust Bowes," Verney said, "and you put me in a position where I virtually had to reply with another letter, to let you know that the contract was coming. Naturally, the letter was carefully worded, but all the same, I felt strongly that discretion was required."

"I tried to find a messenger—not Bowes, but someone who wasn't connected with us," Holme said. "I made a mistake in the first instance, and picked on one of those honest types who want to know exactly what's going on even when it's not their business . . ."

I went rigid. The honest type sounded remarkably like John Wilton. Holme's voice continued, slightly self-justifying.

"In the end, we just had to rely on Bristow. He can't read too well and probably wouldn't try to look at any letters he was asked to carry. Actually, I shouldn't think Bowes did. Why should he, after all? But Sir Richard here wasn't happy. I've kept your contract carefully hidden, Mr. Forster."

No, I thought. Holme wasn't quite among equals. He gave the impression of being just, barely, within their social boundaries, and hanging on to his position with fingertips and teeth.

"I preferred not to have it on my own person," Verney said candidly. "Fortunately, Holme here was willing to keep it on his."

"You'd better give it to me immediately after supper, Holme," Forster said. "You should have done so at once."

"Oh, you needn't wait till after supper; I can hand it

119

over now." Holme gave Verney a grin. It was an impertinent kind of grin, to which Verney did not respond. "And *you* needn't have worried about carrying it. There's ways and means of keeping things secret when they're on your person."

He turned sideways, revealing a booted foot, and with some difficulty tugged the boot off. He took a moment to fill his mouth again with pie, and then plunged his hand inside the boot, apparently doing something to the inner sole. Then he turned the boot upside down and shook it, and what looked like a wooden plug came out into his palm. He put this on the table and reached inside the boot again. He then grunted crossly, picked up a spoon and hit the upended heel with it, several times. At last, he drew out a piece of folded paper caught between two fingers, which he handed to Forster.

I watched this performance with increasing amazement, and forgetting to be afraid, I tried so hard to get a good view of the document that I made the tapestry stir, and drew back quickly. I had seen a seal, but no other details. I waited while Forster read the document to himself. When he finally spoke, his words were not informative.

"Thank you. I suppose this will do, though it's so discreet that I could still have trouble extracting the money if anyone chose to be difficult. But it's better than nothing. All right. I accept it."

"It's the best you'll get," Verney told him. "It's a promise of reimbursement when matters have reached a satisfactory conclusion, and the signatures of the principals. Since they won't allow their names to be spoken even in private, you can imagine how eager they were to sign anything, no matter how discreetly worded."

"I said, I accept it," Forster repeated, folding the

paper away inside his doublet. "The fact that it is addressed to me and involves such a large sum of money would be interesting to some people. I agree: it's still a lever. I fancy the payment will be forthcoming."

"Of course it will. There was no need for the contract anyway," Verney said shortly. Then, maddeningly, there followed a silence during which the three of them continued merely to consume their supper.

Growing stiff with the effort of keeping my feet turned so that they wouldn't poke at the hangings, I tried to make sense of all these cryptic remarks. Something was going on that ought not to be—a child of two could have told that—but what? The emphasis seemed to be on money more than anything else. Quite possibly, this dubious trio were merely pawns in a plot to steal money or land from Dudley. In fact, since the avaricious Forster was involved, such an explanation seemed more than likely. But I had overheard what I surely should not and I shuddered to think what would happen if I were found.

I longed to escape from my perch, but I dared not stir or even breathe carelessly. I discovered that I was also hungry. The supper was inviting. They had salad as well as pie and what looked like almond fritters with cream awaiting their attention as a dessert. The kitchen had functioned well for a change. To my alarm, my stomach rumbled. Fortunately they didn't hear it.

After some time, they began to talk to each other again, but once more, what with Holme's unpleasant habit of speaking with his mouth full, and the sound of the worsening wind and rain, I heard little of what was said. What I did hear appeared to concern the buying and selling of wool by people I didn't know, and then the harvest prospects and how promising the Cumnor apple orchard looked. The rest of that supper seemed interminable.

I had to wait until Forster and his guests had left the table and the maids had cleared. Not until the candles were out and the house quiet, did I dare to leave my hiding place. I then realised how little thought I had given to the matter of getting back to my room. Outside, it was still raining, and in any case, the outer doors were locked at sunset. I could not return across the courtyard. Within the house, the doors would be left unfastened, but I now realised that I must traverse the house in the dark, as I dared not take a candle. I went to the door of the little dining room and paused, uneasily, not wanting to step out into the antechamber beyond.

I was not unduly timid, but few people like the dark, and this monastery-turned-dwelling-place was not friendly. Besides, I was afraid of making a noise or disturbing the dogs, who would be inside in such weather; what if one of them barked? If I were found creeping about in Forster's or Mrs. Owen's quarters at night like this, excuses would be impossible.

However, I must get back to Amy's wing somehow. Trembling, I set off.

Fortunately, the dogs now knew me well. They came up and sniffed at me in the dark, and one let out a subdued woof of greeting, but no one heard and the dog was quiet after I had petted him. As I crept through Mrs. Owen's parlour—most of the rooms led out of one another—I accidentally kicked a footstool over. I also, at one point, startled a cat which sprang away with a yowl. No one heard that either, but by the time I reached my bedroom door, the sweat was streaming down my back, and I entered my room almost at a run.

Dale was there, waiting for me by candlelight, still fully dressed, her eyes watchful and scared.

"Oh, ma'am, wherever have you been? That Pinto's been asking for you. I referred her to Lady Dudley and Lady Dudley said Pinto wasn't to bother; that it was all right. But I've been worried!"

"Well, here I am, safe enough. I can't tell you where I've been, Dale, but I haven't been doing anything wrong." Forster and his friends wouldn't agree with that, I thought grimly. "Now, I want you to fetch the cold supper that's waiting for me, and then I want to sleep."

I ate my supper and went to bed. I felt wretched. I was lost in a world of mystery and hidden dangers, full of uncertainty. I must make a report to Lady Dudley in the morning, but what on earth was I to say? How much could I tell her? How much, indeed, did I know? I had learned very little.

Between my doubts and fears, and my sense of responsibility for her, I felt more lonely than I had been even in the days after Gerald died.

When I slept that night, I dreamed not of Gerald but of Matthew de la Roche, so vividly and in such a manner that I woke to find a deep pulse beating within me as though the act of love in my unguarded night-time vision had been real.

I also woke to find that overnight, some—not all, but some—of my ideas had crystallised.

Not into certainty, much as I longed for certainty, but into doubt renewed, and a deepening dread.

§ 8 §

A Time of Waiting

"I did manage to overhear a little of their talk, Lady Dudley. I hid behind the dining-room tapestries," I said. It raised a very small, difficult smile. I had gone to Amy as soon as I awoke, and found her far from well. Pinto and I changed the dressing on her nipple and gave her a painkilling draught but she was clearly miserable. She wouldn't let me taste the gruel Pinto brought her for breakfast. "What if it *is* poisoned? It will shorten my pain."

Presently, she found an excuse to send Pinto out of the room. She told me that she had guessed, from what Dale had told her the night before, that I had gone to Forster's wing to try and learn something, and said, "Go on."

"There's very little to tell. Your name was never mentioned, Lady Dudley, and nor was your husband's name. Holme gave Mr. Forster a document of some kind and there was talk of the difficulties of finding messengers for confidential letters and some discussion of money owing to Mr. Forster which he is afraid he may never receive. There was nothing, Lady

124

Dudley, absolutely *nothing* to suggest that . . . that what you suspect may be true."

"To suggest that they are planning my murder. You can say it outright, Ursula."

"Lady Dudley, there was nothing to suggest that they were planning anyone's murder."

Amy made a movement with her hand. "Thank you, Ursula. You tried. I'm grateful. I'd like to rest now. Send Pinto to me."

I went back to my own quarters and sat down, once again trying my best to think clearly.

I had not exactly lied to Lady Dudley, but I had certainly edited my report. There was no point in alarming her when I had learned nothing definite and therefore could do nothing definite. The indications were so vague.

All the same, they were there. Something questionable was afoot. Forster, Verney and Holme were acting on behalf of people they called their principals, and these principals were afraid to have their names mentioned, even in private, an extreme degree of caution which suggested that whatever the matter in hand might be, it was dangerous or dubious or both. It also suggested that the names in question belonged to people of position.

There had been that reference to Dr. Bayly too. He had defamed Forster's name. By saying that Forster was trying to murder Amy? Forster was outraged. But if Bayly were right, it would be most inconvenient for Forster to have the doctor bruiting the truth round the countryside! The mysterious matter in which Verney, Holme and Forster were concerned, might be only a financial swindle. But what if, after all, it were something to do with Amy, and something sinister, at that?

If someone with a famous name were prepared to pay what Forster had described as a large sum of money to bring about Amy's death, then who was it likely to be?

Dudley, of course. I couldn't believe that he had got Elizabeth with child, but he might be afraid that she would slip away from him into the arms of some foreign prince. Yes, that was possible. In that case, he might indeed want to speed Amy's departure.

Now I found a new powder train of thought in my head. Oh no, I said to myself desperately, no, please, not that, *no*.

I had begun to admire Elizabeth very greatly, and besides, she was the queen. If she were involved in such a thing and it became known, the whole country could be overturned.

No, I said to myself. She would never be so foolish, so insane. Surely, surely, however much she desired Dudley, Elizabeth would wait for him?

People in love were often insane. It was one of the arguments in favour of arranged marriages. Aunt Tabitha had often said so. She had cited my mother's misfortune, frequently, as the sad result of passion without permission.

Dale now came to help me with my toilette for the day. I had gone to Lady Dudley in my wrapper, and while Dale brushed my hair and assisted me into sleeves and bodice and kirtle, I went on struggling with my thoughts. I had now lived for some time with the unpleasant idea that Dudley had sent me here to create an appearance of uxorious anxiety for Amy, while he plotted her death. Could he also be trying to convince *Elizabeth* of his innocence?

This made quite a lot of sense, and was comforting, for in that case, Elizabeth herself would be innocent. But how was I to know? My ideas now went uselessly round and round and no inspiration came.

Amy slept for a while that morning and woke feeling a little better. We were called to help her get up and put on a loose gown, then she went as usual to her prie-dieu. I braced myself for more heartrending prayers. But no, this time, to my surprise, there was a change. With a new air of calm, she simply said a paternoster and then repeated "Thy will be done" twice. She settled in a chair and asked me to read to her.

Later on, Verney sent a somewhat perfunctory request to pay his respects that morning, but Amy said she wasn't feeling quite well enough to see visitors. After dinner, I saw Verney and Holme ride away.

That was a Friday. I spent the weekend fretting. I had no definite information, only suspicion, and I didn't know how reasonable that suspicion was. I was at sea—in a fog, I said sourly to myself, and without a rudder. There had been intrigues in Sir Thomas Gresham's household, and life at Faldene had been markedly unpleasant, but in neither establishment had I come across any murderous plots. I didn't, as it were, know the hallmarks.

I needed advice, but to whom could I turn? Lying awake at night, wrestling with the problem, I thought of doing the boldest possible thing and writing to Dudley himself. If he knew of my suspicions, perhaps he would abandon any plots he was considering. If he wasn't after all plotting anything, he might start enquiries and find out what was really going on. But if he was guilty . . . In that case, he might find a way to get rid of me as well as Amy! In the small hours of the night, my mind played with horrors.

When dawn came, these ghastly thoughts always seemed ridiculous, but as soon as night fell again over the old, chill walls of Cumnor, and the candles were lit, and the shadows gathered in the corners, they returned.

Suppose, instead of to Dudley, I were to write to the

queen? However, the tiny, hateful fear that after all she *was* a party to some evil scheme, would not quite go away. I could scarcely believe it, but while even the smallest question remained, I dared not approach her either.

But there was Cecil! As I tossed restlessly in my bed on Sunday night, I remembered that Cecil and his wife had said I should go to them if ever I were in any difficulty. Yes. I would ask the advice of Sir William Cecil, and John Wilton should be my messenger.

It now transpired that at Cumnor Place, writing a letter, which I had always regarded as a simple and everyday task, was nearly as complicated as mounting a siege.

Amy Dudley, though hardly an intellectual, was not stupid either, and on her good days, one could tell that in health she would have been a pretty young woman with quite a practical turn of mind and a pleasant sense of humour. Even ill and frightened, she was still capable, as I had now seen, of surprisingly dignified moments.

She was not, however, well educated. Certainly Amy could read and write but she never practised either skill beyond occasionally writing her signature or verifying someone else's. Forster or Ellis read letters out to her when necessary. I gathered from her servants that before she became ill, she had taken an interest in estate matters and had often dictated letters to a clerk, but now Forster and Ellis (who was steward as well as butler) had taken over all such tasks and dismissed the clerk. That was when the writing room fell into disuse and was locked up. The only pens, ink or paper in Amy's home were in that room, and if I wanted to write a letter, I needed the key.

Amy had mislaid it. She was in pain again that day, and was lying on her bed. I did not persist, beyond saying gently that with her permission I would look in likely places myself. She nodded and then leaned back, closing her eyes. I tried various drawers and presses in her bedchamber but found nothing, and went to the parlour to try my luck there. I was upending vases in case the key were inside one of them when Pinto came in and caught me and demanded angrily to know what I thought I was doing.

"Looking for the writing-room key. Do you know where it is, by any chance?"

"The writing-room key?" Pinto drew herself up, flinty eyes gleaming with suspicion. "And what might you be wanting with that, may I ask?"

"I want to write a letter."

"You? A letter?"

I stared at her in amazement. Literacy was normal in my family. Even my aunt and uncle, who held me so light, made little demur over letting me study with my cousins. The Blanchards had a similar attitude and Sir Thomas Gresham took literacy for granted. Now it struck me that Pinto, whose own command of it was so poor, and who so hated to hear me read, probably regarded my abilities as presumptuous accomplishments in a woman. If I wanted to write a letter, I was up to no good.

"I have a little girl," I said quietly. "She lives in Sussex, with her nurse. I just want to write to Bridget—that's the nurse—to ask after them and send my love to my daughter Meg. I've heard nothing from them for so long," I added, and did not have to act my sadness because it was real. I would put a letter to Bridget in with the one to Sir William Cecil, I thought, and ask John to deliver that as well.

"Oh. I see." For the first time, I detected a very faint air of apology in Pinto. I followed it up.

"Pinto, I wish you weren't so suspicious of me. Believe me, I am here in good faith, to help you look

129

after your mistress. I have a very real regard for her and I think I could have regard for you, too, if you would let me."

The flinty eyes went cold again. "I'd be a fool to trust anyone who comes from *him.*"

"Sir Robin Dudley?"

"That's right," said Pinto harshly. "I've been with my lady since she was little. Used to serve her mother, I did. She's all I've got and I love her and I won't see her cozened by anyone who *may* mean ill to her. I've no means of being sure and I won't take chances."

"I wouldn't expect you to, but how do I harm her by writing to my daughter's nurse?" She stared at me blankly, trying to assimilate this new idea of me as a mother, anxious for news of my child. "Pinto," I said, "please, I do have a regard for Lady Dudley. I wish you would believe me."

She went on staring. Then she said abruptly, "Oh, what's it matter? I'm going to lose her anyhow. She's dying. I've got the writing-room key. I'll fetch it for you. Write to who you please."

As she turned away, I thought I heard her sob.

It was a careful letter. The Cecils, being in constant contact with the queen and the court, must know I was at Cumnor, but I explained anyway, stating that I had been asked to stay with Lady Dudley and try to persuade her that no one meant harm to her, that the current rumours lied. Then I said that now that I was here, I was no longer sure of this myself; that by chance I had overheard a scrap of conversation which frightened me. I needed help and advice. I mentioned no names. There was no need. Cecil would guess at Dudley's name, anyway, but no one could accuse me of indiscretion.

When I had sealed the letter, I penned a few lines to Bridget, too, and went to find John Wilton.

130

He was in the stable. John had started life as a groom and seemed to be content, taking care of Bay Star and the other horses we had brought with us and which were still at Cumnor. I found him seated on a mounting block, burnishing a bridle and whistling cheerfully. My commission made him less cheerful, however.

"You're writing to Cecil, ma'am?" He studied my face carefully. "Does that mean something's worrying you?"

"Yes, John, it does. I need advice, but to get it I must ask for it. Will you come back as fast as you can?" Somehow, I felt better when John was near. He was so trustworthy.

"I'll do that, ma'am. I hope I don't have to chase about too much to find the court, that's all."

"There's a letter for Bridget, as well. You'll have to take it into Sussex and you'll want to see your sister, of course, but please—don't be too long. You might collect Cecil's answer on the way back. He may need a day or two to think."

"Don't you worry, Mistress Blanchard," said John.

He was on his way in less than half an hour. I walked beside Bay Star to the gatehouse and out into the road to say farewell, and as he rode off, he turned in the saddle and doffed his cap in a parting salute. I saw his spiky hair sticking up, outlined against the clear September sky. I envied him, riding off into a sunny day while I must go back to Amy's room with its shadowy fears and its odour of disease.

I found Amy in tears, enduring a bad attack of pain and in great distress of mind as well.

"I'm dying. Dr. Bayly was right. Well, Robin will be glad! I wish he would come to see me. I wouldn't be frightened of him now, why should I? If he strangled me with his own hands he'd only be saving me from

131

misery. I wish I could die quickly and get it over. It's so disgusting and oh God, oh God, it's like a spear going through me."

Over the next few days, there were several scenes like this. They kept us all busy. I wondered, now and then, whether John had found Cecil or not and when he would come back, but I was too preoccupied to think about it much.

Amy's condition was not the only focus of interest that week, however. Abingdon Fair was approaching and apparently it was a big and exciting occasion to which everyone looked forward. The weather had turned fine again; people looked anxiously at the sky and hoped it would hold.

I said to Dale that I was glad the servants were to have an outing, especially the younger ones, because the grim atmosphere of the house wasn't good for them. Dale told me that both Forster and Mrs. Owen had given leave to their own servants to go on the Sunday if they liked and that Forster intended to visit the fair himself that day. Gathering from her faintly aggrieved tone that she wanted to visit it too, I gave my consent before she asked for it. Pinto said she would stay at home and I decided to do likewise.

On the Sunday morning, Amy woke up early, said that she felt well enough to rise and dress, told Pinto to assemble all the servants in the parlour and then, in the tone of voice that means an order, announced that every single one of us, without exception, including Pinto and myself, was to go to the fair, straight after church, and stay away all day.

"But, Lady Dudley," I said protestingly.

"Don't argue!" said Amy, almost fiercely. "Do as you're told!"

Amy had not only told us that we were to go to the fair whether we liked it or not; she had even dragged herself through the house to see Mrs. Owen and Mrs.

Odingsell and tell them that she wanted them to go as well. Both, however, had declined. Mrs. Owen couldn't be bothered, she said (I had once heard the groom Roger Brockley remark that Mrs. Owen was so idle that to get her to take a journey you'd need a door-to-door litter carried by six Nubian slaves, which was rude, but true).

Mrs. Odingsell had refused on the grounds, I gathered, that the Sabbath was no day for respectable gentlewomen to be gallivanting to fairs; on Sundays, decent people stayed at home and read devotional works.

"Such nonsense!" Amy fumed. "Time was, people went to church on Sundays and then spent the rest of the day in harmless amusements and no one questioned it. Now there is all this long-faced talk of enjoyment being a sin on the Sabbath. I have no patience with it! Ursula, I've told you that I want you to go. Do as I say!"

There was no question of Amy attending church—she hadn't done so now for weeks—but the rest of us must set out shortly for the service, and then, it seemed, we must proceed to Abingdon. Pinto had gone to mix a painkiller for her mistress to take before we left. I stood worriedly beside Amy's chair. She was sitting very upright, her face determined.

"You'll be alone all day," I said. "Do you really mean . . . ?"

"Yes, I do. Why not? You all do so much for me; why shouldn't I give you all a day off at the fair? And I won't be alone. I wish I were! It's what I want. But Mrs. Owen will be here, it seems! If I want to, I'll have her in to dine with me. The cook's leaving a cold meal."

"But . . ."

"Oh, *Ursula!*" said Amy.

I knelt beside her chair. "What is it, Lady Dudley?

There is something behind this, isn't there? Can't you tell me?"

Amy studied me with those brilliant, sunken eyes. Then she said, "When you first came, Ursula, I thought you meant ill to me. I thought . . ."

"I know," I said. "It isn't true, Lady Dudley, really it isn't."

"No, no, I realised that long ago. You've been good to me. But someone means ill, all the same. I don't trust Forster or that man Verney. You said that when you overheard their talk, they spoke of messages so secret that it was hard to find messengers they could trust, and there was a document for Forster and some mention of money to be paid to him. Ursula, I may be ignorant, and ill, but I am not silly. Something secret was being discussed and it could well be something dishonest. Would you agree with that?"

"You're certainly not silly," I said uncomfortably. "I would call you very shrewd."

"Yes, you had your doubts, too." Amy nodded. "You wanted to protect me, but I saw it in your eyes. And for a long time, I've seen something in Forster's eyes too, something that disturbs me. Ursula, he was the one who first told his servants they could all go out today. Then he suggested that Mrs. Owen should tell her staff the same thing, which she did, and after that, he suggested it to me. That was several days ago now. It was all his idea in the first place."

"Was it now!" I hadn't known that.

"Yes. As if he wanted to empty the house as far as possible. But it doesn't matter. I'm dying and I know it and lately I have suffered so much that . . . I no longer fear death." The brilliant eyes filled with tears. "I think I fear life more—life which drags on and on in pain from which there's no escape. If when I'm alone someone comes to stab me, they'd be doing me a kindness. So I'm going to help Forster send everyone away for a day. If he—or anyone—is waiting to kill me, let them have their chance. Let them release me from this body that's falling to pieces while I'm still alive in it. I want to go free."

"What?" I was horrified. "Lady Dudley, if you really believe that, then someone *must* stay with you. It can't be true," I said resolutely, trying to convince myself, "but if it is, then you don't really want it to happen. If someone . . . attacked you, you wouldn't want to die. You'd be terrified. You'd cry out for help. You'd . . ."

Amy wiped her eyes. "And could you supply the help?" she asked. She sounded almost amused. "You'd be the only one here. Everyone else will obey me, including Pinto. Could you alone fight off my assassins?"

I was silent.

"You couldn't," said Amy. "I'll tell you what would happen if you were known to be here. You were sent here by Robin. You would be accused of murdering me yourself."

"That would be ridiculous! He sent me here openly. I'm known to be his employee. He would hardly instruct *me* to do away with you!"

"No," said Amy, "I don't suppose he would. But ordinary people, in alehouses and round wellheads and dinner tables, do you think any of them would work that out? I believe I am in danger, Ursula, but I will not let you share it."

"This is all nonsense," I said, but even as I spoke, I remembered that during that curious, elusive conversation between Forster, Verney and Holme, they had mentioned Abingdon Fair. Forster had said that one year it had rained throughout the entire fair, and Verney had said that would be a disaster. It assuredly would be, if they wanted an empty house in which to commit a murder without being interrupted! The

135

servants might refuse to be sent out into a downpour! I heard my voice trail away.

"Ursula," said Amy, quite calmly, as though this were a commonplace conversation about what to have for dinner, "I believe that if any attempt on my life is being planned, it will take place when everyone is at the fair. I am, if you like, opening the door to it. If you don't want to risk being hanged, go to Abingdon, and stay in the company of the others every minute, and come home with them at sundown."

§9§

The Small Cold Voice

I went to the fair under protest and, to all intents and purposes, under guard.

We set out on foot straight after the church service in the morning, in a crowd consisting of nearly everyone who made up the three Cumnor households. Lady Dudley, Mrs. Owen and Mrs. Odingsell had stayed at home, of course, and Forster had gone separately, on horseback, but all the rest of us were in the party.

Once we were in Abingdon, people went this way and that in small groups. Dale and I were accompanied and hemmed in by Pinto, the manservant Bowes, who was lean and taciturn and alert, and Roger Brockley, the groom who was so good at looking tactfully blank. Brockley was a well-built man, with wiry brown hair just touched with grey at the temples. He had a scattering of gold freckles, a high, back-sloping forehead and a conscientious nature. He was the kind of man who has his own opinions and he didn't seem to dislike me, but he had had his orders and would carry them out.

137

Amy had not only insisted that I attend the fair; she had also apparently decided that I couldn't be trusted to do as I was told. She had informed Pinto that I might want to return before the others did and that I wasn't to be allowed to do so.

Pinto, of course, had interpreted this to mean that Amy was afraid of me. She didn't actually say so but I saw it in her face. What she did say, in my hearing, to Bowes and Brockley, was that her mistress had insisted that she was to be left alone today and that it wasn't anyone's place to question her or to go back too soon. Mrs. Blanchard, she added, might attempt to do this but her mistress was not to be upset by disobedience. Amy's fears were common knowledge in Cumnor Place, and so was the fact that Dudley had sent me there. Brockley was on Amy's payroll and Bowes was on Forster's, but they were equally prepared to take orders from Lady Dudley. They might or might not share Pinto's suspicions, but Lady Dudley wanted me under surveillance, and they clearly didn't intend to let me out of their sight.

Pinto was a blinkered soul. She was so sure that if there were danger, it must lie in me; therefore she could not entertain any other possibility. Dale was annoyed on my behalf and the two of them weren't speaking.

Abingdon Fair was one of the great local events of the year. The whole of the little riverside town was caught up in it, with flags across all the streets, and jolly processions of apprentices and tradesmen, accompanied by musicians, wending their way through every now and then, to advertise their trades.

The meadows beside the Thames had been cleared of sheep and cattle for the day and entirely given over to the fair. At one end, all through the day, there were sporting contests such as high-jumping, wrestling and archery. At the other, there was a horse fair and a sale of livestock.

In between, market stalls sold hot pies, sweetmeats, jams and cordials and simples; gloves, hats, belts and ribbons; linen and woollen cloth and hanks of yarn; cheap scent and cheaper jewellery; fresh cheese, elderflower and dandelion wine, ale and butter and new-laid eggs. There was a woman selling basketware, a hardware merchant offering tools and rope and kitchen pots; a potter who had brought his wheel along was making his products on the spot, and a nervous silversmith who had put his goods on display had two hulking sons and a large growling dog to discourage the lightfingered. Whatever you happened to want, the fair was a likely place to find it.

When the Cumnor party arrived, we were held up as we made our way through the main street by slow-moving farm wagons bringing pigs and coops of poultry and goods to be sold. There were entertainments, too. Just after we reached the town, a bear-baiting started in the middle of the main street, and a troupe of travelling players commenced a drama in front of the abbey.

By midday, the fair was hot and noisy. Vendors bawled their wares; actors ranted and clashed swords in a mock fight which looked alarmingly real; horses whinnied, dogs bayed and poultry cackled. Onlookers watching the sports applauded spectacular vaults and good archery shots and a medley of smells filled the air, of spiced meat and fresh pastry; ale and farm animals and human sweat; dust and perfume and the tang of the river.

As my watchful escort and I threaded our way among the thronged stalls, the sun flashed off the river, and I could feel it scorching through my cap. I had eaten an over-flavoured pie which I didn't want and, in an attempt to lull my companions' suspicions by appearing properly interested in the fair, bought a workbasket which I didn't really want, either. I now had to carry it. Dale was already burdened with purchases of her own: a length of linen and a pot of honey.

I had a menacing twinge above one eye; possibly the start of a sick headache. There was so much noise, so many smells and so much conflict in my mind. Amy had been right to think that I would want to disobey her and go back to Cumnor early. But how?

All through the church service and all the way to Abingdon, I had felt, more and more, that I ought to be with Amy. She was wrong to say that I would be no protection. Mrs. Odingsell and Mrs. Owen were both at Cumnor. If I could get both or even one of them into Amy's company on some pretext, surely we would amount to an adequate bodyguard. I might distrust Forster but I really couldn't see his righteous sister-in-law being a party to murder. Amy would be safe with the three of us, and under the eyes of Mrs. Owen and Mrs. Odingsell my reputation would be safe, too.

Time was passing, however. It had taken us an hour and a half to walk to Abingdon, and noon was now gone. Even if I escaped from my guardians immediately, and I could see no prospect of this, it would take me another hour and a half to get back. I couldn't get hold of a horse because ladies on their own didn't hire horses. If Amy were right, and she might be, oh yes, she might be, then God alone knew what was happening at Cumnor meanwhile.

"Shall we watch the potter?" Bowes enquired. "It always makes me marvel, the way the clay just grows under their hands. I'd say it was witchcraft if I didn't know better. Over here, now."

I went unprotestingly across the crushed grass,

thinking irritably that we might as well watch the potter as do anything else. Then Dale pulled at Bowes's arm. "Look, a juggler!"

The juggler hadn't been there a moment ago; he had evidently just set up his pitch. Dressed in a medieval motley of red and yellow, with dagged sleeves and a crazy coxcomb of a cap and announcing his presence with the help of a small boy with a drum, he had placed himself between a stall selling preserves and another one peddling cures for everything from warts to impotence, and he was collecting an audience. Bowes let himself be distracted from the potter, and we all pressed forward to watch. The juggler was tossing up brightly coloured skittles and while he juggled, he danced, ducking and twirling, catching skittles behind his back, even twisting round to catch one on the tip of his nose.

Children in the crowd squealed with wonder and excitement and a big farmer with a toddler on his shoulders pushed in between me and Bowes, who was on my left. He was followed closely by an equally massive wife, with another child holding to her skirt and a baby in her arms. Unable to see past her husband, she moved to one side and paused by my right shoulder.

Casually, I took a step backwards.

Bowes had been on my left but all the others were on my right. The farmer had obscured me from Bowes, and the farmer's wife now hid me from the rest. I swallowed, drew a long breath, waited for a few brief seconds until the juggler started a new routine, and then I edged away into the crowd behind me, and was free.

Most people were in their best clothes but I had had the good sense to put on one of my everyday dresses with no farthingale and no hot, prickly ruff, and my shoes were comfortable, too. I slipped quickly behind

141

a row of stalls and then made my way at a fast walk, across the meadow and out into the streets of Abingdon, and presently, into the fields beyond.

I would go by the field paths, I decided, because the others wouldn't take long to realise I had gone and they would give chase. By not taking the road, I might evade them. The paths were rough, though, and twice I had to walk in the wrong direction for some way before I found a gap in a bank or a place to cross a ditch. I became hot and irritated and the workbasket I was clutching was a nuisance. I got rid of it, eventually, in one of the ditches. My headache, I noticed, had disappeared as soon as I got away from the others. Finally, I returned to the main track, keeping an ear open for sounds of pursuit.

I could be there before half past two, I thought. If only Amy were still all right. She had said she might have Mrs. Owen in to dine with her; if so, that would help.

Hurrying along, thinking as I went, I didn't hear the approaching horsemen. They came across a field from my left and took me by surprise, leaping the bank and ditch into the road and landing almost on top of me. The foremost horse knocked me aside with its shoulder and I lost my footing and almost fell into the ditch. The riders paid no heed to me but thundered on their way as though I didn't exist. I sat beside the ditch, rubbing a wrenched ankle and staring after them. I had had a momentary glimpse of the horse which had knocked me down, and the man on its back. The horse was a good-looking chestnut, and the man's hawklike profile, though so briefly seen, reminded me of . . .

Sir Richard Verney. Had the riders been Verney and Holme? If so, they were going, at speed, straight towards Cumnor. They would arrive there long before I did.

My ankle hurt. I stood up, put my weight on it and hastily sat down again to massage it anew. I was still engaged in this when I heard the sound I had been listening for earlier: familiar voices. Round a bend in the road hurried Pinto, Dale, Bowes and Brockley, all perspiring in their Sunday best. They rushed up to me, exclaiming.

"So there you are. What a pace you set us!" Bowes had pulled off his cap and his balding scalp was bright red from the sun. "Mrs. Blanchard, you shouldn't have done this," he said reprovingly.

"Oh, ma'am, whatever are you about? This Pinto creature has been saying such things. I can't abide to listen to her! But to go off alone like that . . ."

"Oh, you wicked creature. I knew you would make off if you could. Didn't I say so, Mr. Bowes? We lost you at the fair but we knew which way you'd go! We saw you in the fields, in the distance. That's her, I said, and we've got to catch her up before she reaches Cumnor and works some mischief there . . ."

"Things like that she's been saying and I'm ashamed to have heard them, ma'am!"

"You've hurt yourself," said Brockley.

Roger Brockley did at least seem to be regarding me with a glimmer of human sympathy. I gave him a grateful glance.

"I've turned my ankle," I said. Once again I tried to stand and, to my relief, it felt better. "It's nothing much. And you've no right to call me a wicked creature, Pinto. That was insulting. Yes, I want to go back to Cumnor to be with Lady Dudley. I know she ordered me to come to Abingdon but I have other orders to obey as well. Those other orders were to *look after her.* That's what I'm paid for and none of you had any business to interfere!"

"You're being paid by her husband, deny it if you can, you deceitful thing!" cried Pinto.

"Now, now. It's true that a gentlewoman like Mrs. Blanchard shouldn't be running about the countryside alone but there's no need to forget your manners," said Brockley severely.

"I am certainly being paid by Sir Robin Dudley," I said, "but his orders *were* to comfort and protect Lady Dudley, whether Pinto believes it or not. And now . . ."

I stopped. I wanted so very much to share my load of worry with someone, but John Wilton wasn't back yet and I had had no word from Cecil. I feared to trust anyone beyond those two: my manservant and the Secretary of State.

In the people now standing round me in the road, I dared not confide. I thought they were honest, and I included Bowes in that—he had a respectable air even if he did work for Anthony Forster—but none of them was skilled enough in clear thinking. Amy's voice echoed in my head, commenting on the intellectual shortcomings of people in alehouses and round wellheads. And the queen's voice spoke in my mind, too: *What touches Sir Robin's honour, touches mine.*

Then came the moment of which I am ashamed to this day. I know I cannot actually be accused of betraying Amy. Between my ankle and my companions, I had no hope now of getting back to Cumnor, and even if I did, if those horsemen really were Verney and Holme, and they were making for Cumnor with evil intent, they were far ahead of me. Until I had seen them, some part of me had still clung to the hope that perhaps I was wrong, and Amy was wrong, and no harm was intended to her after all, by anyone. Now, that hope had died. I believed fully in her danger, and with that, my mind had horrifyingly cleared.

Even if my companions had arrived with fast horses, on which we might yet reach Cumnor in time, I would still have turned back to Abingdon rather than say to them, "I think the danger lies in Sir Richard Verney."

Verney was Dudley's man, and if they believed me at all, they would have shouted to the skies that behind the threat to Amy were Dudley *and the queen*.

If what I feared were true, they might well come to that conclusion anyway, in the end, but I did not intend to be a part of it.

For as I stood there, a small cold voice was speaking in my mind.

Imagine Elizabeth discredited, while Lady Catherine Grey and Mary Stuart fight over her crown. Imagine civil war let loose.

Imagine Mary Stuart triumphant, a Catholic queen on England's throne. Remember what our last Catholic sovereign, Mary Tudor, did to heretics.

It may happen anyway but do you want to make it sure? Do you, Ursula, want to be the one who sets off the explosive and blows the frail new peace of the realm to ruin?

If I deserted Amy in my mind, and perhaps I did, it was not for personal gain but for the sake of England, although a part of me still longs to ask for her forgiveness.

I did not try to make any of them understand just why I had wanted so desperately to return to Cumnor. I merely shrugged. "We'll go back to Abingdon," I said. "If I can walk that far, that is."

Walking seemed to improve my ankle further, but once back in the town, I sat down outside a tavern and stayed there for the whole afternoon. Pinto and Dale remained with me, sulking at each other, and Bowes wandered off. Brockley, though, fetched us cakes and cider from the inn, and although he went to see more of the fair, he came back several times to ask if I were all right. Later on, Bowes reappeared and between them, he and Brockley got our little party a lift most of the way back in a wagon which had brought a Cumnor tenant and his family to the fair.

We were home ahead of anyone else. As we made our way up the track from the gatehouse, I saw with disquiet that one or more horses had passed that way much more recently than the morning. I did not draw attention to it.

In the courtyard, the dogs frisked to greet us. We separated, Bowes going to Forster's wing and Brockley to the stableyard. Pinto, Dale and I went in a silent and ill-tempered group to Amy's entrance.

She was there at the foot of the staircase, a sad, huddled heap. She did not look as though she had been thrown down the stairs, for her clothing was perfectly tidy, white headdress neatly in place, the russet taffeta skirts of her Sunday gown decently disposed. She seemed oddly small, no bigger than a child. Her head was twisted at a frightening angle and her eyes were open and blank. She was quite dead.

Tragedy and farce have a way of mixing themselves up. In our grief and horror, we lost our dignity completely. Pinto sat down on the floor and had hysterics, Dale slapped her and I swore at them both. Then, leaving them to it, I hurried, still limping, out across the courtyard to the Forster wing, and was promptly accosted again by the dogs, barking and prancing, apparently under the impression that the excitement they had sensed was some kind of game.

Hearing the disturbance, Brockley ran from the stableyard. "Take these damn dogs away!" I shouted. I hobbled into the cloister and through the Forster entrance, calling for Mrs. Odingsell in a voice urgent enough to bring her at once, with Bowes on her heels. Briefly and breathlessly, I told them what had happened. Bowes at once sped off to the scene. Mrs.

Odingsell took my arm, led me into a sitting room and sat me down on a settle, and with an unusual air of human sympathy, brought me a goblet of wine.

"Drink that. You're very shaken. Now then, say it again, slowly. You have found Lady Dudley lying at the foot of her staircase? You're sure she isn't just in a swoon?"

"Quite sure," I said, shuddering, remembering the ghastly, unnatural angle of Amy's neck. I gulped at the wine, and asked the obvious question, which someone else would ask even if I didn't. "Mrs. Odingsell, has anyone been here this afternoon?"

"Not that I know of. I was reading the Bible in my room, but I should have heard if there were callers. The dogs would have barked. The whole day has been very quiet."

Her cold grey eyes met mine. She was lying; I knew that perfectly well. Someone had ridden in or out very recently. The droppings on the track from the gatehouse had been fresh, and all the grooms, and Forster, were in Abingdon. And yes, the dogs would have barked, and from any room overlooking the courtyard, as her chamber did, one would hear the clatter of hoofs when someone arrived on horseback.

"I will come over to Lady Dudley's wing with you, but finish your wine first," she said. "I feel sure that this is just a dreadful accident. Lady Dudley's health was poor. She could have felt dizzy and fallen, or perhaps—well, she has had her fits of despair. I told her once that she should trust in God, and she said to me, quite angrily and very shockingly, that she had tried and God had failed her. One can only hope that she has done nothing foolish. But we should remember that there are worse scandals than suicide. If any really shocking scandal should attach to this sad death, it would be very terrible, and not just for this house and for Sir Robin as her husband. It would be

147

terrible on a far greater scale than that. Do you understand me?"

I didn't then, and don't now, think Mrs. Odingsell
would ever have been party to a homicide if she knew
about it in advance. But afterwards, when the dead
were dead and could not be restored to life? In that
case, I thought, Mrs. Odingsell, the ardent Protestant,
might well be party to anything that would keep the
door of England's throne room firmly shut in the face
of Mary Stuart.

"Oh yes. I understand," I said wearily.

The rest of the household began to return from
Abingdon shortly after that. Mr. Forster arrived and
was all horror and outrage, sending Bowes off at once
to ride to court and find Dudley. Poor Bowes was
barely allowed time for a bite of food. "Get as far as
you can tonight but reach Sir Robin tomorrow without fail," Forster said. "The court is at Windsor."

I wished I'd known that when I sent John off, and
wondered anxiously when he would come back. He
would have had to find the court and then go on to
Sussex. Today was Sunday and he might return by
Wednesday, but not, I thought, before. I shouldn't
have sent him to Sussex as well, I said angrily to
myself. However, the moment I used Meg as an
excuse for wanting to write a letter, I had known that I
wanted desperately to hear news of my daughter. I
had seized the opportunity. And I doubted whether it
would have saved Amy, even if Cecil had replied bv
immediate messenger. Perhaps it had made no difference after all.

Meanwhile, Forster had ordered Amy to be carried
to her room and laid upon her bed. Everyone was
distracted. Even the indolent Mrs. Owen, who apparently had dined with Amy and then gone back to her
part of the house to sleep all afternoon and was only

woken by the sound of Pinto's hysterics, was very upset, while Pinto just cried on and on, most pitifully.

Dale berated her for saying that I meant harm to Lady Dudley when, if only I had been allowed to stay with her, I might have prevented the tragedy. Pinto agreed, and clung to me, begging forgiveness, which in a way was nearly as upsetting as her accusations. I had longed for them to cease, but not like this.

We had a haphazard supper which no one wanted to eat, and we went to bed although I doubt if any of us slept well.

The following morning, no one really knew what to do with themselves. Pinto wouldn't eat and kept on crying. While Dale and I were toying with our breakfast pottage, Forster and Mrs. Odingsell brought us an early visitor.

"Master Blount!" I exclaimed, starting to my feet.

It was indeed Dudley's cousin by marriage, Thomas Blount, neatly dressed with a sword at his side, but unattended, in his unpretentious way.

He knew of the tragedy already, from the landlord of an Abingdon inn where he had slept the previous night. Bowes, who must have passed him on the road, had called at the inn for a cup of ale ("I told him to make all the haste he could; he had no right to waste his time like that! He'd better not charge that ale to his expenses!" Forster barked) and told the landlord of Amy's death.

"It was too late then to ride on to Cumnor," Blount said, as we took him up to see Amy, "but I set out at dawn this morning. So it's really true. Oh, poor soul, poor soul. I was on my way to see her. Her husband wanted me to bring some money to Cumnor. I have it with me."

"I'll take charge of it, Mr. Blount," said Forster, predictably.

149

I hated Dudley at that moment. He had plotted his wife's death, I thought, made use of me as a shield, and cynically sent money for Amy just at the time when his hired murderers were putting an end to her. I had no doubt of his guilt and only prayed that Elizabeth might not share it. Whether she did or not, her interests and those of the realm were the same, and for that reason I must not tell what I knew, or guessed. It all but choked me.

Mr. Blount asked what had happened and we told him how we had come back from Abingdon and found her at the foot of the stairs. Pinto had decided that it must have been an accident. One thing she would not hear of, and that was the idea that Amy had deliberately thrown herself down the stairs. "My mistress was too good a gentlewoman to commit such a sin!" she said indignantly.

In Pinto's mind, if Dudley had had an agent in the house, then I was the said agent. I had been in Abingdon when Amy died and was therefore innocent, and in that case she thought Dudley was innocent too. I supposed I should be relieved.

Presently, we covered Amy's face and withdrew to the parlour, leaving her alone.

"Mrs. Blanchard," Forster said, "will you order some refreshments for us all?"

"Mrs. Blanchard!" said Blount. "Oh, how remiss of me. Even in these circumstances I should not have forgotten that I had another sad message to deliver."

"A sad message? For . . . for me?" I asked, alarmed. "Not about my daughter?"

"Your daughter? Why, no, Mrs. Blanchard. Dudley did mention to me that you had a daughter. I trust she is in the best of health. This concerns your manservant John Wilton."

"John! He's away on an errand for me. What do you mean, a sad message about him? What's happened?"

Blount looked at me so gravely that I was frightened. "On my way from Windsor, yesterday," he said, "I broke my journey for a meal at an inn called the Cockspur, in between Wallingford and Maidenhead."

"I know it," I said.

"Your man, John Wilton, was carried there a few days ago. I seem," said Blount, "to have been greeted by news of violent events at every inn I patronised on my journey! Mr. Wilton had been set upon by footpads, and he was badly hurt. The landlord, Dexter, is a good fellow, and has had him cared for. Just before I arrived, he was able to say who he was, and explain that he came from Cumnor. When I appeared, Dexter recognised me and remembered that Mr. Wilton and myself were in the same party when we took refuge at the inn during the storm, so he spoke to me. I said I would carry the news to Cumnor."

I was too upset to speak. Mr. Blount looked at me anxiously. "There will be an inquest on poor Lady Dudley, you know, and you'll have to be here for that, but I saw Wilton, and his injuries are serious. There's a bill to settle at the inn, too, for his care and the stabling for his horse. The horse was found loose. I think you should go to the Cockspur."

§10§

The Cockspur Inn

I was there the same day. Forster found me a mount without demur and sent me off escorted by Roger Brockley. Brockley, in fact, caused the only difficulty. Since coming to Cumnor Place, I had not ridden, and only now did I discover that he was a sweetly old-fashioned soul who did not think, to quote his own words, that ladies ought to charge about the countryside like wild things. If they needed to travel, they should go by litter or coach or on their escort's pillion. He wanted me to ride behind him or, if I *must* ride my own horse, then I had better take the lazy white gelding which had been provided for Dale, and which had remained at Cumnor along with Bay Star.

"I'm in a hurry," I snapped at him. "I'm not going to go at walking pace on your pillion or ride that four-legged snail, either. We almost had to tow it to get it here. Let me remind you, Brockley, that her majesty the queen is a noted horsewoman. I am following her example."

"There's no man alive more patriotic than I am . . ." Brockley began. He couldn't be more than forty, but he had a deep, serious voice, and between that and the silver strands at his temples, he was capable of exuding as much gravitas as a Roman senator twice his age. His back-sloping forehead shone with earnestness. "But . . ."

"Listen, Brockley, I have a sick servant awaiting my help and if you were lying injured in an inn you might like your employer to take an interest!"

This silenced him and we set out at last, carrying just a few overnight things in our saddlebags. For all my anxiety, I took a malicious pleasure in demonstrating how fast a lady on a modern sidesaddle could gallop. We reached the Cockspur in three hours.

Leaving Brockley to see to the horses, I went straight inside to find the landlord, Dexter. He took me into the tiny parlour we had used on the day of the thunderstorm.

"I'm glad you've come, Mistress Blanchard. I'd have sent for you sooner but it wasn't till Master Wilton came round enough to talk a bit that we knew who to send to, or where. Then, luckily, Master Blount turned up. It's a bad business, mistress."

"I want to see him," I said. "But first, tell me just what happened."

"Well, it was a week ago—yes, last Monday. He came in with a party of gentlemen, and they stayed the night. He'd fallen in with them on the road and was riding with them, the way people do, for company and protection. There's always the chance of a bit of highway robbery."

I nodded. Thomas Blount, carrying money for Amy, had trusted to the sword at his side, but most people journeyed in parties if they could.

"Well, they went off again in the morning, all together. A while later, I had an errand up the road that way. I took a cart to a woodyard for some firewood and I had my dog Watcher with me. It was

153

Watcher found Master Wilton. He'd been dumped under a bush, a good bowshot off the road, about a mile and half from here. My hound was ranging this way and that, the way dogs do, and suddenly he set up such a barking and howling that I went to see. I was that horrified, I can tell you. Well, I got him into the cart and brought him back, and we did what we could for him, until he could speak to us. He's never done more than mumble—I wouldn't say he's ever been properly conscious—but we did finally make out the name Cumnor, and then your name, and by then I'd remembered your party staying here, with Master Wilton and Master Blount included. But then, as I said, Master Blount came along and said he'd see you were informed."

"If he was riding in company," I said, "how did he come to be attacked like that? Who were the gentlemen he was with?"

"Oh, they weren't nothing to do with it. Very proper, dignified gentlemen they were! No, no. I wondered about all that myself, Mistress Blanchard, but when I was bringing Master Wilton back, we passed a hind clearing a ditch and I reckoned I'd seen him there when I went by the first time. So I called out to him, saying what had happened and asking if he'd seen the riders go by. He said he'd seen a man go past, riding pretty fast, as if he was in a hurry . . ."

"He was," I said. "His errand was urgent. Well, at the time, anyway. It doesn't matter now."

"According to the ditcher, if it was Wilton he saw, then he was alone. He was on the Windsor road, but the track forks before that—the left fork goes north—and the others were maybe bound that way. He had no money on him and we reckon he was killed for that. We've got his horse, though. One of my people found it roaming about a few hours later. It's in our stable— a nice little bay mare."

154

"Yes, Master Blount mentioned that." Bay Star was safe, but it was John who mattered, poor John, who had never reached either Cecil or Bridget with my letters. "I'd like to see Master Wilton now," I said.

"This way," said Dexter, leading me to the door. "But . . . I warn you again, mistress. It's bad."

John was lying on a truckle bed in an upper room. It was a tiny place, with plank walls and no ceiling, just sloping cobwebby rafters and thatch above. The day was hot again, and with the dormer window shut, the room was stifling. There was a foul sickroom smell. I sat down on a stool by the bed and looked at his injuries, and knew that John was not just a servant but a dear and trusted friend and that to see him like this was anguish.

He lay quiet, with closed eyes, sleeping or unconscious, breathing noisily. There were huge dark bruises and contusions all over his face, the marks not of fists but surely of a cudgel. His spiky hair was hidden by a bandage which held a pad over his right ear. Blood and something yellowish had seeped through it.

"That's not all," the landlord whispered, as if afraid to rouse him. He reached past me and turned back the coverlet to expose John's tough, wiry body, now relaxed in unconsciousness. There were more bruises on his right side and arm. "He was wearing a dagger when he left here," said Dexter. "I'd say he tried to fight back and they did that disarming him."

"He would certainly have tried to fight back," I said.

Someone had fixed a kind of nappy on him, to protect the bedding as far as possible. Tears sprang to my eyes. It was a sensible thing to do, of course it was, but it was such a bitter indignity for a grown man.

However, neither the bruises nor the nappy-cloth

were serious compared to the second bandage, the one round his lower chest. This, too, was stained, and as I leaned to look at it, I found the source of the smell in the room.

"He was stabbed as well," said the landlord. "It missed the heart, but . . ." He made a helpless gesture. "We did fetch a doctor. He said Master Wilton had a fever, which we knew, and suggested a herbal potion and an ointment. We'd already given him both of them. My wife Annie is good at such things. Then he charged a fat fee and went away to his dinner."

"You will include the fee in your bill, of course." I looked at John again, anxiously. "I want to see the stab wound," I said. "I want to know just how bad things are."

"I'll call Annie," Dexter said.

Annie Dexter was as thin and bony as her husband was cylindrical. She came armed with warm water and unguents and clean linen and said it was time to change his dressings and perhaps I could help her.

Well, I had asked to see and I saw.

The head injury was clearly grave, though not especially repulsive to look at. The stains on the bandage had oozed from his ear. However, the stab wound was both serious and horrible to behold. I had to grit my teeth to drive off an attack of faintness. Mercifully, John remained more or less unconscious. He moaned a little and jerked once or twice when we were bathing him, but he did not open his eyes. When we had finished, Annie took the used dressings and the stained water away and I met Dexter's gaze.

"There isn't much chance, is there?" I said quietly. "The stab wound has gone bad and his skull . . ."

"Is dented. But God works miracles sometimes. You mustn't give up hope, Mistress Blanchard. Would you like to come downstairs again or will you sit with him awhile?"

"I'll sit here. You go and make out your account."

I stayed with John all the rest of the day. He did not wake, although Annie said he would swallow fluid if it were spooned carefully into his mouth. She brought milk and thin broth and I gave them to him at intervals. She brought some fresh wadding too, linen wrapped round pieces of fleece, and we changed him, as though he were an outsize baby. I left the room only once, to take a meal. No one could have eaten in the midst of that smell. I had to force my food down as it was. I paid John's bill up to date, backed by a generous gratuity, and asked for a pallet to be put beside his bed so that I could tend him during the night.

Brockley was intending to sleep in the stable hayloft, as grooms usually do, but when in the evening I went to see if all were well with him and the horses, he asked if my room were satisfactory. When I informed him that I was sharing John's, on a pallet on the floor, he literally threw up his hands in horror. To deal with that, I marched him upstairs and showed John to him.

"John Wilton was on an errand for me when this happened. I am responsible, Brockley. I don't want to hear another word from you," I said.

Brockley lifted the dressing to examine the stab wound, and his attitude was altering already. "This looks like a sword-thrust and it's gone well-nigh through him. I'm sorry, madam. I didn't realise things were this serious, but you need to sleep. You take a room, in the proper fashion, and I'll use that pallet. I'll call you if there's need. You should have fetched me before. A man needs another man to tend him, it's only right."

"You have the horses to look after, Brockley."

"There's an ostler and four stableboys down there. They can manage. They'd better, or I'll have their hides."

"Brockley," I said. "Thank you."

Annie found me a room on the floor just below. I was very tired and fell asleep more quickly than I expected. It was still very warm and I left the shutters open.

When I woke, the dawn was creeping in, and there was a soft, insistent tapping at the door. I wrapped a robe about me and drew back the bolt. Brockley was outside, candle in hand.

"Will you come, madam? He's awake."

"Awake!"

"I doubt it'll last. I've seen something like it before. I was manservant once to a gentleman who took part in tournaments and got himself killed in an accident. His case wasn't so different from this and he came round for a while but . . . oh well. These things are in the hands of God. Anyway, please come."

I followed him up to the attic, where candlelight and daybreak now mingled. John's eyes were open but one pupil was huge and dark while the other was shrunk to a pinpoint. I wasn't sure that he could see.

"John? It's Ursula Blanchard."

He stirred and murmured something and I thought his eyes were trying to focus on my face.

"He knows you, I think," said Brockley. "Talk to him."

"John?" I said again. "You were set upon by robbers. You're in the Cockspur Inn. I'm here and I'm caring for you myself now. Oh, John, I am so sorry. To think that this should happen to you when you were carrying a letter for me."

He tried to speak. I bent closer. "What is it, John? I can't hear."

He tried once more. The effort made the sweat spring on his forehead and his words came out in a blurred whisper, confused with the rasping of his breath. I could make nothing of them. They were only

158

syllables with no meaning. Once, I thought he said his own name. His uneven gaze focused painfully on my face, pitiful with intensity, with the desire to communicate. Then, from the incomprehensible mumblings, came two lucid words, whispered, forced out as if through a barrier.

"Red hair."

Across the bed, my eyes met Brockley's. Brockley said quietly, "Were you attacked by a red-haired man?"

Although he had a country accent, Brockley spoke clearly, and John understood him, answering, "Yes."

There was a pause, as though he were marshalling his strength. Then the difficult whisper came again.

"Bludgeoned me. Blood in my eyes. Didn't see who stuck . . . the sword in me . . ."

His voice faded and his eyes closed. "John," I said urgently. "Please! These robbers should be brought to justice. Can you remember anything else?"

On the pillow his head turned restlessly from side to side. He muttered again, but once more it made no sense. Beside me, Brockley too strained to hear, as the whisper dissolved in a rattling breath. Again John's head turned from side to side and his body began to shudder.

"Take hold of him!" said Brockley sharply. "Put your arms round him. Comfort him. Madam," he added belatedly.

I did as he said, and held John Wilton as he died.

Before we returned to Cumnor, I asked for John's belongings and, when given them, I examined his jacket. Both my letters were there, untouched. He had not been killed for the letter to Cecil, that was certain. His money was gone, though. Robbers, then. Just commonplace robbers, one apparently with red hair.

I reported to Master Dexter what John had said,

and he shrugged. "Robbers come in all shapes and shades, and likely enough that one's washed his hair in walnut juice by now and he's going round as dark as a crow. Look, Mistress Blanchard, there'll be an inquest on him but you were away in Cumnor when it all happened; you need not hurry back to be here for it. I take it you've another inquest to attend, that on poor Lady Dudley, and one is enough, I'd say! But will you arrange the funeral? It being warm weather still . . ."

"It shouldn't be delayed. I understand," I said. People pass so quickly, I thought, from being sick or hurt and in need of loving care, to being embarrassing heaps of debris which must be put underground quickly before they breed disease. Gerald too had had to be laid away without delay.

The inn was not far from the parish church, St. Anne's. Escorted by Brockley, I went there and gave the necessary instructions and paid in advance, saying I would return when I could, and place flowers on the grave.

We went back to the inn to tell Dexter what had been arranged and take a fortifying cup of ale before Brockley went to saddle up, while I packed John's belongings. I asked Dexter for writing materials so that I could write down what I thought John's last words were and sign it so that it could be read out at the inquest.

"Though I couldn't make out the very last thing he tried to whisper," I told Dexter. "Could you?" I said, turning to Brockley.

"Well, madam, it sounded like 'bald' but it didn't make much sense. He'd just said his attacker had red hair—I heard that right enough—so bald he can't have been."

"But there was more than one! He said he didn't see who stabbed him. It must have been a whole gang.

Perhaps he was trying to tell us what the leaders were like." I could see them in my mind, two ferocious robbers, one with unkempt, flaming hair; the other bald like Mr. Ellis the butler at Cumnor. "Well, it had better be reported. I'll set it down anyway. Perhaps I ought to come back for the inquest after all," I said uncertainly.

Brockley shook his head, and humour for once glinted through his gravity, the same humour which had said that Mrs. Owen was too lazy to go to the fair except in a litter carried by slaves. "No, Mr. Dexter's right. One's enough. You'll be bouncing from one inquest to another like a tennis ball between racquets otherwise."

"I agree with that." Dexter gave us all some more ale and nodded at Brockley in a friendly way. "Mistress Blanchard, you've a good fellow here, and if you want a replacement for John Wilton," he added unexpectedly, "I think you could do worse than ask Master Brockley if the job takes his fancy."

§11§

The Huntress

In my room at Cumnor, or what had been my room, for I would not sleep there again, Fran Dale was folding clothes neatly into panniers, ready for the packhorse, while I went through drawers and cupboards to make sure that we had left nothing behind.

Amy was in her tomb, and the inquest on her death was all over. The jury had been sober and honest; made up of men who had Amy's interests at heart. Two of her half-brothers were on it: one of them her mother's son by a previous marriage; the other Arthur Robsart, dressed in black without ornament, his face serious as I had never seen it before; no sign now of either the fashionable gallant or the careless lover.

The inquest was a farce. Since only I (and possibly Mrs. Odingsell) knew that horsemen had come to Cumnor on the day of Amy's death, and only I had heard Amy say she wished to be alone to give any intending murderers their chance; and since loyalty to the queen kept me (and probably Mrs. Odingsell too) from repeating what we knew, there was no trace of evidence that Amy had died through foul play.

If there had been, however, I doubt if either coroner or jury would have wanted to pursue the matter. According to Thomas Blount, Dudley had sent the strictest instructions that they were to find out the truth, and the queen had banished him from court until the inquiry was over, but I still had a strong impression that the jurymen knew very well that if their verdict even hinted at the possibility of murder the result could be a national disaster.

Instead, they examined with great care the theory that Amy, grieving over her husband's neglect and mortally ill, and in pain as well, had deliberately sent us all away so that she could commit suicide by throwing herself down two flights of stairs.

Mr. Hyde, Forster's tiresome brother-in-law, stated in evidence that Lady Dudley was deeply unhappy, citing as proof the fact that he had often called and tried to cheer her, without success. Inquests are hardly entertainment, and I didn't expect that anything in the course of this one would amuse me. However, when I heard that and recalled Mr. Hyde's tasteless methods of cheering people up, I found it quite hard not to laugh, until it occurred to me to wonder if Forster had covertly encouraged Mr. Hyde's damaging visits, knowing how they would upset Amy, because he was looking ahead to a possible inquest. A suspicion of suicide might suit him very well. I was angry then, but there was nothing I could do.

The jury decided against a suicide verdict, however. Pinto, who was terrified that her mistress would not be accorded a proper Christian burial, indignantly denied that Amy, who was so pious and spent so much time in prayer, would ever entertain such a wicked thought, while Dr. Bayly, called to testify on Amy's state of health, said that it would be a foolish way to commit suicide because the chances were that it wouldn't work.

It was the only time I ever saw Bayly. He was one of those big, opinionated men with too many chins, and I didn't take to him, but he did something to keep Amy from the horror of burial in unblessed earth. The jury's final conclusion was that she had simply slipped, or felt dizzy, as sick people often did, and had fallen, and been unlucky (or lucky, some would say, since she had at least not had to die of her disease) in the outcome.

Perhaps that was the truth. I did not think so, but I had lain awake, turning everything over in my mind, for many a night now, and still the wary, glittering, powerful and yet curiously vulnerable figure of Elizabeth blocked the road to candour. England needed her, and her name must not be smirched.

Now the verdict was given I could set it all aside. Amy no longer concerned me. I had attended the huge and elaborate funeral in Oxford and I had wept genuine tears for her, but I was free of her now, and of Cumnor. Dudley, who had been exiled to his house at Kew and banned from the queen's presence until the inquest was over, had come to Oxford for the funeral, solemn of face and dressed in mourning, head to foot. There he had given me my outstanding pay plus something extra and also given me a letter in which he formally made me a present of Bay Star "because," said the letter, repeating what he had said verbally, "I hear from Bowes and Cousin Blount that you did all you could for my wife and performed your duties most admirably, and I would reward you for this."

I hated him for his hypocritical mourning and his long face, but I accepted graciously. I needed the money and I was thankful to have a good horse. Now that I was well mounted and in funds, I had written to the court and obtained leave of absence until the end of October, so that I could go to Sussex, see my daughter and give Bridget a further good supply of money. I also wanted to see John Wilton's sister, Alice, and perform the sad duty of telling her of John's death.

In Sussex, I might even hear news of Matthew, whose house was in that county. If I could learn where he lived, I might venture to send him a message, although I wasn't sure about that. His total silence since he left Cumnor was not encouraging. He had thought it over, I said to myself dismally, and decided that after all I was too difficult a woman for him, or perhaps he had met someone else.

Well, I had sent him away myself and would do better not to brood. When I went back to court at the end of my leave of absence, I would if necessary approach Arundel and learn through him how matters stood. I might even find a message waiting for me!

For the moment, I had much to think about. I had missed John's funeral, but on the way to Sussex, I would visit the grave in the little churchyard of St. Anne's, near the Cockspur Inn. Dudley's party had left for London direct from Oxford, but I had had to return to Cumnor to clear my room. I had arranged an escort for myself and Dale. Taking Dexter's advice, I had asked Brockley to enter my service in place of John and he had agreed. He was not John, who was part of my lost past, and I knew, with some irritation, that he thought I needed watching over and guiding, but I also knew too that like John he was honest, and I was glad to have him.

There was a tap at my door, and Pinto came in. She too had been generously paid off by Dudley and she was going to Norfolk to rejoin Amy's mother, who was taking her on as an extra lady's maid and had even sent an escort for her.

"I've come to say goodbye," she said. "We're ready to go. They're bringing the horses to the door now."

"Goodbye," said Dale stiffly. She had never forgiven Pinto for being so suspicious of me.

Pinto glanced at her doubtfully and then said to me, "I want to say again that I'm sorry I made a mistake about you, Mrs. Blanchard. I see now you meant no ill to my lady. Only I did love her so and she was so good to me and . . ."

"If there's one thing I can't abide," remarked Dale to the pannier she was filling, "it's jealousy."

"Stop it, Dale. It's all right, Pinto. I'm glad you're provided for and I hope you'll be happy."

"I hope you'll be happy too, Mrs. Blanchard." She did not include Dale in her wellwishing. She held out a folded sheet of paper to me. "One of the maids says she found this, lying under the hangings of the bed in the guest room Mr. Blount was using till he went to Oxford. I don't know if it's important. I can't find Mr. Forster, so can I leave it with you? I have to go now."

"Yes, of course." I took it from her. "Well, good luck, Pinto, and a safe journey."

Her suspicions had been hurtful and although I said the right things, I couldn't quite manage to kiss her goodbye. Fortunately she didn't seem to expect it. She took her leave, and Dale went downstairs after her, I rather think so that she could watch Pinto ride out of our lives.

Once alone, I stood for a moment, looking at the letter in my hand. Then I unfolded it.

As Pinto had handed it to me, the doubled sheet had partly opened and I had recognised the writing inside. It was the same as that on Dudley's note to me. I make no apology for what I did next. I could do nothing now for Amy, but I still longed to know how she had died. I wanted it so much that I was still prepared to listen behind wallhangings or read other people's letters or do anything else which would bring me information. I opened the letter out, and read it.

I can't say what I expected to find. I had no suspicions of Blount, and the letter had probably been written to him. I think I was clutching at the vague possibility that it might turn out to belong to Forster, who after all lived here and had often been in and out of the room even when Blount was occupying it.

Even so, I could hardly have supposed that Dudley would put down in black ink and his own handwriting detailed instructions for doing away with Amy or helping Verney to do so. However, if the letter did belong to Forster, there might be something, I thought: an oblique reference, perhaps, a cryptic phrase which would have meaning for a partly informed person such as myself; some revealing slip . . .

I read the letter through and then sat down on the bed, holding it in my hand, shattered. Some revealing slip. Oh yes, indeed, but what it had revealed was not at all what I expected. Quite the reverse.

The letter was most certainly the property of Thomas Blount. In fact, it was the missive containing the strict instructions which Blount had mentioned, to arrange an inquest and find out the truth.

It was most unpleasant reading. It made me hate Dudley more passionately than ever. All right, Amy had had her limitations. She had had some native shrewdness, but little education and her health was poor. However, she had been good, and she was beautiful when Dudley married her, and if he had let her, I think she would have loved him truly always. She deserved better of him than this. I looked at the first paragraph again.

> Cousin Blount—immediately upon your departing from me, there came to me Bowes, by whom I do understand that my wife is dead and,

as he saith, by a fall from a pair of stairs. Little
other understanding can I have of him. The
greatness and the suddenness of the misfortune
doth so perplex me, until I do hear from you
how the matter standeth or how this evil should
light upon me, considering what the malicious
world will bruit, as I can take no rest . . . I have
no way to purge myself of the malicious talk that
I know the wicked world will use, but one,
which is the very plain truth to be known . . .

"My wife." Just "my wife." Not *Amy* and certainly
not *poor Amy*. No anxious hope that she might at least
have died quickly and not lain helpless for a long time
first. No hint of grief. I remembered how when he first
asked me to come to Cumnor, he had spoken of Amy
with underlying exasperation, and said that their
marriage hadn't prospered. Very well, they were estranged, but couldn't he, I said to myself furiously,
just have *pretended* that he felt sorry for her? Even if
you had quarrelled with someone, or become bored
by them, wouldn't you still be distressed to learn that
they had suffered a fatal accident when they were ill
and alone? In all decency he should at least have put
up a pretence!

Instead, his sole reference to "misfortune" read as
though he considered the misfortune to be his, because he was afraid that people would say he had
arranged it. *Considering what the malicious world will
bruit . . . the malicious talk that I know the wicked
world will use . . .*

The subsequent paragraphs were no better. The
grammar was confused and hasty, as though he had
dashed it off in a panic. He wanted the "discreetest
and most substantial men" for the jury, "no light or
slight persons," and he wanted things to proceed in
every respect "by order and law." The manner of

Amy's death "marvellously troubled" him; he asked whether Blount thought it happened "by evil chance or villainy." He had sent for various friends and relatives of Amy's to watch over the inquest proceedings—true enough, since her half-brothers had been there. It was perhaps Dudley rather than Blount who had summoned them.

The letter breathed fear for his reputation, and behind and beyond that, I smelt fear for his career and even for his neck. These were the words of a man taken by surprise, and too horrified even to counterfeit suitable feelings about his own wife. I looked through the disagreeable missive again. Amy's name wasn't mentioned anywhere at all. In the second paragraph, there was an impersonal recommendation that "the body be viewed and searched." "The body." Just "the body." Not Amy, not a woman he had been married to for ten years, not someone to whom he had once made love.

If he had arranged her death, the news of it would not have frightened him into near-incoherence, and one might reasonably suppose that a husband who has just done away with his wife and wishes to cover his traces would put down a few conventional phrases of regret for her passing.

However, he was too upset to think of anything beyond the harm that scandal could do. Harm to him, that was. Elizabeth's reputation didn't mean much more to him than Amy's neck, judging from what I had just read.

Dudley was innocent. The very self-centredness of the letter proved that, dealing a backhanded blow to all my suspicions. He had not sent Verney or anyone else to murder his wife. If Verney and Holme had been here that day, they had come for some other reason, probably quite harmless. Probably, they didn't know that anyone had seen them, and were now keeping quiet for fear of drawing suspicion on themselves and Dudley.

Amy had died by accident or else flung herself downstairs, trusting that the fall would kill her, and it had obliged. I need never have written to Cecil in that panicky fashion, need never have sent John to London.

I folded Dudley's letter again and went to give it to Forster, to send to Blount in London.

If I hadn't written to Cecil, if I hadn't sent John to London, he would still have been alive.

The funeral for Lady Dudley, held in the Church of Our Lady in Oxford on 22 September, was all pomp and ceremony, the church hung with black cloth, and a long, slow procession with a choir solemnly singing as they came, and the coffin itself borne by eight tall yeomen.

John had had no family at hand. His burial two days later beside the small grey church of St. Anne's had been very quiet. There were yew trees along the fence at one side of the graveyard, but the path through the middle was bordered with cherry trees. John lay near to one, and I was glad to think of the blossom tossing above his resting place in springtime and blowing down to make a coverlet of petals when their hour was gone.

We had brought him flowers; sprays of late roses, for summer was dying. We tied the horses to a tree outside the churchyard and we all went in together, Dale, Brockley and myself, to put the offering on the newly heaped mound.

I was riding Bay Star, and had used some of Dudley's gratuity to buy a packhorse and a cob, a sturdy fleabitten grey, for Brockley. For Dale, I had somewhat high-handedly borrowed the wretched white gelding. At least she wasn't likely to fall off it.

Dale said, "Perhaps you'd like to be alone here for a bit, ma'am. You knew him longer than we did."

I nodded, and they withdrew to wait in the road with the horses. I stayed where I was, kneeling in the grass. When they were out of earshot, I spoke to John.

"John, I'm so sorry. Wherever you are, please forgive me. It need not have happened. I was wrong, foolish, imagining things. I lost my head and sent you off on a stupid errand and now you're dead and I can't even do anything to bring your murderers to justice. I can't scour the forests for a robber with red hair, and perhaps a bald associate! I would if I could. Please, please forgive me."

I was being a fool all over again. John, if he was anywhere, was in the hands of God, and what lay in the ground beside me was only his cast-off clay. He couldn't hear me and nowadays it was not the thing to pray to the dead, or for them, either. That was Popish. I was too unhappy to be bothered with labels, though. I clasped my hands and closed my eyes and said a paternoster for John and asked God to look after him.

Then I rose and rejoined the others. "To the Cockspur," I said. "We'll have dinner there and set out for Sussex in the morning."

We found the inn humming. A noisy family party, apparently on their way home from a wedding, and encumbered with two elderly ladies, one young pregnant one, two horse-litters and three very drunk gentlemen, had just arrived and seemed to have taken over every corner. The dogs were barking excitedly; the stableyard cats had taken refuge on the roof of the hayloft to get away from the shouting and singing and the trampling hoofs and we could hardly get into the yard for the crowd of people and animals and equipages.

171

"You've picked a bad time," said Dexter candidly, pushing his way between the two litters to reach us. "I've already got the house full, with a couple of merchants and their wives, and a travelling packman and an archdeacon with his chaplain, and the stabling's stuffed full of horses and grooms. Mistress Blanchard, can you and your woman make do with the little attic place where we put your man Wilton? It's all that's left. I daresay we can get Brockley here into the hayloft if we use a shoehorn. The horses must go into the meadow. There'll be supper enough if mutton suits you. I sent to the farm up the road and bought a sheep and got them to kill it. I just hope no one else arrives because I hate turning business away, but . . ."

"The attic will do very well," I said, "and we can certainly turn the horses out for the night. We're too tired to ride any further if we can avoid it."

"Bay Star can't stay out," said Brockley firmly. "She's too fine bred and it's going to rain."

"See my ostler," said the harassed Dexter, as someone called his name in peremptory tones. "He'll maybe get somebody else to put their horse in the meadow. Excuse me . . ."

The ostler appeared, at an unhurried pace. He was a thin, brown, weathered man who never seemed to be in a rush, even in the midst of chaos like this. He recognised us, greeted us by name, gave Dale a hand down from her saddle and patted Bay Star. He also agreed with Brockley's opinion about her.

"We'll find a corner inside for your pretty little mare, Mrs. Blanchard. Your man's right. The night's going to be wet and chilly and she's got Arabian blood, I fancy. They always feel the cold. I was sorry about Mr. Wilton, madam. It's a thousand pities he wasn't taking the same road as the gentlemen he was with when he came here. They'd have been protection for him. Now, one of them had a half-Arabian, a very handsome beast."

He ran Bay Star's stirrups up and ducked his head under her saddle flap to undo the girth. "Beautiful head it had," he said, stepping back and tossing the girth over the saddle before lifting the saddle right off. "Skin so fine you could see every vein on its face, and very striking colouring. You get that sometimes with Arabian blood. This one was piebald."

There was a click inside my head, like a key going home in a lock. For three seconds, three heartbeats, I stood still, absorbing what he had just said, and wondering. Then I heard myself ask, oh, so very casually, "Really? That sounds familiar somehow. I wonder if they were people my husband used to know?"

"I never heard their names, madam."

"I can't recall the names either," I said, still very casually, "but did one of them have red hair?"

"Red hair? Yes, in a manner of speaking. Not fire-red, but ginger, yes, one of those gentlemen was ginger."

The world turned upside down.

There was no parlour vacant but I called Brockley up to the attic where Dale and I were to sleep and told them what I meant to do. I expected them to say I was insane, and they did. Brockley indeed interrupted me quite brusquely before I had finished explaining.

"Madam, the inquest on Mr. Wilton brought in a verdict of murder by a person or persons unknown. There's been a hue and cry out for a band of robbers, possibly including a red-haired man and a bald one, but no one's been found. How can we hope to trace them? In any case, you shouldn't try. Such things are not a lady's business."

173

"That's quite right, ma'am. Madness I call it, though I'm sorry to be disrespectful and I know I'm speaking out of turn. And what about your little girl in Sussex? And Mr. Wilton's sister?"

And Matthew, I thought. And Matthew.

"I know," I said, "and in due course, Dale, Sussex is where we'll go. Of course it's important! But so is this. Brockley, please listen and this time let me finish! The whole point is that I don't think John *was* killed by robbers. I think he was killed by that party of gentlemen he was with. I think that last word he tried to whisper could have been 'piebald' instead of just 'bald.' Neither of us could hear it properly. Now I learn that one of those men was ginger haired and another had a striking piebald horse. It's suggestive, you must admit."

"I admit nothing of the kind, madam. He was delirious, near death. He could have said anything. If what Mr. Dexter said is right, he parted from his companions before he was killed. I understood Dexter to say that a ditcher saw Mr. Wilton go by on his own. Respectable gentlemen, the kind of folk who ride blood horses, don't murder for money along the highway."

"Brockley, I haven't the faintest idea how or why they did it. Perhaps they're a new kind of robber band, who've taken to going about looking respectable so as to tempt unwary travellers to trust them. John was carrying quite a full purse. I know it sounds unlikely. I know I'd be wasting my time if I went to the Sheriff of Berkshire or anyone else with such a story. They'd say what you have just said: that John was delirious. I intend to find out who those so-called gentlemen were, all the same. Are you coming with me or do I go without you?"

"I'll take your orders, madam, naturally. Someone," said Brockley pointedly, "must guard you, for your own sake."

"And Dale, what about you?"

"Of course I'll go where you go, ma'am, but I just don't understand *why.*" Poor Dale had found our long ride very tiring indeed. I didn't know how old she was, but at a guess, she was in her forties and she had always worked hard. For once, I could sympathise with her aggrieved air. I spoke gently.

"We're not setting out tonight, anyway. If you sleep soundly, Dale, you'll feel better in the morning. As for why—there are things I can't altogether explain. You will have to trust me, both of you."

Dudley was innocent, although I hadn't thought so when I let myself be turned back to Abingdon Fair. The small cold voice inside me had said that I could not save Amy and must not even seek justice for her, because the good of the realm came first, and I had listened.

In the same circumstances I would do the same again, and it had made no difference anyway, but the guilt would be with me always. The least I could do was to seek justice for John, who had also died by violence, because of my mistaken belief that Dudley was a murderer. For John, I would become a huntress, implacable as Artemis herself.

"The first thing I need to do," I said, "is find the exact place where John was found, and look at it. Maybe that will tell us how they managed it. Brockley, please go and find Dexter and give him my compliments, and say that although I understand how busy he is, I desperately need five minutes of his time."

§12§

The Cold Scent

Dexter was hurried and impatient and clearly growing tired of being inconvenienced by John Wilton and those connected with him. He couldn't conceive why I should want an exact description of the place where John was found, and came very near to saying that he didn't have time to supply one. I exerted myself to be charming and apologetic, however, and in the end he provided short, brusque directions. I didn't ask him to take us there next day, because judging by his irritated air, I would ask in vain. I thanked him graciously and left it there, and hoped we'd find the place without him.

We set off early, through a damp grey morning. The land in this part of England is all rolling hills and broad, shallow vales. Much of it is wooded, but there are farms in plenty, too, with cornfields and hay meadows and patches of open heath where sheep and cattle graze. The road onwards from the Cockspur went past the church and roughly south-east, through woods and fields, for a mile or so, and then forked.

To the left, the way turned north, and according to

176

Dexter it led to one of the main northbound highways. To the right, the road took a long curve round a heathland of wiry grass with a few spinneys and some clumps of gorse. The curve, which at the beginning almost bent the road back westwards, probably followed some old land boundary, but eventually it settled again into a south-easterly direction, which would ultimately lead to the Thames and Windsor. John had been found to the left of the road, under a gorse clump, just at the end of the long curve. Dexter's instructions had been concise enough, and the place was easy to find. We couldn't pinpoint the precise gorse clump where the dog had found him, but it didn't seem to matter.

"So. What next?" said Brockley.

What next indeed? The implacable huntress was feeling a good deal less implacable this morning. Low clouds scudded overhead, borne on a chilly wind, and rain spattered. My spirits were as joyless as the sky. What was I doing here?

It was three weeks since John had been discovered, mortally hurt, under one of these bushes. What had I hoped to find? Had I thought the tracks of his assailants would still be here, and even if they were, how would a few footprints, or hoofprints, guide me to a party of dubious gentlemen who had ridden away all that time ago and very likely split up since then? Did I think one of them might have been careless enough to drop a dagger with a family crest engraved into the handle, or a prayerbook with his name inside, and left it here for me to pick up?

"Madam. Whoever did it was in ambush here, waiting for an unwary traveller," Brockley said. "It's a lonely enough place and they could have been hidden in those trees over there." He pointed to a little spinney about thirty yards off. "I don't see how his assailants could have been the companions he left

177

back at the fork. How did they get here ahead of him?"

He was right, of course. I had been foolish.

And then I saw.

I at once realised that I didn't want to see it; that a large part of me would have been relieved to find no clues and to give up the whole enterprise. However, it was there: a path, faint, overhung by bushes and trailing grass, but a path all the same. It joined the road a little to our left, and led off across the heath, going roughly north-eastwards. I pointed to it, saying, "I want to see where that goes."

They humoured me, like the attendants of a lunatic. We rode along the little track, and before long I saw that my guess had been right. That unobtrusive path cut across the heath, joining the two ends of the curve on the road, as a bowstring joins the two ends of a bow. It rejoined the road, in fact, at the fork, making a narrow central prong, almost invisible because of the bushes and the grass.

It was a short cut. From time to time, people in a hurry avoided going round the curve and walked or rode this way instead. They had made the path. Indeed, horsemen who knew the lie of the land could have beaten John to the far end of the curve even without a path. They could also have done it without being seen either by John or the ditcher. There were spinneys, and a concealing hump in the ground between track and road. Brockley's argument did not hold.

I explained what I was thinking. Brockley frowned. "I don't doubt it's possible, madam. You think they set on him here at the fork, and he got away from them, but they took the short cut and were waiting for him at the far end of that curve."

"Yes. He was going fast, so the ditcher told Dexter,"

I said. "Suppose he was trying to escape from someone?"

"Well, again, madam, it's possible, but . . ."

He stopped. While we talked, we had both been looking about us and it was Brockley, this time, who saw something. Close to where we stood, at the meeting place of the three paths, the ends of several twigs had been sheared off clean from a bush, and the cut pieces were still lying on the ground.

"That wasn't recent," Brockley said. "It's not raw; the weather's been at it for a week, or maybe three. It's not proof, of course, but I grant you, it looks like—"

"Someone's been here, slashing about with a blade," I said. I felt odd. Part of me had come alert, like a hound that picks up a scent, but another part of me once again wanted to run away, to subside into feminine diffidence and say, "But I can't do anything about this! Who would expect it of me?" The answer to that was that if the evidence were there, then *I* would expect it of me.

I remembered the sword-thrust through John's body. These sheared twigs weren't evidence, exactly, but they were suggestive.

"If someone was here, laying about him with a sword," I said, *"why* was he laying about with it? What if he were one of John's attackers, and this is where he missed his stroke and sliced the bush instead? While John stuck in his spurs and rode for his life."

"They took a risk," Brockley said, "going for him on the highway, either here or where he was actually stabbed. This road's not empty."

This was true. At that very moment, there was a cart plodding slowly towards us, and a farmer on a shaggy pony had passed us a few minutes earlier, with a civil good day

"That," Brockley said slowly, thinking it out, "could be why they never made sure he was dead. Perhaps they saw someone coming, so they shoved him under the gorse and got themselves out of sight fast. I wonder why they started on him just here?" He stood up in his stirrups and scanned our surroundings. "There's a pond over there," he said.

We rode over to look. The pond was only about fifty yards off, in the angle between the northward track and the narrow short cut. It was dark and scummy: weight a body and throw it in, and it would vanish. John's assailants probably had been disturbed, or they would surely have brought him back here anyway. Instead, they had had to leave him under a bush where he might be found, and was.

"You think they meant to put him here," I said.

"It could be," said Brockley, doubtfully.

Dale looked as though the conversation had become completely beyond her. She sat on the white gelding's back—we had dubbed the animal White Snail—with an expression of long-suffering gloom. Brockley gazed up at the dismal sky as though seeking inspiration there.

"Did he have any weapons?" he asked me at length.

"He had a dagger but it was gone when he was found," I said bleakly.

"He might have tried to defend himself, then. I did get to know him a little at Cumnor, and I should say that he would. If he did," said Brockley, once more with that fugitive glint of humour, "we are looking for a group of gentlemen, one with ginger hair, one with a well-bred piebald horse and possibly more than one with recent scars from a dagger."

"Yes. Exactly," I said. I couldn't smile.

"Madam," said Brockley, "you believe that John Wilton was attacked by his gentlemanly companions.

You may be right, but are you really determined on pursuing them?"

Dale looked hopeful. She was praying that I would say no, that I had had second thoughts and that we should set out for Sussex forthwith. I wanted to do that, too. I wanted to see Meg and, if I could, find Matthew. How could I put either of them aside for the sake of this ridiculous hunt, which might take heaven knew how long and would almost certainly fail anyway, and if it didn't, might take me into peril? If these men had killed John, then they were dangerous. I remembered the bruises on his body and the horrible, rotten wound which had killed him.

I remembered how I had denied justice to Amy.

"I am determined to go on," I said. My voice was formal. It was an undertaking, as though I had sworn an oath before a priest. All three of us knew it. Even Brockley heard the grim intent in my tone, and acknowledged it. He bent his head. "In that case, madam, may I make a suggestion?"

"Indeed you may."

"We must begin, must we not, by picking up the scent, so to speak, of these violent gentlemen? We must find which route they took."

"Yes." I thought. "They went northwards—no, that was what Dexter said, because he thought they'd parted from John at the fork, but that isn't what happened. They could equally well have been going south."

"So we should enquire along both roads," said Brockley. "In villages, at inns. Someone must have noticed them. Although," he added with a sigh, "it was weeks ago. The scent may well be cold."

"This is absurd," said Brockley.

We were conducting what I suppose one could call a

council of war, sitting on our horses just outside a small hamlet a few miles from Henley. We were all tired, and earlier that day Dale had actually succeeded in falling off White Snail, which I had believed to be impossible. I had scolded her for being such a terrible rider, and said that one of these days I must get Brockley to give her some proper tuition, but I knew that really she was exhausted. I was not much better myself. The ankle I had turned on the day of the fair had not given trouble at first, but I had turned it again since, dismounting too quickly, and now it ached persistently. As luck would have it, it was the left ankle, which took my weight at the trot.

We had been hunting for two days, searching along both the northward and the Windsor roads for traces of our elusive group of gentlemen. We had now enquired at two posting inns, four village taverns, six farms, three blacksmiths—one of their horses might have cast a shoe—and about two dozen cottages. However, it had been too long ago and no one remembered them now, except for one old woman, and her testimony hardly made sense.

We had begun our hunt by tossing a coin to see which road we should investigate first, and accordingly started with the northward route. After failing to find a trace within five miles, we spent a night in one of the inns, bought cold food for today's noon meal and returned to the Windsor track, to meet with another complete blank, until the afternoon, when we rode into the hamlet which was now just behind us, and found a group of village women engaged in a stormy altercation.

At the centre of the wrangle was a fierce old beldame with a jutting chin and a grubby headdress. She was standing at the door of a dirty-looking cottage, shouting and gesticulating with a spindle, from which a broken strand of wool trailed and

182

floated. A younger woman, much cleaner, sturdy, rosy and very angry, was standing in front of her, arms akimbo, and shouting back. The rest seemed to be interested onlookers.

Halting on the fringes of the uproar, we gathered that the younger woman was complaining because the older one did nothing "but sit there spinning at your door all day, staring at what other folks are doing, and making up mucky tales about them! Yes, my Peggy does go walking with young Walter Rigden and we know about it and so does Walter's father and the two of them'll get wed next spring and you can just keep your foul mouth shut in future and your filthy ideas to yourself, you old besom!"

"Don't you call me names! Oh, I daresay you don't care what your Peggy gets up to! I know what *you* got up to in your day, Milly Mogridge. You were no better than you should be. Like mother like daughter . . ."

"How dare you, you . . . !"

"How dare I tell the truth? Ho, yes, the *truth!* And I don't tell all I know, either. There's not much I don't know about what goes on in this place and there's plenty I could tell but I don't, and . . ."

Somebody in the crowd growled, "Bloody old witch!" and the crone rounded on the voice.

"Who said that?"

Several of the women shuffled uneasily backwards, and someone made the sign to ward off the evil eye.

Brockley spurred forward and straight into the midst of it all. "Excuse me, good women!" He swept off his cap, and smiled round at them. As I watched in amazement, thinking that I would never have believed that Brockley could be so ingratiating, it struck me that he was a personable man. The entire gathering had transferred its attention from the wrangle to my manservant. The affronted mother of the over-passionate Peggy had unfolded her arms and was gazing at him with marked interest, and despite her advanced years and aggressive temperament, the beldame had produced a toothless simper.

"It is possible," declared Brockley, "that you goodwives may be of help to us—especially one with such great powers of observation as yourself." He bowed to the beldame. "We are sorry to intrude, but I and Mistress Blanchard, whose servant I have the honour to be, are on an errand of vital importance. Three weeks or so ago, did you, mistress," addressing the old dame, "or any of you . . ." throwing his enquiry to the crowd, "chance to see, riding through this village, three gentlemen, one on a fine piebald horse, and one with ginger hair?"

Astonishingly, the old dame had, except that it wasn't three weeks ago, but the Saturday before last.

Brockley thanked her and I handed him some silver to press into the old woman's palm. As he gave it to her, he spoke quietly to her and she said something in answer. He looked round at the others. "Her husband's dead and she has no children to help her. You're her neighbours; surely you know that. Try being kind to her and don't talk nonsense about witches. She's lonely."

As we rode on, Brockley said, "I hope I had an effect but I doubt it. That old woman reminds me of my mother."

"Your mother?" That the dignified Brockley's mother could in any way have resembled that unprepossessing crone, I found hard to believe.

"Oh yes," he said. "She was another lonely one, after my father died and I was working away from home. She lost all her teeth, which made her ugly, and children threw stones at her, so she grew bitter. Then she started getting at her neighbours; finding things out about them and dropping hints. Then someone said the word 'witch' and it was luck that I went to visit her just in time to get her away before she was arrested. It happens so easily. Witches, indeed! It's all a lot of nonsense, witchcraft is. That old dame will end up hanged if she isn't careful. Well, I did my best."

It seemed that Roger Brockley shared not only John Wilton's honesty, but also his willingness to remonstrate with people who were doing things he didn't approve of.

"Is your mother still alive?" I asked.

"No. I rented her a cottage in another village, but it was strange to her and she pined. She was gone in three months, but in her bed, quietly. It could have been worse. Never mind that now." We had left the hamlet and now he pulled up at the roadside. Dale and I stopped beside him, and that was when he said, "It's absurd."

"What is?" I asked.

"What that poor old woman told us. A week last Saturday, she said. That was the fourteenth of September. But John Wilton was attacked on . . ." he did a quick calculation on his fingers ". . . on the third. Where were they in between? Somewhere hereabouts, most likely. But where? And why?"

Dale said tiredly, "I suppose they stopped with someone. They didn't go to an inn, so they must have."

"That's possible," said Brockley thoughtfully.

I looked about me. This was quite a well-populated stretch of countryside. We had called at farmhouses and cottages near the roads, but there were plenty more, down side lanes. I could see roofs in the distance, in all directions, and hearthsmokes climbing into the sky. "They could have stayed anywhere!" I said.

"But they were gentlemen," Dale persisted. "With at least one fine horse. They might have stayed at a manor house, a big place. Well, we've only seen two or three of those."

We hadn't called at any of them. We had been thinking of our three gentlemen as travellers, who would have pressed on along the road. It simply hadn't occurred to us to turn off to the large houses whose gables and chimneys we had only glimpsed once or twice since they were all well back from the main routes.

"We can't just ride up to strange houses and push our way in and start asking questions about their guests," I said. "It's not like asking innkeepers or blacksmiths about passing strangers."

There was a silence. In the middle of it, Dale gave a sigh, and for the second time that day, slid gently out of White Snail's saddle and sank into a heap on the ground.

Brockley handed me his reins and dismounted. Dale sat up, apparently unhurt, but there were tears in her eyes. "I'm that stiff and sore. I can't abide to go on riding, day after day, like this. I just let go, I couldn't help it. I'm sorry, ma'am, but I couldn't, I couldn't."

"Dale's worn out," said Brockley, "and this morning, madam, you complained of your ankle. We passed one of those big houses not a mile back. Let us go and ask for hospitality and make some enquiries at the same time. You're one of the queen's ladies, madam. It's more natural for you to go to a manor house, than to an inn. If we learn nothing there, we can go back later to the other big houses we've passed."

"Up you get, Dale," I said. She looked at me miserably, but Brockley held out his hand to her and she came slowly to her feet and let him help her back into the saddle. "It's not far," I said, "and then you can take your ease."

* * *

We had to turn back through the village and then take a lane to the right. The house Brockley had glimpsed was smaller than Cumnor Place but proved to be much better run. There was a neat, thatched lodge and gatehouse, with a porter, whose young son ran on ahead of us to announce us. We followed, arriving in due course at a pretty manor house, half honey-coloured brick and half white plaster patterned with black timbers. Tall, ornamental chimneys rose from the slate roof, and beyond a wall to the right I caught sight of a knot garden, most beautifully laid out with beds shaped as stars and crescent moons. When we reached the front door, two grooms were already there to show Brockley where to take the horses, and a lady stood on the front steps to greet us.

She was older than I, perhaps in her thirties. Her dark red dress had no farthingale and over it she wore an apron stained with what looked like fruit juices, but her cap and her small ruff were white and clean. She had the mature, tranquil features of a woman happy in marriage and secure in things material. She smiled at us. "I am Kate Westley, and this is Springwood House, the home of my husband Edward Westley. You are travellers in trouble, I hear. Please dismount and come inside."

As Dale and I got down, I explained, nervously, "We are on a journey to Sussex, but I have twisted my ankle and my woman, Dale, is unwell. We need to rest, if we can trespass on your kindness. I am Mistress Ursula Blanchard, widow, and although at present I have leave of absence, I am one of the queen's Ladies of the Presence Chamber."

Our credentials were established, not that Kate Westley seemed much concerned by them. She had noted the pallor of Dale's face at once and was already shepherding us indoors. I allowed myself to

187

limp, which wasn't difficult, because the ache was real.

Just inside the door was a wide vestibule, much lighter than Amy's entrance hall at Cumnor Place, with a floor of polished boards, and some well-kept panelling. The doors out of the vestibule were set wide. To the left there was a parlour and the door to the right led into a dining hall, with a long table and a sideboard and fresh rushes strewn on the floor. I smelt beeswax polish, strong and sweet, mingled with a faint trace of something more exotic and elusive, some rare strewing herb, perhaps. The queen would like this house, I thought. Elizabeth detested unpleasant smells and it was clear that here, every effort was made to please the nose and not offend it.

Within moments, both Dale and I were seated in a large parlour and our hostess had sent a maid to fetch restorative doses of herbs mixed into wine. Dale was invited to loosen her stays and Mistress Westley examined my ankle. I was relieved to see that it was genuinely puffy.

"I'll get a cold compress for that. Dear me. Have you been riding with it like that? Ah, here comes Madge with the wine. You had better both have some of this. It is a recipe of my own. It contains a tincture of marjoram and camomile—I grow the herbs myself—and it both calms and refreshes. It's quite palatable, too," she added. Kate Westley had a delightful smile. It was difficult to imagine this well-ordered house sheltering questionable people.

"I am sorry to impose on you like this," I said, as I sipped at my goblet. The mixture was indeed palatable. "We are really most grateful."

"Oh, please don't be formal. We're always glad to welcome chance travellers." Madge had now brought a bowl of cold water and some linen and towels, and Kate, sitting down on the end of the settle, put a towel on her aproned lap, took my foot into her hands and began to bathe it. "You will stay overnight, I trust—longer if necessary."

"You are very kind, Mistress Westley." I glanced at Dale, who was sipping wine with her eyes closed. She would be glad of a full day's rest, I thought. A house of any size was, of course, supposed to welcome wayfarers, but at Faldene, the greeting was usually more dutiful than warm. Aunt Tabitha could learn from Kate Westley. "I hope," I said, "that we are not causing you any difficulty. If you have other guests . . ."

"We haven't, and my husband would be horrified if I didn't look after you properly. He will be home soon; he is going round his fields. I often go with him, but I have been making preserves today. We have had a fine fruit crop this year. You must taste some of our apples and cherries. They are quite famous in the district."

I laughed. "Do people make excuse to call at this time of year? Perhaps we're very lucky that you have no other chance guests at present."

It wasn't a very good way of asking the question but I could hardly just say, "Who else has stayed here lately?" I must not be too blunt. I felt that even this sounded a little obvious, and to my stretched nerves it seemed that Kate Westley paused half a second too long before she said, "We haven't had anyone to stay for weeks. You are a welcome change—though I am sorry for your ill health. Now, I'll bandage this for you, and then I think we must get you and your woman there upstairs to a bedchamber to rest quietly until supper."

"You are indeed kind," I said.

No one could fault the hospitality of the Westleys. Dale and I were shown up a wide, polished staircase

189

to a walnut-panelled guest room. The big bed had embroidered hangings and the window looked out on an orchard. It must be beautiful in spring, I thought, when the trees were in bloom.

Hot water was brought so that we could wash away our travel-grime, and our panniers were borne upstairs. After a couple of hours, Dale, restored by sleep, did my hair and helped me into a fresh gown before we joined the family at table.

The master of the house, Edward Westley, had returned by now and proved to be a beaming, thickset individual, tanned by weather and full of concern for the welfare of his unexpected guests. The children were at supper too: two little girls of perhaps four and seven; a boy of about nine and his elder brother, who must have been twelve or so, and was already leggy with approaching manhood. The girls were accompanied by a young nursemaid, little more than a child herself, and very much inclined to bob respectful curtsies to me. A tutor, middle aged, quiet spoken and inky fingered, came in with the boys.

The children showed no fear of parents or tutor. When their father asked the boys how their Latin studies had progressed, they chattered freely of how Arthur had mastered the ablative absolute, and when the tutor interrupted to regret that Paul, the older boy, had not had the same success with the gerund, he did it kindly and Edward Westley laughed.

"Never mind. It will exercise your brain and you won't need gerunds anyway when you're full-grown and I'm in my dotage, and you're running the farm for me," he said unconcernedly.

We were asked if we felt better, and where we were bound. I said we were recovering, and were very grateful for their hospitality. I explained, without going into details, that I was on leave from the court, and had been on a visit to Oxfordshire but was now going to see my daughter Meg in Sussex.

The table almost creaked under the weight of the food; the maids who waited were deft and willing. I had never been in a more pleasant household.

However, that night, the memory of that fractional pause when I asked Kate Westley if any other guests had been there lately, came back to me. In the morning, I asked Dale if she would like another day out of the saddle, and on receiving a hearty "Yes, please," I asked Mistress Westley if we could accept her offer and stay for a second night.

"But of course! As long as you need to—just as I said. You are more than welcome!"

I thanked her and after sending Dale upstairs again to rest a little more, I made for the stableyard where I found Brockley. He had White Snail outside, tied to a stable door, and was rubbing the gelding down with a wisp.

"I've arranged for us to stay another night. I just might find something out."

Brockley continued to work, with sweeping strokes of the wisp. "Very well, madam. I've been cultivating the grooms. They go out of an evening for a jar of ale in the village near here. I'll go with them tonight if I can. Maybe they'll gossip."

"I wonder," said Kate Westley, when I went back to the house, "if you'd like to help me this morning. I'm preserving cherries and making an apple syrup. We'll be in the kitchen, and there are plenty of stools to sit on, if your ankle is worrying you."

I said, truthfully enough, that my ankle was improving but would be all the better if I kept my weight off it for a little longer, but that I would be delighted to work in the kitchen with her and chat.

"We shall enjoy each other's company," said Kate.

We did. The kitchen was sunny, with a vaulted stone ceiling and a generous hearth. There was a cook and a spitboy and a couple of maids but it was clear that they were all accustomed to having the mistress of the house among them, and that they worked as a team, on friendly terms. While Kate carefully boiled cherries with red wine, sliced apples and sugar, I perched on a stool by the hearth with a long-handled spoon and stirred a simmering pot of apples. When the apples were fluffy, they had to be simmered again, with sugar, until the mixture thickened and it was time to spoon the syrup into jars.

With Gerald, I had mostly lived in town lodgings, in London or Antwerp, and we didn't grow things. I had helped often enough in the kitchens at Faldene but I couldn't remember ever being shown how to preserve fruit.

"I'm learning something new," I said to Kate.

I stirred and poured and then peeled apples for another potful, and as the quiet domestic morning wore on, I became convinced that, after all, this house was as innocent and happy as it seemed. What I had thought was Kate Westley's suspicious hesitation yesterday, could only have been my imagination. I was glad that my quest had brought me here. I needed this. Working here amid these pleasant, normal women, breathing in the heavy sweetness of simmering fruit, I found an unexpected peace, a sense of healing. I had not realised, until now, how the fears and sorrows of the last few weeks had lacerated my spirit.

I was no further on with my search and perhaps I never would be, but perhaps, after all, it didn't matter as much as I had thought. Brockley was probably right. It was not a lady's business. Ladies made apple syrup, or attended to their children . . .

Or served Queen Elizabeth, by dancing for her and

walking with her. And if they were lucky, were wooed by someone like Matthew. Where was Matthew now? Was he thinking of me at all? In that spacious kitchen, with the early autumn sun streaming through the window, my quest began to fall away from me, and I was not sorry.

The following morning, Dale said bravely that she could face the saddle again, and with many expressions of gratitude, the three of us set out again. We rode along the lane, back to the main road, and then, by mutual consent, we reined in. Dale and Brockley looked at me expectantly and I wondered what to say. I had decided during the night that we would put the search aside and set out for Sussex at once. However, I must make some comment on what I had, or rather hadn't, discovered.

"I did ask about recent guests," I said, "but Mistress Westley said they hadn't had any for weeks. There's no sign that the men we're looking for were here."

"Oh, they've been here right enough," said Brockley.

I stared at him. He responded with a smile which was little short of smug.

"What? How do you know? Well, come along, Brockley. Let's hear it!"

Brockley considered me thoughtfully. "Up to now, madam," he said, "though you've believed that Mr. Wilton was murdered by this respectable-seeming trio, one with red hair and one with a piebald horse, I've been doubtful. I'm not doubtful any more. They've been here, and yet it seems that these people, the Westleys, don't care to mention them, and that looks to me as if all isn't as it should be. I owe you an apology, madam."

"Never mind about that!" I almost shouted. My interest in hunting had reawoken in a hurry. I was like

193

an old hound who hears a horn. "It's nice to be vindicated, but what have you found out, and how?"

"I got it from the grooms, madam. You remember I said I meant to go to the tavern with them? Over the beer, I talked about Bay Star and Arabian blood and out it came. Three men, one mounted on a striking piebald, spent almost two weeks here not long ago. And one of them was hurt."

"Was he now?" I said.

Brockley nodded. "Dick Lane—he's the young stable lad—said one of them had a bandage round one forearm, and when he arrived he was reeling in the saddle. He had a black eye, too. Lane took his horse from him and got a close sight of him. The boy reckoned he'd been in a fight. Well, we reckoned that John Wilton would have fought back."

"Yes. And that's why they stayed so long, to let the injured man recover!" I added, with relief, "I expect they spun the Westleys a tale. I can't see the Westleys protecting a murderer but they're kind people who might help someone who said he'd done damage in a fair fight, and was afraid of the law and hadn't meant to get into trouble. That would explain why they didn't want to talk about their guests."

"Especially, madam, if the guests were friends of theirs."

"Why should we think that?" I didn't want the Westleys to have friends like the men who had killed John and robbed him. "If the man who was hurt felt too ill to go any further, he and his companions could well just have called at the first big house they saw and asked for help."

"Lane's quite a bit of a gossip, madam, especially after a pint or two," said Brockley disapprovingly. "My father was in service, like me, and he always said a good servant usually knows most of his master's business but never talks about it. He wouldn't have thought much of Lane and neither do I, though, as I said, he's only young. No doubt he'll learn. It was useful to us, anyway. According to Lane, as they were all getting off their horses, one of them said what good luck it was that Springwood was their next port of call. They were coming here, madam, all along."

§13§

House to House

"What are our plans now, madam?" Brockley enquired.

I considered, sitting in my saddle and fretting. The hunt was on again. We had picked up a scent and must follow it. I owed that both to my dead manservant and to the shade of Amy.

I sighed inwardly and once more put Meg aside, and Matthew too.

"It's the twenty-seventh of September," I said. "I need not return to court until the end of October. During that time I must get to Sussex and spend some days there. I think I have to set a time limit. Another fortnight—yes, I can give another two weeks to this business and let's hope it will be much less. All I need to know is who our murderously inclined friends are and perhaps get some idea of where they might be now. Then I will report what I know—to a county sheriff, perhaps, or I may ask advice at court." Brockley nodded, apparently finding all this reasonable. "Our *friends*," I said, with ironic emphasis, "did apparently stay at Springwood House, and then passed through the village. That means they were going towards Windsor. We'd better search for them along that line. We can take it at an easy pace, Dale. Don't worry."

It was a misty, brooding morning, with the promise of autumn in it. The rolling hills faded away into greyness in the distance; a line of trees on a nearby skyline were ghostly shapes, with no colour. The air was damp and still, but it wasn't particularly cold. Riding was pleasant enough and I could think without interference. I was trying to make sense of what little we had learned so far, though I wasn't very successful. All that I achieved was a long list of unanswered questions.

To start with, I just could not see the Westleys conniving to protect murderers. Whether they knew their injured visitor or not, they couldn't possibly have known how he really got his wounds, but it did seem that our quarry had intended going to Springwood House. That didn't necessarily mean that they already knew the Westleys, though, only that they had business which had taken them there. Either way, however, I couldn't believe that we were trailing a trio of sophisticated robbers. People like that just didn't fit together with the Westleys.

I then paused in my reasoning again, because the next idea taking shadowy shape in my mind was disagreeable. I faced it eventually. If our quarry were not robbers, then who were they? Whatever their mysterious business at Springwood might be, could it nevertheless, unknown to the Westleys, be somehow connected with their crime? Had John's money been stolen just to make robbery appear to be the motive?

The Westleys had evidently wanted to conceal the visit. Was that because they thought the wounded man had been hurt in a way which might get him into trouble and they were sorry for him? Or for some

197

other reason? It was odd, I thought, puzzling over it, that the Westleys hadn't sworn their servants to secrecy. Lane had been quite open with Brockley, who had said there was another groom with them, who had evidently not protested.

Perhaps the Westleys were wise. Impressing secrecy on one's servants is apt to arouse their curiosity. Maybe Edward and Kate had thought it best to let the wounded man and his friends simply sink back into the haze of commonplace events. That way, they would be more forgettable.

When I had reached this point in my deliberations, I shared my thoughts with the others, and they agreed with my conclusions, such as they were, but none of us could get any further. We must wait until we knew more.

We made a number of enquiries that day. We called at more taverns and blacksmiths', where we asked openly if a group of gentlemen, one on a fine piebald horse, had been seen lately. We had become better at it by this time and developed quite a convincing and detailed story of friends who might have passed this way ahead of us.

We also visited two manor houses, using the excuse that we had lost our way while attempting short cuts, and wanted directions, and here we were more round-about in our questions. In the big houses, the trio might be known, or might have come on a dubious errand. Someone might find a way to warn them of our enquiries.

"If they did attack John, they're not safe people to annoy," said Brockley, expressing my own feelings precisely.

That day yielded nothing. The road was always fairly busy, with folk travelling on foot, on horseback, in wagons and carts, and no one remembered any particular party of riders. Of the two big houses, one was full of very busy people and when I asked its young, bustling and officious mistress if she had many unexpected callers ("Living so near the Windsor road, I expect you have a stream of them!") she said roundly that she didn't encourage them; it interfered with getting things done. She couldn't think how we had missed our way; *that* was the main Windsor Road, down there on the other side of the fields; you could see carts going by from here, and we could have a cup of buttermilk each if we liked but we must forgive her, she had a thousand things to do.

The other was occupied by a childless old widower who was crippled by the joint evil and alone except for his servants. When he heard us arrive, he shouted to his butler to bring us to him. He was delighted to see us and here we had no need to ask questions; before we were well over the threshold, he was telling us what a pleasure it was to see fresh faces; he hadn't had a visitor for three months at least. He pounded on the floor with his stick to bring the butler back and demanded wine and cold chicken and fresh bread for us. The bread was all right, if coarse, but the wine was acid and the chicken underdone.

"Poor old man," said Brockley, when, with some difficulty, we had made our escape. "He must be very lonely. He must have constant indigestion as well! I pity our friends if they stayed there. Only, madam, I don't think they did. I doubt they were at either place."

We spent a night at a village inn—a very uncomfortable one—and started off again in the morning, making at once for the next set of ornate brick chimneys we could see amid the rolling fields and woodlands. We took a lane which led in the right direction, and from a small boy who was moving sheep into an adjacent field, we found that it did indeed go to the manor house, and that it was called Lockhill.

We came to another village before we reached Lockhill. It contained about a dozen thatched hovels and a couple of slightly bigger houses, one of which was a vicarage attached to a church smaller than itself. The village also had an alehouse and a well and, at the far end of the single street, a blacksmith, who plied his trade in a cave-like building made of the mellow local stone. Iron goods such as spades, rakes and firebaskets hung on the walls to advertise his wares. Here, for the first time, we struck ore.

"A fellow on a piebald?" said the smith, through clouds of steam from a piece of hot iron which he was tempering in cold water. "And one with ginger hair? Oh, aye, they've been through here. A matter of a fortnight back, that'll be. The ginger-haired man was on a grey and it had a shoe hanging by only two nails. I saw to it for him. The others tied their horses up outside and hung about waiting. They didn't go to the alehouse, daft things. Mistress Lambert makes a decent brew, not like that Pocky Peter that had the place afore her and used to water it, till we had him marched out and made to drink a gallon of his own ale and poured the rest over his head . . ."

He was not the sort of man who can ever keep to the point, but Brockley eventually got him back to it, and then he asked us what our friends were called. I snatched a name from my recent past. "The one who is a friend of my family is called Mr. Pinto."

"Pinto? That's a funny-sounding thing to call anyone. No, none of them mentioned that. The one with the piebald, he was Will Johnson; I heard the others use both names."

"Why, yes. Mr. Pinto had a . . . a cousin Johnson. My husband knew them quite well," I said mendaciously. "Well, well, what a tiny world it is. Perhaps we shall catch them up in due course. Were they going to Lockhill?"

"Aye, that's right. They went straight on up there. Likely you'll get news of them there. Important, is it?"

I shook my head. "No, not very. It was just by chance that I heard these old friends might be ahead of us on the road. We'll ask after them."

I decided not to use the short-cut story this time but to play the card of feeble health once more, because just after we left the smith, Dale confided to me that she had a headache. "I'm forty, ma'am, but I still have my monthly courses and I've just started one."

"Dale's not feeling quite well," I said to Brockley. "We'll ask for shelter for her sake."

The track led uphill, past fields and hedgerows which had a slightly unkempt air; not as bad as those round the house of the old widower, but still untidy. The ditch beside the track was overgrown and we saw a field of corn stubble which had been harvested carelessly, with patches of wheat standing uncut in the corners.

The house itself was smaller than it appeared from a distance. The gatehouse opened straight on to the main courtyard, with no intervening path. A mastiff on a chain leaped at us, snarling, making the horses snort and sidle, and Dale didn't so much dismount as slither to the ground with fright. She was leaning on the Snail's shoulder in a way which looked convincingly like near-collapse, when a thickset butler appeared and shouted at the dog to be quiet. It ignored him and continued to bay, whereupon the man enquired our business in another bellow.

On hearing of the sorry plight of exhaustion which had overtaken poor Mistress Blanchard and her maid, he became sympathetic, however. He helped me down, directed Brockley to the stableyard, swore at the dog and took Dale and myself inside to present us, he said, to Mistress Ann Mason, the lady of the house.

Lockhill was the very opposite of the Springwood household. It was chaotic. We stepped through the main door straight into a big hall which was strewn haphazardly with gloves and boots and goblets and jugs and letters and hooped chests with fabric trailing from under their lids. Books lay open, as though the life lived here was too frenetic ever to have time to tidy up after itself. Ann Mason, who had heard us arriving and came to meet us as we entered, was quite young and very pregnant, but except for her mounded stomach, she was thin with overwork, her brown stuff dress spattered with flour from the kitchen, fluff from a spinning wheel and dribbles from the baby on her arm.

A crowd of children came with her, screaming and giggling, accompanied by a couple of small dogs which added to the uproar by yelping alongside them. A harassed-looking tutor appeared and tried to round up the children, but without success.

"I am so sorry for the noise," said Mistress Mason, joggling the baby, pushing a dog out of the way with her foot and leading us through to a parlour where the spinning wheel stood beside a basket of fleece. There seemed to be wool flecks and dog hairs on everything and someone had carelessly left a bucket of soaking nappy cloths beside the hearth. "The children do become a little excited at times but Dr. Crichton, their tutor, is much opposed to the idea of beating them."

Normally, I would have agreed with Dr. Crichton. I had been beaten and so had Gerald, and we had agreed that Meg should not be treated in the same way. However, as the shrieking horde tore into the parlour after us and out again, and poor Dale flinched at the racket, I began to wonder why the Masons didn't chastise their offspring themselves or else pension off their tutor and get a firmer one.

Mistress Mason promised us food and drink and went herself to see about it. While she was gone, a door opened somewhere close by, footsteps approached and a tall, ascetic-looking man wandered into the room. He was holding a book in one hand and keeping his place with the thumb of the other, and his lean face was scored with fretful lines. He was halfway through a querulous plea that he was trying to translate a most difficult piece of Italian verse and why could Ann not do *something,* my dear, about this unconscionable din, when he noticed us.

Ann Mason came back clutching a loaded tray. She apologised anxiously and introduced us to her husband, Leonard Mason. He listened courteously to our account of headaches and exhaustion on a long journey, requested his wife to make us comfortable and provide us with beds for the night, and then took himself off again.

"He has gone back to his study," said Mistress Mason, and added, in a hushed and awestricken voice, "He is translating Dante's verses, from the Italian into English. He is a scholar of languages. He also studies the devices of Leonardo da Vinci, whose namesake he is. He has a brilliant mind." Another chorus of youthful shouts and shrieks, interspersed with excited canine barks, broke out in the distance and she sighed.

"He can never understand why the children are so uproarious," she said wanly. "None of them are at all studious. I try to protect him from distraction as much as I can."

She did her best for us. We were given food and

drink, and shown to a bedchamber. It was a pleasant enough room, with plastered walls and a high, beamed ceiling, but it was in sorry need of dusting. With exclamations of annoyance, Mistress Mason went to find a maid to clean it, and after a long delay, came back with a cloth and did it herself. There was aired linen ready, however, and I helped our hostess to make up the bed so that Dale, who really was quite poorly, could lie down.

Once Dale was settled, I went downstairs with Mistress Mason, explaining that my maid was mostly the one in need of rest; that I was now quite restored. I sat with her while she worked at her spinning wheel and encouraged her to talk.

In the course of the next hour or two, I learned a good deal about Lockhill. Every house has its own character, and Lockhill was like two houses in one. In fact, it resembled one of the Norman castles whose design my cousins' tutor had explained to us, drawing diagrams to show us what he meant by the keep and the outer bailey. At Lockhill, the keep and the bailey were mental rather than physical concepts, but they were real for all that.

The outer bailey was presided over by Mistress Ann Mason, who lived in a harassed whirl of household duties, disobedient dogs, too many children and not nearly enough staff, and tried to protect the castle keep, represented by Master Leonard Mason. Leonard Mason cared for books and languages and abstruse scientific concepts to the exclusion of all else. From what his wife let fall and from what I observed myself that day, it seemed clear that he preferred to keep as detached as possible from all matters of the house, the land and his own children, and spent most of his time virtually barricaded into his study where he worked with his books and drawings. If he wanted exercise, he walked or rode alone and often ate by himself in the study.

It was no wonder, I thought, that Mistress Mason seemed so overburdened and the estate so neglected. More was left to her than she could possibly do, and the best fertiliser for any field is its owner's eye. Crops fail easily when the farmer pays no heed to them.

Although I learned so much about Lockhill and the Masons, I discovered nothing else. I trailed my lures, but the hawk would not fly. Not one word would Ann Mason speak concerning any previous guests. I asked after Will Johnson by name, saying that he had been a friend of my husband, and that I believed he had recently passed through this district, with a companion who had a fine piebald horse, but she showed no sign of recognition; I asked if unexpected visitors were frequent and she said no. I ran out of ideas.

I also became very uneasy. The smith had been quite specific. A party of three men, of whom one had ginger hair and another riding a piebald, had been coming to this house. He could have been wrong, perhaps. Maybe they had taken another track and bypassed the manor house. In that case, they probably weren't going in the Windsor direction after all. I wished I could consult a map.

At supper, blessedly quiet because the children had taken theirs earlier (I had heard them taking it, in their own room, and shuddered at the sound of their table behaviour), Leonard Mason joined us. This was evidently unusual and he was only doing it to be polite to me. I asked him about "my husband's friends," expressing surprise that they had not called here. I received the same null answer. They had not been seen.

Mason, however, did show an interest in my family in another way. He asked my maiden name and on

205

learning that I was a Faldene, said he had met my Uncle Herbert in London. "Even a recluse like myself must occasionally bestir himself to do such things as sell wool," he said. "I was haggling over my fleeces and your uncle was doing the same thing. I found that he and I also have shares in the same merchant vessel. Indeed, we have a number of things in common." He gazed at me, speculatively.

It was Ann Mason who said, in a voice both warm and timid, "The Faldene family have a loyalty still to the old religion. Perhaps Mistress Blanchard feels the same." Her husband frowned at her and she turned pink, but added bravely, "There is no harm. There is no secret about our own worship, after all. If Mistress Blanchard belongs to our flock, surely we should make her welcome. Were you not wondering the same thing yourself?" she asked her husband. Ann Mason was clearly one of those gentle ladies who nevertheless turn into steel when it is a matter of their deepest beliefs.

"I confess I was," Leonard Mason said, "though I would have approached the matter with more caution. Well, Mistress Blanchard. Please speak for yourself!"

"I follow the Anglican religion," I said, "but I mind my own business." I hesitated. I badly wanted the Masons to feel they could trust me. If they did, they might talk more freely. "The law's the law," I said, "but I must admit I sometimes miss the old mass. I was brought up with it, after all." It went against the grain to say it, but I forced the words out. "I believe my uncle and aunt still hear it," I said casually. "I can understand why."

"Really? You feel like that?" Mason too appeared to hesitate. Then he said, "If you would really care to hear a mass—well, I may say that I pay a regular fine in order to avoid attending Anglican services. So far no one has enquired into my private religious observances at home. Dr. Crichton is a priest, and celebrates mass for us each Sunday. Tomorrow is Sunday. Would you like to join us? It will be before breakfast, in the room that opens off our parlour."

This was going further than I meant. I didn't want to accept the invitation, but on the other hand, it might be worth it. I also thought, with amusement, that this probably explained why they kept their disaster of a tutor on.

Dale, sitting at the lower end of the table, was regarding me in horror. I smiled at her reassuringly. "Dale will not attend," I said, "but I will. At what o'clock?"

"I'm doing it to gain their confidence, that's all," I said to Dale as soon as we were alone in our room. "Don't worry. And don't talk about it, either."

Dale didn't like it, though. Next morning, she dressed me in what I can only call a speaking silence. I gave her shoulder an understanding pat, and went downstairs alone.

The mass was a very simple affair, held in a small bare room. The altar was an ordinary table with a white cloth over it. There were some candles in plain candlesticks and a modest crucifix, and nothing more. Dr. Crichton recited the service from memory, without a prayerbook. The whole family and most of the servants were there and the children, for once, behaved themselves—except that the baby cried.

It was all very gentle and devout and seemed innocuous, ten thousand miles away from the horror in Chichester, which Uncle Herbert had described to me. It was absurd to think that the Masons were paying a fine for simply not attending the official parish church, and even more absurd to realise that if

I chose to report them, they could be fined a hundred marks for hearing a mass and maybe four hundred marks for any further offence. Why could not people worship in whatever way they wanted and let others do the same?

Why could Queen Mary not have left her subjects alone? If she had, the law now might be easier on those who clung to the rituals of their forefathers.

Harmless . . . but I was ill at ease and only hoped that I might gain something from it. In this, however, I was disappointed. At breakfast, I took some cold beef and game pie and remarked that my husband's friend William Johnson had been very partial to venison. Mason said, "Really? I prefer pheasant myself," and that was all.

We took our leave. We paused in Lockhill village to attend the Anglican service there and then once more took to the road. As we went, I asked Brockley if the Lockhill grooms were as chatty as the ones at Springwood.

"No," he said sourly. "If our friends were here, then for all I could find out from the grooms, they made themselves invisible."

"The smith thought they were coming here," I said. "I've even wondered . . . when John was lying in that inn, trying to tell us things, and we found it so hard to understand him, I thought at one point that he said his own name—John. But suppose he was saying 'Johnson?' I believe we're following the right men, but where on earth have they gone?"

"It's a funny thing, ma'am," said Dale. "We do know they went to that other place, Springwood, and that was Catholic, like Lockhill."

Brockley turned to her in surprise. "Yes, Lockhill's Catholic," I said. "I heard mass with them this morning."

"You *what?*" I eyed him coldly and he recovered himself. "Madam," he added belatedly.

"I was trying to get them to trust me a little more, though it didn't work. I expect your discretion, Brockley."

"That you will have, madam, and I accept what you were trying to do, but I have to say I can't approve."

"No. A Popish mass!" Dale broke in. "I don't know how you could abide to do such a thing, ma'am, but that's not what I set out to say. I meant, it's odd: that house and Springwood both being Catholic."

"What makes you think Springwood was Catholic?" I asked.

"Because I smelt incense there. I didn't at Lockhill—I don't think they used any, did they?—but it was quite strong at Springwood."

Of course. That was it. That was the fugitive, exotic fragrance in the Westley manor house. Not a rare strewing herb, but incense, only so overwhelmed by the freshness of beeswax polish, that I hadn't recognised it, although I had smelt it often enough at Faldene. Probably mass had been celebrated at Springwood shortly before we arrived.

I became aware, at this point, of a very unpleasant physical sensation, as though I had swallowed a lump of ice which now lay in the pit of my stomach and refused to melt.

What might a party of gentlemen be doing, if they were riding from one Catholic household to another through Elizabeth's England, on business so secret that none of their hosts would mention it, or even mention that the gentlemen in question had passed that way? And what kind of business might induce these secretive travellers to murder a harmless fellow wayfarer?

Well, one could hazard guesses. They weren't, for

209

instance, just itinerant priests holding masses in private for the devout. There had to be more to it than that.

I had been frightened at Cumnor but this was worse. Much, much worse.

I had begun, dimly, to perceive the nature of the enemy.

I think I was more thankful than otherwise, when shortly after that, we lost the spoor.

§14§

Lost and Found

It was when we reached Windsor. We had traced our quarry that far with some success. We crossed the Thames at Henley and there we heard of them when we asked the wherrymen and lightermen who ferried people and goods across and up and down the river. We found a lighter crew who had taken a party of horsemen over, they said, roughly a couple of weeks ago. Yes, one of the horses had been piebald. They remembered it and weren't likely to forget it, either, the vicious brute. It had kicked one of them. The lighterman pushed his scruffy, water-stained breeches up to his knee to show the remains of what must have been a spectacular bruise.

We also picked up traces at the next town, Maidenhead, where we found an innkeeper who thought they had stopped there for a meal, but after Windsor, the trail petered out. Up to then, we had had a kind of direction, but now our quarry could have gone towards Southampton on one main road, or towards Dover on another, or taken a secondary track into Sussex and we would have to guess which. We spent two more days asking questions along the first few miles of each route, but learned nothing. We returned to Windsor, where we were staying in an inn, and considered the matter.

The court was still at Windsor but I did not feel inclined to call there, in case I were somehow kept from leaving again. The queen could be capricious. Now that the trail was lost, Sussex was calling with an insistent voice. I must see Meg; I must see John Wilton's sister; and it had also occurred to me that if I could find Matthew, I might, just might, ask his advice. I would have to be careful; after all he was Catholic, too. If my frightening guesses were right, however, then I had found the spoor of treason. Matthew would understand that. It was high time for me to go to Sussex and nothing must hinder me.

Brockley, when I told him this, said, "Should you not report what you know to somebody in authority first?"

I had hired a parlour and a meal for three. Constant association had made us draw close and we now ate together habitually. Brockley considered me gravely across the table.

"I don't think we know enough," I said. "There are things which I *think* are so—but that's guesswork."

"You've maybe guessed more than you have told us," Brockley said, "but even guesses might be worth passing on."

"I wonder," I said.

"We've found out a few things, ma'am," Dale said. "Those two houses, being Catholic; I'm sure that means something." So, privately, was I.

A maidservant came in with a hot mutton pie and served us, which stopped the discussion for the time being. While portions of pie were cut and put before us, I studied Brockley. He had a good deal of sense, and although he was not yet old, he was mature enough to have a considerable experience of life. He hadn't had a formal education in the Latin and Greek sense, but he had worked as groom and manservant in more than one big house and had had at times to receive written instructions and act on them. I now knew that he could read very well and write a fair hand, albeit slowly. His advice was worth heeding.

Well, sometimes. If Brockley had worn bonnets, he would have had a few bees in them. As the maidservant went away, he said, "Simply report to someone of standing where we've been and why, and what we observed. That's my advice to you, madam. Then it's out of your hands and you can finally forget about chasing after these men yourself, which is not becoming to a lady."

"I knew you'd say that before long," I told him.

"I fancy," said Brockley, "that you climbed trees when you were a child."

I was familiar now with the way he made sallies with a straight face so that only the glint in his blue-grey eyes betrayed him. I smiled. "I swarmed down a wall covered with ivy even when I was grown up," I said. "I had a runaway marriage."

"Indeed, madam?"

"Yes. Our families lived near each other, in Sussex. Gerald was about to leave for London where he was taking up his post in the household of Sir Thomas Gresham," I said. "We had already planned to slip off together and marry secretly, but we used to meet out on the downland, and someone saw us and told my aunt and uncle that there was something between me and Master Gerald Blanchard. I went home that day and found them waiting for me, furious. Gerald was meant to marry my cousin Mary, you see. I was shut up in my room, up in the attic. The busybody who told them had told Gerald's family too. He quarrelled

with his father and brother, and left his home that
same day and came for me. He knew which my
window was. He threw pebbles at it and when I
looked out and saw him there in the moonlight, I
climbed down the ivy to join him. He took me to
where John Wilton was waiting with horses, and we
went off together then and there. We married in
Guildford."

"How you dared!" said Dale admiringly.

"I was more afraid to stay than go, I think," I said,
"and Gerald never failed me. Never, until the smallpox took him."

I didn't want to remember that, the ravaging fever
which burned away his senses so that he no longer
knew me; the pustules which ran into each other and
turned his handsome face into a horror on which I
could hardly bear to look.

"You've lost your husband and your protector,"
said Brockley earnestly, "but a lady needs to be
protected, madam. There must surely be someone at
court to whom you could pass on this quest of yours."

I thought this over, knowing that it was good sense.
"I could ask to see Cecil," I said doubtfully. "I could
go to the queen! But . . ."

"Why do you hesitate, madam?" Brockley asked.
"It is only a matter of stating facts. We visited such
and such places; we noticed this and that. You guess at
such and such. Do you guess at something serious? Of
much import?"

"Yes, very much so, and because of that . . ." I was
working it out, trying to understand my own uncertainty. Then I saw. "It's because what I guess is of
great import that I'm unhappy about speaking before
I'm sure." I had never even told Brockley or Dale of
the letter John was taking to Cecil for me, or of my old
suspicions of Dudley. My companions thought John
had just been taking a letter to Bridget. I couldn't

possibly talk to them about treason while it was still only a theory.

"It's still all so vague," I said. "If I speak, and I am wrong, I shall do no good and cause trouble for people like the Westleys and the Masons. I don't want to do that. At least, I want to think it over before I go any further. We will go to Sussex. Perhaps when we come back, I'll have a clearer mind."

Perhaps, by then, I would have talked to Matthew. Two days later, we were in Sussex.

"That's the place," I said, jogging impatiently ahead.

I had done my duty by John and visited his relatives, his sister, Mistress Alice Juniper and her husband Tom, on their smallholding, which was a few miles south-east of Faldene.

The Junipers were kind people. When I visited Sussex before joining the court, I had stayed in their little farmstead with its beaten earth floors and the one main room downstairs, which adjoined the cow-byre and was divided from it only by a half-wall of split logs. The place was always full of the warm cattle smell, and if we sat by the fire for a while in the evening, we could hear the cows chewing cud, and the firelight sometimes caught the tip of a horn or the gleam of a liquid eye beyond the partition. I was more at ease there than I ever would have been at Faldene, with its polished floorboards, its family pride and its cold heart.

Telling his people of John's death was harrowing. I did not tell them of my suspicions or of our chase, but simply said he had been attacked by robbers, and that I had taken so long to reach them because I had to stay at Cumnor for the inquest and the funeral and couldn't get away at once.

They had heard of Lady Dudley's death; it seemed

that the whole of England was ringing with the news that the queen's sweet Robin had now become a widower by way of a most convenient accident. They accepted what I said without question.

It was done now. Alice had cried and I had tried to comfort her, and Tom had called down curses on the murderers of his brother-in-law. We had spent a night and stayed on to midday dinner, and let them talk John's death over and ask all the questions they wished. Now, at last, *at last,* I could ride back to Westwater, the hamlet not far from Faldene, where I had settled Bridget and Meg in their cottage.

While there, I might enquire of the Westwater vicar whether he had heard of a Master de la Roche anywhere in Sussex. I had asked the Junipers, who had not, but said, "We live very quietly. We hear bits of news at markets—we heard of Lady Dudley dying, that way—but there's plenty gets by us, or takes a while to reach us. They'd know at Faldene, I expect, but if you don't want to go there . . ."

"No, I don't!" I said.

"Then try at the church in Westwater. Vicars all know each other and they talk about their new parishioners, like as not."

It was a cool, bright, early autumn day. The downs above the chalky track were turning to brown and gold as the grass and bracken changed colour. The cottage was at one end of the hamlet and was the first to come into view. It stood a little apart from the rest. It had been recently built and the thatch still had the gold tint of newness. It was not the kind of great house in which Meg ought rightly to be growing up, but it had been the best I could do for her as yet. At least, with Bridget, she would have safety and affection and it couldn't harm her to learn how to cook meals and tend a garden. I might repair the other deficiencies later. For the moment, I wanted only to see her running to meet me and to leap down from the saddle and sweep her up into my arms.

As we came near, I saw that the garden had been planted with herbs and vegetables and glimpsed a henhouse at the back. Bridget had been doing what I told her. At the gate I shouted, "Hallo!" but there was no reply.

"Visiting neighbours?" Brockley hazarded. "Or is there a market anywhere near?"

"At Faldene village, every week," I said. "It's on Wednesday. This is Friday."

Then the door opened and out came Bridget at a run, although she was a plump woman past her youth. Skirts held clear of her feet, she pelted towards us and arrived gasping. "Oh, Mistress Blanchard! You've come! You had my letter then, oh dear, oh dear, I've been at my wits' end . . ."

"What is it? What's the matter, Bridget?" I swung down from Bay Star, looping her reins over my arm. Bridget's round face was normally not expressive but anxiety was now written clearly all over it. My nostrils informed me, to my regret, that she had slipped back into her old ways as regards personal washing, and I noticed that the strands of hair escaping from her linen headdress were greasy and that her skirts and headdress were none too clean either. Just now, however, this was not the point. "Bridget?" I said, as the nursemaid showed signs of bursting into tears instead of answering. "What *is* it? What letter? Where's Meg?"

I was looking round for her as I spoke, but nothing stirred within the open door of the cottage and no little girl came running from the garden.

Bridget recoiled. "You've *not* had word, then? But you're here, ma'am, you've come . . ."

"I've been on the road for a long time. Where did you write to?"

"To Cumnor, a week ago now. I paid a boy to go, from the village here. Oh, Mistress Blanchard!"

"Bridget! In God's name tell me what's wrong! Is Meg ill? Or . . . ?"

Oh no, please God, no. Children are always vulnerable to sickness. Suddenly I was terrified, imagining my daughter mortally sick, or dead, perhaps of the smallpox, like her father.

"No, ma'am, she's not ill that I know of, but she's not here. They took her away!"

"Who did? Bridget, you're not making sense. Where is she?"

"She's at Faldene, ma'am. Your uncle and aunt came over a week ago and took her away with them. They said her place was at Faldene. They said this cottage wasn't good enough for her and they talked a lot about her immortal soul. I couldn't stop them, ma'am. I tried but they wouldn't listen and poor little Meg, she cried so!"

"Faldene!" I said, furious.

"You will stay here," I commanded Bridget. "Wait to hear from me. Oh, you'd better have this."

In my saddlebag was a package containing some fabrics which I had bought in Windsor, so that Meg could have more new clothes. She was a dark-haired child, and I had found some woollen cloth and some satin, both in shades of crimson, which would suit her to perfection. The sight of it, when Meg herself wasn't there to be delighted and to have the rich coloured fabrics held against her, nearly made me cry but I held the tears back and gave the materials to Bridget to look after. Then I found my purse and handed her in addition seven pounds in half-angels and shillings, at which her eyes widened.

"We're going on to Faldene," I told her. "We'll

bring Meg back if we can. Be ready for her, and while you're at it, Bridget, for God's sake heat some water over the fire and *wash.*" I fished in my saddlebag again. "Here's some soap, so you've no excuse."

"Oh, ma'am, I'm that sorry, but these days it's getting chilly and my mother always said that if you once get a cold on your chest . . ."

"Do as you're told, Bridget! We'll be back as soon as we can."

Westwater was at one end of the long, forested valley known as Faldene Vale. Faldene House was three miles away, at the other end. There was a track through the woods and along this we sped as fast as the packhorse and White Snail with their respective bouncing loads could go. Dale, gasping and holding on to her saddle, expressed outrage as we went.

"They've stolen your daughter, ma'am? Well, I never heard of such a thing! Oops! I've lost my stirrup!"

We paused while Brockley reunited Dale's foot with its support. "Why would they do that?" Dale demanded, while he made sure that the Snail's girth was secure as well.

"I can think of several reasons, but spite is highly likely," I said. "Now come *on!*"

"We'll get her back, madam, never fear!" said Brockley.

"I hope so!" I said.

I was frightened as much as angry, frightened for Meg. She had lost her father and been parted from me—that was enough for any child to bear—but I had at least left her with a goodhearted nurse. How would she fare in Faldene, of all places, with Aunt Tabitha and Uncle Herbert? I pictured her bewildered and bereft and bullied, unable to understand Aunt Tabitha's rigid rules of conduct, constantly offending by mistake, wondering why those she trusted had let her be taken away by such unkind people. I remembered my own childhood experiences at Aunt Tabitha's hands. Faldene was the last place I wanted to go to and now I couldn't get there fast enough. I grabbed the White Snail's bridle, and shouted, "Come on!" once again.

We emerged from the woods at a point where paths crossed. One led on to the gatehouse; others ran left and right to the fields which quilted the valley's sides. The corn had been cut and the cattle had been turned in to the stubble. I saw village women gleaning, baskets on their arms, moving here and there and stooping to collect the leftover grain.

"This is your family home, madam?" Brockley asked respectfully.

"Yes. It's supposed to have been given to one of my ancestors by King Harold, before the time of William the Conqueror," I said. "In fact, before Harold himself became king, if the legends are true. I shan't be particularly welcome here, though, I fear."

At the gatehouse, Harry Fenn the porter, white haired ever since I could remember, square, muscular and completely unsmiling, stepped out of his doorway and into our path. Harry Fenn never had been one of my favourite people, nor I his. He was a devoted servant of the house but his devotion had been to my grandparents when they were alive, and was now given to Uncle Herbert and Aunt Tabitha. He regarded me, as they did, as a stain on their pure escutcheon.

"Ah. Mistress Ursula. Well, this is a surprise."

"Is it?" I said. I had no doubt at all that he knew that Meg was here, in which case my arrival couldn't be as surprising as all that.

He took hold of Bay Star's bridle. "You'd best wait here while I go up to the house and say you've arrived.

I'm not sure that the mistress will be able to receive you. Down you get."

"No, thank you. We'll ride straight up."

"I've had my orders, Mistress Ursula."

I was right. He knew all about Meg. I glanced at Brockley.

"You heard my mistress," said Brockley, and raised his riding whip. Harry, scowling, snatched his hand off the rein.

"I prefer to make this a surprise attack," I said, and spurred on.

There had been changes since I was last there. Someone had introduced topiary into the formal garden, shaping the yew bushes there into cockerels and horses' heads. The ivy which had once covered the walls of the house, climbing almost to the top of the crenellated towers which stood at each end of the frontage, and tapping against the mullioned windows, had been stripped away. The house would be lighter inside, I thought, but outside, the grey stone walls, bare of creeper, seemed harsh.

On impulse, I led us round to the back, where there was a stableyard and courtyard combined, lying between the two side wings of the house, with the stables forming the fourth side. Doors into the yard were often left open. On the way, I had worked out how I might compel my aunt and uncle to hand Meg back to me, but it would save much unpleasant argument if I could simply dismount, run into the house, find her and whisk her away.

The entrance was an archway through the stable block. We clattered under it, to find the yard busy. Horses were outside, being rubbed down in the open air where the men could see what they were doing, and one horse was having a front fetlock carefully bathed in cold water.

I pulled Bay Star up so sharply that she tossed her

head in protest. The horse having its fetlock bathed was a piebald, and a more spectacular animal I had never seen.

In the last few days, I had once or twice thought that if I had committed a murder, I would prefer not to make my escape on a horse as conspicuous as the piebald apparently was. But of course, William Johnson and his friends had no idea that they were being chased, and if the famous piebald looked like this—and could there be two of them?—then no wonder its owner wanted to keep it.

"Piebald" is an irritating word. It makes one think of foodstuffs—a parti-coloured egg, perhaps, or a pie with a very smooth crust. Nothing in that word came anywhere near describing the sheer beauty of this animal. Its coat was glossy raven black splashed dramatically with snow; the fine head, held so proudly, and the long sloping shoulders spoke of desert blood and effortless speed. It was a gelding, but had been gelded late, judging from the crest on its strong neck, and its jaunty tail was a waterfall of mingled black and white like foam glimpsed in shadow. It was quite superb.

I stared and stared and I heard Brockley gasp. The grooms had all paused and looked round at us. With no attempt at finesse, I pointed to the piebald and demanded, "Who owns that?"

I didn't know its groom and he didn't know me but I spoke so peremptorily that he was startled into answering. "It belongs to a Master Johnson, from Withysham."

"Withysham?" I was nonplussed and then remembered that Withysham had been taken over as a country house. Alice Juniper had told me, of course, when I stayed with her before I went to court. "Oh, yes. It's occupied now. By a . . . a Master Johnson?"

"Well, he lives there," said the groom snappily,

resenting this catechism. "Him and others. There's quite a few of 'em. They visit here now and then. Master Johnson and some others came through here ten days back or thereabout. Looked as if they'd been on a journey. They called in because his horse was lame. They dined here and left the horse to be cared for. He borrowed a nag to get home on. Ma'am," he added dubiously, as if wondering whether I were entitled to terms of respect, or not.

"Ursula!" said Aunt Tabitha's voice behind me. "To what do we owe this unexpected pleasure?"

She had appeared suddenly, from a back door. I swung Bay Star round to face her. I was dazed. The pursuit of John's assailants and the desire for reunion with my daughter had till a few moments ago been two different things. Now they had collided, and I was seeing stars, as though I had dashed my head against a stone wall.

However, at the sight of Aunt Tabitha, I found myself concentrating once again on Meg. I had lost the advantage of surprise. I had no hope now of snatching my child away before I was caught. I opted instead for a direct challenge. "Good day, Aunt Tabitha. I have come to fetch my daughter. Will you bring her to me, please?"

It was a brave attempt and of course it failed. Aunt Tabitha wasn't to be impressed by any high-handed tactics on my part. She was, as ever, thin and active, with a fastidiously disapproving twist to her mouth as though she had just eaten a particularly sour crabapple. Except when in a temper, she believed in the proprieties.

"So you have discovered that she is here. Well, Ursula, this is a serious family matter and you can hardly expect to hold a discussion on it in a matter of moments, least of all out here. How do you come to

223

be here unannounced, by the way? Fenn should have known better."

"Harry Fenn had no choice, Aunt Tabitha. I was prepared to ride him down. I repeat: I have come for my daughter. How did you find out where she was?"

"I saw her with you once, if you remember, when you came to see Anna's grave, though you did not care to call on the people who supported both you and your mother, only to be rewarded with base ingratitude, and who offered to take you back when your husband died, in spite of everything."

To answer that would have taken a long time and done nothing to improve family relations. It was better ignored. Slowly, I dismounted and signalled Dale to get down as well. We handed our horses to Brockley. He was emanating unspoken outrage in Aunt Tabitha's direction in a way which I found comforting, but my aunt, of course, was unaware of it.

"Are you telling me," I asked her, "that you chanced to go to Westwater, and saw Meg and recognised her from that one brief glimpse?"

"No. You wrote to that stupid woman you left her with, and she went to the vicar in Westwater to get help with reading the letter. Some weeks later, he was dining with dear Dr. Bryant, who is still our vicar here at Faldene, and mentioned the matter. Dr. Bryant realised at once that it concerned you and your child. There was some further delay because Dr. Bryant considered for a while before he came to us, and we in turn considered before making up our minds. We called at the cottage to see it for ourselves, and we were shocked to see the child in such a place. I can tell you, Ursula, that we did wonder if we should simply leave her there. After all, you have disowned us; why should we not disown you and yours?"

"No reason at all," I said candidly.

My aunt ignored my tone. "Better counsels prevailed in the end," she said. "Two weeks ago, we finally decided that we should forgive you, and do our best for your daughter. We then brought her here. You should thank me."

I didn't thank her. I stood there choking at her effrontery, and silently, unjustly, cursing Bridget for being unlettered and too simple and honest to understand things like family feuds and clerical grapevines. The Junipers had been right. Vicars did all know each other.

I cursed myself for leaving Meg in Westwater, so near Faldene. Stricken by Gerald's death, I had rushed to a familiar place, even though it was infested by Faldenes. I had been a fool, and now Meg was paying for it.

"I repeat," said my aunt, "we cannot hold a discussion of this kind out here. Come inside."

I beckoned to Dale and we followed my aunt into the great hall, which was still the centre of Faldene life, just as the hall always was in medieval days. It was a big room, decorated in somewhat boastful fashion with the swords and pikes of forebears who had fought at Crécy and Agincourt. My mother had once told me that when she was sent home from court in disgrace, carrying me, her parents marched her into the hall and pointed at these relics, and told her that she had betrayed all those noble names.

She had considered it unfair because some of the noble names in question had been anything but monuments of purity and of this there was physical evidence. The Faldene family had a tendency to thick eyebrows. This was all right for men—Uncle Herbert's eyebrows made his face quite impressive—but it was a great trial to the women. My mother and I had escaped the Faldene eyebrows but my female

225

cousins, especially Mary, all had them and Mary in particular spent much time plucking her eyebrows into a more ladylike shape. The same characteristic occurred quite often among the local villagers and labouring families. It was all too evident that in bygone days some of the Faldene men had been large with their favours.

The hall was handsome, though, and well lit, with big windows looking out to the front and a row of narrower ones to the yard at the rear. A maidservant—a stranger, new since my day—came at once with cups of wine on a tray. I sat down and nodded to Dale to take a seat and a cup of wine as well. She did so warily. She had heard enough about Aunt Tabitha to be nervous of her and was now eyeing her as though she were a keg of gunpowder in dangerous proximity to a bonfire.

I sipped my wine grimly and repeated that I wished to see my daughter. "Where is she, Aunt Tabitha?"

"At her needlework. She is sharing your youngest cousin's governess, who just now is teaching them embroidery. She is perfectly well and far better off here than in that cottage, grubbing in the ground and feeding hens like a peasant's child. How could you leave her with that idle, dirty creature Bridget?"

"Bridget is not idle, Aunt Tabitha."

I could hardly deny the charge of dirtiness. Aunt Tabitha noticed the omission and her blue eyes flashed triumphantly.

I gulped at my wine. I had spent the most of the first two decades of my life under my aunt's control. I had come here borne up by fury and fear for Meg and by the new independence I had learned with Gerald and at court. Now, old habits of mind were closing me in again like tight stays. I had to force myself to speak firmly.

"Aunt Tabitha, I came here to fetch Meg. She is my daughter and it is for me to say how and where she shall live. You should not have brought her here."

"You need not be so abrupt. Naturally, you can see her. But," said Aunt Tabitha, her eyes snapping anew, "make no mistake. You are not taking her away with you. She isn't going back to that cottage. You were always wilful, Ursula, and not prepared to accept the place to which God was pleased to call you, or to accept the teaching of the true Church. Well, you may destroy your own soul if you choose, but we shall save Meg's. You were the fruit of sin but she at least is not, and she is after all our great-niece. We brought her here so that she might be reared in clean conditions and properly educated, and taught the true faith instead of being condemned to eternal damnation as a heretic. We shall not let her go."

I opened my mouth to say, "No, you hypocrite, you brought her here to hurt me. You want to humiliate her and turn her into the unpaid servant that I refused to be. Give her back at once, or I'll report you for having had mass said in this house." That was the ploy I had thought of on the way to Faldene from the cottage and I believed it would work. The Masons were getting away with it, but if the authorities received a formal complaint, they were duty bound to act.

She looked at me with those chilly, righteous eyes, and my body cringed, remembering other passages of arms with Aunt Tabitha, and how they had so often ended. I wasn't even sure I was physically safe from her even now. I was in her house, and Brockley was out of hearing. If she called a couple of strong servants and made them hold me while she "brought me to my senses" with a birch as she had so often done when I was a girl, I couldn't prevent her.

So I held my tongue, despising myself for my weakness. I had lost control of the situation and how I was to rescue Meg now, I could not imagine. Out in the yard, a horse squealed and a man cursed and I glanced through the window in time to see a groom rubbing his thigh while the piebald horse rolled its eyes and laid back its ears at him.

The piebald.

With that, the small cold voice whose existence I had never suspected until the day I fled from Abingdon Fair, spoke to me again. I would be wise, it said, not to quarrel with Aunt Tabitha; and not just because I feared her.

There are things you want to find out. The words fell into my mind like tiny drops of cold rain. I had followed William Johnson and his friends from house to house through southern England and I had arrived at a theory which explained their purpose. *You are seeking confirmation. The answer may be here. You know one way to seek it, but you will need to stay the night. Don't provoke your aunt just now.*

But what of Meg!

One night. With luck, you will only need one night.

Quietly, I said, "I just want to see my child. I want to see for myself that Meg is well."

Aunt Tabitha rose. "You are very impatient. Very well. I will take you to her now," she said.

"Oh, Meg," I said. "My dearest, darling Meg. You've grown so much!"

I had missed those stages of growth. I did not know my daughter as I should. It was months since I had last held her in my arms. I pulled her close to me.

At first sight of me, to my distress, she had been stiff and timid, putting her sewing aside to curtsy in formal fashion, hesitant to run into my arms even when I opened them wide for her, but I was embracing her now. Aunt Tabitha, doing the considerate thing for once, had let me be alone with her, although I knew that she wasn't far away.

"I'm so very glad to be with you again, sweetheart! Are people being kind to you?"

I set her back from me so that I could look at her. She was clean and prettily dressed, but her little face was too serious. She took after Gerald. Her dark hair was like his, rougher in texture than mine. The sight of her brought him back vividly. That small square rosy-brown face and brown eyes were meant for laughter, though, not for this strange gravity. She curtsied again.

"Indeed, everyone has been very kind, Mother. Aunt Tabitha says I must be grateful to have come here."

"I'm sure she does," I said. I had held her very tightly a moment ago, and she had not shown any discomfort, but there was one thing I must make sure about. "You look lovely," I said, "but I hope your shift is as clean as your dress. Let me look."

A moment later, holding her to me, I breathed a silent prayer of relief. In two weeks, my small daughter had been reproved and lectured out of natural spontaneity, and I knew she had done some weeping, for her brown eyes were sad and somehow dimmed, but I did not think she had been beaten.

No serious harm had been done to her, and she would only be here for one more night, I said to myself. Tonight, I must stay here and satisfy the small, cold voice, and so, perforce, must Meg stay, but tomorrow I would get us both away somehow.

I wasn't sure how. I was hunting dangerous men, and if the guesses I secretly made were right, it might be just as well that I hadn't used illegal celebrations of mass as a lever. I had already shown a surprising degree of interest in the piebald horse. I should be careful. My fear of Aunt Tabitha could have saved me from a bad mistake.

However, escape we would, all the same. I would not take Meg back to the cottage, but to Tom and Alice Juniper instead. Tomorrow, we would both be free of Faldene.

I stayed with Meg for some time, playing with her, and making much of her, and presently saw her to bed, then I went back to Aunt Tabitha. Forcing myself to smile, I said that on reflection, and because I must in fact start my journey back to court the next day, I felt it best to leave Meg at Faldene for the time being. I asked if I could spend the night there, as it was late for setting out again and there was no inn in Faldene village.

"Of course," said my aunt, frostily. Always one for doing the correct thing, was Aunt Tabitha.

It still felt as though I were betraying Meg, but John's murderers must not go free, and the stakes might be higher even than that. I was still the implacable huntress.

Uncle Herbert, who had been in his study working at his ledgers, emerged for supper. Unlike my aunt, he had altered lately, putting on more weight and becoming very fleshy round the jowls. His fashionable puffed Venetian breeches and his elaborately padded doublet made him look even bigger. He was hobbling—"Gout, my girl. I've gone and developed gout"—and he wasn't pleased to see me.

"So *you're* here. If you think you're taking your wench away, you're mistaken. We've taken her in hand now."

He became a little more amiable (if not much) when Aunt Tabitha assured him that I had agreed to the new arrangement.

"I'll never say you're welcome here, not after the

way you've gone on, but we treat family members civilly, however they behave, and we care for their neglected children, too."

I said I was sure their intentions were good. Making my tongue frame the words was almost physically painful but if I had to dissemble, I would do it properly. We sat down to eat, and over the meal, my aunt and uncle made conversation, bringing me up to date on family news. The eldest son was in London, conducting business for Uncle Herbert, whose gout now made riding difficult, and the second son had a place in the ambassador's household in France. Cousin Mary had at last been married off, although her husband had only comparatively modest means. "The Blanchards are well connected, and could have brought us many advantages. We much regret the loss of the Blanchard match," said my aunt.

This was provocation and I gave way, in a small degree, to the urge for retaliation. "But you had a Blanchard match," I said, "if only you had given me a dowry to sweeten Gerald's family."

They did not actually say, "You? Unthinkable!" but their expressions said it for them before they returned their attention to their food.

"However," Aunt Tabitha said after a pause, "Mary is settled after a fashion. Her sister Honoria has had another daughter and . . ."

When they had finished talking about my cousins, Uncle Herbert showed some interest in my life at court and asked what the queen was like at close quarters. I answered politely, and carefully.

I went to bed early.

I hadn't been given the best guest chamber, or even the second best. Instead, Aunt Tabitha showed me into the old attic room with the plain uncurtained bed which I had once shared with my mother and was now invited to share with Dale. If I hadn't already known that I wasn't a favoured visitor, this would have made it clear.

I ventured a pleasantry. "I saw that the ivy's been removed. Still, I won't be wanting to climb down it tonight, Aunt Tabitha."

My aunt had no sense of humour. "You were always a hoyden. I tried to whip it out of you but you never change. I don't trust you. Don't think you can steal Meg away in the dark, by the way. Our mastiffs don't know you, and they are loose at night."

"You may rest assured," I said, "that I shan't leave the house until tomorrow."

It was true enough. I wouldn't be staying in my room either, but my purpose this time lay on the premises.

I was tired but I must stay awake somehow. I didn't want to tell Dale what I intended, so I said I wasn't sleepy and would sit up by the window for a while and keep a candle burning.

I let the fresh air blow in on my face, while I gazed out on the perilous slope of tiles down which I had slithered, five years ago, clutching at a venturesome ivy stem which had crept over the top of the wall on to the roof, and finally trusting myself to the creeper on the wall itself, in order to make my escape.

I remembered how Gerald had taken me across the gardens and how we had scrambled over the bank and ditch which bounded the grounds, out to where John was waiting with the horses; and how I had fallen into the ditch in the dark, and Gerald had jumped in to help me climb out; and how, down there, with only the stars to see, we had stopped to kiss and cling.

It was all over now, all lost and long ago and Meg was my only reminder.

I shook myself fully awake, because it was deep in the night by now. Dale was fast asleep and it was time to tackle the errand I had set myself.

I put on soft slippers, lit a fresh candle from the guttering old one, and blew the old one out. Then I made my way stealthily out and down through the sleeping house. It was just as alarming as my creep through the house at Cumnor Place, after listening behind the hangings, but I forced myself not to be afraid of the dancing shadows as my candle streamed and wavered in draughts. I knew my way. I also knew that Uncle Herbert's study would be locked. I hoped that he still kept the key where he had kept it before my marriage, when I used to help him with his accounts. It should be hanging on a nail inside a closet door at the top of the first flight of stairs.

I found that inside the closet door there were now three nails, adorned with keys, all very similar. I took the lot and crept down to the hall. It was hushed and empty. A waxing moon looked in through a window and cast a pale light across the floor. I hoped no one sleeping in either of the two wings was suffering from toothache or insomnia because if they were to look out of their windows they might catch sight of my flickering candle crossing the hall.

My uncle's study led off the hall. I crept to the door and held the candle in one hand, while I tried the keys. The second worked. A faint rattle as it slid home, a click as it turned, and I was in, back amid the familiar smell of paper and ink. The candlelight revealed things well remembered: the desk, old and scored, with inkstains here and there; the silver writing set, with inkstand and sander, quills in their tall holder and a trimming knife in a shaped trough; my uncle's carved chair; the panelled walls and the shelves full of leatherbound ledgers; the padlocked cupboard which I knew held the money-chest.

I wasn't concerned with the money-chest. I was after the ledgers. I pulled the curtain across the window to conceal my candle, and set to work.

My uncle had done some rearranging and it took a
minute or two to find the current ledgers, but presently, heart pounding and ears alert for any sound
elsewhere in the house, I was sitting at his desk to
examine his records. If my guess were right, then what
I wanted would be here in some form. Uncle Herbert's accounts were always so very meticulous, and
he did full-scale balance sheets at the end of each year,
showing exactly what had come in and how it had
been disposed of. He might disguise the item—he was
almost bound to—but it would be there.

I found it almost at once. It was an entry in a
current ledger labelled "Expenditure, July to Decem-
ber 1560." It was dated 3 September. The entry read:
"Donation to charity, for the furtherance of instruction in lawful religion—200 marks."

One man's lawful religion was another man's heresy. Uncle Herbert, I thought, unlike Aunt Tabitha,
had a certain sense of humour. But 200 marks! Over
£130 pounds. "Generous of you, Uncle Herbert," I
muttered. "Unusually generous. You were never one
for giving much to charity."

Searching rapidly back through the ledger and those
of the year before I found that Uncle Herbert had, as
usual, made a few charitable donations. A man in his
social position was virtually obliged to make them,
although my uncle, who gave the servants his cast-offs
at Christmas, wasn't going to be bountiful to the poor
in any circumstances. He had kept his genuine donations small.

Five pounds for the relief of poor people in the
parish of Faldene—that was an annual one which I
remembered from the past, and he only kept it up
because his father had started it and to discontinue it
would have looked bad. Five shillings—my dear
uncle, what a skinflint you are!—to clothe poor
women in London. A pound to a hospital in Chichest-

er; ten pounds for the care of orphans and widows in the county of Sussex. Among these modest offerings, that 200 marks shone forth like a beacon.

I turned back to the entry in question and began to shiver. Family was family, however obnoxious, and much as I detested Uncle Herbert and Aunt Tabitha, I did not want to bring them into the kind of danger that this promised. I wanted to harm the Westleys and the Masons even less.

However, there was John, and not only John. It was wider than that now. If this meant what I thought it did . . .

Perhaps it didn't. Perhaps I had read more into this entry than was really there, although I had been looking for it. I had guessed and guessed right. It was so much: *two hundred marks!*

For a few moments, engrossed in the possible meaning of my discovery, I had ceased to keep alert for sounds elsewhere in the house. I had also forgotten Uncle Herbert's talent for treading softly and creeping up on people undetected. I only realised that someone else had come into the room when the draught from the open door made the flame of my own candle stream. I sprang up and turned.

There in the doorway, wheezing slightly, as though he had come across the hall too fast, a fur-trimmed gown wrapped over his nightshirt, and a thick palm shielding his candle, was Uncle Herbert.

"And what, Ursula, is the meaning of this? I looked out of my bedchamber window and I saw a light moving across the hall. What are you doing out of your bed at this time of night, and what are you doing in my study, and what the *devil* are you doing with my ledgers?"

Shaking with fright, I did my best. "You have taken Meg into your charge against my will, Uncle Herbert. I . . . I was looking to see if you have recorded money set aside for her, or money already spent on her." As a lie, it was pitifully lame. I tried to infuse my voice with vigour. I was a mother, defending her offspring. "Frankly, Uncle, I do not wish you to have charge of Meg and I would remind you that you have no rights over her and . . ."

I was not only frightened, but tired, and was making mistakes all the way. I hadn't kept alert for footsteps and I hadn't had the sense to slam the ledger. He stepped to the table and looked at the open page.

"Why were you studying *this* page in particular?"

"I wasn't. I was just reading it through." The item concerning the two hundred marks seemed to rewrite itself in giant letters and spring off the page to meet us.

"If you wished to know what we were spending on Meg, you could have asked us," he said. "You had no need to creep about in the night like a miscreant for that. My head groom tells me that when you arrived here, you showed a remarkable interest in William Johnson's piebald horse. Why was that?"

I managed not to jump. The stance of my uncle's bulky body, enlarged by the shadow which the candles threw on the wall behind him, suddenly seemed extraordinarily menacing.

I thought of John then, and was overtaken, without warning, by sheer rage. I lost my temper, so completely that it overwhelmed my sense of danger. I flung the truth in my uncle's face.

"I was interested in that piebald horse because I've been trying to trace its rider and his friends. They've been travelling about and apparently calling at houses of Catholic persuasion. I don't know why but no one will speak of their purpose or even admit they've been there, and at a guess, they've been collecting money for the Catholic cause. Tell me, Uncle Herbert: that two hundred marks you so generously gave away on the third of September—what was it for? It wasn't a contribution to a possible Catholic uprising, was it, by any chance?"

My uncle's thick brows drew close together, forming a line of heavy shadow across his fleshy face. "And if it was," he said, "do you think that you would be allowed to hinder it?"

"No," I said recklessly, "and I have a feeling that someone else, quite recently, wasn't allowed to hinder it either. Johnson and his friends murdered a servant of mine, John Wilton, perhaps because he found out what they were doing. I've been hunting his slayers across country. I now understand that Johnson lives at Withysham, and that he has dined here. You've had a murderer at your table, Uncle Herbert!"

"I know nothing of that," said my uncle, "but if you are right, well, such things happen when great causes are afoot. The safety of many may depend, alas, on the death of one." He sighed, with unconvincing regret.

I leaned against the desk, my knees quaking. I had been carried away by anger. I'd let it happen because—well, this was Faldene, where I had grown up, and I had known my Uncle Herbert all my life. I didn't like him and he didn't like me, but nevertheless, however reluctantly, he and my aunt had reared me. Like the heavy eyebrows, a strong sense of family was a Faldene characteristic, and this one I shared. I just hadn't believed that he would really harm me. I was less certain now. "So you . . . condone murder?" I said.

"I wish to see the country returned to the true faith and ruled by a Catholic queen."

It was an evasive answer, to say the least of it. "Queen Mary is dead," I said. "Elizabeth is on the throne now."

"For the time being," said my uncle with a chesty chuckle, "but not necessarily for good; not if she surrenders to lust for her Master of Horse, as seems very likely. Meanwhile," he added, "I must decide what to do with you." There was a silence. In the candlelight, he stared at my face. "What were you ever in this house," he said at last, "other than a symbol of your mother's disgrace? Are you now to be the ruin of all our hopes as well?"

There was another silence. My heart raced with the desire to fight or flee. I wondered how much danger I was really in, and whether I could get hold of the candlestick or the inkstand to use as a weapon, but neither was within arm's reach.

The silence was broken not by either of us but by the arrival of a third person, also with a candle. "Herbert?" said Aunt Tabitha's voice. "You said you thought someone had gone into your study with a light and you went to see and when you didn't come back . . . Ursula!"

"She's been reading my ledgers," said my uncle. "She seems to think it is somehow her business that we have been contributing to the cause of our faith."

I found my voice again. "It is my business. Those who were collecting the money killed my manservant, John Wilton."

"What is she talking about?" demanded Aunt Tabitha.

Uncle Herbert explained. My aunt, standing there in an oyster-satin wrapper and a white nightcap, holding her candle, stared at me with fury. "Your manservant is nothing to do with us. How dare you pry and poke into your uncle's affairs? You were always an ingrate, but this!"

"That isn't the point," said Uncle Herbert. "Of course she's an ingrate; there's nothing new about that. What is new is that she is now in a position to do us harm. We have a viper in our midst."

"I'm one of the queen's ladies," I said. "I am to return to court at the end of October. If I don't present myself then, enquiries will be made."

My aunt frowned, pursing her prim lips. "I think, Herbert, that we need advice. I would not, myself, wish to harm this wretched girl. She is our niece, however sorry the state of her soul. I think we must keep her under lock and key until we have had time to consult Withysham on the matter."

Withysham, I thought, feeling panic rise up in me. Withysham, where William Johnson lives. Where John Wilton's murderers live.

"It could then be taken out of our hands," Uncle Herbert said thoughtfully.

I became aware, not for the first time, of the curious, delicate balance of power between my uncle and aunt, and also, of the weird and convoluted nature of Aunt Tabitha's morality. You don't smother illegitimate babies; you rear them as servants. You love God, and are prepared to hand over to the most terrible of deaths anyone who doesn't share your views on the fine detail of doctrine. You don't strangle your inconvenient niece; you consign her to someone else who may or may not do it for you, but either way you're not responsible.

My uncle gripped my upper arm. "And don't trouble yourself to call for help," he said. "All the servants are loyal to us."

I did try to resist, more by instinct than because I had any real hope of escape. Even if I broke away and got out of a window, the mastiffs were loose. I couldn't break away, anyhow. Even stamping on Uncle Herbert's gouty foot didn't work. He let out a torrent of swear words but he kept his grip on my arm.

It was two to one and they were determined. The only effect my efforts had was to make Aunt Tabitha say breathlessly, as she hung on to my other arm, "The attic room is too far to drag her. Put her somewhere nearer! I'll fetch her woman. I daresay she's Ursula's confidante. They ought to be kept together."

I spent the rest of the night in the best spare bedchamber after all, with Dale for company.

§15§

Upon Conditions

The best spare bedchamber was in one of the towers, at the corner of the frontage and the south wing. It was on the first floor, and its mullioned windows, like those in the hall, looked both to the front and into the courtyard. It had a huge fourposter bed equipped with a down mattress and hung with blue velvet embroidered in silver. There was a tall walnut clothes cupboard, a generous fireplace, fur rugs on the floor on either side of the bed, a stone-topped washstand with a silver basin and ewer, three branched candlesticks of silver with fresh candles in them. It was a most luxurious prison.

However, it was still a prison, and Dale and I were the frightened captives. We huddled together in the big bed, and I explained as much as I could to her: my suspicions, and what I had learned from the ledgers. I wished I could have kept her out of it, but my aunt and uncle assumed that she was in my confidence, so I might as well make it true. She was caught up in this now and had the right to know why.

"I'm sure they won't actually harm us," I said,

reassuringly. One thing I had not said was that my uncle had turned to Withysham, and therefore to William Johnson, for advice. I must not alarm her too much. "But we may be kept here for some time. I've brought you into an uncomfortable situation, Dale. I'm sorry."

"You didn't mean to, ma'am." Even hand in hand with me as we were then, for comfort, Dale remained the perfect lady's maid. "I'm sure all will turn out well. After all, you are a Lady of the Queen's Presence Chamber."

"I told them that," I said. "I hope they were listening!"

We fell asleep eventually, out of sheer exhaustion, and only awoke when someone entered the room in the morning. It turned out to be Aunt Tabitha, in person, with breakfast on a tray, followed by a maidservant with hot washing water, and another one with our clothes.

Neither my aunt nor the maidservants spoke to us, however. They set down their burdens and withdrew. Dale seemed inclined to huddle in the bed but I ordered her to take some breakfast and then to see to my toilette and her own. "Don't fret," I said.

This was good advice, although hard to follow. There was nothing to do but peer restlessly from the windows and try to work out what was going on from what little I could observe. I saw Uncle Herbert in the courtyard, giving a letter to one of the grooms, and saw the groom saddle up and ride off. To Withysham, presumably. The thought made me feel ill.

We were given more food at noon, and once again I was trying to eat something and urging Dale to do the same when we heard hoofs. The groom had returned, and was not alone. Four other horsemen came with him. I looked from the front windows and saw the five riders pass. I took in at once that the tallest of them had a small ginger beard and ginger hair just visible under a dashing blue hat with a feather in it. Darting to the other window, I saw them enter the yard.

Another of the horsemen, the moment he saw one of the grooms, called out loudly, "How is Magpie? Is he sound yet?" and at once I tensed. Magpie had to be the piebald. That man, then, was Will Johnson. I stared at him, taking him in. He dismounted and I could see him clearly: a stocky, strutting fellow with a thick neck. He pulled his hat off in order to scratch his scalp, revealing a round dark head.

Three men had been concerned in John's murder. One was Johnson. One, almost certainly, was the ginger-haired man. Down there in the courtyard, behaving just like ordinary men, walking, talking, asking anxiously after the progress of a lame horse, were two, at least, of the men who had attacked John, plunging a blade into him and leaving him under a gorse bush like a sack of unwanted rubbish. For a moment I almost forgot my own danger. My eyes fastened on them, as though I hoped to skewer them with a stare and let their lives out of them.

Was the third there as well, and if so which one was he? Apart from the groom, whom I recognised as belonging to Faldene, there were two others. One, who had also dismounted and was leading his horse away himself, was quite young and still had a few boyish spots on his face. The fourth I couldn't see at once because both he and the ginger-haired man were slow to dismount, and Ginger Hair was in the way.

Then, at last, Ginger Hair threw his leg over his horse's back and swung to the ground. The last man in the group, who was still in his saddle, leaning forward to speak to Will Johnson, came into view at last.

243

He too was tall, but looser-knit and wider of shoulder than Ginger Hair. As I watched, he straightened up, took his feet out of the stirrups and joined the others on the ground, turning his face towards me as he did so. I took in his features: the long chin, the dramatic black eyebrows.

Then he looked up and saw me at the window, as I stood paralysed, while the blood withdrew from my face and tears of shock pricked my eyes.

Oh God. What a trick for fate to play on me. How can *he* be with *them?* What on earth is Matthew de la Roche doing here in the company of Will Johnson?

However, if the sight of Matthew had paralysed me, the sight of me had a galvanic effect on him. He let go of his horse's reins altogether and ran into the house. A moment later I heard his voice, shouting to someone, and within seconds, or so it seemed, Uncle Herbert was opening the bedchamber door and standing back to let Matthew stride through. By then, I had stumbled from the window to sit on the side of the bed with my hands clasped tightly together to stop them from shaking.

Matthew looked over his shoulder at my uncle, and barked, "Leave us!" Uncle Herbert obeyed at once, taking orders under his own roof as though Matthew were the master here and my uncle merely the butler. Matthew came to me, sat down beside me and took my hands. I snatched them away.

"Don't! Ursula, my dear, my very dear. I have wanted so much to see you again but not like this. I was told that Herbert Faldene's niece was here but I didn't know it was you. Herbert has many nieces. I was told she had . . . had . . ."

"Learned things you didn't want known?"

"Oh, *Ursula,*" said Matthew, which wasn't an answer.

"Your Sussex home," I said. "You never told me

244

where it was. It's Withysham, isn't it? *You're* the new owner of Withysham?"

"Yes, but what of it?"

"When my uncle didn't know what to do with me, he said he would consult Withysham. I thought he meant that man Johnson but he didn't: he meant you, didn't he? You're the one in charge. My uncle left the room when you told him to. Johnson's your subordinate. Those men you came with, they're your . . your retainers, aren't they?"

As I faced him, my heart was turning somersaults. He was still Matthew. His features, his body, were those to which I had been so powerfully drawn. I had walked and laughed and danced with him; I had had dreams of making love with him. After I had parted from him at Cumnor, I had longed for a letter from him, and I had hoped to find one when I returned to court. When I looked into his sparkling dark eyes now I wanted to dive into them as if into a sunlit pool, and drown there, but there were things that must be said and questions that must be asked.

"It is certainly true," Matthew said, "that I own Withysham and that Johnson and the other men who rode here with me just now are in my employ. They would commonly accompany me when there was any . . . emergency."

"Are you using Withysham as . . . as some kind of headquarters?"

He didn't answer. His eyes were kind but worried; I had the impression that he didn't know what to reply.

I had hoped to find him in Sussex and ask his advice! I almost burst into hysterical laughter but fought it down and pressed on. "I don't know what Uncle Herbert has said to you. I rather think he expects you to . . ."

Kill me. The words wouldn't come out. "Never mind," I said. "I want you to tell me something and

245

please tell the truth. You rode into the courtyard just now with that red-haired man and Will Johnson. Were you with them when they travelled, not long ago, down through Oxfordshire and Berkshire? Were you with them when they stayed at an inn called the Cockspur, not very far from Maidenhead? *And did you help them kill a man called John Wilton?"*

Some time later, although I had stopped crying because my feelings had been bludgeoned numb, I was still sitting upright on the side of the bed, resisting the invitation of Matthew's arms and refusing to rest my head on his shoulder.

Round and round we had gone and now we were starting another treadmill circuit.

"My love, my sweeting. Let me say it once again. I was not one of the men you have been following through the southern counties. They were led by William Johnson—I admit he is my second cousin, who has come to live at Withysham with me—and two gentlemen of our joint household, Mr. Brett and young Mr. Fletcher. I have been at Withysham all the time. I have dealt with tradesmen from outside and dined here several times, and at other houses too. Lately, I've been making an effort to get to know my neighbours. You may question whom you will. I had no hand in the death of your servant Mr. Wilton, and if I had been there it wouldn't have happened. Will and his companions reported the matter to me and I have censured them . . ."

"Censured! John is *dead."*

"I know, and I deeply regret it. My cousin and his associates were extremely foolish."

"So you said. It seems," I said bitterly, repeating what Matthew had already told me, several times over, "that they shared a room with John at the Cockspur, and that their foolishness took the form of discussing their errand when they thought he was asleep. He heard them speak of raising money for the Catholic cause, but he wasn't asleep, and in the morning, when they all set out again, he took it upon himself to remonstrate with them. Yes, that's very like John. He used to argue with people who did things he didn't approve of, regardless of who they were. And so they killed him."

"If I had been there, I assure you, there would have been no unwise talk and therefore no killing, which, I repeat, I deplore as much as you do."

"Do you? Suppose you had been there and the unwise talk somehow happened anyway? What would you have done then?"

"Making sure that such things don't occur is the very root of efficiency. I am efficient," said Matthew.

There was a silence, during which I took in that he was offering this efficiency of his as a matter for pride, even attempting a smile as he said it, and that, sickeningly, I could see straight through him. He was peacocking, presenting his accomplishments, in this case efficiency, in an effort to impress me as a man impresses a woman. He was saying in effect, "Don't look at the wider scene, don't think of such things as affairs of state or religious conflict; let me fill your horizon; let your vision be bounded by me!"

However, John lay mute and still in his grave, when he should still have been alive under the sky. I shook myself free of the snare. "That is no answer! Your men were raising money for Mary Stuart and the Catholic cause in England. They were acting on your orders; you've said so. Does Mary Stuart pay you?"

"No, Ursula. I work for my faith of my own free will."

"Do you? I suppose I should be relieved to hear it, but in England, it's still treason. Well, John would present a serious danger. I can see that. And so, now, do I. What is to happen to me, Matthew? Tell me that!"

"Oh, my God. My darling Ursula. There is no question of harm coming to you. You can't think that! Of course I shall not let anyone hurt you."

"I rather think my uncle and aunt believe otherwise."

"Your uncle is a loyal supporter of the faith, but as a man I don't care for him much," said Matthew frankly. "Why oh why did you enquire into his affairs as you did? I know all about your encounter last night. He sent a letter to me by his groom. It told me everything, except your name."

"I enquired because I wanted to know," I said. "Matthew, don't you *understand* that this is treason, and that decent people are being drawn into it? I'm thinking of two households in particular, the Masons and the Westleys. Did they give money? What *exactly* did they think it was for, by the way? I find it hard to imagine either of them wanting a civil war, but when Mary Stuart and the Catholic cause are bracketed together, they amount to just that. Perhaps," I said with scorn, "your poor dupes thought it was just to pay priests to go about and teach! I think my uncle knows better because it was plain enough from what he said to me that he supports Mary's claim to the throne. I noticed that none of the charitable people your men called on would mention that they'd been there, but even giving money to train priests could get people into serious trouble. Is that the way you've been tricking money out of the innocent? By leaving Mary Stuart out of it and just talking about the faith?"

I had struck home. The red ran up under his skin and his dark eyes became hard and bright with anger. "Tricking is an ugly word, Ursula. Yes, we asked for money to support and train priests. My men also

248

asked people about the kind of support they might be willing to give if ever Elizabeth . . ."

"Queen Elizabeth," I said in a shaking voice.

"So be it, if you wish! If *Queen* Elizabeth were to die childless, or the realm should turn against her and Mary Stuart land on these shores, we want to know what support she would find. Yes, we mentioned Mary, of course we did! Most of the people visited contributed, although some said they could only decide about giving further support when the time actually came. And yes, my men did warn people, for their own safety, not to mention their visit to anyone—although whether those contributions and half-promises were treason, is a matter of opinion. Which is the higher loyalty: that to the crown or that to God? I believe, as many others do, that the rightful queen of England is Mary Stuart and that the Catholic religion is the true one which must one day return. The way will be shown. Something will happen. Anyone may die, at any time, even a queen . . ."

"Even Mary Stuart?" I said hopefully. He paid no heed.

"The people of England may well turn against the queen, especially if she marries Dudley, as now seems all too likely."

"My uncle said that," I said sourly.

"Did he? Well, it's true. If that day ever dawns, money will be needed for arms and to pay Mary's army, when she comes to take her own in the name of God and true doctrine. That is what I—and others— are doing. We are making sure that the money is gathered and ready in her coffers against the moment which we know that God will send."

"Did you or some friend of yours arrange the murder of Lady Dudley, by any chance?" I demanded. "Hoping to encourage the queen towards disaster? I trust she'll be too clever for you, that's all."

He stared at me. "Oh, my God," I said. "Is that what you were doing at Cumnor Place? Helping to plot her death?"

"Helping to . . . ? Murder Amy Dudley?" I had obviously disconcerted him. "What are you talking about? I came to Cumnor Place to see you! I know nothing of Lady Dudley's death except of course that the news of it has reached me. The verdict was accident, or so I heard, and if the verdict's wrong then I assume that Dudley had her killed, with an eye on becoming King of England."

"Well, he didn't," I told him. "I can assure you of that. I've known that for some time, never mind how, and since then, I've believed it was accident or suicide. Now I'm beginning to wonder!"

"What are you saying?" Matthew shouted. "I repeat: I came to Cumnor Place to find you, *you!* Do you think I, or any of us, would murder an innocent, sick woman!"

"Your cousin and his friends murdered an innocent and honest man!"

"I tell you they had no choice!"

"And what," I asked him, "if I had turned out to be one of Uncle Herbert's other nieces—he has half a dozen by marriage, the daughters of my Aunt Tabitha's sister and brother—instead of being myself? What would you have done to her?"

"It is easier to control a woman than a man. I would not have let her be harmed, either," Matthew said angrily. "But we must protect ourselves, yes, of course. We take risks too!" He saw my angry eyes, and he caught my shoulders and shook me. "Yes, we do and you know it! Tell me, if you get the chance, will you go running to the authorities with all this information? Would you like to think of me under the disembowelling knife?"

250

I began to cry once more. My feelings were not numb after all. His physical presence was as powerful as ever. Even while we talked of these terrible things, even while I was being angry or contemptuous, or seeing through him, I was conscious of his warmth, of his smell, masculine and glorious enough to make my head swim. Even while he made excuses for John's murderers, I still wanted to reach out with a fingertip and trace the line of his eyebrows, the angle of his jaw. When he was angry, his magnetism was only greater. It pulled me towards him as though I were a fish on a line. Look too long into those dark, diamond-shaped eyes and I would not be able to fight him any more, but I tried.

"Matthew, Matthew, can't you see that Mary Stuart can't be put on the throne without bloodshed and destruction; that this true faith of yours can't be restored without . . . without *horror,* the sort of horror that makes even John's death look kindly? I told you, I never saw a burning, but Uncle Herbert described one to me and Aunt Tabitha made me listen . . ."

"My heart, it need not be like that. It will all be different. Philip of Spain was here then. The English hated him because he didn't belong here, but Mary Stuart is of the true Tudor line, and people will follow her. Ursula, listen to me. I will not harm you, and I did not murder John or want him murdered. I promise you . . ."

Round and round and round. Someone brought yet another meal and I believe I ate some of it although I can't remember what the dishes were. Another hour and I was as exhausted as though I had gone three successive nights without sleep and ridden fifty miles on every day in between.

He *would* not see, perhaps could not see, that the

251

dreams he and his friends harboured would be for the people of England a nightmare. He had been reared in his beliefs so intensely that they were stamped into his mind. He could not think in any other pattern, could not see that if the attempt to stamp the pattern on others led to dreadful things, then that simple fact brought his beliefs into question.

"Ursula, it is simply a matter of what is true. People must not, for the sake of their own souls, be left in error. I would be the most loyal of subjects to Elizabeth, if only she would change her ways and bring back the old faith but . . ."

"But she can't, Matthew, even if she wanted to. In the eyes of the Catholic world, her parents weren't legally married and therefore she is not lawfully queen."

"I'm sure that after all this time some sort of status quo could be agreed."

"No, it couldn't," I said, remembering my first day at court, when Elizabeth had stamped up and down a gallery, afire with rage because of Mary Stuart's pretensions, and remembering too Elizabeth's own ruthless reading of the situation. "It couldn't," I said, "because such people as Mary Stuart, and probably Philip of Spain, too, don't want to take England over just for the sake of God. They want it because the grass is good and the sheep and cattle thrive and because we have tin and iron. You are so innocent!"

"No, Ursula, you are too cynical."

"I am not. What would happen to Elizabeth if Mary Stuart were to take the throne?"

"Honourable captivity, I suppose."

"While those who still supported her plotted on her behalf? Her honourable captivity, Matthew, would be in a prison two yards long and six feet underground! Oh, God, why can't you see . . . ?"

But he couldn't. His body was that of a very adult and experienced man; his mind was intelligent, but his faith was as simple as that of a child. He was puzzled and wounded because I had challenged it.

And this, like his anger, only made his attractiveness greater. I wanted to hold and comfort that child; I wanted to kiss the wound better. There was no aspect of him that I did not want to take into myself and hold there for ever.

At last I came to what, after all, was for me the major point at issue. "Matthew, what happens to me now?"

He ran a hand, a strong, long-fingered hand, through his hair. "Ursula, if you were to walk free from this house today, where would you go? What would you do?"

I said nothing. The answer was obvious, and hideous. He made it for me.

"You would go straight to the court of Queen Elizabeth and report what you know. What good do you think that would do? It would place me—and I believe you have some feeling for me—in danger of a traitor's death. It would bring down peril on the heads of the Westleys and the Masons, and you say you don't want to do that. It would be all quite useless, for I am only one of many who are engaged in this fundgathering. I have volunteered to take charge of one little group. There are others, although I don't know who they are. It would make no difference to anything in the end."

"It might bring John's murderers to justice."

"You are prepared to sacrifice the Westleys and the Masons—and me—for that? I understand how you feel about him, but nothing now can bring him back."

I wept again, unable to see a way through, unable to see anything but a fog of exhaustion and despair.

Then I felt his arm round my shoulders and heard his voice say, "Well, one thing's clear. I can't leave you here. I don't think I trust your aunt and uncle . . ."

On the edge of hysterical laughter, I hiccupped, "No, nor do I!"

"And nor," said Matthew calmly, "can I set you free. However, there are other alternatives. One is simply to keep you at Withysham for the time being. You would have to stay until I could finish my work in this country for Mary Stuart and could sell Withysham and get away to France. You would be well treated, but not allowed to leave until it was safe for us. That is one possibility. It's what I would have done had you been one of your uncle's other nieces. However, for you, there is another."

"Is there? What?"

"Again, it means coming to Withysham, but in order," said Matthew simply, "to marry me."

"Marry you?"

"Why not? Didn't we begin to talk of just that, at Richmond and Cumnor? Then we could go to France together. I think I must give Withysham up either way, but then, I only came to England and bought it to please my mother. I'll be happy enough to exchange it for a home on the other side of the Channel. Especially if it's a home I can share with you."

"Marry you? But what difference would that make?" I asked wearily. "I'd be a prisoner for life instead of only for a time, that's all."

"Oh Ursula, no. It isn't all. A prisoner? You have been married before; so have I. We both know what marriage is. Marry me and I will spread before you such a banquet of the senses that you will desire nothing else. We will be lovers and soon there will be children. I will be a father to your child. You will be mistress of my household. You will have the life you ought to have, that all women ought to have. Believe me, I will so gladden your days, that all the hard questions that worry you now, of royal successions and this or that faith will fade away. Your husband and your home and your children will fill your world. In France you will be as free as any other lady. Your servants, your woman—" he glanced at Dale where she sat, as unobtrusively as possible, in a corner of the room listening to us with amazement—"and the manservant your uncle told me you brought with you, they can remain with you. Indeed, it is best that they come to France too. There, if they gossip, it won't matter. What do you say?"

I said nothing at all. He repeated it, lovingly, his anger all gone, and drew me tightly against him, nuzzling into my hair. I did not resist. I was dizzy with the swift change in my fortunes. From the prospect of imprisonment or even death—yes, I had feared it could come to that—to the prospect of marriage was a big reversal on its own.

I was confronted with more still, however. I could not yet quite grasp it.

"I must think," I said at last. "I can't answer you just like that."

"Shall I leave you alone to think? There is a man on guard outside your door. You have only to knock when you want to speak to me again."

I nodded. He took my face between his hands and kissed me before he left the room and I didn't stop him. The choice was already made, was inescapable, and this delay was only for the sake of appearances.

And to gather strength. For what lay ahead seemed impossible, as impossible as throwing myself off a cliff.

I threw myself on to the bed and told Dale not to disturb me. I lay there for hours, thinking.

At eight o'clock that evening, I faced it. How I

would do it, I couldn't imagine, but somehow I must find a way. There was a hand mirror on the toilet table and I looked at myself in it. My eyes were red rimmed, but the rest of my face was white and hollowed, like the scooped rind of an orange. I knocked on the door and demanded, first of all, washing water and a fresh white headdress.

Then, when with Dale's help I had made myself as presentable as possible, I asked to see Matthew. He came in with his usual long, swift stride, and this time sat on the window seat, facing me. His own face was drawn. "Before you say anything," he said, "I want to say this. I love you. Truly. Please believe that. Now, Ursula, my very dear love, say what you want to say."

"I'll marry you," I said. And then, before the relief and joy which at once appeared in his eyes could entirely take him over, I added, "But there are conditions. Unless you can meet them, there can be no wedding."

He tensed warily. "What are they?"

"I never want to set eyes on Johnson, Brett or Fletcher again. They are not to be, ever, under the same roof as myself. Send them off to collect some more money, if you like, but get rid of them. The further they go, the better I'll be pleased."

"It had occurred to me that you would not want to have Johnson or the others near you," Matthew said. "They are leaving Withysham at dawn tomorrow, for the midlands."

"Good," I said. "That's not all. The second thing is that my uncle and aunt must not be at the wedding, either."

"I wouldn't think of it! I've been talking to your uncle. I fear that you are right and that he really wouldn't be unduly surprised—or shocked—if I made away with you. Is there anything else?"

256

"Yes, there is, and it's very important. Did you know that my uncle and aunt have brought my daughter Meg here against my wishes? I left her with her nurse Bridget, in a cottage in Westwater, and they fetched her away without my consent."

"No, I didn't know."

"Well, they did, and she's here now. They will say, if challenged, that the cottage was unsuitable for her and that they brought her here to rear her as a lady and save her soul from heresy, but it isn't true."

"Are you sure?"

"Quite sure. Oh, I daresay they've even convinced themselves that it's all for Meg's own good and that they're devoted relatives trying to do their best for her. They like to look well in their own eyes and other people's." I realised as soon as I had said it, that this was probably the key to my aunt and uncle. They had always been good at outward virtue. "The truth," I said, "is that they brought her here to strike back at me for stealing my cousin Mary's bridegroom and denying them my unpaid services as a dogsbody. They will make use of her, and in the process make her as miserable as I was. I have the impression that you have some influence over them. Please use it to release Meg."

Matthew was bemused. "I was supposing, as a matter of fact, that you would bring your daughter to Withysham. I was going to ask you where she was."

"Meg must certainly come to Withysham," I said, "but not immediately. She has been too much upset and disturbed lately. She can come to me after we are married and I have settled down a little and taken the reins of the household. If I marry you," I said, "I will do it with the most whole heart that I can. For the moment, I wish Meg to return to the Westwater cottage and to the care of Bridget. Bridget is at the

257

cottage now. She is to be brought here, so that Meg can return to Westwater in her company. Meg," I said dictatorially, "is not to travel, even three miles, in a stranger's care."

Matthew laughed. "You know your own mind, it seems!"

"Yes, I do. Are my terms acceptable?"

"I think I'm relieved that they are so reasonable! Is there anything else?"

I shook my head.

"Then I agree. Are we now betrothed?"

"Yes."

"I ought to give you a ring," he said, and pulled at a heavy ring of gold set with rubies, which he wore on his right hand. It resisted, however, and he stopped.

"No, not this one. I'll find you something better when we get to Withysham. I won this at cards—Sir Richard Verney had run out of money and he was gambling with his jewellery. Somehow it doesn't have the right history to be a betrothal ring."

"It doesn't matter," I said. "May I now see my manservant Roger Brockley and tell him of his future?"

"How much does he know?" Matthew asked.

"Nothing of my midnight visit to my uncle's office, and nothing of your fundraising. He knows only that we have been hunting John Wilton's killers."

Matthew frowned, seeing, I think, that controlling the tongues of all three of us might be harder than he expected. "It is safer for him if he remains in ignorance," he said. He turned to Dale, who was again sitting in her corner, listening, as before, in an amazed silence. "You will keep your mistress's counsel, I trust."

I gave Dale a small nod and she stammered out a nervous: "Oh yes, sir, of course, sir."

"Good," said Matthew. "Tell me, Ursula, what do you propose to say to Brockley?"

Presently, when Brockley had been summoned, I cleared my throat and declared to him that for the last few days, I had been under a dreadful misapprehension. "I'm thankful to say that it has been proved to my satisfaction that my old servant John Wilton was not murdered, and I can only conclude that he was set upon by footpads as we at first supposed."

"I'm glad to hear it, madam." Brockley was searching my face and I saw him also glance aside at Dale. Dale looked down at the floor. "I've been asking to see you, madam," Brockley said. "I was told you were unwell."

"Were you? It was nothing—just a passing indisposition." I smiled to reassure him. "I have news of much greater importance. Here with me you see Master Matthew de la Roche, with whom I was acquainted at the court, and who visited me at Cumnor Place." I held out my hand to Matthew and he took it. "He is my uncle's neighbour, from Withysham, only a few miles away. He called today and we met again. My quest, mistaken though it was, has brought us together. We are to be married."

"The day after tomorrow," confirmed Matthew. "At Withysham. We leave for Withysham in the morning."

This came as a shock to me. So soon! I ploughed determinedly on, speaking now to both Dale and Brockley, saying that I hoped they would both go on serving me as always and would be as loyal to Matthew as they had always been to me.

Dale murmured, "Of course, ma'am, of course," but addressing Brockley was like talking to a stone. I never saw disbelief so clearly displayed on a human countenance as it was on Brockley's just then. However, he commanded himself, offered his congratulations and promised fidelity to us both in time to come.

"Then," I said, "as Master de la Roche has said, we set out for Withysham in the morning."

"Directly after breakfast," said Matthew.

However, we didn't set out for Withysham in the morning directly after breakfast, or even after dinner. During the night, within the bedcurtains, I told Dale what I intended, and listened to her staggered exclamations. "Oh, ma'am! Oh, dear. Yes, of course it's what you must do but oh, dear, how will you ever manage it? I can see how it is between you and Master de la Roche. Oh. ma'am!"

She was a conventional soul, was Dale, but so was I, at heart. Her reactions mirrored my own. Not only could I not see how to manage it; I was afraid I couldn't bring myself to try.

By dawn, the malady of the sick headache which had vanished during my marriage to Gerald, but shown signs of reappearing at Cumnor, had pounced. I woke in agony, with the worst headache I had ever had in my life.

It was as though my brows had been bound in iron and someone was hitting me rhythmically over the left eye with a very large hammer. Aunt Tabitha, marching into the room to fetch me down to breakfast, found me still lying in bed. Being Aunt Tabitha, she wouldn't believe I was ill, and tried to pull me out of bed, whereupon I was violently sick at her feet, and partly on them, which gave me a certain amount of savage satisfaction.

She went away in stockinged feet, leaving her contaminated shoes behind, and uttering exclamations of disgust, and called Matthew. He had stayed overnight, intending to escort me to Withysham himself. He came to my bedside and looked at my furrowed brow and green-tinged face with consternation.

"Ursula! What is it, what's the matter?"

"It's a sick headache," I said. My eyes were half closed because the light hurt them. "It'll pass. I have them, sometimes."

"What helps it? There must be something!" He rounded on Aunt Tabitha. "Did she have these turns when she lived here? What did you do for them?"

Aunt Tabitha had never done very much for them, but at Cumnor, Dale had tried with some success a remedy which she had learned with a previous employer who had a similar affliction. "An infusion of camomile might help," she said.

"Do you have camomile?" Matthew demanded of my aunt.

"Yes, we grow it," Aunt Tabitha said.

"Then go to the kitchen and get a draught made up!" Matthew snapped to Dale.

As Dale went out, I said weakly to Matthew, "Has Bridget been sent for?"

"Yes, she has." It was Aunt Tabitha who answered, in a very angry voice. "It seems that we must let your child go back to that hovel and that woman. Your uncle insists."

She meant that Matthew had insisted and that Uncle Herbert was doing what he was told. I found some pleasure in that.

"When Bridget comes," I said weakly, "I must see her. I wish to tell her about us and give her instructions for looking after Meg. There are clothes to be made up for Meg before she comes to Withysham, and a lot of other things I want to point out, too." I didn't want to sit up, because the slightest movement, even the effort of raising my voice, set the hammers pounding at my skull, but I put out a hand and

261

clutched Matthew's doublet sleeve. "However ill I am, I must see Bridget."

"I can tell her to wash, if that's what you're worrying about," said Aunt Tabitha with a sniff.

"Other things. A lot of things. I'm Meg's mother," I said, persisting as best I could through pain and fragility.

"Surely we could ride to Westwater later, after the wedding, and you can tell her then," Matthew said. "I assure you that she will take Meg back there today, as you asked."

"I must see Bridget!" I whispered frantically.

"Hush, hush!" Matthew turned once more to Aunt Tabitha. "We must humour the invalid," he said. "If she wants to see the nursemaid, she shall."

Dale was back before long, with a steaming goblet. She also brought a basin, which was just as well, for as soon as I had swallowed the draught, I brought it up again.

It went on, hour after hour of pain and retching. Bridget arrived and was brought to me, and I explained matters to her and gave her her instructions, and now, looking back, I wonder how I did it, through those waves of pain.

Meg was brought in to say goodbye, and I kissed her and told her that although I wasn't well, I would soon be better and that meanwhile, she was going back to the cottage with Bridget and must be a good girl, and I would soon send for her. Then Bridget took her away, and I lay back and suffered.

Aunt Tabitha and Dale stayed with me. My uncle never put in an appearance, and Matthew left the room, saying that I needed to be quiet, but looked in now and then, obviously worrying about me. I was beginning to be worried about myself. By afternoon I had nothing left in my stomach and was bringing up only a thin, watery stuff, and my stomach muscles were aching as though I had been repeatedly punched in the midriff.

Finally, Aunt Tabitha went away too. She had stayed, it soon became clear, because she kept on hoping that I would recover, get up and leave the house. She had made a few acid remarks about undutiful nieces who didn't want their guardians at their wedding, but I don't think she really cared. She wanted to be rid of me. I would have been equally thankful to be rid of her but it was well after noon before she finally left me and Dale alone.

Then Dale, sitting on the edge of the bed and holding the basin for me through yet another spasm of retching, sighed with relief and said, "Now I can talk to you freely. Mistress Blanchard, when I went down to get that draught for you, I saw Brockley. I talked to him."

"What did you say? I want him to know everything and as soon as possible."

"Well, ma'am," said Dale doubtfully, "I've told him all I can. You said last night, after we were left alone, that he'd got to know, whatever you'd pretended to him when Master de la Roche was here, but all the same, I hope I did the right thing, just telling him myself instead of leaving it to you. Only, the chance was there and . . ."

"Of course you did the right thing! Oh, bless you, Dale. How did you manage it?"

"Why, I saw him out in the yard and just stepped out to speak to him. No one stopped me. Master de la Roche was in too much of a fuss over you to think of keeping an eye on me! Brockley was grooming Bay Star and he came straight over to me to ask how you were. He's very kind. I like Mr. Brockley, ma'am . . ."

"Never mind that! What did you say to him?"

"Why, ma'am, I told him, as quick as I could, everything I could remember of what you've told me, about what these men we've been following are really about and how your uncle's mixed up in it, and Master de la Roche too. Ma'am, Brockley says it's a terrible thing you've set yourself to do, but likely you're doing right and he'll help if he can. We agreed we'd both help, not just because you pay us, but because we think it's right."

"Thank you, Dale," I said.

It was Dale, I think, who cured me, although with words rather than camomile. Presently, the headache and the nausea eased and I found that I could sleep. In the morning, I was well.

§16⒟

An Eye for Country

"Yes," I said to Dale when we woke. "I can get up." The headache had disappeared completely and I was slightly hungry. I felt a little weak, but I knew from experience that it would pass. My mind now was calm. I remembered Gerald telling me how he had chosen loyalty to Gresham and the queen and to his family, above the interests of those he conscripted into helping him. He had had to choose his loyalties and hold by them. So must I.

When Aunt Tabitha came with a dish of bread rolls and a bowl of thin meat broth, and enquired sarcastically if I felt equal now to taking some breakfast and setting out for Withysham, I said yes. In due course I came downstairs to find Matthew waiting for me in the hall. The gladness in his eyes when he saw me on my feet was very touching.

"Meg is safe at Westwater and the three of whom we spoke the other day have left on their errand to the midlands," said Matthew quietly. "You need not fear an encounter. Are you all right? You're very pale."

265

"It's the aftermath of yesterday," I said. "I shall soon be myself again."

Normally, this would have been true, but I knew that my wan looks today were partly fear. The risk I faced was a risk not only to me but to Dale and Brockley as well. The responsibility was heavy.

Poor Matthew. If I did bring it off, it would be because I had taken advantage of him. Although he seemed so sophisticated, such a man of the world, he nevertheless had in him that curious simplicity, that childlike streak. I saw myself as he would see me, cold and unwomanly. The image was not pretty.

However, there was no turning back. Our horses were ready, Bay Star, White Snail and Brockley's fleabitten cob, Speckle. Matthew, concerned for me, made us ride slowly. Just once, Brockley managed a few words with me, unheard by anyone else.

"You truly mean to go through with this, ma'am?"

"Yes, Brockley."

"God guide you," he said sincerely. And then, in a practical tone, he said, "When we're at this place Withysham, we'll have to survey the country. We must use what we find."

"Thank you, Brockley," I said.

The place which had once been Withysham Abbey was encircled by a ditch, with a ten-foot stone wall on the inner rim, and the entrance was through an elaborate gatehouse, with a short tunnel under the porter's living quarters and an office to one side, where he sat when he was on duty. The gate was open because carts were going in and out and we rode through behind a load of wine barrels. I looked keenly about me. The place had stood empty when I was a girl and I had been inside the walls before, as a trespasser, climbing over a fallen stretch of wall, but I could remember no details and now I needed to take in as much as I could.

Inside, the space was quite large. To either side of the gatehouse was a paddock, one harbouring a dozen placidly grazing cows. The path led between these and on across a stretch of grass to what had been the old abbey buildings, now altered to make a house. There was an archway leading presumably to a main courtyard, but a second path branched off to the right and apparently went round to the back, probably to a stableyard. Beside the house, a garden was being laid out, with men digging over beds and putting up trellises, and beyond that were a few ruinous arches and the bases of stone pillars which marked the site of what had been the abbey church.

"The stone was taken to build the village church, over there," said Matthew, riding beside me. He pointed to a tower visible beyond the outer wall. "In the old days, the villagers shared the abbey church and had their own entrance. Now they have St. Thomas's in Withysham village. I keep the law on church attendance and go to the services regularly, but I've had a small chapel made inside the house— it's in what used to be the guest parlour, in the oldest part of the building—and that's where we shall take our vows later. I arranged the ceremony for today, as I said I would, hoping and praying that you would be well enough in time. Oh, Ursula, I am so thankful that you are better. I prayed for you again and again yesterday. Everything is ready for us. As far as the vicar of St. Thomas's is concerned, by the way, we were married quietly at Faldene."

"I take it that you hear mass in your chapel?" I said.

"I do indeed. I have a resident priest in the house, an elderly man, who is also an uncle of mine: Armand de la Roche. He celebrates mass for me. Ursula, believe me, before long you will love it as I do."

267

"Perhaps," I said bleakly, and he said no more. We rode under the arch into what was indeed a courtyard, very neatly kept, and all at once we were surrounded by the usual bustle of arrival at a big house, with barking dogs and scuttling poultry and people coming out to greet us. We were clearly expected; while I lay retching in Faldene's best guest room, the comings and goings between Faldene and Withysham must have been brisk.

Brockley led the horses away, while Dale and I were taken indoors. I was introduced to Uncle Armand, who was an aged Frenchman in a black cassock; to a tall, quiet Englishman with stooped shoulders, who was the steward, Mr. Malton; and to the housekeeper, French like Uncle Armand, and known as Madame Montaigle. She was hard of feature, with greying hair and a brisk, businesslike manner, except when she looked at Matthew. Then, the hard lines of her face softened and her pale eyes became sentimental. She clearly adored him.

I was going to hurt these people, dreadfully.

There certainly had been some comings and goings. The wine barrels I had seen being delivered were for the wedding feast, and a room had been set aside for me in which I could be dressed. Madame Montaigle had found, sponged and pressed a very beautiful gown, which she said had belonged to Matthew's mother. It was pale blue satin, embroidered with little golden flowers, opening over an underskirt of cream with more embroidered gold flowers. I would be appropriately fine for the occasion.

Madame's attitude towards me was a mixture of the doubtful (will this girl make my wonderful Matthew happy?) and the anxious to please (you are Matthew's bride and I welcome you for his sake). I wondered how he had explained his hurried nuptials to her but suspected he had simply given orders without explanations. Dale regarded Madame with suspicion at first, but Madame just gave my waiting-woman a little push and said, "Silly one—" she pronounced it *seely oo-unn*—"I am not going to steal your place! But a bride should have more than just one woman to prepare her!"

Dale thawed after that, and between them they gave me a bath, dried me and dabbed me with rosewater, and then I was carefully pinned into the dress and some essential stitching was done. Matthew's mother had been bigger than I was. We were short of time and some of the pins had to stay.

Since I was a widow, it wasn't correct for me to wear my hair loose, but while I was in the bath, Matthew sent a maidservant to the door with a jewelled net for me to wear. "He says to tell you, ma'am," said the maidservant, peeping round the screen and dropping a curtsy, "that this sort of headdress suits you and he'd like you to have this for the ceremony." It was a gold silk net very like the one I had worn at Cumnor, but the net was much thicker, and it was studded not only with pearls but with red rubies and green peridots. I looked at the glittering thing, thinking that it was like a symbol of my marriage: jewelled and beautiful, but a net all the same, like a spider's web, in which, unless I were very careful, I would be caught.

Part of me wanted to be caught, but then I thought of the three men who had killed John, moving along the roads of England, suborning people like the Westleys and the Masons into treason, spreading a web of their own across England. The gems in that web were false, the glitter a meretricious bait. Matthew did not think so, but Matthew was wrong. I must not turn back.

I wonder how many brides, as they don their

wedding gowns, constantly let their gaze stray to the window and scan the view, taking in the detail of what lies outside with the eye of a general planning a campaign, and looking for features of strategic advantage?

Dale, folding my hair into the shining mesh, said how pretty it looked, better than loose hair by far. I agreed with her and noted secretly and with regret that the outer wall had, as far as I could see, been completely repaired. Trespassers would find it hard to climb in now; and getting out would be just as difficult. I couldn't even see any convenient trees.

Madame Montaigle fastened a small linen ruff round my throat and admired the embroidery on my sleeves, and I agreed with her too, while wondering whether I could create a diversion by starting a fire.

My eyes returned most often to the paddocks. Their gates, both of them, opened on to the path from the gatehouse, and the gatehouse was probably not shut at all during the day. Matthew was not only having a garden made; he was having new outhouses built, and cartloads of this and that, plants, stones, timbers, were constantly coming in.

There were possibilities there, I thought. I found an excuse to ask Madame if she had any hartshorn, since I had been unwell the previous day and did not want to feel faint during the ceremony or the feast, and when she went to look for it, I took the opportunity to mutter a few instructions to Dale.

"Oh, ma'am!" said Dale.

"It's important!" I said tersely.

I was married. In the tiny chapel of Withysham House, a low, dark room with a floor sunk several steps below the level of the ground outside, I stood beside Matthew and declared before Uncle Armand and the assembled household that I took Matthew de la Roche to be my lawful wedded husband. "I never did give you a betrothal ring, but let this make up for it. It belonged to my mother, just as your dress did," Matthew whispered as he slid a thick gold wedding ring on to my hand. "This has the right kind of history," he said.

Then I took part, for the second time in only a few days, in an entirely unlawful mass. Dale and Brockley were present as well, although they did not take the sacrament and I could see the words "I can't abide this" written in Dale's indignant eyes.

I sat beside Matthew through the ensuing feast, held in what had once been the abbey's refectory and was now the household dining hall, a long, light first-floor room with windows on both sides, opening out from the top of a flight of wide, shallow stone steps. I smiled, laughed, ate, drank. I dined in privileged fashion, from a silver dish, and salted my food with a silver spoon. I remember that one of the pins which was holding my gown in place suddenly ran into me, causing me to let out a yelp, and how I then amused the company with a description of how we had struggled to make the gown fit.

Matthew's was a musical household. Mr. Malton— he preferred to be addressed as Mr. rather than Master, he told me—played the harpsichord expertly. Uncle Armand could perform on pipe and tabor both at once, and a lanky young man who was introduced to me as a fulltime music instructor, played a spinet. They all played dance music together, and I led the dance with my bridegroom. I felt as though I were splitting into two, for part of me really had the emotions of a bride.

And now, here I was in Matthew's bedchamber, which had been strewn with sweet herbs, and Dale and Madame Montaigle were preparing me for my nuptial night.

271

I think Dale felt that events had moved too fast for her and that she was lost in a world as weird and alarming as Dante's Inferno, but she was loyal to me and she had carried out my orders. She had somehow procured for me a piece of sponge and some vinegar, which she had put in one of the rock crystal bottles in my little toilet box. I managed to soak the sponge in the vinegar and push it into myself without Madame seeing. It was supposed to prevent pregnancy and I hoped it would work. I didn't want to conceive Matthew's child.

It was very different from my first marriage. The friends who had sheltered Gerald and myself had given us a wedding feast, with quite a gathering of their own friends as guests. I had thrown my garter to the guests, and Gerald and I had been escorted to bed amid a hilarious chorus of advice and encouragement, until Gerald pretended to be angry and threw his shoes at them to chase them out of the room.

This time there were no guests apart from Matthew's own household, and even the dancing had been decorous. Madame Montaigle and Dale drew back the bedcovers for me and I slipped in, and then they left me. Presently, Matthew entered, alone, candle in hand. He put the candle down on a chest and said, "Well, here I am."

"And here *I* am," I said, shakily. I had known this moment would be shattering but I hadn't quite bargained, even so, for the sheer reality of him. This was my husband. This was our wedding night. And I wanted him; oh God, how I wanted him. The sensation that I was splitting in two was growing worse; my mind was being riven from top to bottom like a tree struck by lightning. A faint hammer blow of pain over my left eye warned me that I was in danger of another sick headache. I thrust it away by a fierce act of will. No. I would have this. *I would have this.*

272

I did, and I am glad of it. I take the memory out, often, and look at it. I always want to weep, but again and again I drive the lovely knife home into my heart.

He slipped under the sheets with me and we came together at once, easily and naturally, arms and legs entwining, body enfolding body and mouth joined to mouth. For one brief moment I remembered Gerald and then he was gone. There was only Matthew. I had been hungry so long and he was, as he had promised to be, a banquet. He smelled sharp and spicy both at once, like a mixture of sweat and leather and cinnamon; beneath my hands his body was both hard and pliable, his strength reassuring.

We longed for union too much to delay it at first; it took only a little while to have me groaning with desire and Matthew too hard and eager to hold back. He slid into me, and we grappled fiercely, urging each other on: go deeper, climb higher, go faster, grip harder, go *on,* until we exploded together and fell apart, breathless and exalted.

To rest, and caress, and drowse, and rebuild our longing, and at length to come together again, this time slowly and delicately; satisfying ourselves even more intensely and falling, afterwards, into sleep as deep as an ocean.

I woke at dawn and slipped out of the bed. Beyond its curtains, out of sight, I stealthily renewed the sponge and vinegar. Then I crept back to Matthew and he stirred as I put my arms round him. He woke and we were together again.

I was being drawn away from my intent as though in the powerful undertow of a breaking wave. I can't do this, I said to myself, I can't go through with it.

Then Matthew said lazily, "You will like France, Ursula. I promise. We'll go to the Loire valley, where I used to live. I have relatives there. I came to England for my mother's sake but it's never been home. I miss

273

my French cousins and uncles and aunts. They'll be a family for you, Ursula. You never really had one before, did you?"

He had meant to distract me from the past but instead, he threw it into relief. In an instant I saw clearly all that I would lose if I went with him. My own land, my own faith. Elizabeth. And it mattered.

As day strengthened beyond the medieval lancet windows, I turned to him and looked into his eyes, holding back from the temptation to let them bewitch me, but striving to make mine limpid and loving so as to bewitch him. "Matthew, I think I should say . . . I am your wife now and I know it is better that I look forward and not back. I will try to be a good wife to you. I should like to be part of a family. It sounds quite wonderful."

"Ursula, sweeting . . ."

It was so difficult to go on gazing into his eyes that I turned over and settled down with my back against his belly, curved into his body, close and warm but not, now, face to face. He put his arm over me. "I think I'll be glad when we're there," I said. "I'm a little frightened, Matthew. Shouldn't we be prepared to go soon—or at short notice? If what you are doing is found out . . ." I let the sentence trail away.

"It won't be. But if it was, we could get away, don't worry. If we couldn't risk the main ports, there are such things as Catholic fishermen. I know where to turn for help."

I produced a convincing chuckle. "We'd be hard put to it to get Dale to the coast in a hurry. She really is a terrible rider. She bumps in the saddle like a sack of cabbages."

"You have such a salty turn of phrase, darling. And now we are lying like two spoons fitted together," he said drowsily. "You are my little saltspoon."

"Mmm." I was talking with a purpose, however,

and persisted. "Dale's had plenty of practice, these last few days, but it's made no difference. I once suggested that Brockley should give her some proper lessons. Can he, Matthew? Just in the paddocks inside the walls, of course."

"Of course he can. Why not?" said Matthew. "Never mind about Dale now. There's something else we should be doing . . ."

He rolled me gently over again and I yielded to him. My own deception sickened me and yet, looking back, I note that in those strange, brief, bittersweet days of my marriage, I did not again succumb to headache or nausea. It seemed that my deepest self, the part that ultimately gives or withholds consent concerning all vital decisions, the part that sometimes drives people to martyrdom, had made its choice.

"We make progress, sir, madam," said Roger Brockley, bringing Speckle up to the paddock fence to talk to us as Matthew and I paused on our way back from our morning ride round the Withysham home farm. "It was well done, madam, to put her on a better horse; lazy ones like the Snail may be safe, but they're tiring. She does better astride too; she feels firmer in the saddle that way. Generally speaking, I don't care for the sight of women in breeches, but on Dale, they're quite pleasing. Don't sag!" he added, raising his voice so that Dale, who was riding in a circle at a slow jog, could hear him. "The mare won't obey you if you slouch!"

He turned back to me and his level blue-grey gaze met mine intently. "We've met one snag, though. She says the stirrup leathers pinch her. I wonder, madam, if I could trouble you for your opinion?" He turned civilly to Matthew. "If the mistress could just slip down and walk across the paddock, I think Dale would appreciate it. The leather is nipping her legs,"

275

he explained, "and she's shy about showing them in front of a man."

"By all means," said Matthew, amused. "I'll stay here!" I dismounted, handed my reins to Matthew and went round to the gate. Brockley, calling to Dale to pull up, joined me and we set off across the grass towards her.

"Not a very good excuse, but the best I could think of," Brockley said. "Dale told me that you want to speak to me privately."

"I do. It's time we planned our move."

I had had to be cautious. Despite my diplomatic assertion, on that first morning, that I had accepted the situation, I knew that Matthew was watching me not only with love but also with vigilance. I had to make that vigilance relax. Therefore, I had deliberately let myself form a routine. Each morning, after prayers and breakfast, I went to the kitchen to give orders for the day, and since then, except for the one Sunday I had so far spent at Withysham, when we went to church, Matthew at my request took me out riding. I needed the air and exercise, I told him. Next week, I had said, I would ask him to come with me to Westwater and then, if he was agreeable, we would fetch Meg. "I won't visit her meanwhile; it could unsettle her. She is used to her quiet life with Bridget."

I hoped it sounded convincing, as though I had completely given in. I also hoped I hadn't overdone it. It was a balancing act.

After the daily ride, I would study household accounts with Mr. Malton, the steward, and after dinner, Dale and I would sew, or else I would practise music on the spinet, with instruction from the young music master. In the evening I would play at chess or draughts with Matthew, until supper. Then we went to bed, and the night had its own secret magic.

Oh yes, oh God, *what* magic! How could I forgo it now?

The treacherous thought slid snakelike into my mind that it would be easy, so easy. All I would have to do was surrender to this routine of pleasant days and luminous nights. All I would have to do was nothing. Brockley was glancing at me. I suspected that he half-expected me to change my mind and stay.

"Tomorrow, if the weather allows," I said. "Is Dale ready?"

"Near enough," Brockley said. "Putting her astride has done wonders, but the trouble with the stirrup leather is real enough. I pray to heaven, madam, that our scheme works."

I had been able to give instructions openly about Dale's new mount and her new breeches but other matters were more difficult, which was why I had needed, somehow, to arrange this private conference today. We had indeed laid a scheme but only in rapid undertones across Bay Star's withers when he brought her round to the door for me each morning. In such conditions, polished conspiracy was difficult.

"If we fail," I said, "I doubt we'll get a second chance."

"There's no other way out, either," Brockley added. "I've seen every yard of the walls by now. I did have an idea about starting a fire . . ."

"Did you? So did I."

"Really, madam? I think this is better." He was glancing at me again and I turned my head to look at him directly. Once more, his gaze was intent. "You're sure about this? It is a harsh choice for you. No lady should have to do what you're doing."

"I know, but I'm sure," I said, with steel in my voice.

We exchanged a few more words, putting finishing touches, until we reached Dale, who was waiting for us on the back of the brown mare which Matthew had provided for her instead of the Snail. While Brockley stood tactfully back, she showed me the bruises the leathers had made on her calves. Dale had been embarrassed at the idea of wearing breeches to ride astride, but now, except for the bruising, she was obviously relieved. Brockley was right: breeches suited her. I observed too that with all the riding she had done lately, she had lost weight. Her fined-down face was almost handsome. I noticed her glance towards Brockley and exchange a smile with him and it occurred to me that they were the same age and might well be attracted to each other. I wished them well, if so. I would have been glad, just then, to be one of my own servants.

"You need higher boots," I said. "Brockley! Come here. Can you lend Dale some boots high enough to protect her? These stop below the bruising." I let my voice carry to Matthew, waiting by the fence.

"Well, I could—but she'll have to stuff the toes. They'll be bigger all ways, as it were." Brockley, too, spoke clearly. In a lower voice, he added, "I'll have them for her tomorrow. The plan is settled, then?"

"It is. You've put on a wonderful performance this morning, Brockley. What a good strolling player you'd make!"

Brockley looked quite shocked. "I can't say the life of a wandering mummer appeals to me, madam. It's too chancy."

"I'm glad you feel like that," I told him, "because, to be frank, I'm glad you're here! Till tomorrow, then."

I went back to Matthew. "A simple matter enough. All that Dale needs are longer boots with wool in the toes!"

Matthew slid from his own saddle and we walked

back to the house, leading the horses, "How will you spend the rest of the morning?" he asked me.

"With Malton and the estate books. I am getting to understand them, gradually. Then, in the afternoon, Dale and I will start making me a gown from the material you've given me."

"Ah yes, my wedding gift." Two days after our wedding, Matthew had brought me a beautiful roll of rose-pink satin, which had been lying unused in a chest belonging to his mother. He would give me many much better gifts in time to come, he said, but meanwhile, if I would like this . . .

He looked at me with affection. "I shall like to see you in the finished gown. I only wish my mother could have been here to see it."

Matthew wouldn't see it, either. I tried not to think of that.

I worried about the weather. If it turned wet, it would look odd to persist with Dale's riding lessons, but the next day, though grey, was dry and looked as though it would brighten later on. The clouds were high, not lying mistily on the downs as they did when rain really threatened. We breakfasted, as usual, in a small parlour; Matthew went in for more privacy than my aunt and uncle did. The room was like many at Cumnor, with its stone walls and the pointed arches to its windows, and there was the same smell of stone about it, but the atmosphere was different. Withysham was differently positioned and its windows must have been differently angled, too, for it was not shadowy but caught the morning or evening sun in nearly every room.

It had also harboured murderers. I must not forget that.

Dale shared the breakfast, sitting a little apart at the table. I joked with her about her riding lessons. "I was watching you yesterday. You *must* sit up more. I've a good mind to join you when I come back from my own ride and show you how to do a few things myself. General principles are the same, even though I don't ride astride. You wouldn't object, Matthew? Just for fifteen minutes or so before I go to Malton's office. What is Brockley going to work on with you today, Dale?"

"The same as yesterday, madam. He wants me to sit up better, just as you said, and to practise getting a horse going when I want to and stopping when I want to."

I waited for Matthew to say that he didn't object but he did not speak. "I'll stop and enquire after your progress, as usual, anyway," I said, casually, afraid of arousing suspicion and praying that I wasn't going to fall at the very first obstacle. Under my boned bodice, against my heart, I could feel the weight of the bag of gold sovereigns and silver crowns, part of Dudley's last payment, which I had retrieved from my personal chest that morning. I had taken a last look round the bedchamber, to make my farewell to its remembered images of love. It had been a mistake. I had fled the room as if from an enemy.

"Oh, join the lesson if you wish. You ought to give Malton a morning off," Matthew said. "You take him from his other duties and he says how can he leave you alone with the account books, when you ask so many questions?"

A breath of sheer relief went silently out of me. "Oh dear. I'm sorry. Very well, I'll give him a rest." I laughed. "I've probably learned quite enough for the time being. By the way, I've noticed that we're rather extravagant with household candles, but I suppose the big dining chamber needs a great many . . ." Chatting idly about things that didn't matter, I led the conversation away from Dale and her riding lessons.

I can't remember what I talked to Matthew about during our ride. I must have kept the pretence of normality up somehow. When we came back, Brockley and Dale were at the end of the paddock furthest from the gate, engaged in stop and start manoeuvres. Brockley's voice floated towards me.

"No! I want you to put him into a canter straight from a standstill and then stop him before he gets level with that fencepost there. Now, try again. Get him ready. Tighten the reins and sit down well. *Now* . . . oh no, let me show you . . ."

"You know, I don't think Brockley is always a perfect teacher," I said to Matthew in critical tones. "She can't follow what it is he's trying to demonstrate. I'm sure I could do better. Well, I said I might join in for a while. I think I will. I'll see you at dinner, then."

"Of course. Don't overtire yourself," said Matthew, quite unsuspiciously, and opened the paddock gate for me. I took Bay Star in and he closed the gate and then leaned across it for a kiss. "Saltspoon!" he whispered.

I smiled into his eyes, but my own eyes stung as he rode off towards the stableyard. I sat for a moment, watching him go from me, before I turned to join my servants. My friends. My fellow conspirators.

We looked gravely at each other. "We'd better not waste time," said Brockley.

"I have to ask this," I said. "Are you two willing to take the risk? If we fail, I shall of course say that you were only obeying my orders. I'll protect you if I can, but Master de la Roche may well be very angry."

"Let's just go," said Dale in a jittery voice. She tightened her reins and the brown mare threw up her head.

"Easy," said Brockley quietly. "There's an ox-cart full of barrels coming in through the gatehouse, I see.

281

By the look of it, the driver knows the gatekeeper and they're discussing the weather and the gatekeeper's grandfather's rheumatics." Dale let out a slightly hysterical giggle. "We'll have to wait a bit," said Brockley frowning at her. "Madam, you'd better do a little instructing. Dale, you can take the chance of some extra practice. Straight from a standstill into a fast canter, that's what we want. Madam?"

I rode round the field, demonstrating. A few of the men who were laying out the new garden drifted over to watch, but they were well away from the paddock gate, and were not a threat. Every nerve in my body was alert for things that might hinder us.

Dale took her turn and did well. Brockley didn't deserve my disparaging remarks about his instruction. He was a good teacher and the brown mare was much more amenable than White Snail. However, I shook my head at him and told him he wasn't making it *clear* how Dale should use her calves to tell the horse what to do, and then told Dale that now she had boots which would protect her calves from the stirrup leathers, she ought to be able to squeeze firmly.

We were three people practising horsemanship in a paddock, apparently with no thought in our heads beyond the technicality under discussion, but I was watching the ox-cart from the corner of my eye. I saw it move on at last, leaving the gatehouse tunnel clear. Brockley saw it too. "That's enough for today," he said, and we began to walk the horses towards the gate.

Another ox-cart, this one laden with timber, arrived, and blocked the gatehouse like a stopper in a bottle.

"Oh, no," moaned Dale under her breath.

"I think," said Brockley, "that Bay Star has trouble with her off fore. Stop." We halted and he dismounted to examine Bay Star's hoof. Mildly puzzled, she pulled against the bit in order to look round at him. Dear God, I thought, if only we could get on with it.

The second ox-cart had creaked into motion again. Brockley straightened up. "There we are. Just a little pebble." He threw the imaginary pebble away and remounted his cob. The cart rumbled past the paddock and went off towards the new outhouses. There were no more carts behind it.

The porter had gone back into his little office. Brockley opened the paddock gate from the saddle and held it while Dale and I went decorously through. Then we were outside the paddock, on the track. Dale and I, as if to wait for Brockley, turned our horses to face him while he closed the paddock gate. We were now facing the gatehouse, too. It was only a few yards away. Brockley fastened the gate. Then he gathered his reins, spun the cob on its hindquarters to face the gatehouse as well and said, *"Now!"*

With that, we went, all three of us, from a standstill into a canter and then a gallop within six strides, aiming for the gatehouse, the one way out through the encircling wall. At the sound of our hoofs, the porter ran out and tried to reach the gate but we were already tearing through the tunnel, shod hoofs echoing from the walls, and he jumped back as we clattered past. We were through. Bay Star stumbled once and for one appalling moment I thought I would go over her head, but she recovered and I kept my seat, and with scarcely a check, in a flurry of flying clods, we were making off along the track, turning westwards, towards Faldene and Westwater and, ultimately, the road to London.

It was five miles to Faldene and three more to Westwater at the far end of Faldene Vale. The road we wanted, which ran from Chichester to London by way of Guildford, was just beyond Westwater. It wasn't a main highway; in many places it was only a very rough chalk track, but it nevertheless boasted a few hostelries.

"There's a posting inn, two miles northwards from Westwater," I said, addressing the others as we thundered along, three abreast. "That's about ten miles altogether, from here."

"Well, we can't gallop all that way," Brockley replied.

We would certainly be pursued, so we galloped for a good distance to open up the best possible lead before reining back to let the horses get their breath.

It was agony to go slowly, though, and we all kept glancing uneasily back as though expecting the pursuit to burst into sight behind us. The horses sensed our uneasiness, and fretted to be given their heads. Soon, we were galloping once more, and we went through Faldene village flat out. Women came to their doors as we hurtled past and poultry scattered from the road before us. A cat which was washing peacefully in the middle of the track fled for its life and several dogs chased us, barking, for some distance.

We settled, eventually, to a steady canter. The hoofs pounded steadily on the damp earth of the path through the valley, under the trees whose leaves were showing the first autumn tints, and along the side of a stream.

"We may be able to change horses but we can't risk stopping to eat at the inn," I said to the others. "There should be food waiting for us in Bridget's cottage."

"How did you arrange that, madam?" Brockley asked.

Dale, who had been in the room when despite my pounding headache I gave Bridget her instructions, said admiringly, "You were so brave, ma'am. So ill, yet you didn't forget anything. Mr. Brockley, the mistress was wonderful."

"I'm sure she was," said Brockley, and in his voice I heard unmistakable affection for Dale. I had been right. They were attracted. "But just how did you do it, madam?" he asked.

"Before I left Faldene," I said, "I asked for Bridget to be brought there, to collect Meg, and I made up my mind to seize any chance I could of speaking to her without anyone else hearing, except Dale, of course. I was ill, yes, but I turned that to account." My last glimpse of Matthew haunted my mind's eye and I did not feel much like laughing, but the recollection of how I had managed my private word with Bridget did produce a faint amusement. "I moaned that I couldn't speak loudly—which was true—so beckoned her close and said it all in an undertone. I'd been trying to think ahead. I'm sure that Matthew wouldn't harm either of them, but I might arrive at court and find a message waiting to say that unless I held my tongue on what I know, Meg would be taken to France and I'd never see her again. Or else Uncle Herbert might snatch her for much the same purpose. No doubt he'll soon hear what's happened! I told Bridget, as soon as her escort had left her at the cottage, to take Meg on to Tom and Alice Juniper, and not let anyone know where they were going. They should be safe there. I also told her to leave some food, something that would keep, in her larder."

"That was well thought of, madam. *Very* well thought of, if I may say so. Is that Westwater, up there?"

The path had veered away from the stream and now led uphill towards a cluster of thatched roofs. "Yes. You'll recognise it in a moment," I said. "There's Bridget's cottage."

"West*water?* Where do they get their water from?"

"A well," I said. "Not from the stream, I'm thankful to say. I've seen a dead cow lying in that stream, in

285

the past. I thought Westwater would be healthy for Meg because the well water is so pure, but it was too near Faldene, after all. Here we are."

Bridget had done as I told her. We found the place empty; even the poultry had gone. It was useful that the cottage stood somewhat apart from the rest; our visit was unobserved. I dismounted and went in, and found that Bridget had left us a ham, some apples, half a loaf of the black rye bread which keeps so well, a cask of ale and a couple of empty flasks. My orders must have puzzled her, but she had certainly obeyed them. I filled the flasks with ale, found a basket, piled my booty into it, hurried outside again and handed the basket up to Dale. Brockley got down to help me remount, and then stopped short, gazing back the way we had come. "Look down there!" he said.

Standing as it did on a slope, Westwater looked down over the tops of the trees in the valley. They were old, mossy of trunk and massive of bough and most of the path along which we had just raced was hidden beneath them, but in one or two places it widened out and was open to the sky for a little way. Brockley pointed, and I glimpsed movement: the glint of a bridle, the flash of a brightly coloured cap. Riders were on the path behind us, moving at speed. They were little more than a mile away.

"That was quick," said Brockley grimly. "They must have had horses already saddled for some reason. Now what? Madam? You know the district well."

I nodded. "Follow me," I said.

I had lived all my life at Faldene and there wasn't a track, dell or spring for miles that I didn't know.

Brockley threw me up into the saddle and leaped into his own, and I led us at a canter, back down the hill to the woods and the stream. The stream was bordered on both sides by alders and its banks were steep for the most part, but there was one place where they sank somewhat, and it was possible for a horse to shoulder through the alders, get down to the stream, ford it and climb the further bank.

"This way!" I said.

"Hurry!" said Brockley. "They'll be here in minutes."

We pushed through in single file, to avoid damaging the alders more than we could help. Our ears were straining all the time for the sound of hoofbeats. Dale's mare, picking up fear from her mistress, almost balked at the ford but with Dale urging her, Brockley cursing her, and Bay Star to give her a lead, we got her to splash across after only a few moments' delay.

Once up the further bank and through another screen of alders, we were out of sight of the track, and a few yards further on, there was a little dell, surrounded by thick trees and undergrowth. Here I stopped. "We can't be seen from here. We have only to wait. Brockley, hold Bay Star for me. I want to creep back and watch them go by. I have a reason."

"But ma'am . . . !"

"Madam, I can't allow . . ."

"Be quiet, Dale, and yes you can, Brockley, and you will! I shan't be seen, don't worry."

Brockley made an exasperated gesture, of which I took no notice. I slid from my saddle and scrambled out of the dell, going back towards the stream. I paused for a few moments, hopping first on one foot and then on the other, to pull off shoes and stockings, then, kilting my skirts, I waded quickly over, to crouch behind the tangle of alders on the side nearest the track.

They were coming. I could hear the hoofbeats. At once I wished I hadn't ventured back. I had wanted to see if Matthew were with them, wanted to catch one last glimpse of him, but I had been a fool. I was sure

287

that I was hidden, but I was too near, too near. It was too late to change my mind. I shrank as the riders approached, pressing myself against the ground as though I were trying to burrow into it. They were coming fast, but as they came level with my hiding place, someone shouted that he could see Westwater village, and they all slowed to a jog.

"The child lives there with her nurse. I know the cottage; I took them back there! Maybe the nurse'll know something!" That was the voice of one of the Withysham grooms, evidently the man who had escorted Bridget and Meg away from Faldene.

Well, the cottage was empty. They wouldn't be able to frighten Bridget or Meg. I froze as the riders crossed my line of vision. There were six altogether. Withysham was full of grooms and manservants. Third in the line was Matthew. He was close enough to recognise although I couldn't see his face plainly, but as he went past me, I saw him raise his left hand to brush at his left eye.

He could have been rubbing away a piece of grit thrown up by the hoofs but he wasn't. When anyone rubs an eye to clear a speck of dirt away, they do so in a distinctive way, sometimes quite rough. When they brush away tears, it is a different movement, gentler.

I had wanted to see him, one last time. I wished I hadn't. I had expected Matthew to ride after me in anger and fear. Now I saw that he was also riding after me in grief. I muffled my own tears against the ground and stayed like that until the riders were gone.

I crept back across the stream. I dried my wet feet as best I could on my skirts, put on my stockings and shoes again and returned to the others. I knew by the way they looked at me that my feelings were written on my face, but they didn't comment. "They're trying the cottage," I said. "They'll find it empty, and after that, I imagine they'll ride on. They'll be ahead of us on the road."

"That means the inn's impossible even for a change of horses," Brockley said. "Even if we wait until they come back, they might alert the innkeeper. God knows what they'll say!"

"That I'm a runaway wife who has stolen her husband's money, I expect," I said acidly. "Unfortunately, I'm actually carrying some, though it's mine, not his. But there is another possibility." I must not think about Matthew, must not think of that hand, secretly brushing his eyes. "These woods," I told them, "they extend some distance. We can get through them to the Chichester to London road, *south* of here. I doubt if the search will turn south. It'll go north, towards London. Once across, there are ways round among the downs and there are a few remote farms. One of them might shelter us for the night. We can travel on next morning."

I remounted, and we set off. As we did so, Brockley, who had been scanning my unhappy face with some anxiety, suddenly remarked, "We've done very well so far, madam. I think we made a most elegant escape."

"Elegant?" I turned to him. He was now wearing his most expressionless face, with only a gleam in his eyes to tell me that he was laughing.

"Very," he said. "At the start, much depended, did it not, on all of us putting our horses from a standstill into a gallop? The men setting out the gardens came to watch several times, not just today. I had Dale practising the art for three mornings, right under everyone's noses!"

He was trying to make me feel better and to some degree he succeeded. Dale's riding lessons *had* been a piece of most satisfactory cunning. I found that I could smile, just a little.

We crossed the road safely, and found a sheltered

Fiona Buckley

place, in a fold of the downs on the other side, to dismount and eat a meal of sorts while the horses grazed. Then we went on again and as evening drew near we sought beds at a farm, using the old excuse that we had attempted a short cut and lost our way.

The farmer had two sons and a grown-up daughter, and they all clearly wondered why we were trying short cuts when the road was perfectly straight, and found our lack of saddlebags suspicious, but a couple of gold angels worked miracles. They invited us to share their supper and gave us pallets in a loft room. I didn't sleep much. My reawakened body cried in the darkness for the company of Matthew's body. But Matthew was not there and would never be there again.

In the morning we started off again. We avoided Guildford, in case the pursuit had gone on along the road in that direction. This meant making a detour and for a while we missed our way. It took all day to reach Windsor.

When we arrived there, Brockley and Dale were surprised that I would not let us present ourselves at the castle forthwith, insisting instead that we take rooms at an inn.

Puzzled, Brockley said, "Are you not not intending to report to her majesty, then, madam?"

"Not at once," I said. "And when I do, I'll begin, I think, with Sir William Cecil."

§17§

The Card House

I prepared carefully for my return to the court. Dale washed and brushed my hair and packed it smoothly into the net I had been wearing under my hat, and she shook out and brushed all our clothes. Attended by maid and manservant as a lady should be, I arrived at the castle in the early morning, and asked for an audience with the Secretary of State.

The moment I was within the castle walls, the court atmosphere surrounded me, scented with herbs, musty with the smell of the elaborate fabrics on the walls and on the people, full of movement and bustle. It was invigoratingly alive and also, to me, curiously steadying because for some reason I felt at home there.

All the same, reaching Sir William Cecil took some time. I was passed from one official to another, and made to wait in one anteroom after another, until at length, I arrived at a most obstructive and patronising senior clerk who explained to me, as though I were a child, that the Secretary of State was a very busy man and that if I had anything of importance to say—his

expression told me that he found this hard to believe—then I could say it to him.

"I am one of her majesty's ladies," I said. "If I am
refused admittance to Sir William, then I will make
my report to her majesty. But it should properly be to
Sir William Cecil and if he learns through her majesty
that you have refused even to let him know that I wish
to speak to him, you may be reprimanded. Will you
please at least inform him that Mistress Ursula Blanchard wishes to see him—and that in so doing, I am
keeping a promise which I made to him and to Lady
Mildred when they kindly entertained me in their
private quarters!"

I was pleased to see that this haughty speech had
taken him aback. We were asked to wait in another
anteroom, where several clerks, working at desks
under the windows, eyed us all with interest. A leggy
young page came to fetch me. Dale and Brockley must
remain in the anteroom, he said, but if I would come
this way, Sir William would see me. A moment later, I
was in the Secretary of State's private office.

It was a big room, panelled in light brown wood.
The windows faced south-east and at this time of day
let in the October sunlight which streamed through
the leaded panes and cast silvery-gold criss-cross
patterns across the floor. It was pleasant. All the same,
I was uneasy. I stood beside one of the windows, now
and then glancing out. On this fine day, the courtyard
below was well populated. Ladies and courtiers
strolled; a messenger was led quickly across to an
entrance; a man I recognised as the Lord Treasurer,
William Paulet, sauntered by with the Under-
Treasurer, Sir Richard Sackville, and Sir Thomas
Smith, except that Smith lumbered rather than sauntered.

There was grass in the centre of the courtyard, and

in the midst of this, Lady Catherine Grey stood talking to Lady Jane Seymour and Jane's brother Lord Hertford. The three of them were trying to teach a rather dimwitted small pup to beg for titbits.

When I first came to the court, the Cecils had said I should come to them if ever I needed help, and in order to see him, I had reminded Cecil of that promise. However, here in his office, listening to a tale of treason, he was not quite the same as the Cecil to whom I gave that undertaking. Seated behind his desk, with his shelves of books and papers behind him, dressed in workaday russet but with a massive gold chain across his chest to proclaim his authority, he was very much the Secretary of State: judicial, dispassionate and chilly of eye. The lines on his face seemed now to be not so much anxious as harsh.

"Let me be clear on what you have told me, Mistress . . . Blanchard or de la Roche?"

"Legally my correct title is Mistress de la Roche, but I would prefer still to be known as Mistress Blanchard."

"Very well. So, Mistress Blanchard, your servant John Wilton was set upon near an inn called"—he consulted the notes he had been taking and dipped a quill in readiness to make corrections—"the Cockspur, close to Maidenhead. He was carried to the inn and died there. You were sent for and came in time to hear him whisper details which suggested that his assailants were not footpads, but three seeming gentlemen whom he had met on the road. You then set out to find these gentlemen and traced them to a number of large houses—manor houses mainly—where, however, no one wished to talk about them. You believe that some of these places were Catholic in their sympathy. You are reluctant to say which houses they were. Would you care to reconsider that?"

"If you find those three men, John's killers," I said,

"William Johnson, Mr. Brett and Mr. Fletcher—those are their names—then I daresay they will give you that information."

"Indeed they will, Mistress Blanchard." Cecil did not say it cruelly or lingeringly. He said it in an almost dismissive tone which was even more chilling. If arrested, Johnson, Brett and Fletcher would talk. They would have no choice in the matter and that was that.

"I would rather not name those households myself," I said. "I like some of those families. I think they believed they were just helping to finance priests and religious teachings. I *can't* believe they mean harm to her majesty."

"I think you could trust us to be judges of that. However, as you say, the information may well be forthcoming elsewhere. I will not press you now. Your womanly feelings no doubt do you credit," said Cecil. "To continue. You eventually traced—you seem to have quite a gift for investigation, Mistress Blanchard—these men to Withysham in Sussex where you found that their employer was none other than Matthew de la Roche, a remote cousin of Arundel who visited him at Richmond last summer and was, I hear, paying his addresses to you. Was Arundel's name mentioned in connection with this business?"

"No, Sir William."

"I'm relieved to hear it. I've always thought him an honest man, though I know the younger courtiers find him funny. In the days of Queen Mary, you know, when our present queen was the Princess Elizabeth and was accused of plotting against her sister, Arundel was one of her interrogators. But her youth and desperation touched his heart."

For a moment, the dispassionate Secretary of State had softened. "He went down on one knee," Cecil said, "in the middle of questioning her, and said that he could see she was telling the truth and was sorry to trouble her so. I would hate to think that he had turned traitor now. However, de la Roche may have used him as a means of discovering possible supporters among the nobility. Arundel is essentially Catholic himself; he would know who else is, although that's a digression. Now, you also discovered that your Uncle Herbert and Aunt Tabitha at Faldene have had dealings with de la Roche and his trio of associates, Johnson, Brett and Fletcher. You are willing to name your Faldene relatives, I notice."

"I can scarcely avoid it," I said quietly. "It was through my uncle's account books that I confirmed the truth. I accept that I must name them, though it's very unpleasant to think of any member of one's own family being arrested for treason, although they did steal my daughter," I added.

For the first time, Cecil let himself smile a little. "Your daughter is safe and you are not at heart vindictive? Be easy. From what you say, the number of people who have been talked into making contributions may be quite large. We can hardly clap them all in the Tower. Most will just be fined. For the rest—though they may include your uncle—a short stay in the Tower may be thought sufficient. It's the big fat salmon we want. Matthew de la Roche is one of them but I daresay he is now making good his escape to France. There are ways of avoiding the main ports," he said. "If he does escape, will you be glad or sorry?"

"Glad," I said.

"Even though you were forced into marrying him?"

"He thought marriage would bind me to him. That's why I agreed to it. I knew I would be watched, but I thought I would have just a little more chance of escape as his wife than as his prisoner, and I think I

295

was right. He was right, too, in a way. It did bind me to him, though not as tightly as he hoped—I'm here, after all—but I think I should tell you that I arrived in Windsor the day before yesterday. My servants and I went to an inn and waited there for a day. I did it to give Matthew a chance. I hope to God that my husband is by now either on the Channel or already in France. The weather is calm, fortunately."

Cecil's eyebrows shot up in astonishment and his eyes became cold. "You deliberately delayed to give this traitor a chance of escape?"

"Is he really a traitor?" I asked. "He was reared in France. I suppose he might say his loyalties lie there."

"He had taken up residence in England. He is a traitor as far as I am concerned! What were you thinking of, Mistress . . . de la Roche would seem to be the most appropriate name!"

"Of my husband," I said. "He *is* my husband. I have slept in his bed, in his arms. I have known his body. The bodies of traitors are cut open alive and . . . what wife would abandon her husband to that? Yes, I pray he has escaped."

Cecil gazed at me steadily, as though he were trying to fathom the workings of my mind, then he replaced his quill in its holder and leaned back in his chair. "You are really in love with him, then."

"Yes," I said, "and I'm *married* to him. I've been torn apart." I turned to look down into the courtyard once again, unable to meet those too-penetrating blue eyes. "I had the choice between betraying her majesty and betraying my husband. I chose her majesty. I have told you how we hid and how I saw the pursuit go past. I saw Matthew's face. He is still in love with me, too. He was *grieving*. Am I a good citizen, I wonder, or merely a faithless wife?"

"But you *were* compelled into the marriage?"

"Virtually, yes."

"A vow, of marriage or anything else, is not valid if extracted under duress. Whatever your emotions, Mistress . . . er . . ."

"Blanchard, please. I prefer Blanchard."

"I suppose I must say that once again your womanly—in this case your wifely—feelings do you credit." Cecil allowed his features, once more, to relax into an austere smile. "But rest assured, Mistress Blanchard, that you do not owe Master de la Roche the duties of a wife. We can probably get you an annulment. You most certainly did right. Have no doubt of that."

I was silent. He reached for his notes again and glanced through them. "You chose not only her majesty," he said, "but the safety of England. Remember that. The queen will certainly be grateful to you for the sake of her people as well as herself. Now . . . you say that Johnson, Brett and Fletcher were sent away from Withysham before the marriage took place, at your insistence, and that they went to the midlands. You doubt if de la Roche can warn them of your defection in time for them to get away as well."

"Yes. The midlands are a long way from the coast. Even if Matthew's messengers have found them already, and that's not particularly likely, there's a good chance of catching them before they have a chance to reach the sea."

"I fancy you are correct." Cecil spoke with satisfaction. "Messengers will be on their way to both the midlands and the home counties today and the proclamations will be read out in many places before nightfall, tomorrow morning at latest. They will name and describe the wanted men and offer rewards. Our friends will find it hard to slip through the net I mean to spread for them. We must forgive the day of grace you have given Master de la Roche. I can understand your sense of guilt towards him. I hope we can now put a stop to a very dangerous movement. I shall have agents alert for traces of other fundraisers in other parts of the country. As I said, an annulment may well be possible."

I nodded. Even to talk of Matthew brought him back to me so vividly that I could hardly keep my eyes from filling, but I must not break down in this businesslike room. Besides, there were other things to be discussed. "There is another matter I must mention," I said. "It's about Sir Robin Dudley."

"About Dudley?"

"Yes. I imagine that gossip has continued, despite the verdict at the inquest, but I believe he was innocent." I told him of the letter I had seen and he listened thoughtfully, nodding his head from time to time in agreement.

"I agree with your conclusions, I admit. I must say you have a subtle mind, Mistress Blanchard."

"I know that there are many who would like to see Dudley discredited," I said, and recalled Sir Thomas Smith making a remark about a horse-master swanking about in ermine, although I didn't repeat it. Half the court had heard it, anyway. "Some would like to see the queen discredited too," I said seriously. "During the last few days, I have met people who hope, even now, that her majesty will marry Dudley and outrage public opinion so much that it will give Mary Stuart a chance. I am telling you this, Sir William, in case you can, well, warn her."

Cecil nodded. "I will pass on what you say. And now, Mistress . . . Blanchard, I think you should return at once to your duties with her majesty. It will distract your mind from . . . anything from which it needs to be distracted."

Such as Matthew. I kept on having to look away to hide my feelings. I wondered if Cecil realised why I continually turned to the window. Did he think I was so fascinated by the people in the courtyard that I could not attend to him properly? I must stop this. However, just as I was about to return my gaze to Cecil, I noticed a man whom I recognised coming out of a door into the courtyard. I stiffened in surprise, and then in more surprise still as he walked up to Lady Catherine Grey and spoke to her, and she moved away from her companions to talk to him.

"Sir William," I said, "please—could you come and look? I want to know who that man is, down there, talking to Lady Catherine Grey. At least, I know his name. I just want to know who he *is*, if you understand me."

Cecil obligingly rose and stepped round the desk to see. "Which man do you mean? Peter Holme?"

"Yes, that's the one."

"He's one of Lady Catherine's household—he runs messages, performs errands. Why?"

It was like that moment in the inn yard of the Cockspur, when the ostler spoke of the piebald horse and my brain made an instant connection between the word "piebald" and John's half-heard whisper of the syllable "bald." Things hitherto unconnected slid together, whirled in my head and settled into a pattern.

It was too soon to speak of it to Cecil.

"I just wondered," I said. "I've seen him about quite often and never been quite sure where he fitted, that's all. He seems to talk to so many different people."

"Really? You know, Mistress Blanchard, you are a remarkable young woman." Cecil sat down again, linking his hands on the desk before him. "Your name means a she-bear but you remind me of a gaze-hound. You have only to glimpse something that intrigues you, and you are off on the hunt. You have wept for this treasonous husband of yours, have you not? Your eyes are tired and the lids are heavy. I have daughters!

But at the sight of Peter Holme, you changed, as though you had just drunk strong wine. What is it that interests you about him?"

I was being ridiculous. It *couldn't* be. The shape which for a moment I thought I had glimpsed through a confusion of odd little facts couldn't really be there. "I'm sorry," I said. "I'm making a fool of myself, but in the summer, I did see Holme about the court and—" I thought quickly—"and just for a moment, I thought I had recognised him as someone I saw at Withysham. But I'm wrong. Now that I look at him again, I can see that it's not the same man at all. One of the men at Withysham was a similar type, that's all. Sir William, these last few days have taken their toll of me. Could I sit down for a few minutes?"

"Of course." Cecil eyed me doubtfully and gestured me to a stool. "You may well be feeling out of sorts. A restorative would do you no harm."

He went to the door to call for wine, and I sat on the stool and concentrated on my spinning thoughts. Amid the chaos, the half-perceived shape was still there.

Suppose Amy had been murdered after all. If so, then her killers were surely Verney and Holme. Although Verney was Dudley's man he was not, in this case, acting for Dudley. Of that I was sure. That letter had revealed Dudley's mind to me completely and Cecil agreed with my conclusions. Dudley was no victimised saint, but he hadn't had his wife killed. Too careful of his own skin, probably! His father and one of his brothers had died on the block; he knew what the shadow of the axe was like.

In that case, Verney and Holme were acting for someone else. And Holme was Lady Catherine Grey's man.

However much Lady Catherine Grey, the Protestant heir, wished to remain the heir, however passionately she hoped that the queen would never have children, however fiercely she hated the idea of giving place to the upstart Dudley's offspring, could she possibly, all alone, have hatched such a scheme?

I didn't think so. And there inside my head, I saw a little scene. A morning in Richmond Park. Myself, walking with the Spanish ambassador, de Quadra. A few yards away, Peter Holme was walking with Sir Thomas Smith and Edward Stanley, Earl of Derby, and de Quadra was drawing my attention to them. De Quadra was a wary man. If he wasn't sure of his facts, he might well hesitate to speak openly. Had he, obliquely, been trying to warn me of danger from those three? Of danger, perhaps, to Amy?

Cecil came back to his desk and a moment later the leggy page brought some wine. I sipped it, obliged now to take my time and look suitably wan, when every fibre in my body wanted to rush to the court-yard and accost Lady Catherine Grey.

By the time I had finally left Cecil's office, gathered up Brockley and Dale from the anteroom and made my way down to the courtyard, Lady Catherine Grey had disappeared, although Lady Jane Seymour and Lord Hertford were still talking together and petting the dog, which evidently belonged to Jane. I made straight for them and asked where I might find Lady Catherine.

"Ursula! You're back!" Lady Jane Seymour greeted me with pleasure.

"Yes, as you see." I didn't want to stop and talk, however, still less discuss my experiences at Cumnor. "Just now," I said, "I urgently need to speak to Lady Catherine. Has she gone to the queen?"

"No, the queen's out hunting in the park. Catherine hasn't been very well lately," said Jane. "She decided not to go."

"Not well? What's the matter with her?" Jane was the one, I thought, who was fragile. Before her last illness, my mother had had that transparent skin and hectic colour, more like a red stain than a glow of health. I was sorry to see it on Jane, who was a likeable girl.

"No particular illness," said Lord Hertford worriedly. Jane's brother was a pleasant young man, although he struck me as somewhat vacillating. "She seems melancholy," he said, "and has at times felt too weak to get up for two or three days at a time."

"We try to keep her amused. Any kind of sad news distresses her," Jane said. "She cried for days when she heard of Lady Dudley's death, although she had never met her. My brother here has been quite anxious."

"She is so sensitive and warmhearted," said Lord Hertford.

A more unlikely description of Lady Catherine Grey I could hardly imagine. If Lord Hertford wasn't a simpleton, I decided, he must be besotted, or else Jane had been working hard on him on Lady Catherine's behalf. "I will look for her in her rooms," I said.

I went indoors with Dale and Brockley, wondering how to gain admittance to Lady Catherine. She didn't think very much of me and might well decline to see me. I shared my problem with the others, however, and Dale offered a suggestion.

"Oh, ma'am, she'll surely see you if you say it's the queen's business. It is, I suppose?" Dale was longing to know what all this was about. Brockley shushed her reprovingly.

"It's the queen's business, yes," I said. This I could not share with either of them. "Once again," I said, "you will have to await me in an anteroom."

The ploy was successful. The maid who opened Lady Catherine's door withdrew to give my message but reappeared after a moment and let me in. In a luxurious but closed-in chamber, with too many hangings and too much clutter on the toilet table, Lady Catherine was seated on a stool with her mousy-fair tresses loose on her shoulders. The maid had evidently been brushing them. It was true that Lady Catherine was pale, I thought. She regarded me with languid impatience.

"So here you are again, Mistress Blanchard, and you're hardly back, it seems, before you are running confidential errands for her majesty. How can I help this particular errand?"

"It's delicate," I said. "I think it best if I speak to you in complete privacy, Lady Catherine. You will agree, once you hear what it concerns."

Lady Catherine jerked her head, and the maid, a downtrodden, tired sort of woman, well paid, no doubt, but probably much nagged, left the room. "Well," said Lady Catherine, tossing back her hair. "What is all this about?"

"It's about Peter Holme," I said. "He came to Cumnor Place with Sir Richard Verney. I have also seen him—indeed, had him pointed out to me—in the company of Sir Thomas Smith and the Earl of Derby, Edward Stanley. Tell me, how much do you know, Lady Catherine, about the death of Amy Dudley?"

I don't know exactly what reaction I expected. After all, it was perfectly possible that I was wrong; that the pattern I thought I had seen was accidental, like the patterns of the constellations in the night sky, in which case she would be naturally amazed and indignant. On the other hand, I might be right. If so, I had supposed that she would fence with me, ask me what I was talking about, and perhaps present such a blank wall of incomprehension, real or pretended, that I might never know for certain whether I had guessed the truth, or not.

What I didn't expect her to do was to collapse like a badly constructed house of cards. She stared at me and began to tremble, while her mouth sagged open. Then it stiffened into an unbecoming square, and she started to bawl. I stepped forward, seized her shoulders and shook her. "Stop that noise! You'll have half the court in here! I wonder if Amy cried like this when she was about to be murdered?"

Not altogether to my surprise, this produced an even louder bawling, which rose to a shriek. I shook her again and put my palm over her mouth until she stopped. Her eyes, huge and blue and terrified, peered at me over my hand.

"Now," I said. "I'm going to let go, but keep quiet."

I released her, and she sat there with her hair trailing wildly and tears trickling down her blanched face, looking, I thought, less like the heir to the throne than a young but very guilty witch on her execution morning. "I repeat," I said, "what do you know about the death of Amy Dudley?"

Much too late, she tried to regain lost territory.

"How dare you come in here like this and shout at me and bully me? I don't know what you're talking about. I haven't been well; I'm easily confused. I . . ."

"Do you usually burst into tears and shriek aloud when someone asks you a simple question? That's all I did—just ask. I wasn't shouting and I wasn't bullying. Now, I'll ask you again. *What do you know about the death of Amy Dudley?* Oh, come along, Lady Catherine. Don't tell me again that you don't know what I mean."

"But I don't. I don't!"

"I was living at Cumnor Place when she died." I said. "Now, listen."

I gave her the whole story, as far as Amy Dudley

was concerned, from the beginning, from the moment when I first saw Peter Holme in Richmond Park. I told her how Verney and Holme had visited Cumnor and how they nearly rode me down on my way back from Abingdon Fair; and, in graphic detail, I told her about Amy's illness, and her desperate prayers, and how she had asked to be left alone so that the murderers whose existence she had surmised, might put her out of her pain. And how she had looked, lying at the foot of the stairs.

"I can only hope," I said, "that she didn't, at the last, cry out in fear and struggle for her life. But for all her brave words, I should think that being ill and in pain would make violence harder to bear, not easier. Most people, when it comes to it, would rather die in their beds than be murdered."

Lady Catherine Grey didn't want to hear. Once, she put her hands over her ears, but I seized her wrists and jerked them down again, telling her that no, she would listen, whether she liked it or not.

At the end, I stood back and leaned against the toilet table, arms folded. "Well, *Lady* Catherine. So what is it you know? You helped to arrange it, didn't you? You're the Protestant heir. You would like to remain the heir, was that it? You were afraid Lady Dudley would soon die naturally—yes? I'm on the right track, am I not?—and that the queen and Dudley would then marry and produce a child to be heir instead of you? So you conspired to make sure that Lady Dudley died *un*naturally and scandalously, instead . . ."

"It wasn't like that!"

"Then what was it like?"

"Oh, God!" wept Lady Catherine, wringing her hands. I watched this with interest, because although I had heard of people doing this, I had never before seen a demonstration.

305

"I'm waiting," I said.

"Don't tell anyone! Promise you won't tell anyone! Lord Hertford would be so horrified and he ... we ... hope ..."

"To be married? Never mind that now. You wanted Lady Dudley to die, did you not? And not of her disease?"

"No one could have wanted her to die of her disease! She was so very ill, and in pain—you know she was, you saw her, you've just told me all about it!" Lady Catherine was gabbling. "It was a kindness, really."

"Like putting down a sick dog? But you never saw her. Did someone tell you that it would be a kindness? You never mounted this little plot all on your own, did you? Who else was in it? The Earl of Derby? Sir Thomas Smith?"

"I shan't name any names," said Lady Catherine, with an attempt at dignity. I laughed.

"You need not. Didn't I just say that I saw Peter Holme with those two? As a matter of fact, the Spanish ambassador noticed them as well. He drew my attention to them. He knew something. Things get about in this court. A few words overheard at a card game; someone seen in unexpected company too often and the rumours start. Derby and Smith were together quite a lot; it was such an odd combination that people remarked on it. Maybe Holme was seen with them and perhaps with Sir Richard Verney too, and I know that Holme and Verney went to Cumnor more than once. Lady Dudley told me that. Someone somewhere began to add things together.

"Sir Thomas Smith," I said thoughtfully, "detests Dudley, and so does the Earl of Derby. Smith wants the queen to make a good Protestant marriage and Derby wants her to make a Catholic one and you

306

don't want her to make one at all, but you all, equally, regarded Dudley as a threat, unless he could be ruined by a good scandal. Who thought of the scheme first and approached the others? You may as well tell me, Lady Catherine. The queen will make you tell, anyway."

"Not the queen!" Catherine squealed in fright. "No, you can't, you mustn't! She hates me already!" She dissolved into sobs, but coherent words did presently emerge. "It wasn't real! Until I heard it had actually happened, it wasn't real! I didn't know how I'd feel. I've had nightmares every night since! I dream someone's creeping up in the dark to kill me in my bed. I didn't know it would be like this! It wasn't real, I tell you!"

No wonder she'd seemed unwell lately. Reality had come home to her, crashed on her head like a falling brick, when it was too late. I thought she was only just beginning to see that she had stepped on to a road which might lead to the Tower or the block. Her sister, Lady Jane Grey, had died under the axe at the age of sixteen, because their parents, especially her mother, Lady Frances Grey, Henry VIII's fiercely ambitious niece, had tried to challenge Queen Mary Tudor's right to the throne, and put Jane there instead.

The same plot had led to the deaths of Robin Dudley's father and his brother Guildford. Their father had married Guildford to Jane in the hope of seeing his son become king. That should have given Catherine a sense of self-preservation, as it had done to her brother-in-law Robin. But no, it seemed that she had to be caught out first, before it belatedly occurred to her that the paths of ambition had risks.

"What was Sir Richard Verney's motive?" I asked with interest. "I know Dudley treats him rudely, and he strikes me as a proud man. He's also a gambler and

Fiona Buckley

constantly in debt. Did he join in for money? I fancy money was what bought Anthony Forster's help, in Cumnor Place."

"It all began as a joke!" wailed Lady Catherine.

"A joke? Lady Catherine, Amy was found dead at the foot of a flight of stairs, with her neck broken!"

Lady Catherine continued to blubber. Through it, I understood her to say that Derby and Sir Thomas had really thought of it first, and she had become part of it because she happened to say, in jest—"only in jest, that's all, that's all!"—that it would be quite a good thing if someone were to arrange for Amy to die in a way that would make everyone think Dudley responsible because that would put an end to his ambitions.

"Just tell me," I said, "in order and calmly, if you can. Tell me how it all came about. Now's your chance to put yourself in a good light, if there is one!"

She stared at me with hatred, but she did as I said. It was informative. I had never before asked myself how a conspiracy might come into being, how whispered hints became practical action; how "if only this or that would happen" might change into "let's see that it does."

Here was my answer. Once more, I saw the spoor of treason, saw how it prowled from one victim to another, a predator of fair aspect, sinking its teeth in the foolish prey who let it approach and tried to stroke it.

"We . . . we were just talking," Lady Catherine stammered. "In the anteroom one morning, waiting for the queen to appear. I mean, I was talking to Sir Thomas and to Derby. They . . . they said they had already been thinking about Dudley and the queen, and Amy, and that with the illness Amy had, it would be a mercy if she died soon and hardly a crime to end it for her, and . . ."

"Yes, and?"

308

"I asked if they were serious." Lady Catherine unconsciously favoured me with precisely the big-eyed, limpid gaze which she must have turned on to Sir Thomas and Derby. "And Derby said, well, are *you*? So I said, yes, only of course, I couldn't possibly arrange a thing like that, and then Derby said, God help you if ever you repeat this, but it could be done, only we need some reliable agents to do the . . . to do . . ."

"The actual work," I said, substituting the word "actual" for the word "dirty" at the last moment.

"Yes. And that's when I offered them Holme's services. Holme will do anything for me. He's my half-brother."

"Your what?"

"Half-brother. He's a love-child. My father acknowledged him and paid for his education but his mother died when he was small and I don't think her family were very kind to him."

This, I thought, explained Holme's odd air of being just, but only just, a gentleman. So he was illegitimate, and his mother's family hadn't been kind to him. That hit home as far as I was concerned. I knew what that was like. "But he's in your service now?" I said.

"Yes. His mother's family sent him to me when he was a boy. I didn't want him at first, but when he came, I liked him. I was nice to him, and he adores me," said Lady Catherine defiantly.

"Quite. So you agreed to help Sir Thomas Smith and the Earl of Derby in the scheme they were hatching, and told Holme to take their orders? Did you offer money too?"

"I paid Peter. The others hired Verney. They paid Forster, as well. That was for, well, making it easy to reach Lady Dudley. You see . . ." said Lady Catherine, trembling hands clutched together in a fold of embroidered satin underskirt, "to begin with—Sir Thomas told me this—the idea was to get *Forster* to do it. They asked Verney to sound him out. Verney was in on the scheme from the start, long before I was. He had terrible debts. Gambling debts, I mean—you were right about that. He owed Derby a lot, as a matter of fact. Derby said he would wipe out the debts as part of the payment if Verney would help him in a scheme to benefit the realm by spoiling Dudley's ambitions. Verney was only too willing. Yes, he did—does—resent Dudley's manner towards him. He'd often been to Cumnor on errands for Dudley and he knows Forster quite well. He said Forster would do anything for money . . ."

"Just as I supposed," I said, thinking of the money which had undoubtedly gone into Forster's pocket rather than into Lady Dudley's furnishings or food. "Dudley clearly has some shockingly disloyal servants. How thankful I am that neither Verney nor Forster are in *my* employment! Well? Please do go on."

"Forster couldn't do it," Lady Catherine said. "He tried, though this was before I came into it, of course, and I never heard all the details. But . . ."

"He tried poison, I take it. Lady Dudley told me she had had bouts of sickness and pains in her limbs."

"I think, from what Derby said, that Forster didn't know how much to give to make it look like illness. There was some doctor or other who got suspicious and started to spread rumours."

"Dr. Bayly," I said. So Amy had been right. She had only been mistaken in thinking that Dudley was responsible.

"In the end, Forster backed off and said he wouldn't do more than just leave doors open! That almost put a stop to the whole thing," Lady Catherine said.

She had become interested now in what she was

saying, almost to the point of forgetting that it was a confession. She was an extremely stupid young woman. Recalling the limited nature of Anthony Forster's support, she sounded positively aggrieved.

"You mean," I said, "that Forster wasn't willing actually to break Lady Dudley's neck with his own well-washed hands?"

"Why must you put things in such a nasty way?"

"They're such nasty things! I'm glad to hear that Forster has some traces of a conscience! Perhaps the fact that he's actually Dudley's treasurer weighed with him just a little!"

Lady Catherine looked at me as though I had kicked her, and said sulkily, "We had endless trouble with Forster. At one point—this was later—he wanted a contract, a promise of payment in writing, with my signature on it, and Sir Thomas's and Derby's too. And that was just for . . . for making the job easy for others!"

"Yes, I know he wanted a contract," I said and she stared at me, wrinkling her forehead.

"You can't have known!"

"You'd be surprised. Well, go on. Forster wouldn't soil his hands. What happened next?"

"They—Sir Thomas and Derby—wanted Verney to do it but Verney was difficult. He was offered good money as well as having his debts cancelled, but he refused to act alone."

"How dreadfully annoying!"

"They were still wondering what to do," Catherine said, "when I made my little joke—that's all I meant it to be, just a joke! I mentioned Holme, and said he'd do anything I asked him to, and Derby suggested that I ask him to help Verney. Sir Thomas was against bringing me into it at first. He doesn't have a high opinion of women," Lady Catherine explained.

I thought it possible that he simply didn't have a

high opinion of Lady Catherine. "Tell me," I said. "Did you talk all this out in an *anteroom?* With other people about?"

"No. After . . . after I'd seen that they were serious and they'd seen that I was, Derby said we must talk privately and he settled a time for us to meet in the walled garden. Sir Thomas objected but Derby overrode him. I was rather frightened," said Lady Catherine, as if expecting me to sympathise, "but I went, anyway, and Sir Thomas said all right, we'd got to have Holme; we needed him. A few days later, we managed to walk together for a while when we were strolling in the park with the queen, and I was able to tell them that Holme had agreed."

"They never thought of doing the job themselves, I see!"

"They couldn't," said Lady Catherine, quite scornfully. "They're well-known men; they couldn't risk being seen in the district at the crucial time. Besides . . . well, I don't know about Derby, but Sir Thomas said, at that meeting in the garden, that he could never do such a thing personally; that, in fact, he'd been considering urging us to give up the whole idea. He'd only changed his mind again because Sir William Cecil came back from Scotland just then and the queen hardly even noticed Cecil, because she was so taken up with Dudley. Sir Thomas said that when he saw that, he knew we'd have to go on with it, because something had to be done; sheer loyalty to the queen demanded it."

"God help us all!" I said wanly.

"Verney and Holme made a good partnership," Lady Catherine said. "Verney is Dudley's man. He could visit Cumnor quite freely, and Holme could go as his servant. They went a couple of times, to talk over ways and means with Forster."

I stood there, as upright of body as I wished Lady

Catherine to think I was upright of mind, and longed to sit down and put my head between my knees. The court, which I had found so exciting, where I had felt so at home, was suddenly full of evil, populated by ugly creatures who spun webs for each other and baited them with jewelled lies about the good of the realm and the demands of loyalty and a merciful release for a sick woman.

These creatures danced and dined, laughed and made music, and entered into bloody alliances, and wallowed in hatreds so intense that if it happened that they all hated the same person, the fact that their reasons were utterly different, even in opposition, could not keep them from combining to destroy him. The worst of it was . . .

Lady Catherine said it for me. She had some Tudor shrewdness after all. She had seen the one thing which might save her.

"If this ever becomes public," she said, "if it is ever put about that Lady Dudley was murdered after all, *no one* will believe that the queen and Dudley were not in the plot. And if we're all put in the Tower or . . . or . . ."

"Beheaded?" I said helpfully. I had never detested even William Johnson and his friends as much as I detested this female worm. She gasped when I said "beheaded," and then began to cry again but I was unmoved. "You were saying? Even if you and presumably Smith, Derby, Verney, Holme and Forster are all arrested and possibly executed . . ."

"Don't say that!" Lady Catherine almost shrieked. "Don't you see? If we're all . . . all accused, then the tale will be out. Everyone will say we're just scapegoats and that will just make the scandal worse!"

I remembered again what Amy Dudley had said. Ordinary people, in alehouses and round wellheads and dinner tables, were not good at working things out. Those ordinary people would look at once for the simplest, most obvious explanation—and, yes, for the dirtiest.

Amy had been quite right, and so was Catherine.

I saw no reason to let her take comfort in it, though. Like someone pulling a blanket off a slugabed on a very cold morning, I said, primly, "I can't keep all this to myself. I think I must speak to Cecil, and the queen will certainly have to know." Then I walked out.

As I closed the door I heard her burst into tears of terror, although I could not pity her. But for the wicked scheme in which this silly moppet had been involved, John Wilton might still have been alive.

Whenever I thought of Matthew, I too wanted to cry, even louder than Catherine. I, too, needed sympathy, and I had not plotted murder.

§18§

An Instinct for
Conspiracy

It was rare for anyone to be alone with the queen, but
she had summoned me to this small room at Windsor,
at the end of a gallery in her private quarters. There
was little furniture beyond a chest, a chair and a few
cushions on the deep window seat. If Elizabeth wanted
to see anyone alone, she had, in every palace, places
like this in which to do so. People were within call,
outside the door, but we could not be heard unless we
shouted.

I had gone back to Cecil and told him of my
remarkable interview with Lady Catherine and we
had made our report to Elizabeth together. I had been
surprised, a few days later, to be bidden to this private
audience. Soon, she would be giving a public one and
I would be among her attendants there and we were
both formally dressed, though in contrasting fashion.
I was in black velvet, not as mourning, not nowadays,
but as a foil for the white silk, silver-embroidered
sleeves which had taken me all summer to make.
Elizabeth was in thickly embroidered peach silk, her
narrow waist clasped by a wide Spanish farthingale,

her pointed chin framed, like my own, in a linen ruff, although her ruff was bigger.

We were a contrast in another way, too, for while I stood quietly, hands clasped at my waist, Elizabeth, despite the weight of her gown, was pacing stormily back and forth across the little room. The window looked out on to the Berkshire countryside, green and rolling and peaceful. The queen could hardly have been less in tune with the view.

"The wretched girl was right, of course! Everyone would believe the worst. The three killers of your John Wilton have been apprehended, and your uncle is repenting his stupidity in the Tower, but the murderers of Amy Dudley can never be brought to justice. Or not officially!"

She swung round with a hiss of silken skirts, and her pale face was ablaze with a rage which frightened me even though it was not directed at me. She and I were about the same height, but so forceful was Elizabeth's nature that she always seemed at least a foot taller than myself.

"Catherine Grey!" she spat. "She is worse than any of the men. She was after my throne! Smith swears that he and Derby were acting in my best interests, out of loyalty to me, and that the life they took was forfeit to God in any case. Feeble logic but I think they meant it. Derby has left the court and gone home; he will be advised to stay there. I hear that Cecil has already had high words with Smith. Well, well. One day, no doubt, I will find ways to channel their loyalty in better directions. I can't afford to throw any kind of loyalty away, and that's the truth. But *Catherine!* I would like to see her head upon a block!"

There was a silence, the kind of silence which fills a room, the kind in which appalling images are spawned, like fungi in some lightless dungeon.

"I didn't quite mean that," she said. "No, not the block. But she will never be named my heir; nor will I allow her to marry. I know her temper now. As for the smaller men, Verney and Holme; they obeyed their masters. They will be watched in future, that's all. Their characters, too, are now known. We have much to thank you for, Ursula. Cecil has attended to your reward?"

"Yes, ma'am. He has also made an excellent payment to my servants Brockley and Dale, for the good service they have given me."

"And your daughter? What of your daughter? He mentioned the matter to me. A cottage is not a fitting place for the daughters of my personal gentlewomen. I gave him orders."

"You did indeed, ma'am, and I am grateful. Meg and her nurse are to be installed with friends of Lady Cecil in a household near Richmond. Meg will be reared as a lady and given a dowry, but she will always have her nurse with her, and I will see her regularly."

"Good. One day we will dance at her wedding, perhaps."

There was a silence. Elizabeth paused in her pacing. "I called you here to thank you, and halfway through my thanks I let my temper overtake me. I am sorry, Ursula. You made a great sacrifice, all out of the love you bear to your queen, it seems. You cast your marriage away for me. I will not enquire into your feelings. They are beyond my imagining. Cecil says you are glad that Master de la Roche has escaped. Oh, don't be afraid to admit it! We shan't bite off your head—or cut it off, either!"

"Yes, ma'am, I am glad."

I had put him in such danger. Perhaps my notions of loyalty to Elizabeth could be called twisted, too. He was probably in the Loire valley by now. If I had stayed with him, we would have gone there together.

In the privacy of those few married nights, he had talked to me of the Loire, lazily flowing among its pleasant hills, and had painted for me the life he meant us to have in France. Could I have been happy there after all? I would never know.

"There is something else for which I must thank you, Ursula. You have uncovered two unpleasant plots and while you were about it, you have also cleared Dudley's name, at least as far as I am concerned. The truth must remain confidential, but we are pleased to know that he had no part in the death of his wife."

I said nothing. It was plain enough to the whole court that he still had hopes of Elizabeth but I prayed that she wouldn't take him. A man who could fall in love with one woman and take her to bed, and then dismiss her from his affections as completely as Dudley had dismissed Amy, might do the same to another. What did Elizabeth feel? She was glad he was innocent, but when she spoke of him, her voice was cool and she had used the royal plural. She was enigmatic.

She gave me a sharp-edged smile. "You look puzzled, Ursula. I will tell you something. It's in confidence—but you have already demonstrated that I can put trust in you. You were—and are—in love with de la Roche, but you gave him up. I admire you for it. I too know what it is to love, and what it is to turn away from love. I have known all along that I would never take Robin Dudley, even if Amy had never existed."

I was very puzzled indeed and my face must have shown it.

Elizabeth, regardless of the risk to her farthingale, threw herself carelessly on to the window seat. "It will be a long time before he realises it," she said, "and when he does he will fight it, but he will lose. I can take only his friendship and his support; never his love. And now you are thinking that I am an heroine. Like a lady in a troubadour's romance, or like you, my gallant little Ursula. You think I have set him aside because the realm would never accept him and my duty is to the realm. Is that what you believe?"

"Well—er . . ."

Elizabeth at last gave the view a little consideration, turning away from me to look at it. Then she faced me again and said, "Have Lady Katherine Knollys and Kat Ashley told you that I never speak of my mother?"

"Yes, ma'am."

"No more I do. I shall say very little now, either. However, your mother served her and so I will speak of her to you, just this once, as far as to say that although I keep such silence on the subject of my mother, Queen Anne Boleyn, I think of her. Often. Especially of the way she died, at her husband's order. And I also think, often, of my young stepmother, my father's fifth wife, Kate Howard. She couldn't say no to the men, poor silly creature, but she was kind to me, and she paid a high price for her weakness. One moment, she had an adoring husband. The next, he was signing her death warrant. I pitied her. Have you understood me, Ursula?"

"I . . . don't know, ma'am."

It was too oblique; too much of a message in cipher. Elizabeth gave me another razor-sharp smile.

"Can you imagine, Ursula, what it is like to have memories which are like devoted but insane retainers, who cannot tell friend from foe, and drive away all comers?"

I understood then. I saw, at last, the reason for the strange impression Elizabeth had always made on me, of a young woman forever shut away behind a shield, or a fortress wall.

I didn't altogether believe in it. I thought of Matthew. I had fled from him, but I knew that if I had to live at close quarters with him, seeing him often, I would never be able to hold myself aloof. If Dudley were to remain at court, and apparently this was to happen, how long would the queen resist him? He would conquer in the end, I thought. He would scale the wall, even this one.

And perhaps it was best that he should. Elizabeth needed a husband, and the realm needed an heir.

"Ma'am," I said. "You are the queen! Surely you can overcome even the most obstinate retainers."

"I am the queen, and therefore I stand in the place of my father, who was a king, rather than in the place of my mother and stepmother, who were only consorts?"

"Well . . . something like that, ma'am."

Slowly she shook her head, and I had the odd impression that she was saying no not to me but to some importunate voice within herself.

"One thing a queen need never fear," she said, "is a lonely old age. Your own future may be more solitary than mine. You have been told that now?"

"Yes, ma'am." I was relieved to get away from the delicate subject of Elizabeth's love-life. "It seems that the circumstances of my marriage may not amount to quite enough duress to justify an annulment. I was agreeable to the gentleman's addresses here at court and I was not dragged to the chapel by force, or actually threatened with bodily harm."

"I am sorry," said Elizabeth seriously, "but perhaps we can distract you, in time, from this second bereavement, for Cecil tells me that, for you, it amounts to that. There is work for you here at court, in our service; work which may use the surprising talents you have lately revealed. Have you been told? And are you willing?"

"I have," I said. "And I am."

320

Even with Meg now placed safely, I would still find it hard to make ends meet. I would want to buy gifts for my daughter and I must still pay Bridget's wages; that was the agreement. I also wished to go on employing Brockley and Dale. I had grown to depend on Brockley, and as for dear, staunch Dale; for all her fits of complaining, in her own favourite phrase, I couldn't abide to be without her now.

Indeed, it seemed very likely that it would soon be a case, if I wished to keep either, of keeping both. Any day now, I expected them to ask my consent to marry each other. All the signs were there. Once, I had even glimpsed them exchanging kisses.

However, employing them meant paying them, and I must also maintain myself in a manner befitting a lady of the court. I now realised that Dudley's money wouldn't last for ever, generous though he had been. He really was generous—when he didn't have too much to lose. He had waved away my offer to pay for or replace the White Snail, the horse I had virtually stolen and abandoned at Withysham.

"It wasn't much of a horse. Forget it!" he said.

I was relieved of that anxiety but my financial future still worried me and when Cecil said he had work for me, I was happy enough to undertake it. It would not involve hunting people down across the southern counties this time, fortunately. I would only have to be eyes and ears, at court. I need not again be an implacable huntress. As I knew all too well, there was a bitter side to that.

True, I was grimly glad that John's killers would hang. The description proclaimed in so many market places by Cecil's messengers had included a description of Will Johnson's piebald horse, and it was the horse which within hours had caused the trio to be recognised.

But I was anxious for the Masons and the Westleys,

whose fate I did not yet know, and unexpectedly troubled over Uncle Herbert. My uncle and aunt had not fled with Matthew, but had stayed put at Faldene and tried to brazen it out. Aunt Tabitha had been spared arrest, but even though he had assuredly been ready to let me be murdered, I still felt uncomfortable at the thought of my gouty uncle in a Tower cell. However, I trusted I would not have to suffer such inner turmoil again, and Cecil was offering good money.

I very much wanted, on my own account, to have a few quiet words with the Spanish ambassador, de Quadra. It was not easy, since I did not want to approach him officially, but the resourceful Brockley dropped a hint to one of the ambassador's serving men, and de Quadra himself sought me out, quietly, in the antechamber to the dining hall when we were waiting to go in for our dinner.

"You desire to speak to me, Mistress . . . Blanchard or de la Roche?"

"Blanchard, if you will. Yes. Do you remember, my lord, how before I left for Oxfordshire, you walked beside me in Richmond Park and pointed out three men to me? One was the Earl of Derby, one was Sir Thomas Smith and one was a third man whose name, then, I didn't know."

Because he was a short man, our faces were on a level. I studied him intently, but that quiet, olive-skinned countenance gave me no information. He said nothing.

"I know the man's name now," I said. "Peter Holme." We were speaking French, but so did many at the court. I kept my voice pitched low so that although we were in a crowded room, there was no risk of being overheard. "Those three," I said, "were hatching a scheme together."

A page wandered close to us and stood nearby, looking towards a group of courtiers as though expecting one of them to beckon him over and give him an errand. I fell silent and de Quadra edged us both further away.

"That, Mistress Blanchard, is one of the methods by which I myself find out things of which I am not officially informed."

I didn't pretend to be shocked. Anyone who has indulged in eavesdropping from behind the wall-hangings, has forfeited the right to such delicacy. I smiled.

"For once," he said, "I will avoid subtlety. I am not supposed to know what happened to Lady Dudley and who arranged it, but I do. Does this concern her?"

"Yes, my lord. Tell me, when you pointed those three men out to me, did you already know they were scheming together? Did you draw my attention to them because you had heard something already—about their plans and Lady Dudley?"

"Why do you ask?"

"Because the way you called my attention to them made me, eventually, think of them as possible associates. I wondered if you were trying to warn me, without saying too much, perhaps because you were not sure. If so—I suppose I want to thank you, but I wish you had been more explicit."

"You attribute too much cunning to me, Mistress Blanchard."

"My lord? I don't quite understand."

"I mean, dear Mistress Blanchard, that when I pointed that trio out to you and encouraged you to notice that Peter Holme—I too know his name now—was not of equal social status to the others, I merely wanted to instruct you in habits of observation. I had heard rumours about the threat to Lady

Dudley—I said that at the time. I felt that anyone who went to that household should be alert, for their own sake. But I had no knowledge, then, that Derby, Smith and Holme were conspiring together. When I first heard of Lady Dudley's death, I believed that her husband could be responsible. You sensed the conspiracy yourself, Mistress Blanchard. I think you have an instinct for nosing out such things. Do you intend to remain at court?"

"Yes, my lord."

De Quadra bowed. "I shall be very very careful of you," he said.

❦ Historical Note ❧

No one knows exactly how Amy Robsart came to be found lying with a broken neck at the foot of a flight of stairs in Cumnor Place, Oxfordshire, on 8th September, 1560.

Rumours that her husband Sir Robin Dudley had arranged it were rife, although the panic-stricken letter which he wrote afterwards to his cousin Thomas Blount goes a long way towards exonerating him.

It is possible that the theory advanced by Professor Ian Aird in the *English Historical Review*, 1956, is correct. Professor Aird observed that if Lady Dudley really did have cancer, she may have suffered from the secondary effect of brittle bones, which could have caused her neck to snap spontaneously, or as the result of a fall which would not have been fatal to a healthy person.

On the other hand, there were many people at Queen Elizabeth's court who viewed the prospect of a marriage between the queen and Dudley with absolute horror. If there were any danger that Amy might obligingly die and release him, then the temptation to help her out of the world and create a scandal at the same time, was certainly there.

It is a fact that the queen regarded Lady Catherine Grey with dislike and was so angry when she found that Lady Catherine had clandestinely married Lord Hertford, that she put them both in the Tower.

Sir Thomas Smith prospered under Elizabeth on the whole, and in the early 1560s he went to Paris as her ambassador (not always a comfortable post). Although they were generally united in their loyalty to Elizabeth, Smith did at one point have a quarrel, cause unknown, with Sir William Cecil. The Earl of Derby was always apparently loyal to Elizabeth, although Cecil regarded him with suspicion—perhaps because of his strong Catholic leanings, perhaps for some other reason.

I have taken the liberty of inventing explanations for both of these mysteries.

ઠ Bibliography ઠ

While concocting this extravaganza I tried, nevertheless, to stay within the known facts of history and
therefore studied many books on the life and times of
Elizabeth I. Among the works consulted were:

Amye Robsart and the Earl of Leycester by George
Adlard (1870).

The Elizabethan World by Lacey Baldwin Smith
(Houghton Mifflin Company, 1991).

The Reign of Elizabeth by J. B. Black from *The
Oxford History of England,* edited by Sir George
Clark (Oxford University Press, 1988).

Mary Queen of Scots by Antonia Fraser (Mandarin
Paperbacks, 1989).

The Elements of Herbalism by David Hoffman (Ele-
ment Books, 1990).

Elizabeth and Essex by Elizabeth Jenkins (Panther,
1972).

Elizabeth the Great by Elizabeth Jenkins (Victor Gollancz, 1968).

A History of Oxfordshire by Mary Jessup (Phillimore, 1975).

Elizabeth I by Wallace MacCaffrey (Edward Arnold, 1993).

Seven Hundred Years of English Cooking by Maxine McKendry, edited by Arabella Boxer (Treasurer Press, 1985).

Elizabethan England by Alison Plowden (Reader's Digest Association, 1982).

The Tudor Age by Jasper Ridley (Guild Publishing by arrangement with Constable & Co., 1988).

Elizabeth I by Anne Somerset (Weidenfeld & Nicolson, 1991).

All the Queen's Men by Neville Williams (Weidenfeld & Nicolson, 1972).

The Tudor Age by James A. Williamson (Longman, 1979).